ANOTHER ONE GOES TONIGHT

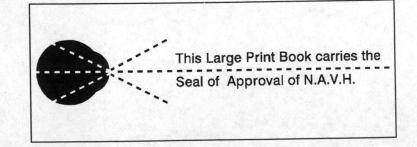

This Large Print Book carries the
Seal of Approval of N.A.V.H.

ANOTHER ONE GOES TONIGHT

PETER LOVESEY

THORNDIKE PRESS

A part of Gale, Cengage Learning

GALE
CENGAGE Learning·

Farmington Hills, Mich • San Francisco • New York • Waterville, Maine
Meriden, Conn • Mason, Ohio • Chicago

LIBRARY OF CONGRESS CATALOGING-IN-PUBLICATION DATA

Names: Lovesey, Peter, author.
Title: Another one goes tonight : a Peter Diamond investigation / by Peter
    Lovesey.
Description: Large print edition. | Waterville, Maine : Thorndike Press, 2016. |
    Series: Thorndike Press large print basic
Identifiers: LCCN 2016024571 | ISBN 9781410492166 (hardcover) | ISBN 1410492168
    (hardcover)
Subjects: LCSH: Diamond, Peter (Fictitious character)—Fiction. | Private
    investigators—England—Bath—Fiction. | Large type books. | Mystery fiction.
    gsafd
Classification: LCC PR6062.O86 A85 2016b | DDC 823/.914—dc23
LC record available at https://lccn.loc.gov/2016024571

Published in 2016 by arrangement with Soho Press, Inc.

Printed in Mexico
1 2 3 4 5 6 7 20 19 18 17 16

ANOTHER ONE GOES TONIGHT

Another one goes tonight.

This time I'm ahead of myself so this isn't a to-do list. Everything is in place, as they say. But being methodical I want something on record to look at when it's all over. You're on your own in this game, so any debriefing is with myself.

The only thing left is to make sure I get the timing right. I'm going for 2 A.M. when he'll be sleeping soundly, guaranteed. Get gloved up, let myself in, do the necessary and get out without leaving any trace. The police have no idea and I'm not doing them any favours.

He'll rest in peace and so will I, with the difference that I'll wake up tomorrow morning.

1

"I've seen a few things on the night shift," Police Sergeant Lew Morgan said, "but this beats them all."

"Shall we stop him?" his driver, PC Aaron Green, asked.

"What for? He's not speeding."

"No helmet."

"He doesn't need one. It's only a trike."

"It's motorised. He's not turning the pedals." Aaron Green wasn't there simply to drive the car. Typical of young bobbies out to impress, he was constantly on the lookout for offenders.

Lew was older and reckoned he was wiser. He took stock. There were reflectors on the pedals and, sure enough, they weren't moving, but the tricycle was. Three hours to go and the boredom was getting to him.

Might as well do the business.

He pressed the control on the dash and triggered the blue flashing lights. "Okay, chummy, let's see if your brakes work."

Their patrol car slowed to tail the offending vehicle and draw in behind. The stretch of minor road near Bathampton was otherwise deserted at 2:30 in the morning.

The tricycle came to a controlled stop. Its rider turned his head in a way that involved rotating most of his upper body. He wasn't young.

"You know what?" Lew said. "That's a fucking deerstalker he's wearing."

"Still illegal," Aaron said.

"Who does he think he is?"

"Fancy dress?"

Lew got out and approached the rider of the tricycle. "Switch off, sir."

"I beg your pardon."

Deaf as well.

Lew shouted, "Switch off," and mimed the action with his hand.

The tricyclist obeyed. The hat was definitely a deerstalker. And the rest of the clothes matched. Lew was no fashion expert but he had an idea he was looking at a Norfolk jacket worn over a check shirt and trousers kept in place by leather gaiters. Like some character out of a television costume drama.

And the voice was vintage BBC. "How can I be of assistance, officer?" How patron-

10

ising was that?

"Do you have a licence to ride this thing?"

"I do not."

Lew almost rubbed his hands. He was going to enjoy this. "You're aware that it's a form of motorcycle?"

"I suppose it might be described as such."

"So you need a licence."

"Actually, no."

"What do you mean, no? You just agreed with me it's a motorcycle."

"In the eyes of the law, it's a beast of another colour, so to speak."

"A *what*?"

"In point of fact this is an EAPC."

Lew was supposed to be the voice of authority here. He wasn't about to show frailty by asking what an EAPC was. "That may be so but it's motor-powered. You were riding without moving your legs."

The man gave the sort of smile that gets the seat by the window. "Only because the poor old pins aren't up to pedalling so far these days."

Lew didn't have any sympathy for the elderly. They did far too well out of the state with their inflation-proof pensions and all the extras. "So it's a motorbike. You're not wearing a helmet either."

"That is true, officer." Far from sounding

11

apologetic, this lawbreaker was oozing confidence.

Lew remained civil, but firm. "Did you know it's also against the law to ride a motorcycle without a helmet?"

Now the silver eyebrows peaked in concern. "You're worried about my safety?"

"I'm not worried. I'm not worried in the least. I'm telling you it's illegal."

"Oh dear." But the concern wasn't for himself, it was for Lew. "I don't suppose you come across many drivers of motorised tricycles."

"That's beside the point, sir."

"Forgive me, officer. I'm trying to save you some embarrassment."

"Trying to save *me*?" Lew said.

"You see I wouldn't be out on the public highway if I knew I was in breach of the law. However, if you'll bear with me a moment . . ." He dipped his right hand towards his jacket pocket.

Lew reacted fast. "Don't do that!"

The startled old man almost fell off the saddle.

"Put your hands where I can see them, on the handlebars. What's in the pocket?"

"Only a piece of paper. I always carry a copy of the official government advice, which I believe is still in force. I was about

12

to invite you to look at it."

"I don't need to."

"That's a shame, because if you did you would see that provided I don't exceed fifteen miles an hour and my vehicle doesn't weigh more than sixty kilograms and the power is not more than two hundred and fifty watts, my choice of transport — contrary to appearance — is not classed as a motorcycle but an electrically assisted pedal cycle."

An EAPC.

All this had been spoken with such self-assurance that Lew knew with a sinking heart it had to be right. The figures the old jerk had quoted were faintly familiar. Out on patrol you don't often come across motorised trikes. This road user was a pain in the arse, but he was in the clear. He didn't require a licence or a helmet.

Lew should have stuck to his first impulse and told young Aaron to drive straight past. Now it was a matter of saving face. He pointed to the large bag strapped to the back of the saddle.

"What's in that?"

"Nothing of interest to the police, I promise you."

"Answer the question, please."

"A plastic box containing a banana and a

13

slice of date and walnut cake. I come prepared, in case I get hungry."

"Is that all?"

"I haven't finished. A flask of tea. Also my binoculars, camera, tripod, an ordnance survey map." He smiled. "And Trixie."

"What's that?"

"You mean, 'Who's that?' Trixie is my late wife."

There was a pause for thought. "In this bag?"

"I always bring her ashes with me. We shared so much in life. She passed away six months ago. Examine her, by all means. And I forgot the puncture repair kit. It's surprising how much the bag holds."

Best insist on the old man handling his own possessions. The power to search at a road check has to involve suspicion of a serious arrestable offence. Lew asked him to unzip the saddlebag. This involved a contortion that was clearly uncomfortable, but Lew wasn't going to get caught out a second time.

The vacuum flask and the sandwich box containing a banana and a wedge of cake were visible on top. And so was the lid of a plastic urn. Lew didn't need to meet Trixie close up.

"What are the binoculars for?"

"Oh, you're thinking I might be a peeping Tom. Absolutely not. I'm well past that sort of nonsense."

"Most people are in bed at this time of night," Lew said.

"But it's not compulsory. We're living in a free country."

"Do you mind telling me where you're going?"

A reasonable question that got an unhelpful answer. "I won't know until I get there, will I?"

Lew was being led into a minefield of embarrassment. He knew it. The only mercy was that Aaron was out of earshot.

The old man added, "They don't stay in one spot. They're moving steadily closer to Bath, you see."

He didn't see. He didn't see at all. But he wasn't so stupid as to ask. He waited for something more, and he got it.

"They can cover as much as a mile in a single night, using hops."

"A mile a night?" Lew pictured a colony of travelling rabbits. What was that film he'd once seen about rabbits on the move? *Watership Down.* "And you hope to see them through your binoculars?"

"Unless I can get really close and observe them with the naked eye. It depends on the terrain."

"If they're always moving, how do you know where to look?"

"I would have thought that was obvious."

"Not to me, sir."

"You can hear them some way off."

"Hear them doing what?"

"Digging their holes."

This was the moment Lew decided to quit. "On this occasion I'm going to leave you to it. For your own safety, I advise you to get a cycle helmet. And keep off the A roads."

"I'm obliged to you, but I always do."

"Go carefully. Other traffic may not see you coming."

The old man looked skywards. "A full moon helps."

You bet it does, you old loony, Lew thought, as he returned to the patrol car. He opened the door, got in and watched in silence as the tricyclist moved off.

Watership Down was a real place somewhere in Hampshire, seventy miles down the M4. The rabbits couldn't have travelled that distance, even at a mile a night. Must have been a different colony. Oh Christ, Lew thought, he's got me thinking it's real.

"You didn't book him, then," Aaron said from the world of modern policing.

"No."

"Let him off with a caution?"

"No need. He's legal."

"How can that be?"

"It's an EAPC."

"Ah."

Like Lew, Aaron wasn't betraying his ignorance. He turned the car and headed back towards the lights of Bath. No more was said for some time.

Eventually Aaron asked, "Did the old bloke say what he was up to?"

"Stalking rabbits."

"To shoot?"

"To watch."

"Like a safari?"

Lew didn't smile. He was smarting from the experience. He realised he hadn't even asked the old boy his name. "It takes all sorts."

A shout from the control room saved them both from more of the same. Some people with a ladder had been seen acting suspiciously near a church north of the city in Julian Road. In the last six months the lead had been stripped from several roofs in Bath. The thieves could make as much as twenty grand from one night's work.

Two patrols were ordered to the scene.

The burst of activity using blues and twos

17

brought much-needed distraction. Aaron jammed his foot down and they arrived first, just as two chancers from Swindon were loading their loot into the back of a pick-up truck.

Gotcha.

The arrest filled an hour profitably and made a success of what had promised to be a long, barren night. The other patrol didn't show up, but Lew and Aaron didn't mind. By the time they had delivered their prisoners to the custody centre in Keynsham and gone through the formalities with the sergeant their shift was almost over.

It wasn't worth going out on the roads again. Their relief would be coming in at 7 A.M.

Cue for a coffee.

Every officer working a shift knows the final hour is the worst possible time to get involved in a fresh incident because it has to be followed through regardless of when you're supposed to go off duty. So Lew and Aaron weren't overjoyed when ordered at 6:19 to investigate a report of a naked man in Beckford Gardens.

"That's all I want, another nutcase," Lew said.

They returned to the car.

"What are we dealing with here — a

18

drunk?" he asked the control room as the early morning traffic moved aside for their flashing lights. "Is he dancing in the street and singing 'I want to break free'?"

The operator giggled. "You tell me when you get there."

To Aaron, he said, "Bet you it's a domestic. His wife kicked him out of bed."

"He could be a sleepwalker."

"Don't talk to me about sleep. I could have been home and horizontal if it wasn't for this."

They crossed North Parade Bridge and turned left on Pulteney Road. Getting to Beckford Gardens wouldn't take long. Questioning a naked man, possibly drunk or asleep, might be a slower process.

"We'd better decide how to deal with him."

"Cover him up?" Aaron said.

"What with?"

"Dunno. We've got high-vis jackets in the back."

"That's what he wants, high visibility."

At the end of Darlington Street the road joins Sydney Place and curls around Sydney Gardens. The traffic was lighter here.

"It's a long one," Aaron said.

"How do you know? We haven't seen it yet."

"The road. Beckford Gardens, I'm talking about Beckford Gardens."

Lew yawned. "Okay. Get us there soon as you can." He closed his eyes.

The next thing he knew was Aaron yelling, "Jeeeez!" followed by the screech of brakes and a lurch as the car tipped sideways.

Lew was thrust forward like one of those dummies you see in films of accident testing. This wasn't in slow motion but to Lew it might have been, because in the milliseconds before his face impacted, his brain flashed images like a slideshow. The sudden braking swung the car out of control. They veered right, mounted the steep bank, bounced off and teetered on two wheels, hurtling left. The crunch was imminent. His head would be crushed unless the airbag inflated. When the car turned over — as it was sure to — he might be crushed anyway.

He expected to die.

How long it was before he regained consciousness he didn't know or care. All he cared about was the excruciating pain in his hip and leg. He opened his eyes to a blur.

Impaired vision.

Fumes of burnt metal told him his sense of smell was unaffected.

Couldn't move his head. Couldn't move anything much. Possible paralysis, then. But how could he be paralysed and feel this pain?

Gradually he became aware that he was in the wrecked patrol car and the reason he couldn't move was the inflated airbag acting like a vice. The blurred vision was an illusion. The windscreen inches from his eyes had cracked into myriad fragments still held together.

Glass chips started raining on his face. Someone was hammering at the thing.

Lew needed to let them know he was there. Urgently. He made a sound that was meant to be a shout and came out as a yelp.

A bigger chunk came down and a hole appeared.

A voice said, "This one's alive."

Next a hatchet was poked through and used to enlarge the hole.

The voice said, "Hang on, mate."

Even in this painful situation Lew thought the remark was stupid. He wasn't going anywhere.

"Can you hear me? We'll get you out of this."

Another yelp was the best he could manage.

A hand came through the hole, groped in

the space, found his face and felt for his mouth. He knew what was going on: the basic first-aid drill of making sure his airways weren't blocked.

"Can you speak?"

Not a syllable anyone would recognise.

"Never mind. I can hear you. I'm going to ask you some questions. One squeak for yes, two for no, okay?"

Wasn't that the system ghost-hunters used? He wanted it known he was still living. He managed a grunt.

"Are you in pain?"

One for yes.

"We'll give you something in a second. Are you bleeding?"

Am I bleeding? Bleeding terrified.

He didn't know, so he didn't answer.

"Can you feel your legs?"

And how! He confirmed it.

"That's good. Tell me where the pain is. Upper body?"

Two grunts.

"Okay, you're making sense. You have pain below the waist, right? Can you move your leg at all?"

Two more.

"But you can feel it, and that's good. We'll get you out of here as soon as we can. In the meantime I'll give you something for

22

the pain."

Extracting him from the wreckage took a week and a day by his reckoning. While the paramedics administered oxygen and morphine and kept talking to him, fire officers with metal cutters worked at the bits that were trapping him. A horrific moment came when they decided to puncture the airbag that was restraining his head. Finding he could move a little, he looked to his right.

He was staring into the mask-like, dust-covered face of Aaron.

The paramedics had discovered Lew's name. He didn't remember telling them, maybe because his brain wasn't functioning well. Or they'd got the information from the control room. They told him their first names, as matey as if they'd all just met at a drinks party. Needing to keep him conscious, they prattled away about things unrelated to the situation, favourite TV programmes, football and music. Some way into the process he managed to get his voice working — and he wasn't wasting words on the rubbish they were going on about.

"My driver — I think he's dead."

"Afraid so. We got to him first but he was gone."

"He was young, not long married."

"Try and stay calm, Lew. We've got a job

23

to do here."

"He was driving okay. I don't know what we hit."

"Looks like you sheered off a wall of turf and turned right over. You may not feel like it right now, Lew, but you're a lucky man."

2

"So what happens now?" Paul Gilbert, the youngest member of the Bath CID team, asked. Everyone was talking about the fatal accident.

"It gets investigated," DCI Keith Halliwell said from across the room. "A police car crashing is big time, a job for Professional Standards. It could go all the way to the IPCC. They'll need to know all kinds of stuff, like what was their speed and were they using blues and twos."

"They'll have a job on their hands with the driver dead," DI John Leaman said in his usual downbeat tone.

"The other guy survived — Lew Morgan," Gilbert said. "He ought to know what happened."

"Yeah — but how much does he remember? He was knocked out. It blanks out everything."

"Not necessarily."

"Are there cameras along Beckford Gardens?"

"Not when I was last there."

"You can tell a lot from skid marks."

"Were they on an emergency?"

"Only if you can call a naked man an emergency."

"Bloody hell — is that what they were attending — some crazy streaker?" Leaman said. "Fancy being killed for that."

"I wonder how the naked man will feel when he hears what happened," Gilbert said.

"He won't give a shit," Leaman said.

True or not, that cynical declaration drew a line under the discussion.

At the same time, the head of CID, Detective Superintendent Peter Diamond, was in denial in the assistant chief constable's office. He'd been called at home before breakfast and told to report as soon as possible. He didn't object to that if there was serious investigative work to be done. The job he'd just been given wasn't what he had in mind.

"Me?" he told Georgina Dallymore, his boss. "You can't cast me as the professional standards man. Everyone in this place will fall about laughing."

"No one here is laughing after the tragedy this morning." Georgina knew how to turn the screw.

"I'm not cut out for this. You need someone who is blameless. My file looks like a jumbo crossword, there are so many black marks on it."

"Nothing was said about your reputation, Peter. You'll be the local investigator acting for the PSD at Portishead," she said as if it was a done deal.

"PSD?" He hated abbreviations.

"Professional Standards Department."

"There's a *department* for it?"

"They asked for a senior officer who can punch his weight, who doesn't shrink from asking questions."

"What's wrong with the collisions experts? They employ them just to investigate crashes."

"The CIU? They're involved, don't worry. But their emphasis is mainly on the mechanical causes, if any. Yours will be on the people, the driver and the sergeant who was with him and whether they were negligent in any way."

"I'm a detective. I come down hard on criminals, not my brother officers."

"Peter, nobody volunteers for a job like this. Think of it as a moral obligation."

27

"Moral? What's moral about it?"

"And when all is said and done," Georgina motored on, "it's what you do better than anyone else — an investigation. Interviewing witnesses, evaluating evidence."

"To stitch up someone I rub shoulders with every day?"

"Not necessarily. If you find they weren't at fault, you say so. You give them a clean bill of health."

"Just so it can be vetted by the PSD and passed to Police Complaints, who will pick it to pieces and say I conspired in a whitewash. This is a no-win job."

"Now you're being cynical."

"Realistic."

Georgina shifted to a more humane approach. "Put yourself in the shoes of the driver's people. They'll want to know how it could have happened and they'll want one of our own to be in charge."

"Did he have family?"

"A wife and a son of only eight months."

Diamond's obdurate face softened and creased. "That's tragic . . . dreadful."

Georgina leaned back in her chair with the look of a chess-player who has made the winning move.

He asked, "Is someone with them?"

"Of course. And there's his co-driver,

Sergeant Morgan, in hospital with multiple fractures and in danger of losing a leg. They're entitled to the best enquiry we can give them. Do you know Lew Morgan?"

"If I do, it's only by sight. In CID, we don't spend much time with the uniformed lot. It's not personal. Our work keeps us at a distance."

"Which is why you're so well placed to carry this out. You're not too close to be swayed. I'm assigning you to this, Peter, and I don't want any more objections."

He'd been about to say he couldn't be spared from the murder squad, but murders had been as rare as pay rises this last two months and Georgina knew. Saying there was a huge backlog of paperwork wouldn't impress her; there was always a backlog. He was stuck with the accident investigation. Better make the best of it. "If I do this, I'm going to need assistance."

"No argument about that," she said, encouraged. "This will be too much for one man. I can deploy a sergeant from uniform to help you."

"No use at all," he said.

"Why on earth do you say that?"

"As you just remarked yourself, anyone from uniform can be swayed. I need neutrals like myself. CID people."

29

She gave him a long look. "You're a devious man."

He waited.

She sighed. "Who are you thinking of — bearing in mind that we want CID to function efficiently while this is going on?"

"Keith Halliwell and Ingeborg Smith."

"Two of your best officers?" She shifted her bottom as if he'd made her uncomfortable.

"John Leaman is perfectly capable of running things without us. He'll jump at the chance."

He'd asked for two, expecting her to limit him to Halliwell, but she surprised him by saying, "Very well. Take Halliwell and Smith." Then she added, "Don't lose any time. You'll want to look at the scene. All the wreckage has to be cleared away before the day is out."

With Keith and Ingeborg he drove out to Beckford Gardens. His two colleagues were every bit as uneasy as he had been about investigating a fatal traffic accident, and said so.

"The technical stuff is taken care of," he told them. "We won't be measuring tyre marks. The Collision Investigation Unit will take care of all that and supply us with the

30

facts. Our job is to talk to the people involved and make sure they acted professionally."

"Person," Ingeborg said.

"What?"

"You said people. My understanding is that there's only one survivor and we won't be talking to him for a while. He's in intensive care."

"Sergeant Morgan," Halliwell added. "Lew Morgan."

"You know him?"

"Been at Bath as long as I have."

They pulled up in Beckford Gardens some way short of the taped-off area. A patrol car parked sideways with beacon lights flashing was blocking the road. Beyond were more police vehicles and lifting gear. "We'll get a sense of the scene as we always do," Diamond said, trying to sound upbeat before they left the car. "Let's treat it as we would a crime scene."

"Except that the body will have been removed," Ingeborg said, making clear she was every bit as unhappy about this assignment as he was. "It's not the same at all, guv. We won't be looking for a murder weapon. Or suspects."

"Or motives," Halliwell chimed in.

"It was a traffic accident," Ingeborg said.

31

"Shocking, but no mystery."

"Hang on, there are things to investigate," Diamond told them. "And there are victims."

"Casualties." Ingeborg was unconvinced.

"One fatal, one critically injured," Diamond said. "As I understand it, they were called out to a so-called emergency about a naked man. In my book, they were victims."

"Who made the call?"

"That's one of the mysteries we have to unravel."

"Whodunit," Halliwell said, and triggered one of those moments when there was imminent danger of Diamond combusting.

This time he just rolled his eyes.

They stepped into the taped-off area.

The stretch where the crash had happened was about halfway along Beckford Gardens, a long narrow road in the north-eastern section of the city known as Bathwick. Houses and bungalows along one side faced bushes and trees on the other. You couldn't see the railway and the canal on the undeveloped side but they weren't far off.

The mangled wreckage of the Ford Focus police car was across the pavement. It had demolished someone's garden wall and come to rest on its side with the front end in their rose-bed. Bits of the bodywork in the familiar blue and yellow Battenburg livery were lying where they had been dropped by the rescue team.

Diamond's hope of treating this as a crime scene had to be swiftly revised. Massive tyres had crisscrossed the surfaces where he would have hoped to find tracks of the original crash. Heavy machinery, a truck-mounted crane and a flat-bed lorry stood close to the centre of things, as well as a fire tender. The car roof had been removed with hydraulic cutters to get at the casualties inside. Fire and rescue officers, police and highways officials couldn't avoid splashing through pools of oil and water as they went about their business removing equipment.

He went over to one of the police and identified himself. He was taken to meet the collision investigator, who looked about seventeen and said his name was Dessie. He was in a high-visibility jacket and hard hat with the word CHIEF across it. Two young women, similarly dressed, except that their hard hats had nothing written on them, were close by, using a laser rangefinder.

"Who do you represent?" Dessie asked. "I'm the specialist here."

"Professional Standards. We won't tread on your toes. Can you run through what happened?"

"Man, you're joking. The only guy who can answer that is in intensive care." Dessie might have been young but he wasn't subdued by rank.

Diamond didn't particularly like being addressed as "man," but equally Dessie probably didn't appreciate people who called themselves Professional Standards muscling in on his territory. "You must have formed an opinion. A police car doesn't smash into a wall for no reason."

"Take your pick," Dessie said, spreading his hands. "Driver fell asleep at the wheel, had a stroke, an epileptic fit, an attack of cramp, a visual problem, a call on his mobile. His brakes failed, his steering went. A stone shattered the windscreen. A deer ran across the road. Or a cat, or a dog, or a runaway ostrich."

"A naked man?" Halliwell said before Diamond could turn ballistic.

"Don't come clever with me," Dessie said, regardless that he was being clever with them.

"That's what the call was about — a naked man."

"Sure, and they were expecting him. He wouldn't have caused the crash."

"If he stepped out from behind one of

those parked cars, he would," Halliwell said. "Anyone, clothed or not, would have made them hit the brakes and very likely go out of control."

"That's one more scenario. I'm trained to keep an open mind."

"Perhaps you should tell us what you've learned so far," Diamond said through gritted teeth.

"Now you're talking, man. I've noted three points of interest. I can walk you through if you want."

"It would help." He resisted the urge to add "sonny."

Dessie was already on his way to a place some thirty metres from the wrecked police car, zigzagging between groups of fire and rescue officers. He was a fast mover.

He stopped where a white Toyota and a silver Renault were parked close to the kerb. Presumably they belonged to people from the adjacent houses. "There's bugger all left to see because of all the vehicles that have come through since," Dessie said when Diamond and the others joined him, "but everything was photographed and measured — skid marks this side of the Toyota indicating that something braked hard here and narrowly avoided hitting the thing. Delta Three — our patrol car — was travelling north along here, on the lookout for the naked man. You can see for yourselves how narrow it is. There isn't much space for overtaking."

With that settled, he marched briskly to the steep grass verge that fringed the road opposite the houses and rose to about five feet above the level of the road surface. Tyre tracks were clearly visible, showing something had mounted the slope and veered back to the road several metres on. "Second point of interest. The tracks show where the front offside wheel mounted the soft shoulder. The indentation is deepest at the high point. When you look at the wheels in a moment you'll see mud and grass adhering to the tyre wall. It's pretty obvious they struck this bank and lost control. The speed they were going and the angle were enough to tip the car over." He headed across the road to the wreck of Delta Three, embedded in what remained of the garden wall.

"It's a miracle anyone got out alive," Ingeborg said when they caught up.

"What you're looking at now is my third and final piece of evidence, the shell of the thing after they were cut out," Dessie told her. "Take note of the mud on the wheels."

The young man was justified in treating them as beginners in accident investigation,

Diamond had to remind himself, but he couldn't take much more of it. "When did you get here?"

"While they were extracting the dead driver. The survivor was already in the ambulance on his way to the Royal United."

"So you didn't see the car in its original state after it hit the wall?"

"Others were here. It was photographed. I won't be short of evidence."

"*We* won't be short of evidence," Diamond told him. "We'll need copies of everything you have. Has anyone from the houses come forward?"

"A few I spoke to," Dessie said. "None of them saw the crash. Several heard it."

"We'd better do some doorstepping."

"Hold on," Dessie said. "That's my call."

"Have you made it?"

"Not yet. I've been far too busy with other stuff."

"And you don't have much help by the look of it. But you're in luck, because we'll knock on doors and share information with you."

The young man blinked.

"Better get on, then," Diamond said. "Can't keep you from your duties any longer."

He waited for Dessie to get out of earshot.

"Something's not right here," he told his companions. "An experienced driver doesn't lose control, even on a 999 job."

"Mechanical failure?" Ingeborg said.

"How often does that happen? Police cars are well maintained."

"We can't rule it out."

"Can't rule out all the other possible causes he was rabbiting on about. We simply have to stop guessing and get some evidence. Now that we've done the tour with Dessie, I want to walk through his points of bloody interest myself. You two had better talk with the gawpers. A few have collected by the tapes. See if they can offer anything helpful."

He crossed the road again to point of interest number two, the place where they'd been shown the tyre tracks. The bank Dessie had called the soft shoulder was much more than that, more than head-high in places. At the top was a long strip of scrubland with well-established trees planted to screen the stark grey walls of the railway embankment beyond. A London-bound train had just thundered past at the level of the rooftops.

He didn't need to study the grooves in the mud. He could understand how the car had been thrown off course and turned over. He was more interested in what had happened immediately prior to that. A higher viewpoint might help. He reached for an overhanging branch, hauled himself up the bank and found he could see much more. The work of hosing away foam and oil continued around the wreck of Delta Three. A flatbed truck was being backed towards it. Difficult to picture the scene before the accident.

The possibility of an animal, a fox or a deer, making a dash across the road from the wild area and causing the driver to slam on his brakes had made sense until now. Unlikely. The railway company had installed railings all the way along, not obvious from below. The bushes hid much of this iron barrier from view. There was only a narrow strip of ground to stand on.

Diamond was forced to think again.

He edged a short way along for a better angle, gripping branches and railings to keep his balance. A fire engine was parked immediately below him and he couldn't see past it.

He hadn't gone far when he was forced to stop for a tangle of metal heaped against the railing. At first he thought some piece of the police car must have broken off in the crash and been flung up here, but it became obvious this wasn't a car part.

Chrome tubing, twisted cable and a circular grooved object that looked like a chain wheel were half-buried in the long grass. He crouched for a closer look. None of it was rusted. The metal had been scraped bare on one piece, gleaming as if it had just happened.

Then he found a bicycle saddle.

This could change everything.

He stood up and looked for Halliwell and Ingeborg. Too far off to get their attention.

And now he noticed that a whole section of the railing a little further on had come off its support and was angled inwards, as if it had been struck hard by the bike. In fact, there was an entire, undamaged bicycle wheel just below it on the grass, the tyre intact. He groped his way towards it.

Had someone been riding this thing? If so, where was he?

The damage to the railing had left a v-shaped gap that Diamond squeezed through.

Tall, coarse grass. Nettles and brambles everywhere.

He cupped his mouth and shouted, "Anyone about?"

No response.

He took out his phone.

Halliwell's voice said, "Guv?" From below,

40

still at the level of the road.

"You'd better join me, both of you, up on the wild bit behind the fire engine. I found something."

He hadn't even pocketed the mobile when he saw a shoe.

Then a leg.

The familiar shock-horror adrenalin surge.

Someone face down in the grass, dead-still.

A corpse?

Diamond squatted, caught his breath, composed himself, tugged at a shoulder.

The pale, wrinkled face of a grey-haired old man, eyes closed, mouth gaping, with dried blood at the edge of the lips. Gently, he turned him on his back.

Dead, apparently, but was he?

What right did he have to decide such a thing?

Do the drill, Diamond told himself. Feel for a pulse. Press two fingers to the side of the neck, in the hollow part beside the Adam's apple.

If there was anything, it was faint and feeble. Could have been the blood circulating through his own fingertips.

No other hint of life. And no obvious injuries other than the blood at the mouth. A cut tongue may have caused that.

He tried opening one of the eyelids. The pale blue eye was motionless, unseeing.

The airways were clear. What else could he do?

CPR.

Mouth-to-mouth resuscitation of an old person, very likely dead, isn't for the squeamish. The urgency of the situation overrode the reluctance. Gently he rotated the body, tipped the chin upwards, leaned over, made contact with the slack, cold lips and breathed into the mouth, enough to cause a slight rise of the chest.

Didn't mean there was life.

He tried a second breath and then started chest compressions, linking his fingers and flattening his palms against the old man's shirt.

Thirty, wasn't it? Thirty compressions followed by two breaths. And you do it as if you mean it, with brute force, regardless that this is a frail old body. Work that ribcage, using the weight from your own upper body and don't even think about his brittle bones splintering. You're the only chance he has, so do all you can to get the blood pulsing around his body.

He'd already lost count, and that was careless. He pumped five more and stopped.

The grey face framed by the grey hair

showed nothing.

He stooped lower for more mouth-to-mouth. The first instinctive revulsion had gone. He cared, he really cared. Hot lips against cold. Two lungfuls of air.

Then back to the compressions. Already he felt the emotional bond that lifesaving creates. He couldn't allow himself to think this might already be a corpse. He and his mate here were not letting go. There had to be life. Come on, old friend, he urged as he worked his aching shoulders, you and I can do this. He was trying to keep counting, but it was next to impossible. Maybe some inner clock was controlling him.

He heard a shout.

Halliwell had scrambled up the bank and was running towards him.

Diamond shouted, "Call an ambulance. There may be a chance."

Paramedics must have attended the crash but they'd long since left with the known casualties. All the attention in the first critical hours had been on the men trapped in the car. No one had thought to climb up here.

He remained on his aching knees beside the unconscious man, working the chest and speaking occasional words of encouragement. So much of him was invested in this

43

rescue bid that he'd actually felt a spasm of anger at Halliwell's interruption. He and his helpless old man were on a mission and nobody had better unsettle them.

Halliwell had put through the call. "They're on the way. Want me to take over?"

"I'm managing. I think there was a pulse."

"He's not looking great."

Ingeborg joined them and had the good idea of wrapping coats around the lower half of the body for warmth. She and Halliwell unzipped their padded jackets.

"Is that the remains of his bike?"

"Must be," Halliwell said. "He was hit by the car and thrown up here."

"What was he doing, an old guy on the road at six in the morning?"

Nobody had an answer. Diamond continued with his task as if it was *his* only chance of keeping alive. He was counting aloud now, almost shouting the numbers to inform his two colleagues that they'd better shut up asking pointless questions that were only a distraction.

Halliwell heard the ambulance siren first and went to meet the paramedics. Diamond continued resolutely with the CPR. There had been no change.

The flashing blue lights drew close and lit up the scene, giving the accident victim an even more deathly look.

The roof of the ambulance was on the same level as the top of the bank. Two paramedics scrambled up.

"I thought there was a faint pulse," Diamond told them between counting.

"You did good," one said as he pulled open the shirt and stuck defibrillator pads to the motionless white chest. "Got to be positive. We'll give him a jerk with this and some more compressions and then get him to the resus bay and see if he was born lucky."

After the ambulance had powered away, siren screaming, massive anti-climax set in. Diamond felt shattered, exhausted, mentally bereft. The people he'd worked with daily for years were like strangers at this minute. The frail old man being rushed to hospital was the only reality. And yet he had to accept that his part in the rescue effort was over.

Recriminations wouldn't be long in following. Someone else should have checked the wild part long before they had got there. The fact that it was across the street from the crash and well above eye level was no excuse.

And now Dessie had been drawn here by

all the activity. He stood gazing at the mangled bicycle parts lying in the long grass. If he felt he should shoulder some blame for missing the hidden victim he wasn't admitting it.

"So here's another point of interest," Ingeborg said acidly.

He gave her a sharp glance. "Arguably, yes."

Nothing more was said for a time. Then Halliwell commented, "Funny sort of push-bike."

"I was thinking the same," Ingeborg said. "Isn't that a third wheel?"

"It's a tricycle," Dessie said. "An adult trike, with a small electric motor." He indicated with his foot. His hands remained in his pockets as if he hadn't yet accepted that this piece of wreckage was part of his remit.

Halliwell squatted and tugged back the grass for a closer look. "There's some kind of bag attached to the handlebars."

"Don't touch," Dessie said. "All the pieces will have to be photographed *in situ* and then taken to our investigation bay. Was he dressed?"

Halliwell and Ingeborg exchanged puzzled glances.

"I get you now," Ingeborg said to Dessie.

"You're thinking of the naked man. Sorry to disappoint. He was clothed."

"Rather eccentrically," Halliwell said, "in an old-fashioned Norfolk overcoat and trousers with gaiters."

"And a deerstalker," Ingeborg added. She'd found one a few yards off in the long grass.

"So what's your expert opinion, Dessie?" Diamond asked. It was taking a huge effort to force himself back to the demands of the job.

"About this? I'll wait for more evidence."

"It's obvious, isn't it?" Halliwell said. "Poor old geezer out for an early-morning ride gets hit by the patrol car and is thrown up here on impact."

"I'll need to see all the technical evidence. There are so many factors — the speed, the visibility, the weather, the skid patterns . . . We always make a computer-aided simulation."

"Which will tell you they swerved to avoid him and mounted the bank and went out of control," Diamond said.

Halliwell said, "I see the patrol car travelling at speed towards the two parked cars, pulling out to pass them and suddenly being faced with the trike. It's early morning, still dark. They won't have seen him coming. They're used to reacting to headlights, not the little lights you get on a bike. Split-second decision. The driver jams on the brakes, pulls the car sharp right and up the verge and still hits the trike."

"Wouldn't he be thrown inwards, towards the centre of the road?" Ingeborg said. "He wouldn't end up here."

"Don't count on it," Diamond said. "If he hit the side of the car swinging towards him at an angle, he'd be bounced this way."

Maybe Dessie had a point. The accident wasn't so straightforward as it had first appeared.

"And he wasn't wearing a helmet," Ingeborg added.

"Crazy," Halliwell said, speaking for all of them.

Dessie went off to fetch a police photographer.

Diamond said to the others, "It's okay trading theories with Dessie. There's some overlap with what we're trying to find out. But let's be clear that he's dealing with the mechanics of the crash. We're concerned with the officers and how professional they were, and suddenly there's a worrying new dimension to it."

"A civilian casualty," Halliwell said.

"Who may have been killed," Ingeborg

added. "And as an ex-journo I know what the papers will make of that."

"Let's not lose time talking about what may or may not happen," Diamond said. The emotional aftermath was still churning him up. "Did you learn anything from the rubbernecks down there?"

They shook their heads. "It happened before anyone was about," Ingeborg said.

"I'm not taking that for granted. One witness could transform this case. We need to knock on doors now. Every door. One thing they'll be able to tell us is if our guys were using blues and twos."

"I doubt if they would have had the siren on," Ingeborg said. "A quiet residential road so early in the morning. Lights, yes, as they were going at speed."

"Even so, we want confirmation, so we ask. And from now on our main priority has to be the tricyclist, a member of the public who was hit by a police car and seriously injured, may have lost his life, in fact. We all know how that will go down."

"Riding a trike at night is asking to be hit," Halliwell said.

Ingeborg turned on him, "Fascist."

"What do you mean? It's crazy."

"It won't be seen that way," Diamond said. "But we need everything we can get

49

on this man. Was he right in the head, sober, capable of riding a bike? If he's local, somebody will know who he is."

"And the naked man?" Halliwell said. "We ought to ask about him. Who's the local fruitcake who likes to get his kit off?"

They started at the houses closest to the crash. Diamond didn't need to knock at the bungalow with the smashed garden wall. The occupant was just emerging with a tray loaded with tea and biscuits. "Would you like one, my darling?" she asked him. She was about eighty, with hair almost as sparse as his.

"That's kind. I haven't been here long," he said. "Give me the tray and I'll pass it to someone who needs it more." He handed it to the nearest fire and rescue man and then turned back to the old lady. "Bit of a shock for you, waking up to this."

"I don't mind," she said. "I grew up in London in the war. You never knew what each new day would bring. I'm sorry for the poor men in that police car. Is it true that one was killed?"

He showed his card and asked if they could speak inside the house. She was only too pleased to cooperate but it didn't take long to discover she knew nothing. The first she had learned of the incident was when she parted her curtains and saw what the patrol car had done to her wall. By then the rescue team was already at work.

"Didn't you hear the crash?"

She shook her head. "I don't wear my hearing aids in bed, my dear."

When asked if she'd ever seen a man on a tricycle riding past, she shook her head. "I'm not much help, am I?"

"Then perhaps you can tell me if any of your neighbours behave strangely. There was a report of a man in the street with no clothes."

"Really? Disgusting." Her eyes lit up. "And to think I missed it."

He tried the next house and was kept on the doorstep by an elderly Asian woman who didn't speak any English. Communication was only achieved with gestures and sound effects. He was thankful his team didn't hear his "Nee Naa Nee Naa Nee Naa" or watch him clap his hands to simulate the car hitting the wall. That was the easy part. The man on the trike was a bigger challenge and the nude neighbour almost impossible to convey without causing offence. All his efforts were rewarded only with disbelieving eyes and a shake of the head.

Finally at the house facing the parked

51

cars, he got a result. The owner, a large, muscled man in a black singlet and combat trousers, had heard the collision while at breakfast and been one of the first on the scene. He'd called the emergency number on his mobile and tried speaking to the two officers in the smashed patrol car, but neither had shown any sign of life until the paramedics arrived. He worked nights at a petrol station on the Warminster Road and hadn't long been home. The white Toyota belonged to him. He was certain the police siren hadn't been used. When asked about the tricyclist, he said he was sure he'd seen an elderly man on a trike.

Diamond's hopes soared. "Today, you mean?"

"No, mate. One morning last week, between six and seven, when I was coming home from work."

"Which day was that?"

"I couldn't tell you. I remember, because he wasn't all that easy to spot. He had one of those LED flashers. He was coming towards me, so he can't have come far."

"Why do you say that?"

"The top of this street is a dead end. It goes a long way and gets a change of name — Hampton Row — but you can't drive any further. It ends in a footbridge across

52

the railway, and that's it."

"Could he have brought the tricycle across the footbridge?"

"Unlikely. Too many steps."

"So it looks as if he starts in Hampton Row. What's it like up there — just an extension of this, with houses one side and rough ground the other?"

"Pretty similar, except they're small terraced houses all the way along." It was said in a superior tone. Beckford Gardens was the smart end.

"No garages, then, where you could store a trike? Thanks. This is useful," Diamond said, thinking it shouldn't be too difficult to trace the tricyclist's home if he lived in one of the terraced houses. He needed to know more about this man who had apparently been the cause of the crash. That was a given. And at a deeper, emotional level, he was tied to the life he still hoped he had helped to save.

"One other question. The police car was on its way here to check on a report of a naked man. Can you think of anyone locally who gets up to stuff like that?"

"Round here? Unlikely. Who reported it?"

"At this stage I'm not sure. Our control centre ought to know the source of the call but I haven't been able to check yet."

53

"What a weirdo."

"It takes all sorts."

Diamond returned outside to see if Ingeborg or Keith Halliwell had discovered anything more. He'd visited the three houses he'd picked for himself. Halliwell had got through his three and learned nothing of use and Ingeborg was still not back.

"Probably getting coffee and cake," Halliwell said.

"If she is, she'd better have something to report." He called the control room and asked if there was news from the hospital of Lew Morgan's condition. The injured sergeant was under sedation. He wouldn't be fit to interview for at least the next twelve hours. "How about the man on the trike?" Diamond asked.

"They're trying to resuscitate him," the operator said.

"I know that. Do we know his name? Was he carrying any form of ID?"

"Apparently not."

He was stung by their lack of urgency. "Someone at your end should have identified him by now. It's not rocket science. How many blokes in Bath own motor-powered tricycles? Was he registered to ride the thing?"

"One moment, sir."

54

He told Halliwell the operator was checking. "Idle bastards. This should save us no end of time and hassle."

The operator got back to him. "An electric bike is an EAPC."

"What's that when it's at home?"

"I'm not quite sure, sir. The thing is, it doesn't have to be registered, taxed or insured."

"Great." He ended the call and told Halliwell.

"Not to worry, guv. As soon as it's on the local news, someone will know who he was. You can't ride a thing like that around Bath without people asking who the hell you are and why you do it."

"Good point." He checked his watch. "Which house did Ingeborg go into?"

"The one with the tiled porch."

"D'you think she's okay?"

"What do you mean?"

"She's been in there the best part of half an hour. The naked man could be in one of these houses."

"She'd kick him where it hurts most, guv."

Halliwell was right. Ingeborg could look after herself. She hated being treated as the helpless female. More than once, Diamond had made the mistake of fretting over her as if she was a daughter. He hardened his heart and watched the lifting gear being attached to the wrecked car, ready to hoist it on to the flat-bed truck. At least one life had been lost, but for the professionals it was just another traffic accident.

There was a movement under the tiled porch.

"Here she comes," Halliwell said, "looking none the worse."

"I hope you've got something for us," Diamond told her when she joined them.

"Afraid not," she said. "It was an old lady in a panic because the carer hadn't arrived. She had no idea what was going on outside."

"So you did some caring?" Halliwell said in a mocking tone, still smarting from being called a fascist.

"I couldn't just walk out. She was in a wheelchair."

Diamond stopped himself from making an approving comment about Ingeborg's feminine side.

"I did ask her the questions," she added, "just in case."

"And the other people you spoke to?"

"No help at all. Just like her, they had questions for *me.*"

He decided to cast the net wider. He wanted to explore the top end of this road, where the man on the trike had come from, leaving Ingeborg and Halliwell to knock on doors at the other end. When he stepped over the DO NOT PASS tape, edged through the gawpers and headed up the street, it was a relief to leave the mayhem behind.

If the truth were told, he needed a chance to collect his thoughts. Accident investigation was new in his experience. At a murder scene, he'd be making the decisions. He'd decide the scale of the investigation, how many CID people to employ. A procedure was observed. As SIO he'd seal the immediate area and control the access and the screening of the body. He'd liaise with the scene-of-crime people, a police photographer, the divisional surgeon and usually a forensic pathologist, and there was no question who conducted the operation.

Here, he'd been one of many response people from the different emergency services. They respected each other, for sure, only they all had jobs to get on with. Nobody wilfully contaminated the scene, but it was a dog's breakfast compared with the painstaking process he was used to. And the noise level had been a pain. In these conditions it was easy to act and hard to think.

He asked himself what he could usefully do before the doctors allowed him to interview the key witness, Lew Morgan. In the next twenty-four hours or so there would be a postmortem on the dead driver. He'd long ago learned that a postmortem was a false dawn. It happened soon after death and you hoped for swift information, but then samples of blood and body fluids were sent for testing and the testers wouldn't be hurried. In this case the cause of death was obvious. All he wanted to know for sure was that the late PC Aaron Green had no trace of alcohol or drugs in his system.

As Halliwell had rightly commented, identifying the civilian victim shouldn't be a problem once the incident had some publicity. Not many people rode the streets of Bath on tricycles. Somebody would be able to put a name to him.

Towards the end of Beckford Gardens he found he'd been misinformed. The street didn't just become a dead end in Hampton Row as the man in combat trousers had claimed. Beckford Gardens ended at a left turn called Rockliffe Road. The man on the trike could easily have come from there.

You need to check every damned thing yourself.

He moved on, muttering. After the Rockliffe Road turn, Beckford Gardens had a change of identity as Cleveland Row and finally Hampton Row. At least the description as a terrace of small dwellings had been accurate. By the look of them, they were two hundred years old or more, some shabby, some nicely renovated. At the far end, where the road went no further, was the bridge over the railway, and he couldn't imagine anyone struggling to hoist a tricycle over that. He climbed the steps and watched a First Great Western express from Paddington shoot beneath him on its way to Bath Spa station. The small boy in him thrilled to the power of the train making the bridge vibrate.

On returning to street level he spotted a postman dressed in shorts, as so many are in all weathers. He went over.

"Morning, postie. Is this your regular route?"

"It is." The postman spoke the words on the move, making clear he hadn't much time to chat.

"It's a part of the city I don't know too well," Diamond said, keeping pace. "I'm in the police, investigating the crash back there."

"I saw." The postman had his attention on the letters in his hand, checking address numbers.

"The driver was killed and two people are

59

in intensive care. One of them was travelling from this direction on a tricycle. Quite early, before seven. Have you ever seen him along here?"

"No." He hadn't even looked up.

Diamond wasn't letting him off so easily. "If he lived in one of these houses, he'd need to park his trike in front. I noticed bikes leaning against some of the railings. I expect you'd have spotted a trike if someone owned one."

"I haven't." Which closed that line of enquiry.

Try the other, then. "Someone called 999 about a naked man in Beckford Gardens. That's why the patrol car was here."

Not a flicker of interest.

"Ring any bells? I'm asking you as someone who knows this neighbourhood."

"Can't help you," the postman said, almost causing another accident by swinging his trolley wide and over Diamond's foot.

"Do you mind? You don't even sound surprised. A man with no clothes on. It's not a common sight."

"I expect he came up from the lido."

A light bulb went on in Diamond's head. Something had been on the local TV news a while back about an old Georgian swim-

60

ming baths beside the Avon that had got into disrepair and was having millions spent on it. There was a trust and they'd staged some kind of open day when over a thousand people had turned up, including folk in costume looking like characters out of Jane Austen. He hadn't connected the report with this row of poky artisan dwellings.

He almost hugged the postman. "Now that could be vital information. Would that be the outdoor pool they're renovating with lottery money? It's round here? I've heard about that, and never seen it. Where exactly is it?"

"You walked straight past."

"You're kidding."

But this postman wasn't the kidding sort. "Them two stone pillars between Fir Tree Cottage and Rose Cottage. Now can I get on with my round?"

"Is it open to the public, then?" he shouted after him.

There may have been a shake of the head. There wasn't anything more.

He'd have to see this for himself, so he stepped out and entered the narrow passage between the terraces. The footpath was steep, and he wouldn't care to make the descent after frost. But after being in that narrow road between the houses and the railway it was good to see the valley open up below him.

Before he had gone far, the lido came into sight among the trees, the view he remembered from the TV, a cream-coloured crescent-shaped facade reflected in the pool. The centrepiece was the supervisor's cottage with a grey tiled roof and arched entrance. Rows of changing cubicles extended either side. They looked elegant in the context of the building, dark, perpendicular spaces at regular intervals, but he guessed the interiors would need updating to modern standards. However, it was not impossible that some resident of Beckford Gardens or Hampton Row was in the habit of going for an early-morning dip — even a skinny-dip.

He didn't need to go right down there. He'd learned all he wanted, so he turned and picked his way up the path. When he reached Hampton Row the postman wasn't around for further questioning.

That one went to plan. Silly old buffer didn't see it coming, didn't know anything about it. Job done. And now it's a matter of acting normally, given that my normal is a little different from everyone else's. The aftermath will be just as testing as the act itself. As long as I act the innocent and sound surprised by his passing I should be fine.

Sleeping reasonably well, without medication. Vivid dreams left me sweating the last couple of nights, but I know the pattern. They won't trouble me for long.

3

His phone sounded. Even after years of using mobiles, Diamond disliked them going off unexpectedly, much preferring the old days when he could leave the office knowing no one could reach him. This time it was Bath Police and for once it was a message he wanted to hear. The emergency control room at Portishead had supplied the phone number of the caller who had spotted the naked man.

He noted it on the palm of his hand.

"And while you're on," he said to the civilian operator, "I'm going to need a printout of all the exchanges between our own control room and Delta Three from the time they came on duty to the moment of the crash."

"I'll need to speak to my supervisor about that," she said.

"Please do — now — and be sure to tell her that this is urgently required by Professional Standards, and not just me."

Back at the accident site, the wrecked car had already been driven away for examination by the police collision unit and the last of the oil was being hosed from the road surface. It wouldn't be long before Beckford Gardens was open to traffic again. The only evidence of the crash would be the broken wall and the inevitable tributes of cut flowers.

He caught up with Ingeborg first. "It's frustrating," she said. "People want to help, but no one saw what happened."

Keith Halliwell joined them and it was obvious from his expression that he too had nothing useful to report.

Diamond told them about the footpath down to the lido. "Could be unrelated, a complete red herring," he said, "but I'm wondering if our naked man came up from there after an early morning dip."

Instead of cooing in admiration, Ingeborg said, "Does it matter? He's a side issue. He may not even exist."

"How do you work that out?" Halliwell said.

"A nuisance call. They get them all the time."

"You're starting to sound like John Leaman."

65

"It's been a depressing morning. Look, whatever you think about that stupid call, it wasn't directly responsible for the crash. The blame for that lies squarely with the driver of the police car or the old man on the trike."

"Hang on a minute. What if no one was to blame?" Halliwell said. "What if a tyre burst or the brakes failed? Let's keep an open mind."

"And you're starting to sound like Dessie." She held up her hands. "Okay, that was a bit sweeping."

Halliwell said, "So we all agree to follow up any lead we can get?"

Diamond had been content to let this little spat play out. Now he showed them the number on his hand.

"Go for it, guv," Halliwell said. "Let's find out if it was genuine."

Ingeborg gave a nod and said no more.

Diamond pressed the numbers and waited.

A man's voice gave a guarded, "Yes?"

Diamond explained who he was.

"Police? It's about time. I called you over three hours ago."

"You made the emergency call, sir?"

"Why? Do you doubt me?" The guarded voice now became aggressive. "I've heard

66

that response times are a disgrace but this must be a record. What time is it now?"

Scarcely believing what he was hearing, Diamond said, "Maybe you're not aware there was a fatal accident up the road."

"Of course I am. I couldn't help hearing it, but an emergency is an emergency. Your job is to get here as soon as possible."

Everyone had their own ideas on Diamond's job this morning. "Could I have your name and address?"

"Don't you know already?"

"When an emergency call is received, we're more concerned with the situation and where it's happening than who the informant is."

"And now you want to know? Heaven help us. Well, I'm Cedric Bellerby and it's obvious where I live, in Beckford Gardens."

"Which number, Mr. Bellerby?"

"Bellerby Lodge, the one with the flagpole. Where are you speaking from? You can probably see it from where you are."

He spotted the Union Jack fluttering high above the rooftops towards the Hampton Row end. He must have walked past without noticing. A fine detective he was.

"I can now. As you're at home, we'll come and see you."

"Now that the horse has bolted."

Diamond acted as if he hadn't heard. In his time he'd locked horns with bigger beasts than Cedric Bellerby. "Be with you in two or three minutes and if you can run to a coffee — or three — we'll be grateful. It's been one of those mornings." He ended the call before there was any comeback.

So all three arrived on the doorstep of Bellerby Lodge, a modest-sized bungalow considering its owner's air of importance. When the man appeared, he, also, was modest-sized except for a black moustache you could have fitted to the hose of a vacuum cleaner. He looked the visitors up and down before allowing them in.

The interesting thing about the front room was two pairs of binoculars on the window-sill. Otherwise it was the conventional three-piece suite, bookcase, TV and fitted carpet. "You said something about coffee," their host told them, "but this won't take more than a couple of minutes if all you want to hear about is the degenerate with no clothes. He's long since made his escape."

"We'll have the coffee first, then," Diamond said cheerfully. "Mine is white with two sugars and the others like it black without."

Outfoxed, Bellerby sighed, shook his head and disappeared to the kitchen. Diamond immediately picked up a pair of binoculars and tried them. They weren't cheap goods. He trained them on the site of the collision more than a hundred yards away and got a sharp image of Dessie, clipboard in hand, taking paces across the road.

He passed the glasses to Ingeborg to have a try. She held them to her eyes for a few seconds before handing them to Halliwell.

The sound of a throat being cleared heralded Bellerby's arrival with the tray.

"Put them down, Keith," Diamond said. To Bellerby he added, "He can't keep his hands to himself. Always fidgeting with things. Are you a birdwatcher, sir?"

"I have them for the magnificent view."

"Of your neighbours?"

He screwed up his face in disapproval. "The valley, from the back of the house."

"But you keep them here, on the window-sill?"

"Not usually. I was observing the goings-on after the car crash."

"And did you see the naked man through the binoculars?"

"That was earlier."

"Before dawn?"

"I'm an early riser."

The coffee was handed round. Halliwell

had replaced the binoculars on the window-sill.

"Your 999 call was timed at six-fourteen," Diamond said. "Not much light, was there?"

"One set of glasses is for night vision."

"Really? What do you study after dark?"

"Wildlife mostly. Foxes, badgers, deer."

"And naked men?"

Bellerby glared back. "It's never happened before. That's why it was such a shock."

"Take us back to when you first caught sight of this offensive spectacle. Where were you — in here?"

"The back bedroom."

"With the wonderful view?"

"Yes."

"May we see?"

He clicked his tongue. "I thought this was just routine, following up on my call."

"We're investigating what you saw, Mr. Bellerby, and what happened after. Do you live alone?"

"What's that got to do with it?"

"If there's a lady in the back bedroom, she may not welcome three strangers coming in."

"My wife and I separated years ago."

Diamond thought of a comment but chose not to make it. "That's all right, then. Lead the way, would you? We won't spill our coffee on the carpet."

Bellerby tried to make a stand. "I don't see the need."

"But I do. We want to know all about this emergency." He took a couple of steps towards the doorway and there was a momentary stand-off. "Don't even think about obstructing us. It won't go down well."

The moustache twitched but its owner backed down, as Diamond had calculated. They were led into a room that may have been built as a bedroom but had no bed. It was better described as an observatory. In front of a large picture window were two cameras on tripods and a telescope mounted on a revolving dais with a seat that also rotated, like a gun position on a warship.

"Well equipped."

"It's my hobby."

Diamond stepped up to the window and the view was every bit as spectacular as Bellerby had claimed. The houses along here had been built at the top of the escarpment overlooking the river and with the naked eye you could see much of northern Bath, the tiers of crescents rising to the dark green of Lansdown on the opposite side.

"Stunning. You had an eye to the location when you moved here."

"It was a factor, yes."

71

"And you didn't expect to look out on a buck-naked man? Neither would I. Very off-putting. Where was he when you first spotted him?"

"Down there to your right," Bellerby said after some hesitation.

"Down where?"

He pointed.

"The Georgian lido?" You wouldn't have guessed Diamond spoke with the authority of a man who had been reminded of its existence less than an hour ago. "They're spending millions of lottery money refurbishing it, aren't they? It will surely become a tourist attraction — the oldest open-air swimming pool in Britain, I was told. I daresay the naked man had sneaked in for an early morning dip."

Bellerby said nothing.

"Rather him than me," Diamond went on. "Too damn cold this time of year. Crazy people do it all the year round. I worked in London years ago and they used to break the ice on the Serpentine to have their daily swim. Is he one of your neighbours?"

"I've no idea," Bellerby said, tight-lipped.

"You'd know if he was. With that powerful telescope you must have got a good sight of him and all his particulars."

"I wasn't using the telescope at the time."

"I forgot. You had the night-vision binoculars. The image wouldn't have been so sharp. Have you seen him before — or any other secret bathers?"

"No."

"Still, it could become a regular thing. You don't want that sort of how-d'ye-do going on in this beautiful valley. Is there local opposition to what's happening to the old lido?"

After a long pause, as if aware he was being drawn into dangerous territory, Bellerby said, "Some of us aren't overjoyed."

"I'm with you there," Diamond said. "Trippers, people hiring the place for parties, booze, loud music and God knows what else going on in your own back yard. It's sure to be a pain. But if you try and stop it now, you're up against the great and the good of the city. There's a trust and all this money being invested."

Bellerby started backtracking. "I don't know why you're making an issue of this."

"Because I need to understand why a naked man was a full-blown emergency. Some people might treat him as a laugh, or at worst a blot on the landscape. You called 999 and asked for the police."

"It was the proper thing to do. Gross indecency. There are laws about that."

73

"Against people exposing themselves? Yes, indeed."

"He could be a sex maniac."

"That's an expression I haven't heard for years."

"A pervert, then. A danger to the public."

"A 999 call?"

"How else am I supposed to report it? You know very well that calling the local police station is no help at all in an emergency. This was going on while I was watching. In a short time he'd be away."

Diamond controlled his contempt. This was the justification that put impossible strains on the emergency service. People didn't trust the first line of help, be it police or general medical practice, to react effectively to their small crises. In a society where so much of life is controlled by the touch of a button they felt entitled to instant action. And then they complained when the response times got longer and longer.

"Where exactly was he when you first spotted him?"

"Down by the pool. It was flagrant nudity."

"Was he alone at the time?"

"He appeared to be. That doesn't excuse it."

"No one's excusing it, Mr. Bellerby. What

74

happened next?"

"He left the lido and started up the footpath. That was when I called 999."

"And then?"

"I continued to observe him so that when the police arrived I could say exactly where he was."

"Sensible." This buffoon had to be humoured to tell his story in full.

"I followed his progress all the way up the footpath towards Hampton Row."

"Still without his kit on?"

He cleared his throat. "By then he'd put on some sort of tracksuit."

This was getting more and more farcical. "He'd dressed before leaving the lido?"

"Yes. I kept him in my sights as long as possible."

"And when he reached Hampton Row you dashed into the front room to see where he went. Is that right?"

"I wouldn't say 'dashed.' I was perfectly calm."

"Put it this way: you moved directly there. Did he come into view?"

"No. Unfortunately there's a bend in the road. I can't see Hampton Row from here. That's where the footpath comes out. I expected he would turn this way, but it seems he didn't. I can only imagine he lives in one of the terraced houses along there."

Ingeborg, who had listened with admirable self-control, said, "Or he could have turned up Rockliffe Avenue."

"I think not. I can see that turn from here. Well, from my front gate."

"So you went outside?" Diamond said.

"To meet the police — as I expected. I told them to come here."

"But the incident wasn't here. It was down at the lido."

"Quite true. But if they were going to make an arrest, they'd have to do it up here. He was already climbing the hill when I made the call."

There was a plodding logic in this, but Diamond had long since lost any sympathy he may have had. Somehow, he had to rein himself in, because this absurd little man could still have vital information. "Think carefully, Mr. Bellerby. What happened next?"

"There was a fearful bang —"

"Before that," Diamond cut him short. "We're here about the events leading up to the crash. Did you hear the approach of the police car? Were they using their siren?"

"I believe not. I would remember, wouldn't I?"

A question impossible for Diamond to

answer. "I'll take that as no. How about their beacon lights?"

"Yes, I saw them flashing, I'm certain. The thought went through my head that this must be the police car answering my call, and then there was the screech of brakes and that almighty bang and the lights weren't flashing any longer."

"You heard the crash but didn't actually see it?"

He nodded. "I was too far off."

"By your front gate?"

"I told you."

"How long for?"

"I don't know. I wasn't timing myself."

"Ten minutes?"

"About that."

"This is important," Diamond said. "I know the crash is strongest in your memory but during the ten-minute wait did anyone else come by?"

Bellerby frowned and then fingered the moustache as if it might aid his thought process. "Yes, there was someone, an elderly man on a tricycle."

"Before the crash? This could be helpful. Which way did he come?"

"From the Hampton Row direction. It was still quite dark but I made sure I got a sight of him in case he was the naked man.

I'm certain he wasn't. He was definitely older and dressed differently as well, in a jacket and deer-stalker hat. Heaven only knows where he'd been or where he was going."

Finally something useful.

Diamond pressed for more details. "Was he travelling fast?"

"Not at all. The tricycle must have had some kind of motor, because he wasn't pedalling, but you could have kept up at a quick walk. His steering wasn't the best, either. He was wandering off course as if he wasn't used to riding the thing."

"Did he have lights?"

"I'm sure he did, front and back, the sort that wink intermittently."

"Did he see you as he went by?"

"He was too busy trying to stay in control. I don't think he noticed me at all."

"But you definitely saw him before the car crash? How long before?"

"Not long."

"I need a more precise answer than that."

"Three or four minutes, at least. I assume he got through before it happened."

"You're wrong about that," Diamond said. "An elderly man was found a short time ago, unconscious."

"Oh my word. Nobody said."

"He and his tricycle were thrown high up on to the embankment."

"Shocking."

"You say you didn't recognise him?"

"It was almost dark and I didn't get a proper look at his face, but I can't recollect anyone from round here riding a tricycle. Poor fellow. Will he recover?"

A fatuous question. Diamond glanced at his colleagues. "We've heard enough for now, I think."

On the drive back to Keynsham, where Bath CID was now inconveniently housed, Halliwell spoke for all of them. "What a toerag. He doesn't get it, does he? Because he made that stupid bloody call, Aaron Green was killed and two others are in intensive care."

"People like him have no idea of consequences," Ingeborg said. "They're so wrapped up in themselves they don't think of the risks each time there's a call-out."

"I can't make out why he got so uptight about a nude bather," Halliwell said. "It's obvious he's some kind of perv himself with his telescope and binoculars. Studying wildlife, for Christ's sake."

"There's more to it," Diamond said. "He has an agenda. He'd like to stop the lido project. Did you see the glint in his eyes when I talked about parties and loud music? Any mud he can throw their way, he will."

"Is that all it was about?"

"It's no help to him if he's the only one who sees the naked flesh. He wants maximum publicity, so he calls 999."

"After the guy has got dressed and left the place. Pointless."

"No," Diamond said. "He had a point. He wanted our lot involved, to get it on record. He could write to the papers or go on local radio and say the lido is being used for nude bathing and the police were called and unless something is done about it, they'll soon be having sex parties and orgies."

"How do I join?" Halliwell said.

Ingeborg rolled her eyes.

"His coffee was rubbish, too," Diamond said. "Let's stop off at the Verona."

In Keynsham police centre, Georgina, the ACC, had told everyone she wished to speak to Diamond the instant he returned. He took a relaxed view and stretched the instant to almost an hour. It had been a long morning.

"This mysterious man on a tricycle," she said when he finally went upstairs and reported. "Who is he?"

80

" 'Who was he?' may be the right question."

"No, no. I'm getting regular updates from the resuscitation bay. He's clinging on to life."

He perked up. "He survived my CPR?"

"Your prompt action may have saved his life. If he does come through this, he'll owe you a debt of gratitude."

"I don't want anyone owing me anything, thanks."

"Don't be so modest, Peter. I gather you found him on a piece of wasteland where nobody else had thought to check."

"They would have got round to it," he said. "Pure chance on my part. I was thinking a fox or a deer may have jumped down and caused the crash. There's an iron fence all the way along the top of the bank, so that's unlikely."

"Getting back to my earlier question, what do we know about him?"

"Very little. My working theory is that he caused the crash. A witness says he was riding unsteadily."

"Someone saw?"

"No, ma'am. They only saw the old man going in that direction."

"Did they know him?"

"No."

"Wasn't he carrying any form of identity?"

"I was too busy pounding his chest to go through his pockets."

"The hospital doesn't seem to have found anything."

"He's a Sherlock Holmes impersonator, going by what he was wearing," he said. "Someone will know. People like him get noticed."

"The worst of it is that this brings a serious new dimension to your investigation," Georgina said. "Deeply alarming."

"You're wishing I hadn't found him?"

"I'm happy for his sake, not for ours. It was bad enough that one of our officers lost his life. With a member of the public critically injured it's almost certain to be referred to the Independent Police Complaints Commission."

"Does that mean I'm free to return to normal duties?"

"Quite the reverse. You must devote every minute of your time to finding out what really happened. We're going to find ourselves under scrutiny. At the earliest opportunity you must get a statement from the driver."

"Difficult. He's dead."

She dismissed her mistake with an impatient, angry sigh. "The other one, then."

"Lew Morgan is still in intensive care."

"I know. I called the hospital in the last twenty minutes. But at some stage he'll be able to talk."

"We can hope."

"See that you're the first in. Did you meet the collision investigator?"

"Dessie? Yes."

"Make sure he's on side. We don't want conflicting versions."

"That's unlikely to happen. Dessie is dealing with the mechanical stuff, recording everything. Scene plans, vehicle components, that sort of thing. He's very young."

She saw danger in the last remark. "Don't underrate him. I have it on good authority that he misses nothing."

Diamond thought of the crashed tricycle and its rider lying unnoticed for three hours but kept the thought to himself.

"He's a civilian, of course," Georgina added, "so don't be tempted to pull rank with him. He's with the top forensic road collision investigation company and they have the highest opinion of him."

"We'll sort things out between us," he said.

"What will you do next?"

"Depends."

"Depends on what?"

"How soon Lew Morgan is fit to talk."

4

Diamond slept fitfully, troubled by recurring images of the old man's grey, lifeless face.

In the morning, he drove — with even more care than usual — to the Royal United Hospital instead of straight to work. After much badgering of the ward sister responsible for Lew Morgan's care, he was told he might be allowed a short visit after the consultant had seen the patient.

It wasn't so simple.

Extra treatment — whatever that meant — was prescribed, meaning a wait of at least an hour. Instead of sitting outside and staring at a wall he had the good idea of checking on the progress, if any, of the tricyclist. He located the Critical Care unit quickly, not far from the room where Lew Morgan was being treated. Understandably, he wasn't allowed inside, even with his police ID.

"What are his chances?" he asked the one nurse willing to be questioned.

She held her hand palm downwards and made a quivering movement.

"Not the best, then?"

"He's old. He must be over seventy, quite well nourished, but the trauma he's been through would test someone half his age. Apparently — don't ask me why — he was lying unconscious for some hours before he was brought in. There are other injuries from the fall and we haven't concluded how serious they are."

"He's still with us. That's something."

She didn't comment, just widened her eyes a fraction.

He took this to mean the patient was clinically alive thanks to the treatment he was getting. Whether he showed vital signs of his own was less certain.

Of course it would aid the investigation if the old boy pulled through, but at this minute Diamond wasn't thinking about the investigation. He passionately wanted the man to survive.

"Did you discover his name?" he asked the nurse. "I was wondering if you found a wallet or a card-case in his pockets."

"There wasn't anything like that," she said. "Some money and a set of keys that

Sister has put in the safe. No, he's our mystery patient until somebody misses him and comes looking."

He went outside and called CID. Ingeborg was in.

"I've been given a statement from the control room, guv," she said. "It's a log of all their exchanges with Delta Three on the night of the crash."

"Good. I asked for that. Anything of special interest?"

"Not really but it gives a picture of the areas they visited. They arrested two men from Swindon stealing lead from a church roof in Julian Road and brought them in to the custody suite. They were still here when the call came in about the naked man. It was almost the end of their turn."

She also had a list from Dessie of the items found in the handlebar bag: binoculars, digital camera, a few tools for the trike, an Ordnance Survey map of Bath, a vacuum flask containing the dregs of some tea and a plastic sandwich box but with only some cake crumbs and a banana skin inside. And a plastic vase.

"A what?"

"A vase about a foot high, with a lid. Dessie thought it might have contained ashes."

"Oh?"

"He said it was typical of the temporary containers provided by crematoria but there was nothing inside."

"Like an urn? How weird."

"Very."

"You mentioned a camera. Have they checked it?"

"Damaged, I'm sorry to say."

"How damaged? It would be good to know if he took any pictures."

"The vacuum flask split and everything was soaked in tea. They're sending the memory card to a data recovery expert but they don't hold out much hope."

"What's a data recovery expert for if he can't recover data?"

"Am I supposed to answer that, guv?" Ingeborg said.

"No need. I was having my usual rant. We've got a few clues now."

"Have we?"

"Come on, Inge. Is this the result of all the hours I've devoted to teaching you the art of detection?"

He heard a nervous laugh. "Sorry, guv, I must have missed something."

"First, there's the obvious clue of the banana."

"But there isn't a banana."

"That's the obvious clue." She'd walked into that like a latter-day Dr. Watson. "He'd eaten it."

"He'd eaten the cake as well."

"Better. What do you deduce from that?"

"He'd got hungry at some point."

"More importantly, he hadn't just started out. He must have been out some time already."

"Okay, that's worth knowing, I agree."

"Now let's turn to the clue of the binoculars," he said.

"You're doing my head in, guv. Does it mean he was another voyeur, like Mr. Bellerby?"

"Spying on people? I doubt it. He wouldn't need an Ordnance Survey map for that. It suggests to me he'd been out most of the night in the country — maybe at a nature reserve, looking at wildlife. Foxes, deer and badgers all like to move about after dark. He had the deerstalker hat and gaiters, so he dressed the part. The camera was in case he got a chance of a picture. My hunch is that this was a keen nature-lover."

"Will that help us identify him?" Ingeborg said without sounding wholly convinced.

"Well, it doesn't give us his name and address," he said, slightly piqued. "I'm a detective, not a clairvoyant."

She hesitated. "Isn't there something else — the clue of the empty cremation urn?"

"For the present, I haven't got that down as a clue."

"Could he have been on his way back from scattering someone's ashes?"

A depressing thought that couldn't be discounted. "I suppose." His thoughts moved on. He was back in the CID groove. "Was anything on TV this morning about the crash?"

"I don't look at TV in the morning."

"Issue a press statement appealing for information, then. I'm serious now, Inge. I want this done right away. Full description of our tricyclist, the eccentric get-up. We can say he was injured early yesterday in a car accident in Beckford Gardens and is now in intensive care. Someone must be missing him by now."

His own last comment stayed with him after he'd pocketed the phone and was returning to Lew Morgan's ward. Was there anyone who would miss the old nature-lover? The cake might suggest there was someone who cared about him. But going out at night — and staying out — could be the mark of a loner.

"Don't get your hopes up," the sister said

when Diamond reached the room where Lew Morgan was being treated. "He's unlikely to remember anything about the crash."

"So I'm wasting my time?"

"It's not surprising. He's being treated with strong painkillers."

"They said he might lose his leg."

"He will, almost certainly." A statement of fact. There's no room for sentiment in the treatment of accident victims.

"Does he remember much?"

She looked at him over her glasses. "It's not our job to question him. We try to stay positive. Are you a close friend?"

"Can't say I am."

"But you're here officially?"

"Between you and me, I'd rather be anywhere else."

"You can try getting him to speak. He knows who he is and where he lives."

"That's a start."

"Be patient, then, get his confidence and let him talk if he wants to. Don't make him anxious. No pressure, please. First, you must put this on." She took a pack from a shelf and handed it to him.

A surgical mask and gown in a sterile bag. He was going to feel odd dressed like that but he didn't question the instruction.

"If you need me," the sister added, "there's a call switch in front of him."

Dressed like someone out of *ER*, he went in. He could just about recognise the patient as the uniformed sergeant he'd seen from time to time at Manvers Street police station. Lew Morgan's eyes were closed and sensor pads were attached to his chest. A console of screens monitoring vital functions was at the head of the bed. An intravenous drip on a stand was connected to his right arm. But his face was clear, apart from bruising and small cuts.

"Lew?"

The eyes opened and looked as if they wanted to close again. Wouldn't anybody's, faced with one more hooded figure with a sterile mask?

"Peter Diamond, from the nick. You may have seen me around."

No answer.

Be patient and get his confidence, she'd advised, so he made the attempt. "Plenty of people send you their best, too many to mention by name. You'll be inundated with get-well cards. I get to be the first to see you because I was given the job of finding out what happened. I'll need all the help you can give me."

No response, except that the eyes remained open.

Diamond had never been good at small talk — and this was a muffled monologue, not a conversation. He would quickly run out of topics that would not upset the patient. "Of course, if there's anyone you'd like to visit you, just say their names and I can arrange it."

Lew didn't seem interested in naming his police buddies. But then his cracked lips moved and at a second try he found his voice. "Did we . . ."

"Yes? I hear you."

". . . get to Beckford Gardens?"

Did we get to Beckford Gardens?

A pause for Diamond to catch up. "You did." Encouraged to have elicited anything at all, he was about to add, "That's where you crashed," and managed to stop himself. Instead, he said, "You definitely got there. Oh yes, there's no argument about that. Mission accomplished."

The mouth curved into something like a smile.

"So you haven't lost your memory." Diamond started mining this promising seam. "You can recall where you were heading. You'd been on the night turn when the call came from the control room soon after six A.M."

Lew's lips twitched, trying, it seemed, to speak again. It took an effort but the words finally came. "Some bollock-naked idiot."

This eased the tension wonderfully. Diamond grinned. "I couldn't put it better myself. Report of a naked man in Beckford Gardens." Instead of being the hospital visitor with the sick patient, he could relate to the guy as one cop to another.

"Aaron at the wheel," Lew volunteered. "PC Aaron Green."

Watch it, Diamond told himself. This was heading into an area the sister would class as upsetting. Fortunately she was on her duties way out of earshot.

"Married," Lew said. "Young kid."

"I know."

"Nothing wrong with his driving."

"I'm sure."

"Tired. Very tired." The eyes closed.

Frustrating. On the brink of saying something helpful he seemed to be drifting off again. Then it became obvious that Lew wasn't speaking of his present condition. Those eyes were squeezed tight in an effort to remember.

They opened again. "Knackered. Both of us," Lew said. He'd been trying to convey the state he and Aaron had been in before the crash.

Anyone who had worked the night turn would understand. Seven A.M. can never come too soon.

"One of those nights," Lew said. "Fucking nutcase."

"Nuisance calls?"

"Old guy on a trike."

Suddenly Diamond was all ears.

". . . dressed as Sherlock fucking Holmes."

"I'm with you, Lew. This is really helpful. Keep going."

"Crazy. Told me he had his wife with him."

Who was the crazy one here? Lew himself had a few of his pages stuck together if he thought he'd had a conversation with the accident victim.

"It was her ashes."

The empty urn Dessie had recovered from the scene. Surreal and impossible as it was, Lew was making some kind of sense. "He spoke to you? Is that right — you and he talked? Did he tell you anything else?"

"Rabbits."

"Yes?" Thrown by the word, Diamond tried to respond as if he understood. It was vital to keep this going. "Like furry creatures with large ears?"

"A mile a night, hopping to Bath," Lew said. Maddeningly, he'd lost the thread just after he'd made the first significant statement.

"Yes?"

"Hear them digging their holes."

Too bad Lew had lost it and was talking rubbish. He needed to be brought back to the scene of the collision. "You were telling me you and Aaron were dog tired. Do you remember what happened when you got to Beckford Gardens?"

"Bushed, yeah."

The troubled brain was working hard.

"Shut my eyes."

"No. Stay with me if you can." Diamond didn't want this ending now. "We're almost through, Lew."

"I'm telling you," Lew said with more force. "My fucking eyes were shut."

"Got you now. Sorry."

"Next thing Aaron yells something and we're fucking turning over. That was it."

"What did he yell?"

" 'Jeez!' Something like that. Ask him."

Chilling. He thought Aaron was still alive. He'd been trapped in the car beside a corpse. Surely he remembered? But the brain has its own way of dealing with shock. He must have suppressed the ghastly memory he couldn't deal with yet.

Diamond changed tack. "The old guy on

95

the trike. Did he cause the accident?"

"Him? What do you mean?"

"He was there, Lew."

"Wasn't."

The only witness to the crash was self-deluding about everything he couldn't cope with. This critically important interview was imploding. "Believe me, he was."

"No."

"I'm telling you."

"Stay out of my head, will you?"

A sharp rebuke. Worse, Lew reached for the call switch and pressed it. The session was about to end.

"I'm on your side, Lew."

But now the eyes registered only mistrust.

Diamond was thinking if the medics had decided an amputation was necessary there might not be another chance in days of getting to the truth. "We're all aware of what you're going through. You know what the police are like. They have to know every detail of what happened."

"Piss off." Lew pressed the button again.

The sister came in, heard what was said and summed up the situation. "I had my doubts it would work. It's too soon. I'm afraid I must ask you to leave."

Diamond didn't argue. "Thanks, anyway." He removed the sterile clothes and gave her

96

a card. "If he changes his mind, these are my contact details."

She glanced at the card and smiled faintly. "I don't suppose he knew he was talking to a superintendent."

"I've heard worse," he said.

On his way back to the car he was seething with frustration. He'd succeeded only in upsetting a critically injured man. The fragmented account of the collision had added little of use to what he already knew. He'd not asked for this bloody job and he was getting nowhere with it.

There was a voice message on his mobile asking him to call Desmond De Lisle. Who the hell was that?

Dessie.

He called the number.

"How's it progressing, squire?" Dessie asked.

"Squire" was slightly less objectionable than "man," but it still rankled. "It isn't. One of the survivors is too far gone to speak and the other isn't making sense. But you were trying to reach me."

"Don't get your hopes up. Nothing to make your day. The smashed car is being worked on as we speak, checking mechanical faults, brakes and what have you. It's not a job you can do in a day or even a

97

week. What I'm calling about is we also have the bits of the trike to play with."

"Does it matter?"

"May do. Something interesting has come up. The trike wasn't factory built. None of the parts are standard manufacture except the tyres. He was riding a homemade machine."

"Strange."

"I think so. And it's expertly done. The welding, the gears, the electrics, are as well built as any commercial bike. Kept in nice condition, too. From all I can tell, looking at the brakes and the mechanics, it was roadworthy."

"Could he have made it himself?"

"Can't answer that, squire, but whoever put it together was hot stuff at metalwork."

"Thanks for letting me know. Have you learned anything else?"

"Not a lot. The tread marks confirm what I showed you at the scene. The patrol car moves out to pass the parked vehicles and immediately brakes hard, gets into a skid, hits the trike, rises up the bank, turns over —"

"Hold on, Dessie. You've added something. You didn't mention the trike when we walked it through."

"Obviously. Because you hadn't found it

at that stage. For him to be flung up there, with all that force, he must get hit broadside on."

"Okay. The big question is why PC Green slammed on the brakes."

"Haven't you worked that out?"

"The trike?"

"Got to be. He was unsighted by the parked cars and didn't see the winking LED lights until the last moment."

"Right. And it's possible the old man was wandering all over the road. I heard from a witness that he wasn't too straight with his steering. Does that fit your reading of it?"

"Tell you later, when we get round to the computer simulation." Dessie paused. "You say there was a witness?"

"Someone saw him ride past higher up the street. They didn't witness the crash."

"Was he breathalysed?"

"The old man? No chance," Diamond said. "I'm not even sure he was breathing when I found him."

"Shouldn't we ask the hospital for a blood sample?"

Slipped up there, Diamond thought with a stab of guilt. Being so new to crash investigation, he'd missed a basic procedure. "Quite right. I'm seeing to it."

"And the driver?"

"What about the driver?"

"You'll need to know if he was legal."

"They're doing a postmortem this morning. The usual body fluids and tissue samples will be sent for testing. I've no reason to think he'd been drinking."

"The shunt was entirely down to the civilian, then," Dessie said with irony. "The police are squeaky-clean."

"That's my strong impression."

"Just bad luck they met a speeding tricyclist."

When he ended the call, Diamond was feeling a long way out of his depth, wondering how "just bad luck" would be received by Professional Standards and the IPCC. He would need all of Dessie's graphics and stats to back up a conclusion as artless as that.

He started the car and drove into work. Please God a really juicy murder had been committed overnight and this whole wretched inquiry could be passed to someone else.

This isn't a compulsion. I'm not psychotic. I can stop at any time. And when I do, the world won't be any the wiser, which will be a personal success. I keep this record of my ordered state of mind at every stage so I can look back at each episode and recall exactly why it was necessary to put an end to a life and how I dealt with it. Of course there are glitches sometimes. I think back to the first and cringe at how naïve I was. Fortunately no one noticed except me.

Right now I'm thinking another one may be beckoning, but not in the near future, not before I've taken time to make all the arrangements. Good preparation is the key.

5

Georgina looked ready to unload a sackful of blame. She crooked a finger at Diamond when he arrived in the temporary CID room. Then she headed straight for the place he called the goldfish bowl and parked herself in his chair.

"Where have you been all morning?"

He glanced at his watch. "It's not that late, is it? I was at the hospital, ma'am. Didn't anyone tell you?"

"Your two assistants aren't here."

"Hard at work on their duties, Keith Halliwell at the autopsy and Ingeborg Smith with the press officer. It's non-stop." Diamond liked her to believe everyone was fully stretched and today it happened to be true. The Critical Care unit, the autopsy room and the press office. No one had been swanning around.

Georgina, in full battle order, was forced to abandon the charge. "And what news is there from the hospital? How is he?"

"Able to speak now."

"Really?" Some of the disapproval vanished from her face. "Is he making sense?"

"On and off. He's well dosed with morphine, or whatever they give them."

"Was he able to tell you his name?"

"I didn't ask."

With a rasping catch of breath she was back on the attack. "That's the first thing to find out."

"I knew it already."

"How is that?"

He frowned. "Have we got our wires crossed, ma'am? I'm speaking about Lew Morgan."

"Morgan?" she said as if the injured sergeant was an alien creature. "For pity's sake, I thought you'd been talking to the civilian you discovered. He's our priority now. It's not just a police car overturning. It involves a member of the public, and that's the worst possible development."

From the looks she was giving him, she blamed Diamond for finding the man. Would her life have been easier if the poor old coot had been left up there to rot? She probably thought so.

She was still on at him. "I thought you were telling me there was an improvement in his condition. Did you see him?"

"He's critical. That's the worst you can be, short of dead. They'd like to do a scan but they don't want to unplug him."

And now she had more worry lines than a Shar-Pei in a dog pound. "This could be catastrophic."

"But we keep calm and carry on."

She glared back. "Don't try me, Peter. This investigation can be taken out of your hands."

If only, he thought.

She shot him another reproachful look. "I'll have to speak to Professional Standards."

"I thought I was Professional Standards."

"You're their instrument. Did you say Ingeborg is with the press officer?"

"I did." Being called an instrument was another first for Diamond and he didn't much like it.

"Doing what?" Georgina asked.

"Issuing a statement about the man on the trike. As you were just saying, we urgently need to know who he is."

Now her eyes bulged as if she'd swallowed her tongue. "You're not making the information public?"

"We have to, ma'am, or we'll never find out who he is. If he rides a trike around

Bath, he must be well-known."

"I can't believe I'm hearing this. The *last* thing we want is publicity. Don't you ever read the newspapers? They love to run headlines about innocent people knocked down by speeding police cars."

"We can't pretend it didn't happen. It's going to get known anyway, so we might as well make it official."

"Show me the statement you're proposing to issue. I want to vet it first."

"Too late for that, ma'am. It's done and dusted. I asked Ingeborg to draft the piece and get it out as soon as possible. That was more than an hour ago. By now it's public knowledge. The media can't resist breaking news."

"I'm speechless. You didn't vet the statement before it went out?"

"I trust my team, ma'am. She's an ex-journalist, as you know. There won't be any grammatical errors."

"That's not the point, and you well know it. I wouldn't have sanctioned this." Georgina got up, walked to the door and looked out. "If it's done and dusted, to use your phrase, why isn't she back at her desk?"

"She'll be with the press officer getting the first responses. Fingers crossed we'll get his name shortly."

"But at what cost? Headlines in the gutter press. I can see it already: PENSIONER CRITICAL AFTER POLICE CAR CRASH. All my efforts promoting our good name undone at a stroke. Attending countless civic functions being nice to people. I might as well give up trying." Unable to think of a better exit-line, Georgina stomped through the CID room and out.

Events didn't pan out as speedily as Diamond had predicted. He was told by John Wigfull, the ex-cop who had returned as their press and PR man, that Ingeborg had gone out for a coffee.

"Did she hand you the press release? Has it gone out?"

"It's on my to-do list," Wigfull said. "My in-tray is heaving." Like Diamond, he never allowed anyone to think he was underemployed.

Theoretically, then, there was still a chance for Georgina to put a stop to the process.

"I didn't hear that, John."

"What?"

" 'On my to-do list.' Get it on the done list before the ACC puts you in her out-tray."

He wasn't a detective for nothing. He found

Ingeborg where he knew she would be: at Verona Coffee, their new place of escape from the police centre. He ordered a cappuccino for himself, tipped in more sugar than was good for him, asked for a triple chocolate muffin as well, and carried them to the table where his usually alert sergeant was so engrossed in the *Guardian* that she hadn't seen him coming.

"Don't tell me," he said. "Murders are down and crimes against women are up. So what's new?"

"Hi, guv." She pushed the paper aside. "How was the hospital?"

"You mean, how were the patients? As expected. Lew Morgan is talking some sense and some nonsense. He's going to lose a leg, poor guy, but I don't think anyone has told him yet."

"That's awful."

"Yes, and I'm not sure if trike man is brain dead. They don't want me to see him."

"Maybe it's a coma. People can go for years like that."

"What a comfort you are."

"I was looking on the bright side."

"If that's the bright side, next time I go for coffee I'll join John Leaman."

"You said Lew spoke some sense. Is there anything I should hear about?"

"Not a lot. He can recall the events leading up to the crash."

"That's all we need to know, isn't it?"

"Except he had his eyes closed and didn't see how they lost control. It had been a long night turn, he said. He heard the driver say 'Jeez!' and opened his eyes and they were already on two wheels."

"Imagine."

"I can, all too easily." Diamond's unease in fast cars was almost a phobia. "But he was also talking about trike man, called him Sherlock fucking Holmes."

"You just said he didn't see anything."

"This is where it gets confusing. He must have got a sight of the old guy in the deerstalker."

"In that instant he opened his eyes, obviously."

"Then he started rambling about hops."

"Hops they make beer from?"

"I didn't think so. I assumed he was thinking of rabbits. He said you could hear them digging their holes."

"Rabbits? Never."

"You'd have to be up close to hear that going on. But let's not forget we already decided the old guy could be a wildlife enthusiast. He was carrying field glasses and a camera. Lew mentioned something else:

they were heading towards Bath at a mile a night."

"What, the rabbits?" She laughed. "Beware the bunny invasion. Where did all this come from?"

"Hallucinating, I reckon."

"But he knew about the man on the bike."

"Evidently. When I asked if he'd seen him in Beckford Gardens, he denied it and turned angry and accused me of trying to get inside his head. He called the sister and she saw he was upset and asked me to leave."

"His head will be clearer next time."

"I wouldn't count on it, with major surgery to come."

"Well, then" — she sat forward in her chair and made a steeple of both hands — "he must have seen trike man being catapulted in the air by the crash and his brain is suppressing it. That's why he got angry with you, because you tried forcing him to confront the ugly reality. If Aaron Green was at fault in his driving, going too fast or not concentrating, Lew wouldn't want it known."

"He did say something about nutcases."

"And we know where he wants to point the blame."

"I welcome your ideas on this, Inge, but

let's not make up our minds before all the evidence is in. We haven't got Dessie's report and we don't know much about trike man — whether he was fit to be out on the roads at night."

"I gave the press release to John Wigfull. We'll get some take-up shortly."

"Let's hope so. And by the way, Georgina Dallymore isn't too thrilled that we went public. She thinks Bath Police will be hung out to dry by the press for injuring a harmless old man."

"She's right about that, only it's better to go public now than wait for it to leak out."

"My feelings exactly, but I just hope we get some information back. I'm in the dog house already. I know where I'll end up if this doesn't succeed and it won't be fragrant."

Keith Halliwell was back from the postmortem when they returned to the police centre. He was able to report that Aaron Green had died from compression of the heart between his sternum and his vertebral column.

"Basically," Halliwell said, "his upper body hit the steering wheel with such force that he died at once."

"And I bet he wasn't wearing the seatbelt," Ingeborg said.

"It's not compulsory for police drivers."

"I know that."

"I can see the reason if you've made an arrest and got a suspect in the car," Diamond said, "but it's stupid not to use one if you're on an emergency call."

"They think it's macho to go without," Ingeborg said. "The younger guys in particular."

"Macho? Lew Morgan was wearing his and it saved his life. He'd have been flung through the windscreen."

"He's still going to lose a leg," Ingeborg said.

Halliwell shook his head. "That's bad. I didn't know."

Diamond said, "I was at the hospital this morning."

"Me, too," Halliwell said. "I could have given you a lift."

Diamond could tell it wasn't meant as a dig. Halliwell came out with things like that from genuine willingness to be helpful. There was an understanding in CID that he stood in for Diamond at all postmortems. The big man was uncomfortable with dissections. But he was also self-conscious about it.

Diamond updated Halliwell on his somewhat surreal conversation with Lew Morgan. Halliwell was unable to throw any light on the matter. Rabbits, he said in his forthright way, were outside his experience. He'd seen them in the lanes around Bath but never travelling with any purpose.

"Me neither," Diamond said. "Maybe we should put it down to the painkillers he was on."

Before lunch, calls started coming in. The first appeal for information had been on BBC Radio Bristol and a number of Bathonians had phoned in to say that the tricyclist in the deerstalker was a well-known local character. This was a beginning, even though no one seemed to know his name or address.

"It's only a matter of time," Ingeborg said. "Someone will know."

Diamond hoped so. He needed the result before the police were hammered by the headlines in next day's papers.

So there was great relief all round when, about two-fifteen, a Mrs. Roberts from Henrietta Road called the radio station to say that the man was almost certainly one of her neighbours. Her contact details were passed to the police.

"He's called Ivor," she told Diamond when he phoned her. "An elderly gentleman all on his own. Lives in a big house up the road from us. All we've got is a two-bedroom flat. Ivor's place is easy to spot because there's a large workshop at the side with a corrugated-iron roof. How he got planning permission is beyond me. It doesn't do anything for the beauty of the street. But I feel sure he must be the person they spoke about on Radio Bristol because of the deerstalker hat and the tricycle. You don't see that too often, do you? His wife died some time towards the end of last year. And as if that isn't enough to bear, poor man, now this happens. Will he pull through?"

"We hope so. Do you know his name?"

"I told you: Ivor."

"The surname."

"I can't help you there. We don't say Mr. this and Mrs. that. We're friendly along here, even though some live in million-pound mansions and others more modestly, like my husband and me. He always gives us a wave as he goes by, but being on his tricycle he doesn't stop for a chat. I heard he was an engineer before he retired."

This checked with Dessie's evidence that the bike was homemade and expertly welded. "How long has he lived there?"

"Quite a long time. We arrived sixteen

113

years ago and they were here then. His wife Trixie was a dignified lady who I never once saw without a hat, rather shy, I always thought. Flat shoes and twin-sets. No make-up. But they were very close. She had an unusual shopping trolley with large wheels that I think she once said he made her. She had a beautiful funeral. Lots of flowers and a white coffin. They buried her up on Lansdown in the cemetery there."

"*Buried* her? Are you sure she wasn't cremated?"

"Absolutely. You can visit the grave. It's very peaceful up there and she's got a lovely headstone."

So much for Lew Morgan's information about Trixie's ashes. And Ingeborg's theory about the scattering of them.

Mrs. Roberts talked on, through his distracted thoughts. "But I was telling you Ivor was the only mourner who went from the house and only a handful came back after. Sad, really. I don't know if they had family."

"Have you seen him riding out early in the morning? The accident happened about six."

"Lord help us, I'm never up as early as that. What would he be doing out at that hour?"

"We don't know. That's why I asked. Does

he drive a car?"

"Years ago he had a beauty, one of those expensive German makes. White, it was, and he kept it beautifully clean, but I haven't seen it for ages. He must have given up the driving when he got older. He gets about on the tricycle these days."

Mrs. Roberts had been a useful source but she'd told him as much as he needed, so he thanked her and ended the call. Ingeborg had already found the house on Google Earth and got the number. The electoral roll gave the name of the occupier: Ivor Pellegrini. His wife Beatrix was still listed.

"Distinctive name," Diamond said. "Stay online and see what else you can find. It would be good to get a picture, to be certain this is the right man."

"I doubt if he's on Facebook, if that's what you're thinking."

"Me?"

She smiled. The boss didn't do his networking electronically.

"But check it, by all means," he said.

"Can we speak to the people next door? They might know more than I can get from the Internet."

And now he grinned. "That's a big admission, coming from you. Okay, we'll try both. You get surfing or tweeting or whatever and

I'll visit Henrietta Road and do some old-fashioned door-stepping."

The buildings in Henrietta Road lined one side only because one of Bath's prized green areas was opposite. Henrietta Park, originally part of the Bathwick Estate, had been gifted to the city in 1897 by one Captain Forester to celebrate Queen Victoria's Diamond Jubilee. The Pleasure Ground Committee had arranged for the ground to be turfed and given paths and a drinking fountain. When the park opened, the villas along the west side of the triangular plot were already in place and their situation was much enhanced by the new amenity. Most had since succumbed to economic constraints and been divided into flats. As properties they were not the grandest in Bath but, as Mrs. Roberts had accurately stated, you would still need more than a million to buy a single villa outright.

She had also been right about the iron-roofed workshop. The advantage to Diamond was that no other villa had such an eyesore in front, so Ivor Pellegrini's home was easy to spot, a handsome three-storey stone building with large sash windows and a corniced entrance with a front door painted yellow.

116

He left his car outside and took a closer look, starting with the workshop. Clearly the retired engineer liked to keep his hand in with some mechanical projects, but whatever was inside couldn't be inspected. The windows were too high to see into, the door was sturdy and fitted with a lock that looked as if it would do for Lubyanka prison. A metal plaque said the building was protected by a response alarm. He spotted the bell under the overlap of the roof.

Switching his attention to the main building, he saw at once that it was fitted with CCTV — and the cameras were not dummies. Nothing remarkable in that. If you had a nice house you might well discourage intruders. He took a stroll round the side.

Unexpectedly, an upstairs window was drawn upwards and a woman looked out and said, "What are you up to?"

"Nothing to worry about, ma'am," Diamond said. "Police officer, making enquiries about the owner of the house."

"Oh yes?" She sounded sceptical.

"I'm right that Mr. Ivor Pellegrini lives here, am I?"

"What of it?"

"We've reason to believe he had an accident yesterday."

"Oh my God. What happened?"

"Are you related to him?"

"Me?" Her voice shrilled in denial. "I'm only the cleaner. I come in twice a week. Nobody told me he was hurt. Is it bad?"

"Before I answer that I'd like to be sure we're talking about the same man. Does Mr. Pellegrini ride a tricycle and wear a deerstalker hat?"

"He does."

"And is there anything to show he's been home in the last twenty-four hours?"

"He hasn't," she said. "The bed hasn't been slept in and I found two days' letters and papers on the doormat when I let myself in."

"You have a front door key?"

"It's all above board. I've been doing for him and his late wife for the best part of ten years. What's happened to the poor man, then? How bad was this accident?"

"Let me in and I'll tell you."

She was Mrs. Tessa Halliday, from Fairfield Park on the northern outskirts, he learned when she had shown him through a carpeted entrance hall into a kitchen almost as big as the new CID room at the police centre. Old-fashioned in style, with a built-in dresser and walk-in pantry, it even had a servant bell box. But the Aga was modern and so were the double-door fridge,

118

dishwasher, hob and hood.

He told her about the accident but without saying a police car had been involved or that Pellegrini had lain unconscious and unnoticed for three hours. Even so, he left her in no doubt that her employer was critically ill and unable to receive visitors.

In turn, she told Diamond that the Pellegrinis — she called them Ivor and Trixie — had lived in Bath most of their married life. They were a devoted couple, regular churchgoers and wholly upright citizens. Ivor had held a senior position with Horstman's, one of Bath's main employers, at their Newbridge works, before the factory closed and was moved to Bristol. Then he'd taken on consultancy work for a number of local firms.

"I know where Horstman's used to be," Diamond said. "Just up the road from where I live in Lower Weston. Good firm, good reputation. Is engineering what he does in the workshop?"

"I couldn't tell you," she said.

"You don't go in there to clean?"

She shook her head. "I'm not even sure Trixie was allowed in there. It's his holy of holics."

"He doesn't go in there to say his prayers, by all accounts. I heard he made her a shop-

119

ping trolley and we think the tricycle was homemade as well."

"He's clever with his hands. Is that what you call engineering, then?"

"I would say so."

"I thought it was just engines and that."

"This is a sensitive question but I'd like you to try and answer it. Have you noticed anything different about Mr. Pellegrini's behaviour since his wife died?"

"What do you mean? Of course he's different and so would you be."

That raw nerve twitched. He didn't inform her how right she was, that he, too, was a widower, deeply scarred by his loss. "He was out on the roads on his tricycle in the small hours of the night. Is he mentally okay?"

She looked surprised. "In the night? Why would he do that?"

"My question, exactly. Eccentric, is he?"

She frowned and thought before answering. "I suppose you might get that impression because of the clothes he wears, but people wear all sorts these days, don't they? There isn't anything wrong with his brain, if that's what you're asking. If he went out at night there must have been a good reason."

"Do you know if he likes a drink or two?"

"Nothing alcoholic, that's for sure. They both had strict views about that."

"Does he have family — anyone we should notify?"

"I can't think of anyone. I went to Trixie's funeral and there weren't any family there, just a few of us from Bath who knew her, some people from the church and some neighbours from long ago. It's sad, but they were a close couple and didn't mix much."

"One last thing," he said. "Is there a photo of Ivor anywhere about the house? I'd like to make absolutely sure he's the man who had the accident."

There was a nice one in the library, she said, and led him upstairs to an even larger room where the two longest walls were lined with books and each had one of those rolling ladders attached to a track for reaching the top shelves. He couldn't resist moving one along a short way.

"Runs well."

"All his own work," she said. "Is that engineering as well?"

"Definitely."

The end walls were used to display pictures, mostly of steam trains. He'd already noticed several shelves of books about railways. "He's a train enthusiast, then?"

Her mouth twitched into a slow smile.

"He's a man."

"I expect it's more than collecting numbers in his case," Diamond said. "He'll know how they work."

"The only thing that interests me is will they go on time," Mrs. Halliday said. "The photo is up the other end."

He was prepared for this but he still felt his flesh prickle. It was of Ivor at the wheel of an open-top sports car in his younger days, darker and with more hair, but definitely trike man. All doubt was removed: this was the accident victim.

He gave her the bad news.

"That's awful," she said. "What will happen now?"

He shrugged.

"Is he going to die?"

"They'll do all they can to keep him alive." He looked at the picture again. "Does he do any driving these days, or does he only use the trike?"

"He gave up some time back. He has an account with a taxi firm for longer trips."

The doorbell rang.

"Who's that?" Mrs. Halliday said.

She'd asked a question Diamond himself wanted answered. "Let's see."

He was down those stairs quicker than hell would scorch a feather.

He opened the front door to a smiling woman holding a plate with something on it covered in tinfoil. But the smile changed to drop-jaw surprise. "I was expecting Ivor. Who on earth are you?"

He told her and said, "I'm afraid he's in hospital."

"Really?" Her face creased in concern. "What's wrong? I'm Elspeth Blake from the church. We do a bit of baking for him since his wife died."

"A road accident. He was knocked off his bike."

Mrs. Halliday piped up in support from somewhere behind him. "They didn't know who he is. I was able to show the officer his picture. What have you cooked for him, Elspeth?"

"A quiche Lorraine," Elspeth Blake said. "Perhaps I should take it to the hospital."

Diamond explained that Pellegrini was too unwell to enjoy a quiche. "Is it still warm? Smells good."

Mrs. Halliday said, "The best thing we can do is let it cool and put it in the freezer for when he comes home."

"I don't think so," Elspeth Blake said, friendly but firm. "I can easily make him something fresh when he's better again."

Unlikely, going by the look of him this

morning, Diamond thought. Pity to let a good quiche go unappreciated. "A not-so-old person might appreciate it while it's still warm — or three not-so-old people. It's my lunchtime. Is it yours, ladies?" He watched for a positive reaction.

Never tangle with a lady on a mission of goodwill. She laughed — and there was real amusement in the laugh — yet she backed away a step. "I hope you're joking. They'll be happy to take it at Julian House."

Impossible to go into competition with Bath's shelter for the homeless. "If you like I can deliver it for you," he offered without any ulterior motive. "I'm going that way shortly."

She gave a smile and a knowing look that said nice try but no chance. She was an attractive redhead in her forties with eyes that glittered behind tinted green-rimmed glasses and anyone would think he'd suggested something far more lewd. "Thanks, but that won't be necessary. I'm going that way myself. Where is Ivor, in the Royal United?"

The question seemed to suggest Diamond might have been making it up about poor Ivor's plight. His try for the quiche had turned him into a con artist in her eyes. "Critical care. It isn't possible to visit."

"We'll pray for him then."

"Good plan."

Elspeth and the appetising quiche left the scene.

He closed the door. "I didn't handle that very well, did I?" he said to Mrs. Halliday. "I thought we were in for a tasty lunch."

"She had other ideas."

"More's the pity. Smelt really good to me. Would you have had a slice if it was offered?"

She didn't admit to it right away. Finally, without a smile, she said, "Possibly."

Not the conspiratorial pact he was trying for. Undeterred, he asked the question he'd been leading up to. "Is there a key to the workshop? I'd like to see inside."

"He keeps it to himself," she said. "I wouldn't know where to look. I must get on. There's a lot more to do."

"I'll take a chair to stand on and see if I can look through the windows."

She gave him a suspicious look. "What do you want to do that for? You know who he is."

"Yes, but I don't know why he was out in the small hours of the night." He returned to the kitchen and found a high stool that was probably used to reach the top shelves. After missing out on the quiche he wasn't going to be denied again. He took the stool outside and positioned it under one of the workshop windows.

He wasn't prepared for what he saw. On a shelf directly under the window were three terracotta-coloured plastic containers that he recognised as cremation urns.

6

Instead of homemade quiche, lunch was a beer and a sandwich in a seedy bar near the railway station.

"Talk about professional standards," Keith Halliwell said, holding his glass to the light to look at the smears. "They could do with some here."

"Brace up," Ingeborg said. "We'll survive."

"Don't count on it," Halliwell said. "And don't even think about using the toilet."

This was an emergency meeting in every sense. The news had broken: BATH MAN CRITICALLY INJURED BY POLICE CAR screamed a headline board they'd seen along the street. After a spate of such incidents across the nation, some fatal, the collision in Beckford Gardens was a hot topic in all the papers. The media were giving it the treatment. Headquarters had been on to Keynsham demanding that report.

"We're expected to deliver," Diamond

127

said, "today."

"If not yesterday," Ingeborg said.

"Bloody ridiculous," Halliwell said.

Diamond didn't argue. He was of the same mind. "Let's lay out what we know for certain."

"A reconstruction?"

"Starting with the 999 call at six in the morning from Cedric Bellerby —"

"It was never an emergency," Halliwell said.

"He believed it was," Ingeborg said.

"He's a moron."

"He made the call. Fact."

"He's just as responsible as our driver or the man on the trike."

Diamond agreed with Ingeborg here. The caller wasn't the issue. "A call about a naked man he'd seen through his binoculars swimming in the lido. The guy was making his way up the hillside towards the street."

"Fully clothed by then," Halliwell said.

"Towards the street," Diamond said in a tone that brooked no more interruption, "where he could have been stopped by our lads and questioned. But while Bellerby was waiting by his front gate, Ivor Pellegrini came by on his trike, pedalling in the direction the patrol car would come from. His steering wasn't the best but his lights were working. To quote Bellerby exactly — and this could be crucial to what happened — he was wandering across the road, too busy trying to control his trike to notice anyone else. What can we put that down to?"

"Drink?" Halliwell said.

"I have it on the authority of his cleaning lady that he doesn't drink."

"Old age? He shouldn't have been on the road at all."

"He was tired," Ingeborg suggested. "He'd been up most of the night and gone further than a man of his age should have done."

"Do we know his age?" Halliwell asked.

"He worked for Horstman's," Diamond said, "and they relocated to Bristol in 2000, when he started work for some of his local contacts, but he seems to be retired now. I reckon he's seventy at least. This matters because if he was riding erratically he could have been the prime cause of the collision."

"Could dementia be a factor?"

"Nothing wrong with his brain, according to Mrs. Halliday."

"Is she any judge?"

"She sees him twice a week."

"To clean his place, not to engage in intellectual debate."

"I met her," Diamond said. "Not much gets past her. If she says he's still got his marbles, I believe her."

"And yet we have the weird stuff Lew Morgan told you."

"The rabbits?"

"And riding about at night with his wife's ashes, which we know is untrue, because she wasn't cremated."

Diamond shook his head and sighed.

Ingeborg threw in a sharp one. "So who was the more confused — Pellegrini or Lew Morgan?"

"Not Lew," Diamond said at once. "What he told me was coherent and most of it checks with the facts. He remembered they were on a call to Beckford Gardens, a shout about a naked man. He was able to give me Aaron's name, and said correctly that he was married with a young kid. He'd obviously met Pellegrini because he remembered the deerstalker and the trike."

"But when did this meeting take place?" Ingeborg asked.

"It wasn't a meeting, it was a crash," Halliwell said.

Nothing was said for a couple of seconds.

"No," Diamond started up again. "That can't be right. Lew wasn't speaking about the crash. In fact, he became angry when I suggested trike man had anything to do with it. He accused me of trying to get inside his

130

head and told me to piss off. Thinking back, he only brought up the topic of trike man to let me know the kind of night they'd endured. 'Fucking nutcase,' as he put it." He paused and swirled the beer in his glass. "I'm thinking they came across Pellegrini at some point earlier in their turn."

Ingeborg frowned. "There was nothing in the control room audio recordings. I've been through them three times and read the transcripts. I know most of it by heart."

Halliwell was grinning. "Never worked in cars, have you, Inge?"

She cocked an eyebrow. "What's that got to do with it?"

"Plenty of stuff goes on that never gets back to the control room."

"Keith's right," Diamond told her. "If they make a road check that turns out to be negative, they won't want it logged. I can see a situation where they ask trike man to pull over, only to discover he's talking bollocks about migrating rabbits and taking his dead wife for an outing. If bullshit like that gets back to the nick, they're a laughing stock."

"So they don't say a word and it doesn't appear on the audio recording," Halliwell said.

Ingeborg glanced away as if she'd lost

131

interest. "Then we'll never know for sure."

"We're not copping out," Diamond said, resolved to achieve something from this session. "Where were they prior to the Beckford Gardens call-out?"

"Back in Keynsham," Ingeborg said, "thinking their shift was over. And before that they were in Julian Road arresting the church-roofers."

"So any meeting with Pellegrini has to precede that. Does the log tell us where they were in the early hours of their shift?"

"Widcombe Hill and the university. They were there some time, dealing with a complaint about rowdy students. Then they attended a break-in in Northwood Avenue."

"All south of the river."

"The river, the canal and the railway," Diamond said.

"Is that significant?" Ingeborg asked.

"Some distance from where the collision took place," Diamond said. "I'm thinking about Pellegrini on his trike. You've studied the audio-recordings, Inge. Was there any time of the night when nothing much seemed to be happening?"

She was silent for a short spell, remembering. "About one forty-five they drove out to Bathampton to check on a domestic — some man complaining his wife was threatening the kids. They sorted that and reported back at two-twenty and there wasn't much communication for a time. The next the control room heard of them was two fifty-five."

"Thirty-five minutes off air. Seems a likely slot. Where could they have met him at that time? Where were they at two fifty-five?"

"On the A4 heading back towards the city."

"From Bathampton. That figures."

"Where exactly was the domestic?" Halliwell asked.

"Meadow Lane, a turning off Bathampton Lane."

"Which is really quiet at night," Halliwell said, "and a good place to stop and search someone."

"It makes sense," Diamond said, encouraged that the team was functioning better. "He's cycling unsteadily along Bathampton Lane and they stop him and maybe breathalyse him and have this ridiculous conversation about hopping rabbits which unsurprisingly doesn't get reported to the control room. He's allowed to continue."

"Towards the A4?" Halliwell said. "I don't think so."

"Pellegrini won't have gone that way. An old man on a trike wouldn't last five minutes on a major road like that."

Ingeborg agreed. "He'd stick to minor roads." She took out her iPhone and started checking possible routes.

"Yet three hours later they get the call to Beckford Gardens and we can definitely place him there."

"On his way home by the back route," she said. "His night tour is over and he's returning to base."

"The back route from Bathampton?" Halliwell said. "Can't say I know one."

Ingeborg was about to enlighten him. "For a man on a trike, Bathampton is the only place where you can cross the railway and the A4 on a reasonably safe road."

"With you there," Halliwell said. "You mean Mill Lane."

"Right. And a bit further on he's over the toll bridge — which is free after ten P.M. — and across the river and he makes his way through Bailbrook and Larkhall on minor roads to Beckford Gardens, where Delta Three happens to be racing towards him on its emergency run. They meet head on."

"There's still something wrong," Halliwell said.

"What?"

"What's he doing there if he's on his way home?" Halliwell said. "He lives in Henrietta Road. If he's sticking to the minor roads you mention he wouldn't need to go to Beckford Gardens."

"It's not far from his home," Ingeborg said. She swiped the screen and satisfied herself.

"It may look all right on your phone —"

"So?"

"It's out of his way. I've walked these roads."

"We all have," Diamond said. Halliwell was right, but he didn't want the sniping to begin again. It was enough of a brain-fag accounting for Pellegrini's movements. "I could be wrong in saying he was on his way home. Perhaps some special reason made him divert to Beckford Gardens." He slapped the table. "Got it!"

A Eureka moment.

He raised a fist in triumph.

His companions simply stared.

"It's the railway," he said. "He was there for the railway. He's an engineer and that's his hobby. I've seen the pictures of trains in his home. If you go to the Hampton Row end of Beckford Gardens, you come to a footbridge. I walked up there and it seems to lead nowhere on the other side. But Pellegrini visited there. He must have parked his trike and climbed the bridge and looked

135

over, along the track."

Ingeborg was working her iPhone again. "It isn't just a bridge, guv. It's got a history. At one time there was a station there called Hampton Row Halt."

Diamond gave her a disbelieving look. Hampton Row Halt — on the main line to London? It didn't sound likely. Leg-pulling wasn't unknown in Bath CID and he'd been caught a few times.

But she was serious. "They closed it in the First World War as an economy measure and it never reopened. Most of it is demolished." She was quoting now. " 'Originally there were two platforms accessible from the iron footbridge that still exists.' "

Now he felt like hugging her. "Brilliant. It would be a place of pilgrimage for a railway buff," Diamond said. "Can I see?"

She handed over the phone but he gave it straight back. "Bring up the map."

"Hampton Row?"

"Bathampton Lane. This is all about the railway."

And there it was on the small screen, just as he'd pictured it. "See how the track runs parallel to the road? That clinches it as far as I'm concerned. He spent his night following the railway line."

There was pleasure in getting there. Solid

detective work, deduction and fact-finding, the things they did best. They touched glasses, buoyed up by discovering why Pellegrini had been out on the roads at night.

But after a short interval, reality set in. The information wouldn't greatly interest Headquarters or the IPCC.

"We now know he had a purpose," Ingeborg said. "That's something. He may be a nerd but he isn't a total nutcase. It wasn't about rabbits digging their holes."

"Why mention them, then?" Halliwell said.

"As a distraction. He didn't want the police knowing what he was really up to."

"Why? It's not illegal looking at railway tracks."

"It is if you trespass on railway property."

"Is that what he was doing?"

Diamond was getting another idea, a troubling scenario too way-out to share with the others in this exacting forum. "Thanks, both of you. This has been useful, very useful."

"What will you tell Headquarters?" Ingeborg said.

"The truth." And he left the intuitive thinking behind and relied on the right half of the brain to summarise their findings. "We've interviewed several witnesses and uncovered nothing to suggest a breach of professional standards. Our lads were on an emergency call and driving responsibly. They had their beacon flashing. Cars parked in the narrow road may have temporarily unsighted them. They appear to have met Pellegrini head on and the car projected him and his tricycle out of sight up the bank. There's one witness account that his riding was unsteady shortly before the collision, but we gather he was a non-drinker so we don't suspect alcohol was a factor. Old age and fatigue are more likely. The same witness informed us that the lights on the trike were working prior to the collision."

"Pretty straightforward, then?"

"They'll also have Dessie's report packed with statistics and graphics."

"All done and dusted," Halliwell said.

"Unless one of the main players recovers enough to make a fuller statement."

Now Halliwell was frowning. "Are you standing us down?"

A nod. "You can go back to normal duties."

The order wasn't expressed diplomatically, but diplomacy had never been Diamond's strongest suit.

"Is that what you'll be doing, guv — normal duties?" Ingeborg asked in a way

that showed she already knew the answer.
He didn't reply.

Trying not to look ahead. One thing leads to another: that's the beauty of this — and the trap. I don't see my life any more as a series of objectives. I'm content to go with the flow and see where it leads and only then make the arrangements. Up to now it has worked like a dream. But the danger is to get so confident that I make a mistake. I can't see how it would happen but I need to be on my guard. So it's a balancing act, being relaxed and vigilant at all times. The apparently aimless progress will confuse anyone with suspicions about me. They always think of murderers as single-minded, blinkered individuals. Psychopaths. I'm not like that at all, as anyone who has met me will tell you.

The academics who make a career out of studying serial murder, as it is crudely known, only get to analyse the failed practitioners. Those like me who are successful and leave no trace — and I can't be the only one —

never get into the textbooks. Who'd be a criminologist, making a science out of losers?

7

Georgina didn't thank Diamond for his report. She still appeared to believe he'd made her life more difficult on purpose by discovering Pellegrini at the collision scene. But she grudgingly said she now had enough to keep Headquarters off her back for a day or two. Dessie had put together an extremely impressive video simulation based on the latest science and she would submit Diamond's findings as an addendum.

Normally he would have raised a storm at being told his report was only a postscript to a PowerPoint presentation. He and his team had come up with crucial information and deserved better. But in his mind he had already moved on. There was a new possibility he was eager to explore.

He was almost out of the door when Georgina said, "Where are you going next?"

"My office. Things have been piling up."

"You're not turning your back on this

inquiry?"

"Would I do that?"

"I want you to continue to monitor it. The progress of the hospital cases. The witness statements. The gossip in the kitchenettes. Be my eyes and ears."

"That could be difficult, ma'am."

"Why?"

"Am I still an instrument?"

She had to think for a moment. "Are you speaking about Professional Standards? That duty has been completed."

"So I can go back to being unprofessional?"

"That isn't what I said at all."

"I'm your eyes and ears, you said."

"There's nothing unprofessional in that."

"Eavesdropping, spying, informing?"

She shook her head. "That's putting it too strongly. I didn't use the word 'informing.' "

"I get it now. The old Yorkshire motto: hear all, see all, say nowt."

She hesitated. "That still isn't right."

"I can use my discretion, then? Bend the rules from time to time?"

"You always have."

"And now with your blessing. Thanks, ma'am."

He was gone.

■ ■ ■ ■

In the morning he turned up again at the Royal United Hospital, but not because he was Georgina's eyes and ears. He didn't plan to see either of the accident victims and he certainly wouldn't hear anything from them. Lew Morgan would be heavily sedated after having his leg amputated. Ivor Pellegrini would still be in a coma. Diamond's purpose in being there was unrelated to what was going on in the hospital. He planned to gain entry to the workshop in Henrietta Road and discover more about its owner, and he'd worked out a way of doing it.

The nurse he'd met before in the Critical Care unit wasn't on duty. A pity. He would have to start over with somebody else. The sister who stopped him at the entrance had an implacable look. Everything from the tilt of her head to the folded arms and the penetrating stare over half-glasses told him he was faced with a daunting task.

"Yes?"

He showed his ID. "I'm the officer who found Mr. Pellegrini and administered CPR."

"Do you want me to congratulate you?"

144

"Just telling you who I am, sister. How is he now?"

"There's no change."

"Still unconscious, then?"

"In a single room on life support. We're doing what we can." Everything about her made clear that she didn't mean to spend time talking. She started to move away.

Diamond followed her into the main ward. "I understand you have his possessions here somewhere. When I say 'possessions' I mean the things he was wearing when he was brought in."

"That's normal," she said as she checked the notes at the foot of someone's bed. "They're safe with us."

"I was told he didn't have much in his pockets, only some money and his house keys."

"I wouldn't know about that. One of my colleagues undressed him." She moved to another bed.

"But you'll know where these things are kept. Locked up, I hope?"

"Of course."

"The thing is, I need his keys."

"Well, you're not having them," she said. "You're not even a close relative."

"He doesn't have any family. His wife died."

145

"That doesn't make you his next of kin."

"I'm the senior investigating officer."

"I don't care if you're the chief constable. Mr. Pellegrini is in my charge and I'm not surrendering the keys of his house to the police. That's final." She turned away from him so fast that her heels squeaked on the flooring. Her calf muscles, stiff with resolution inside black tights, powered her towards the sister's office.

"I thought you were committed to saving life," he called after her and instantly felt ashamed for speaking to a nurse like that. The words had come impetuously when he thought he'd lost his chance.

She stopped and swung about again.

"Any more of that and I'll have you escorted off the premises."

"It's not about me," he said. "It's . . ." He was floundering. He had to invent something fast.

Inspiration came. "It's Hornby."

She produced a thin smile, and it wasn't in friendship. "Mr. Pellegrini's name happens to be Ivor."

"I know that, sister. I'm not speaking about Mr. Pellegrini."

"Well, if you think I'm willing to discuss other patients with you, you can think again."

146

"Hornby isn't a patient. He's been missing ever since Mr. Pellegrini was admitted here."

"Who on earth are you talking about?"

"His cat. A ginger tom."

Her face transformed in a way exceeding his wildest hopes, with lines of concern rippling across her forehead.

He added, "We believe Hornby could be trapped inside the workshop at the front of the house."

"All this time? That's heart-rending." She had compassion after all, and she was obviously a cat person.

"My thought entirely. There's no other explanation, and there isn't a cat-flap. One of the neighbours thought she heard scratching from inside but it's all gone quiet in the past twenty-four hours."

"Oh no." Her lips quivered.

"They can survive a few days without food or water but Hornby has had his few days already." He paused. "I'm sure if Mr. Pellegrini could speak he'd be begging us to do something about it."

"And this is why you're here?"

"I would have forced an entry but I don't have authority. I can't get a warrant to rescue a cat. If I can borrow the keys, I'll return them directly."

She went straight into her office and returned shortly with a transparent bag containing several keys on a ring. "You might need the help of a vet, or the RSPCA. Be careful when you open the door in case he runs straight in the road and gets run over."

"That would be tragic," Diamond said, trying to keep up the pretence as he grasped how real the mythical ginger tom had become.

"I do hope he's survived," the sister said. "You must let me know. They're said to have nine lives but there's no way of telling how many of Hornby's are used already."

Looking back on the case in the light of what followed, as Diamond would eventually, getting inside that workshop was a pivotal moment. He'd gone to some trouble to achieve it, but his justification had been slight. He was curious about Pellegrini, the well-respected engineer with the unorthodox night life. At this early stage, the man wasn't suspected of anything worse than some erratic cycling on the night of the crash. He had his dippy side — like the rabbits — but there was nothing truly incriminating, nothing to justify a search of his premises. At worst, Diamond was nosy; at

148

best, driven by a hunch that the place held dark secrets — and he mistrusted hunches. They were invariably unreliable. Those old cliché phrases about feelings in the bones or having a sixth sense or a nose for crime were inimical to his way of doing things.

Yet he did it.

He found the key that fitted and let himself in.

In deference to the hospital sister's advice, he opened the door just a fraction. Hornby had become rather real in his imagination, too.

No starving cat ran out.

First impression: surprisingly tidy. Each item in its designated place. Maybe all engineers are like this, Diamond told himself as he took stock of a vast array of tools in beautiful condition clipped to a board above the work bench, boxes of shiny screws ranged along the base, strips of wood and metal arranged by size in racks. A blue boiler-suit hung from a hook beside the bench. A stack of engineering magazines, all squared off as if for inspection, were ranged behind a slim computer on a desk at one end.

Along most of one wall was a hinged sheet of chipboard about fifteen feet in length and more than five feet wide. When he unfastened the sides and lowered the thing, trestle legs dropped down. He was looking at a model railway layout, with stations, footbridges, signals, goods sheds, and all in a scenic setting with tiny figures of people, cars, sheep and cattle.

Nothing remarkable in that. Pellegrini wasn't the only man in the world who played with toy trains. We all get our kicks some way. Some people might think collecting ex–Scotland Yard men's memoirs was extreme. Each to his own.

Above the door and extending a long way beyond was a name-plate in green and gold that had once been attached to a steam locomotive. Suitably enough, it was *County of Somerset.* Probably cost a small fortune. Such things are prized by collectors.

Nothing suspicious so far, nothing remotely of interest to the CID. The three plastic urns on a high shelf under the window no longer appeared so sinister. He was starting to doubt whether he'd been right about their original purpose. Someone had decorated them in the distinctive bold, cheerful style of canal-ware. But instead of daffodils and geraniums, each had a brightly coloured locomotive with a white plume of steam. The trains looked lively against the terracotta background. If you have a passion for steam and happen to own some plastic pots, why not?

He switched on the computer and clicked the icon for emails but the storage files were empty. Probably there was another computer in the house that Pellegrini used for mail. This one was for Internet access. Various sites were bookmarked as favourites and they all had engineering or railway connections. Diamond's lack of expertise with computers prevented him from investigating more. He switched off.

Disappointing.

As an afterthought he curled his fingers under the handle of the desk drawer and slid it open. A few sheets of A4 paper printed from the computer and headed Great Western Railway. He gave them a cursory glance and was about to return them to the drawer when he noticed there was printing on the reverse side. Clearly Pellegrini believed in making full use of every sheet.

This wasn't about railways. It seemed to be a printout of an online discussion forum. Someone calling themselves

Bluebeard had written:

You only have to check how many murders go unsolved to know plenty of killers get away with it. It's around fifty a year in the UK, going by official stats over the past ten years. That's a whole load of dangerous people walking free.

The next person, "Lady Macbeth," retorted:

Tip of the iceberg. Think about it. The really clever ones don't get found out. People are being stiffed all the time and it never gets known because the doctor signs it off as natural. Then you don't have to get rid of the body.

Back came Bluebeard:

And if we knew how many are missed by the police because they take them to be accidents, we'd be shocked out of our skins.

Lady Macbeth:

Accidents or suicide. Nobody guesses there's some evil-minded person who pushes the victim off the cliff or over the side of the boat.

Bluebeard:

Are you really a lady? I wouldn't want to

fall out with you.

Lady Macbeth:

Haha.

Bluebeard:

You're on to something, pushing them over the side. Nothing confuses the police and forensic people better than water. They find a floater, as they call them, and unless there are obvious injury marks it's hard to be certain about the cause of death. Drowning is difficult to prove at the best of times and just about impossible when the victim has been dead in the water some time.

Lady Macbeth:

I thought it was simple to tell from the water filling up the lungs.

Bluebeard was sounding increasingly like a pathologist.

Not necessarily. Some people die from cardiac arrest, basically from the shock of submersion through cold water rushing into the mouth and nose. The water might not even get into the lungs. The nervous reflex triggers a heart attack. This happens quite commonly with drunks who fall in.

Lady Macbeth:

I don't call that drowning.

Bluebeard:

It's still a body found in water. I think it's known as dry drowning. A lot of people die in their own baths. Electrocution is a possibility from using a hair dryer or even an electric fire. Most bathrooms don't have power points but there's always some idiot who decides to use an extension lead. You could murder someone by dropping the electrical device in the water.

Lady Macbeth:

I saw that in a TV play.

Bluebeard:

Another water death that comes to mind is a famous case called the Brides in the Bath that happened about a hundred years ago but could still work. This man would marry and take out life insurance

154

on his bride. While she was taking a bath he'd come in and grab her legs, forcing her to slide under the water and die. Then he'd call the doctor and say she must have had a heart attack. It worked so well that he got over-confident and did it too many times. Someone read in the paper about it and he was caught. If he hadn't been so greedy he would have got away with one or two.

Lady Macbeth:

Nasty. You've really studied this.

Bluebeard:

In fact there are so many complicating factors in drowning that the experts use what they call a diagnosis of exclusion. If the body is found in water and there's no other reason for the death, it's assumed to be drowning. As for deciding if a drowning is accidental or deliberate, your average pathologist is at a loss. Useful information for a would-be killer.

Lady Macbeth:

Not for me. It's all too proactive. I'd prefer some method that doesn't require so much effort on my part.

Bluebeard summed up and ended the discussion:

Whatever. Like I said, it just goes to show there must be hundreds of murderers we could easily rub shoulders with. Next time you're in a queue at the supermarket take a look at who's in front of you or more important behind you. I always do.

Diamond flipped through the sheets, his brain buzzing with this discovery. He knew weird things were debated on the Internet but finding them here, printed out as if they needed to be kept and read again, was disturbing.

Another thread was debating ingenious methods used in fiction:

One of the best was in a short story by Roald Dahl called Lamb to the Slaughter but you have to read it yourself. I don't do spoilers. — Calamity Jane

Everyone has heard of that one. What about a colourless, odourless poison like ricin? That's getting into spy stories quite often since it was shown to have been

used by some secret service agent. —
Jonesy

A sharpened icicle driven into the heart
and after it melts. No evidence, see? —
Calamity Jane

Cool. — Clare de Lune

One of the cleverest ideas was in Patricia
Highsmith's Strangers on a Train. I guess
most people have read it or seen the
movie. She sets up a situation where the
killer has no obvious connection with the
victim. I won't spoil it by saying any more.
— Highsmith fan

My number one film. — Tom Ripley

Injecting an air bubble into the bloodstream. Writers have been thinking up this
stuff for more than a century. — Crime
Reader

The writer you mean (let's spare her
blushes) injected an artery with a hypoder-
mic instead of a vein, but it was still neat, I
thought. Like I said I favour poison. There's
so much of it about, in the garden, the
garage, the medicine cabinet. A good

method I once read about was adding the poison to a tube of toothpaste. A drop of pure nicotine killed the victim. You only have to do some background reading to make sure it works quickly and without anyone noticing. — Jonesy

Are you favouring poison or recommending it? This is too creepy for me. — Normal Norm

Diamond folded the papers and pocketed them. Chilling. He'd seen enough to cause him to stand up and look again at that row of plastic pots.

Sinister or innocent?

Each was about nine inches high, in the shape of a classic Grecian urn with a neck and topped with a lid. They could be used for any kind of storage. And since everything in this workshop had a reason for being here, why not these?

Better check.

He moved the chair across the room, stepped up and took a closer look, and he now saw that the train designs were stickers someone had cut out and attached to the plastic.

But there was something more. Something disturbing. Printed labels had been fixed to the lids of all three urns.

Each had a man's name, a lifespan in years and a location.

The first was *Edmund Seaton 1949–2013 Gloucester Castle.*

A rapid rethink was necessary. He'd been right the first time. These, after all, had to be cremation urns.

Diamond reached for Edmund Seaton's pot and felt its weight, mainly to judge whether the ashes were still inside. It lifted so easily that he knew at once that they were not. Just to be certain, he checked *Roger Matthew Carnforth 1943–2014 Oxburgh Hall.* Roger's remains were elsewhere.

And so were the ashes of *Jeremy Marshall-Tomkin 1937–2014 Forthampton Grange.*

Reassuring, really. It would have been macabre to have stored three sets of human ashes in a workshop, however cheerfully the urns were decorated.

He was about to get down when, as an afterthought, he felt for the lid of the first urn and lifted it off.

The pot wasn't empty after all.

Something was inside, but not ashes. A piece of fine, cream-coloured silk was coiled to fit into the space. He lifted it out and stepped down from the chair. The light-weight silk unfurled into a finely pleated, exquisitely tailored, full-length gown. In spite of the way the garment had been stored, there was scarcely a crease to be seen.

At this point, logic abandoned him.

What in the name of sanity was a woman's evening dress doing in a cremation pot in an engineer's workshop?

And whose dress was it? Some unknown woman's? The late Edward Seaton's? Or Ivor Pellegrini's?

Having started this, he had to go on. He climbed on the chair again and checked the other urns. Each contained a coiled silk dress. The one in Roger Matthew Carnforth's urn was pink, Jeremy Marshall-Tomkin's blue. At a loss for an explanation, he replaced all the lids and stepped down, his brain reeling from the discovery.

He hadn't found the answer to Pellegrini's secret life. He'd found a question, a much bigger question.

"Wow — it's stunning," Ingeborg said, holding the creamy silk dress at arm's length. "Gorgeous. I've never seen anything like this."

"I have," Diamond said. "I've seen two more."

He'd left everything else in place in the

workshop and returned the keys to the sister at the RUH with the good news that Hornby had been rescued in time and was now in a good home and on a special diet.

His solo investigation was already compromised. He'd needed a woman's help. And he couldn't get Ingeborg's opinion without upsetting Halliwell. So they were both with him in the privacy of his office.

For the moment, he was getting little else from Ingeborg than "oohs" and "ahs." Keith Halliwell was lost for words as well, but for a different reason, which anyone might take to be that dresses weren't his thing at all.

"I've had longer to think about it than you two," Diamond said, "and I'm still stumped."

"You want our opinion?" Halliwell said finally.

Diamond heard the reserve in the tone. "That's why I called you in."

"I thought Inge and I had been returned to normal duties."

So that was it: hurt feelings.

"The Professional Standards job is done. Finito. This is over and above the call of duty. I'm sounding you out, okay?"

"No," Halliwell said. "It's not okay. I'm pissed off, if you want to know the truth. Either you want us on board or you don't.

Which is it?"

He could feel the degree of hurt. He'd known Halliwell for most of their working lives and now he'd treated him like a rookie. He'd treated both colleagues shabbily.

"Can we rerun this? I'm sorry if it seemed I was excluding you. That wasn't the intention."

"You couldn't have made it more clear," Halliwell said. " 'You can go back to normal duties.' "

He remembered saying the words. "I should have expressed it better. It's not a one-man show. In fact, I'm in real difficulty with it. This guy Pellegrini has got under my skin since I gave him CPR. I want to take a step back, see him for what he is, good or bad, and there's no chance I can do it without you, but it has to be extra to our other work."

"Okay," Halliwell said, with slightly less pique in the voice. "What do we know about Mrs. Pellegrini? I'm assuming the gowns belonged to her."

"Trixie? I wouldn't bet on it," Diamond said. "The neighbour, Mrs. Roberts, gave a dull picture of her, always in a hat, flat shoes and twinsets."

Halliwell managed a grin. "If that's all she wore, I wouldn't call it dull."

"Oh come on." He grinned back. The remark wasn't all that witty but he appreciated it as a peace offering. "She was shy, wore no make-up, used a shopping trolley. None of it goes with glamorous silk dresses."

"Not exactly day wear, are they?" Halliwell was trying to draw Ingeborg into the debate but all her attention was wholly on the dress, smoothing her fingertips along the fine seams.

"They were hidden," Diamond said. "Rolled up and kept out of sight on a high shelf in the workshop where no one went except Pellegrini himself."

"Are you thinking he was a transvestite, guv?"

He blinked at the suggestion. "Hadn't crossed my mind. It's not impossible. He liked dressing up."

Now Ingeborg spoke. "Oh, I hope not. This is made for someone with a figure. Were the others like this, pleated silk?"

"I got the impression they were. One was pink, the other blue."

"If they weren't his, and they weren't his wife's, they belonged to his dead friends," Halliwell said. "It was a secret club for cross-dressers."

"Get away," Ingeborg said. "These were old guys."

"Does that make a difference?"

"It's grotesque."

All this speculation wasn't leading anywhere. "It may not be a bad idea to check the names and find if they really lived in those places," Diamond said. "Gloucester Castle for a start. That was Edmund Seaton's humble pad."

"Doesn't exist," Ingeborg said at once. "I know Gloucester and there was a castle at one time but it's long since gone."

"I wonder if Edmund Seaton ever existed."

"Shall we see if he's listed on the Internet? May I use your computer, guv?"

"Be my guest." He got up.

She draped the dress over her chair-back and sat in front of Diamond's computer. "What were Seaton's dates?"

He had a note of them. "1949 to 2013."

Before using his keyboard she made a point of flicking dust from it with a Kleenex and wiping the screen. Nothing was said.

"Well, it's not obvious," she said after working the keys for some seconds.

"Nothing doing?" Halliwell said.

"What's the local paper in Gloucester?" Diamond asked Ingeborg.

"*The Citizen*."

"Is it online?"

She checked. "Good call, guv." But after a few minutes she said, "Nothing here about an Edmund Seaton."

"A funeral in 2013?"

She shook her head. "I tried that first. We could be making a wrong assumption here. Gloucester Castle is no more but it could be the name of a pub and it wouldn't have to be in Gloucester."

"Or a boat," Halliwell said. "It wouldn't be a bad name for a boat."

"Thanks for that," she said with a twitch of the lips. "We'd never trace a boat."

"The others had fancy addresses, too," Diamond said. "Oxburgh Hall — does that exist?"

Ingeborg tried again, and this time she said, "Bingo — it's a National Trust property in Norfolk."

"Good. Our man was Roger Matthew Carnforth, died 2014. Do these places have a live-in curator?"

Ingeborg had already found the website. "What a stunning place."

They looked over her shoulder at a slide-show of a large building with features of a castle — a moat and battlemented tower and arched entrance — and the solid structure of a large country house.

"Generations of a single family have lived

165

there since it was built in the fifteenth century," she read aloud from the screen.

"The Carnforths?" Diamond said.

"The Bedingfields."

"I'm starting to feel spooked."

Ingeborg wasn't giving up. "Our man could have worked there as a guide. I could phone the place and see if they've heard of him."

Diamond nodded. "Do it."

"What shall I say it's about?"

"Part of an ongoing inquiry."

But no one at Oxburgh Hall had heard of Roger Matthew Carnforth. The National Trust employee was adamant that nobody of that name had been employed there in her time, which stretched back twenty-three years.

"Another dead end," Halliwell said.

"What was the last man's address?" Ingeborg asked.

"Forthampton Grange," Diamond said with resignation. "Tell me it's a brand name for chocolate biscuits and I'll trouble you no more. I've had enough of this game."

She Googled the name, sat back and gazed at the screen as if she'd lost control. "You're not going to like this," she said. "All I'm getting is websites connected to the Great Western Railway."

"Which was wound up seventy years ago when the railways were nationalised," Halliwell said.

But Diamond was galvanized. "Bring up one of the websites. What does it say?"

"Something about a Grange class and some numbers: 4-6-0."

"We've cracked it, then."

"Have we?"

"These aren't the places where these guys lived. They're steam trains."

The other two eyed him as if he'd finally flipped.

"It's all connected to Pellegrini's obsession with the railway," he went on. "Each locomotive was given a name and the names were grouped in classes. Gloucester Castle was one of the Castle class, Oxburgh Hall was one of the Halls and Forthampton was in the Grange class. We can check and I guarantee that's what we'll find."

"How do you know?" Ingeborg asked.

"Must be my age. When I was a kid I was given an electric train set and the engine was called Albert Hall." He smiled at a long-buried memory that surfaced. "I grew up thinking it was a person's name. Albert Hall, right? It was only when Pink Floyd held a gig there and got banned for firing a cannon and nailing the bass drum to the floor that I found out it was a concert hall."

"You liked Pink Floyd?" Ingeborg said, eyes wide.

"Still does," Halliwell said. "Haven't you seen the CDs in his car?"

"That's immaterial," Diamond said. "Check the trains and see if I'm right."

Ingeborg managed to contain herself and obey orders. Presently she said, "Gloucester Castle, yes, a 4073 class locomotive built in May, 1949."

"Good. Now Oxburgh Hall."

She located it almost at once. "The 4900 or Hall class, built 1943."

"And Forthampton Grange?"

She didn't keep them in suspense for long. "Found it. The Grange engines were a smaller-wheeled version of the Hall class. This one dates from 1937."

"The year Jeremy Marshall-Tomkin was born," Diamond said. "Do you see? Each of them is linked to a locomotive built the year he was born. Seaton, 1949, Carnforth 1943 and Marshall-Tomkin 1937." He snapped his fingers. "And I've just remembered. There was a bloody great GWR name-plate fixed to the workshop wall. County of Somerset. No need to look it up. It will date from Pellegrini's year of birth."

"Neat," Halliwell said. "Very neat. But

where does it lead us?"

Ingeborg said, "My guess is that we're talking arrested development here, eternal schoolboys who like playing trains and belong to some sort of club. Sad but less harmful than holding up banks."

"And each of them chose a train as some kind of identity tie-in," Halliwell said. "You could be right, Inge."

"She is," Diamond said. "She must be."

"So where do the urns come in?" Ingeborg said.

"If you were a railway fanatic, where would you want your ashes scattered?"

"Somewhere along the tracks." Then her voice became as shrill as a steam whistle approaching a station. "I'm with you, guv. The railway companies wouldn't allow that. Dangerous for one thing and not very good for their image either. So the club has to do it in secret. Each time one of them dies and is cremated, Pellegrini gets on his trike and pedals out to some quiet spot along the main line to empty the urn. That's what he was doing on the night of the accident."

"Right. And in case he was stopped he had his cover story ready."

"He was studying the wildlife?"

"In the company of his late wife. Hence the urn in the saddlebag."

169

"Which we know didn't contain her ashes, because she wasn't cremated, she was buried," Ingeborg said, picking up the narrative as if she'd known it all along. "We've cracked it, guys. When the urn was found, it was empty. Pellegrini had done the job. He'd already taken the ashes to the top of the footbridge at the end of Hampton Row and tipped them over. If he hadn't crashed, he would have brought the urn back to the workshop and given it a label and a bright new sticker and placed it on the shelf with the others."

Diamond was nodding. He couldn't fault the explanation. The purpose of the night ride was accounted for.

"Mystery solved, then," Halliwell said.

"And no arrest," Ingeborg said. She got up from Diamond's chair and rubbed her hands as if to remove any dust from her fingertips.

The pair of them wanted to draw a line under the crash investigation and move on. Diamond understood why. He was becoming embroiled in a matter that wasn't legitimate CID business. But he wasn't satisfied. "It would be good to find out if this club really exists. There might be current members about."

"Shouldn't be difficult to trace them,"

170

Ingeborg said. "But isn't this more a job for the railway police than us?"

"If you're thinking about people trespassing on railway property, you're right," he said, "but there's another element here."

"The dresses?"

"Exactly. They look special to me."

"They are," she said, glad of a chance to pick up the dress and feel the silk in her hands again. "Believe me, they are. There's some faded writing here, where the beads are sewn in, and I can't make it all out, except the word 'Venise,' which is French for Venice. It's a fashion item for sure."

"So where do they come from?" Diamond said. "How did Pellegrini acquire them and why did he keep them hidden and locked away? I'm sorry but I don't buy the theory that these wannabe engine-drivers also happened to like dressing up in women's evening gowns."

"Do you think they're stolen property?"

"They could be. Or he could have bought them."

"As an investment, like antiques or works of art? Who would know?" Ingeborg answered her own question. "Paloma."

8

Paloma Kean was Peter Diamond's close friend, close enough to be intimate sometimes. But to call them lovers or partners wasn't right. They slept with each other when it suited and the feeling between them was warm and affectionate. Until her divorce, Paloma had been in an abusive relationship and she valued Diamond's respect for her. Although no one in their wildest dreams could describe him as romantic, he was strongly appreciative of her and he could be amusing, qualities that met her needs. On his side, there would always be the memory of his late wife, Steph, the one love of his life. He wasn't looking for anyone to replace Steph and never would, but he liked the company of women and Paloma was attractive, intelligent and forgiving. As long as she would tolerate his rough edges, he was more than happy to share her company and sometimes her bed.

This afternoon, he made clear, he wanted her professional opinion. She had a successful business providing fashion information for film and TV companies. Her collection of images of historical costume was unmatched anywhere. If researchers needed to know about anything from bustles to bustiers she could supply online illustrations and information within minutes. Just about every TV costume drama in the past decade had benefited from Paloma's expertise.

"Where did you nick that from?" was her first question on seeing the coil of pale silk he'd brought with him.

"I'd rather not say, but I need your opinion."

With care, she unfurled the gown, shook it gently and held it at full length in front of her before draping it over her arm to examine the fixings.

"These are Murano beads, the best."

"Is that a clue?"

She didn't answer. She was examining the faded lettering Ingeborg had noticed along a seam close to the beads.

"We're going to my office. I want to see this on a mannequin. If it's what I think it is, an original, you'd better have a good explanation." She was half playful, half suspicious of his conduct.

"Original as in handmade, you mean?" he said as he followed her upstairs.

"I mean a lot more than that."

In the studio was what he would have called a dressmaker's dummy, a headless female torso shape on a stand. As delicately as if she was handling spider threads, Paloma gathered the fabric and arranged it over the mannequin's shoulders, letting it slip into the shape of the dress, weighted by the glass beads. She stepped back. "Isn't that the most exquisite creation you've ever set eyes on?"

"I'm not the best judge."

"Come on, Peter. Anyone can see it's a classic. Is there another piece — a cape, a jacket?"

"I don't think so. This is all there is." He hesitated, the professional detective in him reluctant to volunteer information unless it brought a return. But this was Paloma, he reminded himself, and he was her sometime lover seeking advice. "Where this came from are two other gowns in different colours."

Her eyes switched to full-beam. "You're not serious?"

"Would I lie to you?"

"What have you done, you wicked man — raided the Fashion Museum?"

"An engineer's workshop."

"Get away."

"True. I left the others stuffed in plastic pots, as this was."

"You mean twisted into skeins?"

"Yes."

"It wouldn't do them any harm. They were often carried in small hatboxes. This is made from a single sheet of silk and the pleating is a legend in the rag trade, a secret process that died with the designer. Have you heard of Mariano Fortuny?"

He shook his head.

"I didn't think you would have," she said. "He didn't murder anyone."

That was below the belt but he was too interested to protest.

Paloma told him, "He was a genius from Spain who could turn his hand to anything creative. Funny you should have mentioned engineering, because Fortuny made his reputation as a lighting engineer in the early years of the last century, inventing new methods of stage lighting that were adopted by most of the great theatres and opera houses of Europe. The fashion was a secondary interest, but he married a dressmaker and she had a huge influence. They bought a palazzo in Venice and Fortuny used his analytical skills to revolutionise the preparation of silk fabric, in particular the dyes, using luminous colours and vertical pleating no one has ever matched. He became the designer every woman of taste would kill for. The man himself could have excelled at anything — painting, photography, architecture — and he hated being known only for the dresses he made."

"And this is definitely one of them?"

"I'm certain it is, his Delphos gown, about a hundred years old and inspired by classical sculpture, the pleated robe worn by the charioteer of Delphi. There was a time in the twenties when all the great ladies of the theatre insisted on being seen in a gown like this. I could show you pictures of Sarah Bernhardt, Eleonora Duse, Isadora Duncan, all in their Fortuny dresses."

"So it could be a valuable item?"

"At auction, anything up to ten thousand pounds."

His lips vibrated softly. "Because of the rarity value?"

"And the fact that any woman will look incredible in it." Paloma herself seemed mesmerised. The simple act of turning her eyes away was clearly difficult. "What's going on, Peter?"

"Long story," he said, and at once made clear that she wasn't about to hear it. "A mystery asking to be solved — which is why I'm here. If a dress like this is as special as you say, experts like you must know about it. Is there any chance you can tell me its owner?"

She shook her head.

"I was hoping you could point me in the right direction."

"But you haven't even told me where it comes from. A workshop could be any-where."

"A private address in Bath."

"Is that where they belong?"

"An open question."

"I know of several in the Fashion Museum at the Assembly Rooms but I doubt if this came from there. You said there are two more. Fortuny gowns are masterpieces, Peter. They don't often come on the market, even at the great auction houses."

"Some well-known collector?"

"Not all collectors care to be well known. You say the gowns are shut away in a workshop. Are you thinking they're stolen?"

"I can't say for certain but I have my suspicions."

"Well, they're easy to coil up and take away, but a thief would find it difficult to sell them on, or fence them, or whatever the expression is. Have you checked the police computer to see if they are listed?"

"Not yet. I only found them this afternoon."

She smoothed her fingers between the narrow seams for the pure pleasure of the touch. "Some people aren't interested in making money. They're the ones the tenth commandment was written for."

"Was it?" Long time since he'd looked at the Ten Commandments.

"Thou shalt not covet."

"I remember now: thy neighbour's ox."

"And a few other things, such as his house, wife, manservant, maidservant."

"And you're thinking a Fortuny dress might be coveted by someone?"

"By every woman who ever saw one."

"But this is an old man, retired engineer, living alone."

"Old men have their memories. Is he married?"

"Was, until his wife's death last November, and she wasn't interested in fashion."

"A mistress, then?"

Caught unprepared, he gave it a moment's thought first. "I could be mistaken but he doesn't seem the sort. Railways are his secret passion. He has a toy train layout in the workshop."

She laughed. "I'm with you, then. I doubt

if he's a ladies' man. Can't you question him about the dresses?"

"He's in the RUH, on life support."

Paloma nodded. "I'm starting to understand. Was he attacked?"

"I'd rather not go into that," he said. "So can't you give me any pointers as to how three Fortuny gowns ended up in Bath?"

She smiled. "I could insist on seeing the others before I give an opinion. In truth, I don't know. If you like I can call Denise, my contact at the Fashion Museum, but I'd better warn you. She's highly excitable. Just the mention of Fortuny will send her into ecstasy. She'll demand all the details."

"She can't have them." He'd been invaded by this image of a hyped-up Denise telling the whole of Bath about Pellegrini's double life.

"Fine," Paloma said. "You're probably right."

And yet . . . was he turning down the only chance of a breakthrough? The people at the Fashion Museum were more likely than anyone to know about collectors of rare and valuable items. "Is there any way you could get her opinion without actually saying we found these dresses?"

"Not easy. She'd be quick to pick up on anything like that."

"But you . . ."

"You want me to try after all? All right." She picked up the phone. "Would you like to speak to her yourself?"

"Christ, no."

She smiled. "The look on your face." Then, as the call was answered, she turned away from him and started speaking into the phone. He could hear only her end of the conversation. "Denise? How are you doing? It's been far too long." There followed some chat about a trip to Paris, a frustrating wait until she said, "I'm calling on behalf of a friend who's trying to trace a person from this area with some extremely rare fashion items and I know you have contacts with people who loan things for special exhibitions. Can you think of anyone who specialises in Fortuny? . . . That's what I said, but no, darling, nothing is being offered for sale. If it was, I'd tell you . . . Absolutely not. You'd be the first to know, I promise, cross my heart and hope to die . . ."

Diamond listened in awe of Paloma's convincing rationale.

"I'm not explaining this very well . . . Yes, I did say Fortuny and there's nothing, I repeat nothing, you should know . . . Actually my contact is a man." She swivelled her chair and eyed Diamond.

180

He gave an encouraging smile.

She smiled back and seemed to take wicked delight in watching him as she said, "A rather sad guy who was adopted and is trying to trace his real parents and the only information he has is that one of them lives locally and owned some Fortuny gowns . . . That's the thing. He has no idea, poor lamb. Definitely on the level, yes. A thought like that hasn't crossed his mind, I'm certain. If you could only point him in the right direction, it will make his day, his year . . . You can? Well, that's brilliant!"

Diamond leaned forward, eager not to miss a syllable. He'd already forgiven the bit about the sad guy.

"You're better placed than anybody. You've got to be right. There can't be any others in Bath. We both know you can't get them for love nor money . . . Very rich? Well, they'd have to be . . . Cavendish Crescent? I know it . . . But how public-spirited. When people who possess beautiful things are willing to allow others to appreciate them it restores one's faith in humanity."

This was promising. Generous owners and just up the hill in Cavendish Crescent.

Then Paloma said into the phone. "Dear God, he'll be heartbroken. How long ago was this? . . . A good age, yes, but so sad

181

when it comes. What was her name? . . . Could you spell that? . . . Filiput. Got it. And what happened to the collection after her death? . . . The husband is dead, too? This is too much. I'll have to break the news to my little guy . . . And the dresses? I suppose they were part of the estate . . . Never! What happened, then? . . . What do you mean 'disposed of them'? . . . I'm speaking for myself now, Denise. My little guy's interest was entirely in the couple, not their possessions. But you and I have a right to be concerned. The world needs to keep tabs on irreplaceable items like this."

"Such lies," she said to Diamond after switching off. "I'll roast in hell for this. I think you heard most of it. Good news and bad. There were definitely Fortuny gowns in private hands in Bath. The owner was a woman of East European origin married to an Italian, and the gowns were handed down through three generations. She wasn't really a collector but she treasured them for their sentimental value and she did once lend a gorgeous blue one to the museum for an exhibition about Fortuny and his influence on design."

"Sounds like the one I saw coiled up."

"Yes, she had two in the Delphos style and

one Peplos, a variation with an attached tunic."

"Did I hear you say her name?"

"Filiput. Olga Filiput. She and her husband had a large house in Cavendish Crescent."

"A whole house to themselves."

"Old money. She was over ninety when she died in 2013 and the old man lasted about six months longer. But — and this is the bad bit — during that time he seems to have disposed of a lot of her things, including the Fortuny gowns. When he died, they weren't among the items listed as part of the estate."

"Did they have family?"

"No heirs, apparently."

"And didn't Denise have any information about where the gowns ended up?"

"You don't need to ask," she said. "You know."

"The engineer's workshop. So she has no record of them being acquired by a local engineer?"

"None whatsoever — and Denise wouldn't miss news of a transaction like that. She's alert to everything. You should have heard her when I mentioned Fortuny. Peter, I'm suspicious."

"Me, too." He grasped Paloma's hand and

squeezed it. "You did brilliantly. I owe you a meal out for this."

"Is that the best you can do? I was telling the most horrendous lies for you."

"And a theatre trip."

"Not good enough, big spender."

"A weekend away. A hot-air balloon ride. What more can I offer?"

"I thought you'd never ask. I'll settle for the dress."

Driving home (with the dress), Diamond felt elated by the fresh discoveries, yet wary of where they were taking him. Valuable fashion items owned by one family for three generations end up with rich old lady. Death of old lady. Death of old lady's husband. Items missing from the estate turn up hidden in cremation pots in engineer's workshop. Engineer has a macabre interest in ways of killing. What could you read into that except a rising scale of suspicion? A deal? A dirty deal? Confidence trickery? Theft? Murder? Double murder?

Hold on, he told himself. This is the man whose life I fought for. He and I are linked by the intensity of those desperate moments. I was alone with him, willing him to survive, mouth to mouth, forcing my breath into his lungs, an intimacy you can't forget. Nothing in my world mattered more than his precious life.

A few sheets printed out from the Internet debating methods of murder don't make anyone a killer.

The truth probably lies elsewhere.

How frustrating that the man himself is alive yet unable to speak. No use relying on an improvement in his condition. Even if he does recover, there's no certainty he'll speak sense. He talked bollocks about rabbits. Lew Morgan, an experienced cop well used to dealing with tall stories, decided the man was a nutcase.

But was all the crazy talk just a front, an attempt to distract from a more likely reason for his night ride: the illegal scattering of ashes along the railway? Illegal, but not unworthy. He definitely lied when he said the cremation urn contained his late wife's ashes. The talk of bringing her on the ride must have been his cover story. Maybe the rabbits are no more than an extra touch of idiocy to convince the two policemen he was gaga, and basically harmless.

Or could there be a germ of truth in the story?

Lew Morgan ought to be able to throw more light. He was the last to speak to Pellegrini. That weird conversation in the small hours of the morning could be the key to understanding whether the man was criminal, crazy or misunderstood. The version Lew gave was spoken in snatches when he was still in shock and under sedation.

He had to be given his chance to talk some sense.

The monitoring equipment took up so much room that when Diamond arrived at the ward next morning he had to slot a chair into a space between bags of fluid hanging from drip stands. This time he hadn't been required to dress in the sterile clothes. Lew Morgan was out of intensive care and in a private room, fully conscious and propped up on the adjustable bed. No restrictions had been placed on the visit, even though it was little over a day since the patient's left leg had been amputated above the knee.

He started to introduce himself again as "Peter Diamond from the nick" — without mention of rank — hoping Lew would open up and fill in some of that crucial extra detail. After everything the poor guy had been through, he was unlikely to have any memory of the previous visit and its abrupt, abusive end.

But Lew interrupted him. "I know who you are. You were here a couple of days ago asking questions."

"You were heavily sedated."

"So what's new?"

"You sound brighter."

"High as a fucking kite. Haven't the faintest idea what they're pumping into me except blood and I need plenty of that. Is this still about Aaron's driving? He did nothing wrong, poor sod."

"Glad to hear it. There was nothing at the crash site to suggest any different."

"So what's your problem? I can speak up for Aaron."

"But you told me you didn't see the crash because your eyes were closed."

"That's a fact. When I opened them we were out of control and turning over. He screamed out 'Jeez' and now I know why: that old git on the trike."

"You remember him, then?"

Lew's hands gripped the bedding as he spoke of the still-vivid experience. "He comes out of nowhere. Aaron swings the wheel and takes us up the bank and we swerve across the street on two wheels and hit the wall." He added through gritted teeth, "They tell me the old fuck is on life support. Let me anywhere near and I'll switch him off even if I have to hop there on my one leg."

"It can't have been deliberate," Diamond said.

"How do you bloody know? You weren't there."

"I've been to the scene. There were stationary vehicles. Aaron was unsighted, and so was the tricyclist probably."

"He was an accident waiting to happen. Unsteady."

"How do you know that if your eyes were closed?"

Lew hesitated and screwed up his face in thought. "We stopped him earlier. Fucking demented. He shouldn't have been out."

"I want to ask you about that, Lew. We touched on it when I saw you last but you weren't able to say much. Where was he when you first pulled him over?"

"Out Bathampton way. This was early in the shift, around two-thirty. Bathampton Lane, in fact. He was the only thing on the road but he didn't have a crash helmet, so we stopped to have a word. Well, I did. Aaron stayed in the car."

"What exactly was said?"

"Straight off I could tell he was going to give me lip. The posh voice, calling me officer."

"Patronising?"

"That's the word. I tell him he shouldn't

188

be driving a motorised vehicle without a helmet and he says, cool as you like, he's legal on account of it being an EAPC."

"What's that?"

"Electrically assisted pedal cycle."

"And was he right?"

Lew nodded. "Smug bastard."

"So at that stage he was talking sense?"

"Every fucking thing he said sounded sense the way he spoke it, like I was a peasant, if you know what I mean. He said he had the government guidance about EAPCs on a piece of paper and I reckon he did, but I didn't give him the chance to show me because it was getting to be a battle of wills."

"I can understand."

"I asked about the contents of his saddlebag and he listed every fucking thing as calm as if he was reading the football results. Mostly it was stuff you'd use to look at wildlife, like binoculars, camera and so on. And his food. Banana, slice of cake, flask of tea. Nothing alcoholic. And Trixie."

"His wife."

Lew's eyes widened. "You know about this? Did I tell you before? It was when it became obvious he was nuts. He was talking about Trixie's ashes. He'd brought the urn with him in the saddlebag, so she could join him on the trip."

"Weird."

"I was already wishing I hadn't started with him. Next I asked where he was going and he said he wouldn't know until he got there because they were always on the move."

A warning light flashed in Diamond's brain. He wasn't sure if it was wise to go down the crazy route again. "Who were?"

"He didn't actually say but I took it to be rabbits because he said they covered about a mile each night, using hops. That's got to be rabbits or hares, hasn't it?" Lew seemed to want to discuss this rationally.

"Frogs? Fleas?"

"You're joking, I hope. He wouldn't want binoculars to look at fucking fleas."

"A mile a night? Do rabbits go that far?"

"Hares might. They get up speed, don't they? Hares, rabbits, kangaroos, take your pick. It's all horseshit, anyway. He said they were heading for Bath."

"I find that impossible to believe," Diamond said.

"You're not the only one. And when I asked how he knew where to look for them, he said, as straight-faced as I'm speaking to you now, he could hear them digging their holes. That was when I decided enough was enough. Either he was taking the piss or he was round the twist."

"So you returned to the car?"

"After telling him to keep off the main roads. He said he always did and I told him other traffic might not see him coming. He said a full moon helped. I remember thinking you can say that again, you fucking loony. We watched him start up and ride away and I thought that was the end of it. Shows how wrong you can be, doesn't it?"

"You didn't breathalyse him?"

"No point. As far as the law was concerned he was riding a pushbike. Anyway I'd have spotted the signs if he was over the limit. I'm not new in the job."

"Unsteady, you said."

"I meant his riding, kind of wobbly, due to age, not alcohol. If I'd thought a charge would stick, I'd have done him."

"In the conversation you had, did he mention the railway at any stage?"

"Never a fucking word. Why?"

"We think he was following the main line. It runs close to Bathampton Lane and Beckford Gardens. He's one of these railway enthusiasts."

Lew frowned. "Yeah?" He looked as if this new suggestion was more than he wanted to know.

Diamond spared him a description of Pellegrini's model train set. "Thanks, Lew. You've helped a lot."

"And I bet this isn't the end of it. I'll get plenty more like you giving me a hard time. Headquarters and the IPCC, I shouldn't wonder."

"You know the drill, then."

"I can handle it as long as they jack me up with whatever it is I'm on right now. What did you say you are at the nick — accident investigator?"

"That'll do," Diamond said.

Ivor Pellegrini was fast becoming more villain than victim. He had an unhealthy interest in murder. He was a danger on the roads who had probably caused the death of one police officer and the loss of another's limb. He certainly wasn't senile. He'd refused to be intimidated by a police car stopping him. He'd run rings around Lew Morgan and he'd manifestly lied about the purpose of the cremation urn. The valuable Fortuny gowns hidden in his workshop needed explaining.

All this was painful to think about. There was no logic decreeing that the man whose life you saved had to be worthy of survival. But each offence was wounding.

Just to be certain there was no change in

the patient's condition, Diamond visited the Critical Care unit before leaving the hospital. The redoubtable sister he'd seen before was on duty.

"What is it this time — a get-well card?" she said.

"Would he appreciate one?"

"Not yet."

"He's still out cold, then?"

"That's not a term we use, but yes."

"No improvement at all?"

"Nothing anyone has noted. What's happened to Hornby?"

He took a moment to remember who Hornby was. "He's doing fine now."

"Who's looking after him?"

"Er, family."

"We were told there isn't any family." Nothing got past this sister. Anyone in need of intensive care would be fortunate to have her in charge.

"My family."

"*You* took him in? That's nice."

I took you in as well, sister, Diamond thought, and I'm starting to get a conscience about it. "Cats are easy to board. It's just for a short time, I hope."

"That's what we do at this stage, hope," she said. "It's better than despair." Evidently impressed that Diamond was a caring man, she said, "I can let you see him if you wish."

"Please."

"You'll need kitting out first."

In the protective apron and mask he was escorted to the side room where the patient lay tubed, wired and ventilated and showing no signs of life that were not medically induced. He seemed diminished by all the equipment. With most of his features hidden under the mask inflating the lungs, he was hard to recognise as the man Diamond had attempted to revive a few days before. Grey hair, wrinkles, large ears, arthritic hands with one finger attached to a pulse oximeter.

"Is this what they call a vegetative state?"

"Keep your voice down, superintendent."

He said in a whisper, "Or is it a persistent vegetative state?"

"It's only termed persistent after four weeks."

"How long do you reckon to keep them going?"

"Not my decision, I'm glad to say. Have you seen enough?"

He drove to work with the image difficult to shift from his brain. Strange to think if he hadn't chosen to explore the uncultivated side of Beckford Gardens at the time he did but an hour later, the old man would certainly have been dead and none of the elaborate medical effort would have come into play. For the health professionals there was no dilemma. Life was a universal entitlement and their job was to bend every effort to preserve it. Diamond's own view was less clear. Already he was questioning whether it would have been better for everyone concerned, including the patient, if he hadn't performed CPR. He could recall from his schooldays a couple of lines from a poem by Arthur Hugh Clough he'd been made to learn:

Thou shalt not kill; but need'st not strive
Officiously to keep alive.

When he got to work, his first action was to make a transcript of everything Lew Morgan had told him. He prided himself on his power of recall, but inevitably some of it would go if he didn't commit it to paper, so it all got into record as near to exactness as he could manage.

That done, he stepped into the CID room and asked Ingeborg to make an online search for obituary notices for Mrs. Olga Filiput, a former resident of Cavendish Crescent, who had died about 2013, aged over ninety, and her husband, first name unknown, who had outlived Olga by about six months.

"Is there something I should know about these people, guv?" she asked.

He was so used to getting Inge's help accessing the Internet that he'd asked without thinking. Officially she was back on routine CID duties. His orders. The mystery surrounding Ivor Pellegrini was no longer her concern, or shouldn't be. She didn't need to be involved in suspicions that were Diamond's alone. If Georgina learned he was using his staff to pursue what was little more than a private hunch, he'd be in trouble.

But he'd set this ball rolling and he couldn't stop it now without giving offence. He told Inge what he had learned from Paloma and her Fashion Museum contact, Denise.

"You're really into this, aren't you?" she said. "What do you hope to get from it?"

That word again. His take on hope wasn't the same as the sister's in Critical Care. "In this job, you don't hope for anything if you've got any sense," he said, trying to keep some distance from Ingeborg and sounding lofty and ungrateful in the process. "You make your enquiries and see what emerges."

This is not good, he told himself. If you can't be frank with your closest colleagues you shouldn't be in the job.

The *Bath Chronicle* was online and the death notices easy to access. Ingeborg found the announcement of Olga Filiput's death before Diamond had made his first coffee of the morning.

"It's only brief," she said when he came, mug in hand, to look at her screen, "but it tells us the husband's name among other things. He was Massimo."

"Good work. What does it mean?"

"The name? Like maximum, I think. The greatest."

"I wonder how anyone lives up to that."

She highlighted the notice for him, one among many:

FILIPUT, Olga, beloved wife of Massimo, passed away peacefully on 2 November, aged 92. Funeral service and cremation at Haycombe, Bath, 2:45 p.m. on 17 November.

"Okay," he said. "Now find Massimo's death notice for me."

"I can't," she said. "Not here, anyway. His name would have popped up in the search, but it didn't."

"He went about six months after Olga. That's May, 2014."

"You told me already, guv."

"And you haven't been able to find it?"

"It's not there."

"Massimo — the greatest — and he doesn't even get a death notice in the local rag? Try again."

She sighed. "It doesn't work like that. I made the search under Filiput and Olga was the only one that came up. If I repeat the search I'll get the same result."

"Why didn't the old man get a mention in the paper if she did? They weren't short of the pennies."

"You'd have to ask his family — if there is one."

"Find them, Inge. They'll be a younger generation, so check the social media. It's an unusual surname."

He left her to start the search and it was a longer process. He had time to check with DI John Leaman on what else had been happening in CID. The church-roof lads had appeared in court and been remanded in custody. A spate of burglaries had shocked the affluent residents of St. James's Square. Nothing Leaman and the rest of the team couldn't deal with.

198

"Massimo seems to have been the last of the Filiputs in Bath," Ingeborg told Diamond when he checked with her again. "I drew a blank. I suppose there was no one left to arrange for a death notice."

"The Internet failed us?" he said.

"On the other hand he may have left instructions that he didn't want his funeral announced. Some house-breaker could have seen the notice and raided the home in Cavendish Crescent on the day of the funeral. It wouldn't be the first time that happened."

Tempted to have another dig at Ingeborg about the limitations of the Internet, he spared her and moved on. "Find one of those websites that lists properties that were sold in the last two or three years."

Easy.

Most of the crescent was divided into four-bedroom flats that sold for anything up to £750,000. The only sale of a complete house that fitted the time-slot was at £2.3 million. Ingeborg found the agent who had handled the sale, called them and learned that the Filiput property had been sold by Fathom and Peake, a firm of solicitors.

"We're motoring now," Diamond said. "I mean, *I'm* motoring now, back to Bath."

■ ■ ■ ■

The lawyers' office was in Henry Street, close to the former home of CID. The receptionist asked what the enquiry was and Diamond flashed his ID and said he needed to see the solicitor who had dealt with the late Massimo Filiput's affairs.

"I'm not permitted to disclose client information," she said.

"Ma'am, I'm not asking you to disclose anything. Just press the right buzzer and I'll turn my back if you want."

"It's not as straightforward as that."

"It never is in these places," he said. "Okay, let's try another approach. Who's the most senior person in the building?"

"That would be Miss Hill."

"Not Mr. Peake? I was hoping to go right to the top."

This receptionist was impervious to rapier wit from visitors. "The founders are all deceased."

"Miss Hill, then, if you would be so kind."

One law as rigidly enforced as any on the statute book is that solicitors keep you waiting. He'd thumbed through most of an out-of-date issue of *The Bath Magazine* before a large lady in a black suit invited him into a spacious office smelling of lavender furniture polish. How the world had changed since he'd last spoken to a solicitor. There wasn't a dusty old book or an overflowing in-tray in sight. Just a bare desk and a flat-screen computer.

"It's about Massimo Filiput," Diamond said after shaking a hand that was mainly rings and fingernails. "I believe he instructed you or one of your colleagues."

Hard to believe anyone would instruct Miss Hill. Nothing about her suggested she was the submissive type. Black hair forced into a tight scrunch. Eyes that missed nothing and lips he couldn't imagine smiling if he'd presented her with a box of the finest chocolates and an armful of daffodils.

"Do you know about client confidentiality?" she asked.

"The client's dead," Diamond said.

"I'm aware of that."

Still in motoring mode, he moved rapidly through the gears. "I can get copies of his will, his wife's will, the documents pertaining to the sale of the house. I can check the names of the executors, the beneficiaries and the purchasers. But it all takes time, Miss Hill, and I don't have much of that and neither do you, I'm sure, so let's cut through the red tape, shall we, and do what we can to allay the suspicion?"

She gave him a glare that would have sent a lesser man straight out of the door. "Suspicion of what?"

"Difficult to say without seeing the paperwork. Any malpractice was out of your control, I hope and believe."

"Malpractice?"

"For want of a better word."

Going by Miss Hill's body language any other word in the dictionary would have been an improvement. "Have a care. I don't take insinuations like that from the police or anyone else."

He took a more persuasive line.

"Why don't you go to your files for copies of the wills, and then I can give you chapter and verse? You'll be giving nothing away. You obtained probate on both, so they're public documents now."

"You used the word 'malpractice.' I must warn you that a term like that is actionable."

"Only if it turns out to be unfounded."

"You'd better explain yourself, superintendent."

"Not without the paperwork," Diamond said and threw discretion out of the window. "If you want to turn this into a damaging police investigation involving the Crown Prosecution Service, I can leave now, but I hate to think of the aggro."

"This is highly irregular."

"I couldn't put it better myself."

She picked up her phone and asked for copies of the wills.

"Good call, Miss Hill," Diamond said. "I'm sure you and I can sort this out between us."

She didn't comment, preferring to punish her computer keyboard. Definitely more of a dominatrix than a submissive, Diamond decided. Finally, the receptionist arrived with two box files.

"I drew up both wills myself," Miss Hill told him as she opened the first box. "They were perfectly straightforward. Mrs. Filiput left everything to her husband in the event of her predeceasing him. And he made a similar will in her favour."

"Tidy."

"It's common practice when a husband and a wife without family are making provision for their deaths."

"But she died first, so he inherited everything. Did that mean rewriting his will?"

"No, each of them made their wishes clear for all eventualities."

"Your firm acted as executors for each of them?"

"I thought I made that clear."

"So after Massimo Filiput died, you wound up the estate?"

"Correct."

"You personally?"

She hesitated. "Yes."

"Which must have meant drawing up an inventory of his possessions and selling the house in Cavendish Crescent?"

She nodded. "It fell to me to do everything, even arranging the funeral. They had no family."

"And previously, when Olga Filiput died, did you also make an inventory of her possessions?"

"That had to be done for probate purposes."

"Her clothes? In particular, I'm interested in three antique evening gowns owned by Mrs. Filiput."

"There were far too many items of clothing for me to remember them all."

"The dresses I'm speaking about were valuable items," he said, "made by Fortuny about a century ago, and worth about ten thousand pounds each."

"I told you. I don't recall them."

"Would you mind checking? This could be important."

She made a sound deep in her throat like a distant tsunami. Then she lifted a stack of documents from the filing box and selected one.

Diamond watched and waited.

"Yes," she said. "Antique evening dresses by Fortuny of Venice."

"That's the list of Olga's possessions?"

"Yes."

"Now would you check the documents for Massimo and tell me if the same dresses are included in the inventory of his possessions?"

The tsunami sounded ten miles closer.

She opened the second box and found the relevant list.

She blinked, ran her finger twice down the list and finally looked up. "There's nothing here about gowns."

Just as he expected.

"He could have sold them, I suppose," he said. "If so, it would show in his bank statements. Presumably you have those as well."

You could have made bricks from her silence and built the Great Wall of China in the time she took to move, but in the end she looked for the statements and found them. After a close inspection, shielding the figures with her free hand, she said, "There are no transactions here that aren't accounted for."

"What happened, then?" Diamond asked.

"Could he have given them away? You see the difficulty? Three valuable gowns willed to him by his wife and six months later they have disappeared."

"I hope you're not suggesting we connived at a fraud."

"Not at all. I happen to know where they ended up. You're not under suspicion, but someone else is."

"Who's that?"

He managed an apologetic look. "Can't say for legal reasons."

She inhaled sharply.

He was unmoved. "Is the death certificate in the box? May I see it?"

She was unwilling to give him a sight of anything.

"Anyone can get a copy from the General Register Office," he said. "It's not classified information."

The copy was reluctantly handed across.

" 'Cardiac failure and coronary atheroma.' Heart, then. Much to be expected when you get to ninety-odd." He gave it back. "So what happened to the contents of the house after he died?"

"Everything of value was put into an auction. It realised just under a hundred thousand pounds."

"Would that have been mainly his stuff, or

his wife's? Presumably she left some jewellery?"

"Most of it was antique and must have belonged to her family. Their origins were Austro-Hungarian. There was also period furniture, paintings and books."

"So the auction takings formed part of the estate. After you'd added in the sale of the house and any stocks and shares, building society accounts and so on — and subtracted the taxman's share, and of course your modest fees, how much was left?"

"A little over two and a half million."

"Not bad. And who were the lucky beneficiaries?"

"There was only one. The National Railway Museum."

I was thinking today about the first two. I'm not stony-hearted but I've made it a rule never to mention names or dates in these occasional jottings. I'm not going to forget who I helped on their way. If I ever DO forget, it will be time to stop. No, I remember every one, some with more regret than others.

There are times when I wish I could share my experience with someone else, but it can't happen. If ever I'm feeling isolated, I can glance through these notes and take stock of myself and how I handled matters. It's not as if I'm lonely. There's this area of my life that is private, that's all.

9

In Bath CID there was plenty to moan about since their Manvers Street base had been sold and they'd been moved to this temporary home in the Custody and Crime Investigation Centre in Keynsham. The large white block was surrounded by industrial buildings instead of the homely pubs and coffee shops of Bath. It was open plan, meaning there was no place to hide. And it was home to the custody team, who resented having to make room for visitors. But from time to time someone served up a happy pill, a piece of information that linked unexpectedly with another and opened a whole new line of enquiry.

Diamond had got his new information, but happy he was not.

The more he probed the conduct of Ivor Pellegrini, the more disturbing it appeared. Dark, alien elements kept bobbing to the surface, demanding attention. In a routine investigation Diamond would have given them an airing, examined them for what they were and formed an opinion, but this wasn't routine. He had a personal stake in Pellegrini's well-being. He'd invested so much of himself in the rescue that he couldn't be neutral. They were roped together like climbers and nothing would allow him to sever the rope and move upwards. Detachment wasn't an option.

But the policeman in him knew this was morally wrong. The truth needed to come out. If he couldn't be neutral himself, someone else must take on the job.

He ought to go straight to the incident room and brief his small team. Difficult, with no incident room.

Today he'd offered them a temporary escape from Keynsham: lunch in the city at the Grapes in Westgate Street. Chips, a sandwich and a beer. No expense spared. The building was said (on a beam above the bar) to date from as early as 1302. But to anyone who didn't glance upwards or know the history already, the Grapes was no different inside from any other comfortable, unpretentious boozer.

"Two and a half million to a railway museum?" Halliwell said. "What will they spend it on?"

"Overhauling steam trains."

Ingeborg said, "I can think of more deserving causes."

"You're missing the point," Diamond said.

"We're not, guv," Ingeborg said. "We get it — Pellegrini and Filiput, both train enthusiasts."

"Let's move on, then. We can now make an informed guess how Pellegrini acquired the Fortuny gowns."

Halliwell spelt it out. "The two became friends. They visited each other's houses. Filiput stupidly showed Pellegrini the Fortuny gowns and Pellegrini nicked them, meaning to sell them when he could find a buyer."

Ingeborg turned on him in disbelief. "Are you asking us to believe Filiput was so doddery he wouldn't miss them?"

"He'd turned ninety," Halliwell said.

"And still looked after himself. He wasn't in a care home."

"We don't know the state of his mind."

Trying to be just, Diamond said in Halliwell's support, "A rich old man living alone is easy prey."

Ingeborg said, "We'll have to take your word for that, won't we?"

Diamond gave her a sharp look, but didn't follow it up.

She went on, "Do you think he helped himself to other objects, as well as the gowns?"

"More things could have been removed. I was told the jewellery didn't amount to much after the old man died. Just silver. Nothing gold."

"Can't we get a warrant and search Pellegrini's house?" Halliwell said.

"No chance," Ingeborg said.

Diamond agreed. "The only evidence I have that he's up to no good was obtained by deception. I was out of order. No magistrate would issue a warrant."

Ingeborg added, "And even if you got inside you'd have no way of telling which items were stolen — if any."

"You found out who the gowns belonged to," Halliwell said.

"I was fortunate there," Diamond said. "I had expert help."

"How can we nail this guy, then?"

The force of the question pained Diamond. He was torn apart by professional duty and the strength of his bond to the man he'd rescued from the brink of death.

"I'm not over-worried about more stolen items."

Ingeborg nodded. "Well said, guv. With the owners both dead, anything you recover will only benefit the railway museum."

"So what *are* you worried about?" Halli-well pressed him.

They both looked at Diamond.

"The deaths of all these elderly people."

If he'd thrown his beer in their faces they wouldn't have been more shocked.

His tortured thoughts had progressed from puzzlement to fact-checking to suspi-cion of theft and now suspicion of murder, and it was still based more on hunch than solid evidence. He hated bringing it up but the possibility needed airing.

"You're thinking their deaths weren't natural?" Halliwell said after some seconds.

The printouts of the online forum on methods of murder were still in Diamond's pocket. He divided the pages and passed them across the table.

"Found in the desk drawer in Pellegrini's workshop."

His two colleagues didn't take long to read what was there.

Halliwell was the first to comment and seemed to speak for both of them. "There's enough here to get him a life stretch."

"That's over-egging it. This stuff doesn't make him a killer, but you have to wonder."

"What's yours about?" Ingeborg asked Halliwell. "These are from a forum on the

213

perfect murder."

"Much the same. Methods used in crime stories."

"Let me see." She caught her breath several times as she glanced through the text. "What do you make of it, guv?"

"I keep seeing those cremation urns lined up on a shelf in his workshop . . . like trophies."

"With three names on," Ingeborg said, eyes widening with the horror of what had been suggested. "And Filiput makes four. We may be dealing with a serial killer here."

Diamond had kept his suspicions bottled up for too long. He was relieved to share them with the team at last. They understood how slender the evidence was, but they also trusted him and he could rely on them. He had a suspicion the old man in intensive care could be a murderer and that was enough for Halliwell and Ingeborg. They'd work their socks off for a result. What was more, they would be discreet. The rest of CID wouldn't hear a word before it became necessary.

"I'm getting angry," Ingeborg said. "This is hideous."

"Hideously clever," Halliwell said, "knocking off old people who aren't expected to live much longer anyway."

"Why would he do it?" Ingeborg said. "What's his motive?"

"Greed," Halliwell said. "He gets to know other anoraks like himself, rich ones, and starts nicking their stuff. They're old guys, mostly. When they find out what's going on, he totals them."

"How do you know that? You're guessing."

"None of us are sure of anything yet, except he's a thief."

"And we're not a hundred percent sure of that," Diamond said.

"I'm putting up a theory, that's all," Halliwell said.

"Go on, then. What does he steal from the others?" Ingeborg asked.

"Railway memorabilia, mainly. You have to understand what serious collectors are like. It's a mania. There's a massive trade in bits of old trains, name-plates, steam whistles, uniforms, flags, signals, badges, firemen's shovels."

"Oh, come on. Shovels?"

"I mean it, Inge. You won't get a rusty old shovel for under sixty quid. A name-plate will cost you twenty grand at auction."

"Are you into this stuff yourself, Keith?" Diamond asked in some surprise.

He reddened. "I've got a brother who drives his wife round the bend with it. You

215

should see their house."

"All this is rather persuasive," Ingeborg said. "I'll give you that. But it doesn't explain the really weird part, keeping those urns on a shelf in his workshop."

"That's a power thing," Halliwell said, unstoppable now he'd started. "He's proud of his killing. Some psychopaths like to keep souvenirs of their victims and gloat over them. Possessions, items of clothing, even body hair in one case I read about. He can sit in his workshop and look at those urns and remind himself three men he knew are reduced to ashes because of him."

"I thought we'd agreed he scatters the ashes on the railway track."

"He does. There's no conflict. A group of saddos agree among themselves that after they die they want to become a part of the railway they idolise. Whoever survives will perform this last service for his old friends. Of course, they don't realise Pellegrini isn't just scattering the ashes. He's created a production line."

"And he keeps the urns as mementos," Ingeborg said, grimacing.

"Like I said, he enjoys being in control. But if anyone sees them and asks what they're doing in his workshop, he can say it's his way of remembering old buddies."

She turned to Diamond. "Are we helping, guv?"

"I think there's more."

"More victims?"

"Let's hope not."

She looked as if she was trying to whistle. "His wife, Trixie?"

"It crossed my mind, I have to say. Order a copy of her death certificate just in case, would you, Inge." He took a long sip of his beer, wanting to keep the talk from getting over-heated. "We haven't even discussed the method he might have used. He's a clever man, a trained engineer. It will be methodical and well worked-out."

"He's done his research, we know that," Halliwell said.

"Poison?" Ingeborg said.

"Hard to say," Diamond said.

"Impossible to say after the victims have been cremated," Halliwell said.

"Trixie wasn't," Ingeborg said. "She's buried somewhere local."

"We can't even get a search warrant, so we're not going to get an exhumation order," Halliwell said.

"I may be mistaken over Trixie," Diamond said. "She doesn't fit the pattern for several reasons. The way forward is to find out all we can about these railway enthusiasts, the ones who ended up in the urns I saw. Then there's Filiput. And, of course, Pellegrini himself."

"We know where he is and we know he's not going anywhere," Ingeborg said. "Is there any chance he'll recover?"

"The medics won't say."

"Won't — or can't?"

"To me, he looks a lost cause, but I'm no doctor."

"Shall I dig into his past?" Ingeborg said.

"You're volunteering?"

"I'm fascinated to know how it happened, a guy with a good, analytical brain, successful career, long marriage, who appears to have no empathy whatsoever. He can form friendships and think nothing of killing his so-called friends."

"That's a psychopath for you," Halliwell said.

"Come off it, Keith. That's a meaningless word," she said with scorn. "Any psychologist will tell you it doesn't describe a condition. It may sound scientific but it's no more than a label that says, in effect, these are cold-blooded killers we don't understand."

Halliwell looked blitzed. "I only chipped in to back up what you were saying."

Ingeborg eased up on him. "Sorry. I blew a fuse. Overexcitement. But I intend to find out more about this one."

"And you must," Diamond said. Such commitment had to be encouraged.

She raised a thumb.

"While you're at it," he added, "see if you can make sense of what Pellegrini was saying about the rabbits. I doubt if he has a sense of humour or even much of an imagination. There may be something we've missed."

"Remind me, then," she said. "They were hopping a mile a night and heading towards Bath, right?"

"And he knew where to find them because he could hear them digging their holes. Sounds like fantasy but I'm not certain it was."

"What can I do?" Halliwell asked.

The rivalry between these two was paying dividends. Both wanted a piece of the action.

Encouraged, Diamond asked Halliwell to find out everything he could on the three men named on the urns.

"And what will you be doing, guv?" Ingeborg asked.

"Looking for a railway enthusiast who isn't dead or in a coma."

Not so simple as it sounded.

He discovered that the electronic revolution had transformed the model-train business. All the local shops had closed or gone over to computer games. There was one in Corsham still trading but only through the Internet. Yet the newsagents' shelves were stacked with titles like *Rail Express, Steam News, The Railway Magazine, Heritage Railway, Steam Railway* and *Old Glory.*

Where do you look for a railway enthusiast?

The railway.

Bath Spa station is at the bottom of Manvers Street. Another engineer, the renowned Isambard Kingdom Brunel, sited it there in 1840 at the edge of the city rather than cutting through the centre. His grand design based on a twenty-arch castellated viaduct in the Tudor style made a strong impression, but the interior was plain. The modern revamped ticket hall retains Brunel's supporting structure in a twenty-first-century context with open areas where partitions had been when Diamond first came to Bath. He liked it.

"I'm not here for a ticket," he explained at one of the desks.

"You want to know about trains," the booking clerk said in a voice that had handled the same enquiry a thousand times before.

"People, actually."

"Sorry, my friend. I'm doing a job here. I don't have time to gossip."

"Police," Diamond said, showing his card. "Is there anything like a railway appreciation society in Bath?"

"Never heard of one."

"Railway enthusiasts, then."

"Are there any? You tell me. All I get is railway bellyachers. It's the electrification causing cancellations. They don't understand their journey to London's going to take twenty minutes less when it goes ahead next year. A little bit of hardship now is all they care about."

"This isn't what I want to know," Diamond said.

"There you go, then. You're no different from the rest of them, slagging me off. You'd better try tourist information, under the subway on the other side."

Wondering if this had been such a good idea, Diamond took the short walk to the office on the other side. Would tourist information be any better?

The young woman he approached was clearly dedicated to helping every enquirer, but when she heard what it was about, a trapped expression spread over her features. Personally, she said, she hadn't come across any train enthusiasts, but she would ask her colleague Trudy.

Trudy, rather more senior, looked Diamond up and down as if he might be a sex pest. "What exactly is it you want, sir?"

He went through it again and identified himself as a police officer.

She consulted her computer and turned the screen for him to see.

"Is this what you mean?"

And there it was — the Bath Railway Society, founded in 1957 and clearly still active, with a colour photo of some forty members. Towards the back was a familiar face: definitely Ivor Pellegrini.

His pulse raced as if he'd won the lottery.

"Does it say where they meet?"

She used the mouse and showed him another page. "St. Mary's church hall in Darlington Street."

"Bottom of Bathwick Hill," he said. "I know that." Only a short walk from Pellegrini's house in Henrietta Road.

"Once a month, on the first Thursday."

"Is there someone I can contact — a secretary?"

Trudy clicked and found a name and a number and made a note for him.

"And one more thing: would you print me a copy of the team picture?"

"It won't be as sharp as it is on the screen," she said as she went through the process. Across the room, a printer hummed.

She handed him a sheet of paper. He could still pick out Pellegrini with ease.

"Trudy, you've made my day," he said. "I could hug you."

She gave him that look again.

He called on a Captain Jarrow in North Parade Road, said it was about the railway society and explained that he wasn't a potential member, but a police officer.

He wasn't invited in. This would be a doorstep interview.

"Before you say another word, police officer, I'll make four pertinent points," Captain Jarrow said with the voice of a man well used to addressing inferiors. "One, we're a properly constituted, law-abiding society; two, we keep proper minutes and accounts; three, we pay in advance for the hire of the hall; and four, we always leave it as tidy as when we arrived." Whether this gentleman was an army captain or from the navy, he had the military mind-set.

"And before you say another word yourself," Diamond said, "I have no interest whatsoever in the way you run your club. I need only to know about somebody who I believe is one of your members. He happens to have a keen interest in trains. Ivor Pellegrini."

"Say that again."

"Pellegrini."

"Foreigner, is he?"

"Originally, maybe. He lives in Henrietta Road, not far from where you meet, and he's a retired engineer. He's a bit eccentric. Wears a deerstalker and rides a tricycle."

"A railway buff?"

"Definitely. He has a collection of items from the steam-train days."

"And his name is Pellegrini? Not one of ours."

He couldn't have put it more clearly, and his words carried conviction.

Diamond took the group photo from his pocket to satisfy himself he wasn't mistaken. "He's on your website."

Captain Jarrow gave it a glance. "At least two years out of date. I'm not responsible. I don't do the computer jiggery-pokery. People seem to regard everything they see on a small screen as gospel, but it isn't, and there's the proof. If the police are getting their intelligence from the Internet these days, God help us all."

"So is he a former member? This gentleman here, second row from the back. Don't you have any memory of him?"

His mouth tightened in defiance. "There are certain individuals I've erased from my memory. I'm mortified to discover anyone should assume they belong to our society."

"Was there a falling-out, then?"

"I'd rather not discuss it, if you don't mind."

"But I do mind. I wouldn't be here if it wasn't important. And I don't believe you'd want to be accused of withholding information."

Captain Jarrow's curiosity undermined him. "Is Pellegrini up to no good, then? I've long suspected he had mafia connections."

In Bath? This was one scenario that hadn't occurred to Diamond. "He was critically injured in a road accident."

The only sound for some time was the traffic in North Parade Road.

The captain seemed to decide he'd overstepped the mark. "I wish you'd told me earlier. When you gave his name and said you wanted information on him, I thought straight away he was wanted for some crime or other. Yes, I knew the man. He and certain of his friends were critical of the way we run the society. It was too all-embracing for them. They wanted to specialise. When it became clear that most of us were happy with the way we do things, they decided to defect."

"When you say specialise . . ."

"Limiting their interest to the GWR."

He didn't press for more information. He didn't want to get into the debate that had caused the schism.

"Let me try some other names on you. Were any of these people in the breakaway group as well? Edmund Seaton, Roger Carnforth or Jeremy Marshall-Tomkin?"

Captain Jarrow nodded. He'd lost some of his assertiveness. "All three."

"Did you know they're all dead?"

"I read somewhere that Seaton and Carnforth had passed over. Marshall-Tomkin went as well, did he? Is this what you're investigating? Is someone targeting railway enthusiasts? I'd better warn my members to watch out."

"I've no knowledge how they died. They're simply names that came up."

"Not in our society, they don't. Not any more."

"So they formed their own society, did they?"

"Absolutely not. No properly constituted

society, anyway, with rules and a committee. I believe they meet in each other's homes. Not the same thing at all."

"One other name I'd like to try on you is Massimo Filiput."

"I don't recollect him. Bit of a mouthful. Sounds like another of the *Cosa Nostra*. Was he involved in the accident?"

"No, and he's dead, like the others I mentioned. He was over ninety when he went. Lived in Cavendish Crescent."

There was a pause for thought.

"I'm sure somebody from Cavendish Crescent came to some of the meetings a couple of years ago, but I thought he introduced himself as Max, not the name you said. He was getting on in years, as you indicated. We're none of us spring chickens, but I'd put Max at ninety, easily. Good brain, even so."

"He wasn't a member for long?"

"Two or three meetings. That was the extent of it. I'm trying to remember him. He wore a suit, a rather beautiful grey pinstripe, and a fine silk tie. It made him stand out from the rest of us because we come more casually dressed."

"That's obvious from the group photo."

"You'll understand what I'm saying, then. Yes, if appearance counts for anything, Max had done rather well for himself."

"He left two and a half million to the National Railway Museum," Diamond said.

"Really? What an extravagant gesture."

"It was his entire estate."

"Admirable. Shows commitment to the railway cause."

"Yes, for someone as keen as that, I'd have thought your society would be a natural home. I wonder why he stopped coming."

"I can tell you, if we're talking about the same man. His wife died."

"That checks," Diamond said.

"He had all kinds of family matters to attend to after that. Couldn't find the time to attend meetings. He let us know. Max was a decent sort. I hope you're not about to tell me he went over to Pellegrini's lot."

"It's possible. I've reason to think they visited each other's houses."

"That's too bad. I must say I had my suspicions he had more than a passing interest in the GWR."

"Excuse me. GWR? You mentioned it before." Diamond was hopeless with initials.

"God's Wonderful Railway."

"I don't believe you."

"The Great Western, in fact, but it had several affectionate names. The Great Way Round was another. It served the whole of

228

the West Country and ran right through here until the whole kit and caboodle was nationalised by the socialists in 1948. Anyway, I know Max was interested, but I wasn't sure how far it had gone."

"And you weren't involved?"

"I'm more catholic in my interests. Don't confine myself to a single company. And I wasn't going in with that lot. But then I don't live in a grand house in Cavendish Crescent, or a villa in Henrietta Road, come to that."

"You think only rich men joined their club?"

"Like-minded is a better way of putting it. Definitely isn't open to all, like the BRS."

"BRS?"

"Bath Railway Society. Keep up, officer."

Diamond had got about as much as he was likely to get from Captain Jarrow. In railway parlance, he'd hit the buffers.

The physician who had signed Massimo Filiput's death certificate was still in practice in St. James's Square. She was a crucial witness who had to be visited in person.

Dr. Mukherjee, small in stature but substantial in personality, was in no way fazed by a senior policeman calling. "He died in his sleep," she told Diamond. "I was called in about eight-thirty in the morning by his cleaner —" she consulted her notes on the computer — "a Mrs. Stratford. And I confirmed that life was extinct."

"On the certificate you wrote cardiac failure and —" he stumbled over the words — "coronary atheroma."

"Narrowing of the arteries. His cholesterol level was being monitored. He'd been prescribed statins for some years."

"A routine death, then?"

"A not unusual death at that age."

"No postmortem?"

"There was no call for one. He died from natural causes. He was aware of his condition and so was I."

"The cleaner found him dead in bed?"

"That is correct. She has a key and let herself into the house. Normally he was downstairs when she arrived. On this occasion he was not and the house was silent, so she went upstairs to check. She called me at once." She put her head round the computer. "Why are you interested? Is there a problem over Mr. Filiput's death?"

"Not that I know of, doctor. I wanted to check the circumstances with you, that's all. How long had he been your patient?"

She consulted her screen again. "Since 2009, when I started the practice."

"You saw him on a regular basis?"

"I'm not one of a panel of doctors. Being in private practice, I can limit the number of patients I take on and I make sure I know them personally. I knew Mr. Filiput better than most. He insisted on telling me about his anxieties."

"And was he mentally sound?"

"His brain was working well for a man of his age, if that's what you mean. He suffered some depression after the death of his wife."

"I can sympathise. Did you discuss his worries with him?"

"I did."

"What did they amount to, if that's not breaking a confidence?"

"He felt he was losing his grip, he told me. There were valuable objects in the house and some of them seemed to have gone missing."

"Really?" Diamond sat forward. "Did he name anything?"

"This was the difficulty. There were numerous items belonging to his late wife, so many he felt he couldn't keep track of them all. She had a collection of valuable jewellery and antiques."

"Yet he knew certain things were gone?"

"He believed they were gone. It isn't quite

231

the same thing."

"You suspect otherwise?"

"People adjusting to some big event in their lives such as the loss of a spouse are liable to feel they can't cope. It's part of the process of bereavement."

"Did he suspect someone in particular of stealing them?"

"He didn't put it as strongly as that. Stealing was never mentioned. He spoke of the matter as if he'd put them somewhere and forgotten where."

"Yet you said his brain was sound. Was the short-term memory going?"

"Hardly at all. For a man of his age he was sharp enough. His concentration was the problem, I believe."

"Absent-minded?"

"I wouldn't put it like that. There were areas of his life that he put to the back of his mind. He believed his late wife's possessions were secure in the house, so he didn't pay much attention to them."

"Did it occur to you that they might really have gone missing?"

"Taken by some dishonest person? It crossed my mind, certainly."

"Did you discuss the possibility with him?"

She sighed. "It wasn't easy. I didn't want

to add to his anxieties. I suggested putting them into storage, but he said if he locked them away and never saw them again it would be like a betrayal of his wife."

"I can understand that," Diamond said. "My own wife died a few years ago and I've kept some of her things simply because I know how much she valued them. Forgive me for pressing you on this, but it could be significant. Had anything gone missing that he was able to describe?"

"No. On reflection I suspect the stealing was all in his imagination."

Big mistake, Diamond thought, but he didn't want to speak of what he'd found in Pellegrini's workshop. "Did he ever mention visitors?"

"He had a retired friend called Cyril who came to the house about once a week and played some board game with him. They used to work together at a college in Salisbury."

Cyril? This was new to Diamond. "Did he tell you Cyril's surname?"

"No. I only remember because Cyril is not a name I've come across."

"So they were both former teachers?"

"He preferred the term lecturer."

"What was Cyril's subject?"

"I couldn't tell you. I'm not even sure

what my own patient taught. They used the same staff room but they may have specialised in different things."

"This was a long-term friendship, was it? Did Cyril's visits continue after Mrs. Filiput died?"

"I'm sure they did. He looked forward to them."

"I expect they helped to ease the depression."

"Certainly they would have, if only briefly."

"And how about Mrs. Stratford, the cleaner?" Diamond said. "Obviously you met her on the day she found him dead. Did you know her already?"

"We'd met two or three times at the house. In case you're wondering about her honesty, I formed a good opinion of her. She was cheerful and a good worker. The house always looked immaculate. She sometimes went to the shops and collected prescriptions I gave him. I doubt very much whether she took advantage of him."

"I wonder if anyone else did. He was interested in railways."

"How does that come into it?"

"I'm thinking of visitors to the house, people who shared the interest."

Dr. Mukherjee nodded. "That's possible.

I did notice various pieces of railway equipment in one of the rooms downstairs, signals and station signs and so on. Surely those are the things any railway friends would have stolen if they were so inclined. I don't think he was worried about them disappearing."

"He would have known exactly what was taken," Diamond said.

"I'm sure you're right." She leaned back in her chair. "And now if we've covered everything, I do have patients to see."

He hadn't finished yet. "Were you also the doctor to Mrs. Filiput?"

She glanced down at her watch. "I was."

"She died in November, 2013, six months before his death?"

"Indeed."

"Of natural causes?"

"Not directly."

He waited, intrigued, for her to explain.

"She had a fall," Dr. Mukherjee said. "Balance becomes a problem as one gets older, so in a sense it was a natural cause, but a fall is a violent event, so I can't describe it as natural. She was frail and she was taken to hospital, and she died there the same day. In her case, I didn't sign the certificate."

"Who called the ambulance?"

"Mr. Filiput, I believe. I only heard what

235

had happened afterwards, so I'm not the best person to ask."

"When you say 'she had a fall,' was it at home?"

"I believe so. I was told she fell downstairs and sustained a fractured skull."

"How sad and what a shock for Mr. Filiput."

"Yes, he came to me for tranquillisers. For a man over ninety there was a lot to cope with."

"No family to help?"

"No children. And the old couple outlived any siblings they had. I believe after Mr. Filiput died his entire estate went to a railway museum."

"So I heard. Do you notify social services in a case like this?"

"He didn't want them. Most old people like to be as independent as they can. He had Mrs. Stratford to clean and do shopping and there were friends who kept an eye on him and brought in cooked meals."

"He had it sorted, by the sound of things. I'm obliged to you, doctor," he said, rising and preparing to leave.

"Incidentally . . ." Dr. Mukherjee said, and then paused as if she was having second thoughts.

"Yes?"

236

His hopes soared. He'd always envied the TV detective who got as far as the door on the point of leaving an interview and then thought of one more thing that brought the breakthrough revelation. In this case it wasn't the detective who had thought of one more thing.

Dr. Mukherjee said, "Have you had a blood-pressure check lately?"

"Why?"

"I don't wish to be personal but your skin colour isn't too healthy and you're carrying rather more weight than you should."

He thought of his chips and beer lunch. "You're perfectly right, doctor. I've been told before. Not enough rabbit food."

10

Massimo Filiput had died in his sleep, according to Dr. Mukherjee, and his wife had fallen downstairs and died. Not the story Diamond had expected to hear. He grappled with the new information while taking a brisk, healthy, cholesterol-reducing walk round Queen Square. Neither death had been suspicious in the doctor's eyes, but then the doctor wasn't a detective.

Could Ivor Pellegrini, having researched ingenious methods of murder, have found a way to kill them both? He'd have needed access to the house in Cavendish Crescent. As a friend and fellow railway enthusiast, it wasn't impossible that he was a regular visitor there. Pushing an old lady downstairs didn't seem all that clever, let alone perfect, but — if it was murder — it had worked. Olga Filiput's collection of jewellery and antiques, including the Fortuny gowns, had been inherited by her distracted husband, a soft touch who had stopped breathing six months later, and the gowns had ended up in Pellegrini's workshop.

Filiput's death in his sleep had been less dramatic than a fall, but if there *had* been any wrongdoing, this one might well be styled the perfect murder.

Or was it natural?

One killing? Two? Or no crime at all?

Murder only made sense if Pellegrini had a compelling motive. The most obvious was personal gain. He'd acquired the gowns and hidden them away. He may well have stacked away other valuable items that had once belonged to Olga Filiput. But did he need to steal? Was it worth the risk? Probably not. He appeared to be comfortably off, no doubt on a good pension.

Think of a better motive, Diamond told himself, already on the lookout for a place to sit. The brisk walk round the square hadn't been such a good idea. His calves were giving him hell. He found an empty bench near a group playing boules.

For some minutes he watched the players, evidently friends who did this regularly. Much noise and joking masked a strong competitive element. The dominant personalities were soon apparent: the deadly serious win-at-all-costs man with the tattoos and earrings, and the joker with the beanie hat who laughed off every throw but was secretly trying harder than anyone.

Could the killings — if killings they were — be down to a driven personality? Extraordinary things are done in the name of self-assertion. The dominant ego is capable of distorting and discarding personal feeling and basic human values. Pellegrini was a man in retirement who had spent his whole career solving problems and no doubt getting satisfaction and self-esteem from the achievement. Now cut off from all that, yet still capable, he needed a challenge. Then why not apply his skills and experience to devising a perfect theft, followed by a perfect murder?

Only in theory, of course.

Until an opportunity arrived to put theory to the test.

Once.

Or twice?

Or about five times?

Taken as problem-solving, plotting a murder could be treated like any other engineering project, constructing a turbine or a tunnel. He'd deal with it in the same detached way, assess the objective, do the research, devise a plan and derive personal satisfaction from pulling it off.

Not bad.

On a bookshelf at home Diamond had a small library of famous crimes and among them was the case of two young Americans from privileged backgrounds who in the 1920s murdered another youth for no more reason than self-aggrandisement. They made mistakes and were caught, but the idea of intelligent students killing just for kicks had shocked the nation. One had claimed they had done it just for the excitement of committing a perfect murder and getting away with it.

How many murders had been carried out by smarter operators who didn't get caught?

In the case of Ivor Pellegrini, killing as self-expression made more sense than killing for profit. He'd know what he was doing was morally wrong and dangerous, but the compelling assignment would transcend morality. He'd immerse himself in the challenge. It was about achievement and a job well done. Those cremation pots lined up like trophies fitted the scenario.

Diamond gave himself five minutes more and then strolled back to the car.

The first person he saw in the CID room was Keith Halliwell.

"I've been trawling the newspapers, guv,"

241

Keith told him. "Those three — the ones in the urns — all died within two years of each other."

"Yes, but what of?"

Halliwell didn't give an immediate answer and Diamond knew why. He wanted some credit for his research. "Two of them had short death notices in the *Chronicle* and the other, Jeremy Marshall-Tomkin, was given quite a write-up. He'd been a county councillor at one time and also played some rugby in his younger days. The interesting bit is that at one stage he edited the *Great Western Railway Journal.* It's a quarterly magazine — still selling seventy-odd years after the company closed."

"Who buys it then? They must have an elderly readership."

"It's nostalgia for the great days of steam."

"Right," he said, without really understanding the appeal.

"The point is that Marshall-Tomkin would definitely have been one of the GWR group," Halliwell said.

Diamond came up with the required compliment. "You've done a fine job here, Keith." And immediately added, "Can we get more on the other two?"

"I'm working on it."

"Doing what?"

"There's a website listing every issue of the magazine and all the articles and their authors."

"These two wrote for the magazine?"

"No. But there are letters in each issue. I'm hoping their names crop up there."

"Okay. And now will you answer my first question?"

"What was that?"

"What did they die of?"

"Can't tell you that, I'm afraid."

"What's stopping you?" Diamond's charitable phases never lasted long.

"There's a standard wording they use in the paper. He or she passed away peacefully."

"So what? It's a cliché."

"Or sadly or after a long illness or a short illness. That's all you're told in at least ninety percent of the notices. Marshall-Tomkin went peacefully, Edmund Seaton the same and Roger Carnforth after a short illness."

Diamond took a sharp, impatient breath. "No help at all."

Halliwell shrugged. "The newspaper isn't going to say they were murdered, even if they were."

It was a telling point. Diamond had to grin. "Is something wrong with us, looking for evil at every turn?"

"Somebody needs to, guv."

"Thanks for that. Massimo Filiput is said to have died in his sleep, which would be what . . . ?"

"Peaceful."

"Yes, peaceful. And we can't exclude murder. A peaceful death of an old man means there wouldn't be any call for an autopsy. If there was poison in his system it wouldn't be found. The doctor had no reason to be suspicious."

"Poison isn't used much these days."

"How do you know?"

"It's easy to detect, isn't it?" Halliwell said. "In the past, they used arsenic or cyanide or something similar and sometimes got away with it, but with all the science these days they wouldn't. And, anyway, the classic poisons aren't available any more as flypapers or what have you. You aren't even allowed to buy two packs of aspirin at one time."

"True, but there are drugs prescribed every day that could kill someone. The average house is stocked with pills and potions I'd think twice about taking, and that's not to mention rat bait and weedkiller in the garden shed. The stuff is still out there."

"But would it be a peaceful death?"

Diamond laughed. "Depends. Personally, I'd rather not swallow weedkiller, but some of the other things might do the job painlessly."

Halliwell still looked unconvinced. "Do you mind if I ask something?"

"Go ahead. It's your job."

"You fought hard to save Pellegrini's life. How will you feel if he turns out to have been a serial killer?"

Deep breath. No one was better than Halliwell at putting the boss on the spot.

"Not great." He took a moment to frame a better answer. "Look at it this way, Keith. I found him and did what anyone would. No choice." He shook his head. "It's pulling me apart. My job as the senior detective is to step back from the detail and take a broad view. I want him to be blameless, but each day that passes brings more evidence. He may have carried out one murder or several or none at all. I can't rule out anything. To ignore our suspicions would be dangerous, sloppy and wrong."

"That's tough."

"I'd rather not say any more."

"So what's the strategy?"

"Same as always. Gather the evidence. Follow up every lead. Miss nothing."

"Still off the record?"

"Has to be. We don't have enough to trigger a full-scale enquiry. Georgina would do her nut if she knew I was taking so much of your time and Ingeborg's. But she did tell me to stay in touch with the fallout of the crash."

"She's worried about the IPCC investigation."

"You bet she is."

"Are they setting one up?"

"It's mandatory. This is classed as a death or serious-injury matter."

"Has someone complained?"

"Not that I'm aware of. Georgina is bricking it that they'll discover our guys were at fault."

Mrs. Stratford, the cleaner to the Filiputs, was easy to trace through the electoral register, but difficult to pin down. Her neighbour in the terrace where she lived in Oldfield Park said she was out all day and often didn't get home until after ten. It sounded as if she was a workaholic.

Diamond needed an insider's account of the Filiput household. He couldn't rely only on Dr. Mukherjee. Normally he would have sent one of his DCs to catch up with the cleaner, but this wasn't a normal enquiry. Truth to tell, he was finding an escape from his personal conflict by taking on the dogs-body jobs of the sort he'd done long ago as a probationer in the Met.

Late in the afternoon he cornered Mrs. Stratford in a printworks in Beacon Hill, off Lansdown Road. She was bending over a bin-bag, filling it with the screwed-up waste paper that littered the floor, and she was a surprise, not much over twenty, with the figure of a gymnast and thick copper-coloured hair tied back with a scarf. And she was speaking to herself, which wasn't a good sign. Speaking, not singing. No head-set. He couldn't make out the words except that there seemed to be strong emotion in them, her shoulders flexing with the stress of whatever she was dealing with.

He made a noise deep in his throat and she straightened up and did an about turn as sharply as a sentry.

"Don't you dare come any closer."

"Sorry to startle you," he said.

"I ought to kick you where it hurts most, creeping up on me like that." They were angry, shaming eyes.

"I'd rather you didn't," he said.

"You shouldn't be here. This is closed for business now."

He introduced himself and without giving much away about his real suspicions let her

247

know he was interested in the Filiputs.

She didn't react the way most people do when a police officer speaks to them.

"You can take a running jump."

He ignored this. "I was told you worked for them."

"They're entitled to their privacy."

"They're dead," he said. He was about to add, "They don't care any more," but he stopped himself. This young woman had known the old couple and it seemed she still felt defensive towards them. To him they were only names. "Look, whatever you tell me stays private. I'm police, not press. I need information about their daily routine and I believe you know more than anyone else."

"So?"

Still defiant. He had to reveal more.

"It's possible someone was stealing from them — or at least from Mr. Filiput in the last months of his life."

"And you think I —" She took a threatening step towards him.

"God, no. That isn't what I'm saying."

"I'm not a thief."

"It never crossed my mind."

"What was taken?" she asked — the first sign of interest and maybe the first crack in the stone wall.

"Certain items of his wife's, in particular three valuable gowns."

"She had some nice things."

He sensed she might be ready to open up. "Do you recall Mr. Filiput saying anything of his wife's had gone missing?"

"To me, his cleaner? He had better manners than that."

This was verbal karate, and Diamond wasn't winning. "I was told he couldn't keep track of things and felt inadequate."

"You were told? You already talked to someone else?"

"His doctor."

"She knows more than I do, then."

"I got the impression from her that you were more than just the cleaner."

Her eyes blazed like chip pans. "You bastard. He was old enough to be my grandfather."

The best he could think of to calm her down was, "Hold on, you're not reading me right. All I'm suggesting is you went to some trouble to look after the old couple, shopping for them, and so on."

"Piss off, will you?" she said, giving the sack a shake and moving on. "I'm doing a job here."

"So am I. I thought just now you were willing to help."

"Help with what? Their stolen goods? It's a bit bloody late, isn't it?"

"You might know if anything else was taken."

"You lot are more concerned with property than people."

He let a few seconds pass. "Can we try again, Mrs. Stratford? It's obvious I caught you at a bad time."

"What the hell do you mean by that?"

"You thought you were alone here."

"Talking to myself when you came in?" she said.

"Well . . ."

"I was speaking lines, if you want to know."

"You're an actress?" Something he could work with.

"Actor — or trying to be. Understudying Maggie in *Cat on a Hot Tin Roof.*"

"Maggie who?"

She gave a sharp, angry sigh. "It's the part I play. I was running through a scene with Big Daddy when you interrupted."

"I could see it was strong stuff. Is Maggie the Liz Taylor part?"

Her glare almost pinned him to the wall.

He'd said the wrong thing again.

"The role doesn't belong to her or any other actor. I work from the script and do it

250

my own way."

"And you were well into it when I interrupted."

"That's why you got a mouthful. I can't simply switch off."

"Understood." He'd humoured her enough about the acting. Much more and she'd be asking him to speak the Big Daddy bits. "So you double up your theatre work with some cleaning?"

"If you really want to know, the cleaning is my mainstay. I'd be a fool to pack it in." She was starting to speak in a more measured way now.

"Were you in a production while you worked for the Filiputs?"

"The occasional walk-on at the Theatre Royal. Not much learning of lines."

"That's why you could be generous with your time, I expect."

She nodded. "They were sweet, both of them. They let me fit my cleaning around all the read-throughs and rehearsals."

He wanted to talk about Massimo Filiput. "He was rather lost after she died, I believe."

"Well, it was so sudden, an accident. She fell downstairs, as you probably know."

"Were you there at the time?"

"No, but I saw him next day. The shock was all too clear. He was crying, on and off.

251

I did what I could to help out, took him to see the funeral director and the register office, stuff like that."

"He had friends, didn't he?"

"His railway buddies, you mean?" She rolled her eyes. "I called them his choo-choo chums. They were at the house the afternoon of the accident, a bunch of goofy old men who used to meet in each other's houses and talk about trains."

"When you say a bunch . . . ?"

"Never more than four or five. Personally I can't think of anything more boring than old trains, but Max enjoyed it and after Olga died the meetings kept him going, really."

"Do you remember their names?"

She shook her head. "There was a gay couple. At least, I thought they must be gay because they arrived together and had a rapport that was fairly obvious. Max probably told me their names, but I had no reason to memorise them. I have enough of a job learning lines."

"Gay men, you mean?"

"Women are daft about a lot of things, but they aren't daft about trains."

"Another of the railway people would have been Ivor Pellegrini," he tried prompting her. "Grey-haired, clean-shaven, average height and build."

"They all looked like that to me." Which closed that avenue.

"Did he have any other regular visitors after his wife died?"

"There was Cyril who played Scrabble with him and Cyril's housekeeper, Jessie, who did the driving as well as a bit of cooking for them while she was there."

This was helpful, chiming in with earlier information. "The doctor mentioned Cyril, said he was a teaching colleague, retired."

"Yes, he definitely wasn't one of the railway lot. Nice old boy. We often had a joke. He liked teasing me about all the leading men I was supposed to have been with: 'Didn't I spot you last night in that commercial with George Clooney?' sort of thing."

"And Jessie was Cyril's housekeeper? That's an old-fashioned term."

"His word for it. I was meant to get the message they lived together but didn't share a room. I didn't want to know about his living arrangements, thanks very much. What old men get up to in private is their business."

"Was Jessie his age?"

"Quite a bit younger. Forties, maybe. I guess he employed her to take care of him. That's the deal with a housekeeper, isn't it?

253

And of course she acted as chauffeur as well on the days they visited. He'd given up driving. She was always nicely dressed, short brown hair with blonde highlights, and fun to be with."

"Are they still about?"

"I haven't seen them since Max's funeral. They aren't from Bath."

"So you got to his funeral? That was nice. Who else was there?"

"Very few apart from the ones I just mentioned. It was a low-key event, quite short, at Haycombe cremmy. Nonreligious. No hymns or prayers. Cyril got up and said some nice, witty things, but respectful. The main bit I remember was while the curtains were closing they played a number by The Kinks called 'Last of the Steam-Powered Trains.' There wasn't a dry eye in the house. Oh, and there was a wreath in the shape of a train."

"From his railway friends? They were there?"

"To a man. And we all went back to Cavendish Crescent and shared some bottles of prosecco. They didn't last long."

"Going back a bit, you said you weren't at the house on the day of Olga's accident."

Suddenly she was back in her Tennessee Williams role. "Don't you believe me? What are you hinting at, Mr. Policeman? Do I have to scream to make myself understood? I wasn't there when the old lady died. End of."

"But the railway club were. What about Cyril and Jessie?"

"No. They came on different days. Max used to say steam and Scrabble don't mix."

"Where do they live?"

"Cyril and Jessie? Somewhere this side of Salisbury in the Wylye valley. They're decent people. You can cross them off your list. I'm less confident about the choo-choo lot. After Max's funeral they were like vultures sorting through his photo collection and the old posters."

"Didn't anybody try and stop them?"

"Far from it. There was a po-faced woman there from the solicitors who arranged the funeral and she told everyone the bigger, more collectable items would go into a sale, but Max had said in his will that things like posters and timetables and old photos should be distributed among his railway cronies. She didn't know their worth and wasn't able to share them out so she suggested they helped themselves. It was mayhem after that, really distasteful."

"Collectors aren't going to miss an opportunity like that."

"It was insane. Jessie had a mug of coffee knocked out of her hand. She should have put in a claim for a new skirt, in my opinion."

"Was she wearing black?"

"Purple wool, and it showed. I made sure she sponged it with white vinegar in the kitchen, which is what you do, but there was still a mark."

"I hope he offered to pay."

"He did apologise at the time. She didn't want to make an issue of it. She had to put on one of the overalls I used for work and she was too self-conscious to show herself again. I had to go back to the room where it happened and collect her handbag. She and Cyril left not long after."

"I've got ahead of myself, asking about the funeral," he said. "Would you mind telling me about the morning you found him dead?"

"Why?"

Not easy to answer without giving more away than he planned to tell her.

"I'm piecing together the last months of his life."

His answer seemed to satisfy her. "It came as a shock, but you can't prepare for anything like that." She shook her head, remembering. "I turned up at the house as usual and rang. Sometimes he wasn't up in the mornings, but there was a key I knew about so I let myself in. He wasn't downstairs, so I made a start on clearing up the kitchen. I say that, but it wasn't a mess. He generally left it tidy before going to bed. After twenty minutes or so, he still hadn't appeared, so I made him a coffee and took it up to the bedroom. The door was closed. I knocked, spoke his name, got no response, opened the door a little and saw there was no movement from the bed. He was face up, eyes closed, mouth gaping and it was obvious he wasn't breathing. I called Dr. Mukherjee and she was there inside ten minutes. She was very good, understood I was shaken and sent me to make a fresh cup of tea." She paused and her eyes were moist with the memory — or good acting. "We agreed he'd found the best way to go, at home, in his own bed."

"You said there was a key you knew about. What did you mean by that?"

"His back-up key. He used to worry about locking himself out, so he kept a spare near the front door behind a drainpipe."

"Not the best security."

"You can't tell ninety-year-olds how to run their lives. You can try, but they won't listen. Everything in that house was done as it had been all his life, right down to the loose tea that was the bane of my life. He had something against teabags. He collected all his tea leaves and dried them off and I was supposed to crush them to powder and sprinkle them over the carpets and wait ten minutes before I did the vacuuming. Have you ever heard of that?"

Diamond shook his head. "It must be a generational thing. I may look old to you, but I'm not ninety. What was the point?"

"He reckoned they absorb odours, so they freshen the carpets in some way. Grass works just as well, he said."

"Do you mean grass as in lawns, or cannabis?"

She rolled her eyes in scorn. "Grass clippings from a mower. He was spaced out enough, without smoking pot."

"It might work."

"But we always had plenty of tea leaves, so we never tried grass. Have we finished? I've got loads to do here and I want to get home some time."

I see in the paper that some committee or other has been looking into the problems of old men living alone. They're giving cause for concern. In the next fifteen years the numbers are due to rise by 65 percent. They're not as good as women at managing. When an old man is widowed, he can't adapt. His social life shrinks and he deteriorates mentally and physically and he's unlikely to seek help, poor old soul. The way I see it, I'm performing a service, saving them from misery and the state from a lot of extra expense. Do enough, and I might even make the honours list.

11

"If I wanted to copy the entire contents of someone's computer, is there a simple way to do it?" Diamond asked Ingeborg.

"Hacking, you mean?"

"Not really. That sounds tricky. I said a simple way. They make it look easy in spy films."

"That's different. They're after one file usually, or one document. They go to the actual computer and use some kind of USB device."

"A memory stick?"

"Exactly, but if you wanted to copy everything you'd need more capacity, an external hard drive."

"Is that huge?"

She shook her head. "About the size of my iPhone. It comes with a USB cable. You slot that into the port and you're in business."

"That's what I'm interested in doing."

"I can show you if you like," she said. "It won't take long." They were in his office with his computer between them on the desk. He'd returned there after his encounter with Mrs. Stratford, the cleaner. It was already after six.

"I doubt if showing it to me will make much difference."

"But it's a breeze." She didn't add, "Even you could do it," but she didn't need to. His problems with technology were legendary.

"What I'd really like is for you to come with me and make sure it's done the right way."

"Come where, guv?"

"Henrietta Road."

"Pellegrini's place?" Her eyebrows took flight like game birds. "Wow. You really are into spying."

"I should have thought of it when I was there before. Those printed pages about murder must have come from his computer. I want to check."

"A spot of breaking and entering?"

"It won't be a break-in. I can let us in."

"By going back to that sister at the hospital and asking to borrow Pellegrini's keys again? Will she play ball?"

"No need." He dipped into his pocket and

held up a shiny new key. "I thought I might need to go back, so I did the old trick of making a wax impression, except I used BluTack."

Ingeborg laughed. "James Bond has nothing on you."

They went in his car, stopping off at Weston Lock industrial estate to buy an external hard drive. He saw that Ingeborg had not exaggerated when she said it was no larger than an iPhone.

"You'll be seeing the workshop for yourself," he said to her as they headed over Pulteney Bridge and turned left at the Laura Place fountain. "It says a lot about the man."

"Let's hope nobody sees *us*. You said it's in front of the house?"

"Coming up shortly. Relax, Inge. We're on the side of law and order. We can do stuff like this."

She didn't answer, but the set of her mouth showed she wasn't persuaded.

"In pursuit of the truth," he added.

"Oh yeah?"

Diamond gave up trying. Ingeborg was right, of course. At best this was an unsanctioned undercover operation and at worst a shameful invasion of someone else's home.

They parked on the drive of Pellegrini's

large villa-style house, in a position sheltered from the busy road. Before getting out, he told Ingeborg, "For the record, you were never here. If anyone discovers my part in this, I did it alone."

"Copied the hard drive?"

"All my own work. Nobody thinks I'm *that* clueless . . . do they?"

She didn't comment.

He opened the boot of his car and took out the skein of cream-coloured silk that was the coiled Fortuny dress. After Paloma had unwound it and gone into ecstasies she had reluctantly twisted it back into its compact shape for him and he'd been driving about with it since.

At the workshop door, they hesitated when Ingeborg pointed to the notice about the response alarm. Diamond showed her where the bell was, above their heads. It hadn't been tripped the first time he'd let himself in, so he had to assume they'd be all right with a key that fitted. He took a deep breath, inserted and turned it.

The door opened and no bells went off.

Inside, he took a torch from his pocket and showed her the locomotive name-plate above the door.

The model railway track.

And the three cremation urns.

He stood on a chair and returned the coiled gown to the urn it had come from.

"I'd better start work," Ingeborg said and sat at the computer. "You want everything that's on here?"

"Please." He shone the torch beam at the keyboard.

She brought up a page that meant nothing to Diamond. "It has a hundred gigabytes of memory, of which only a small percentage has been used."

"Do we need to know that?"

"It tells us what we're dealing with."

"Plug in the thing, Inge, and let's get started."

He tried to interest himself in what she was doing, but it was all a mystery to him. He just wanted the job done and to be out of there.

Clumsy as usual, he rested his arm on the stack of magazines and sent half of them skittering across the floor.

"Bugger."

"Careful how you put them back," Ingeborg said. "They were all squared up."

"Can you manage without the torch?"

She was working with the lighted screen. "I can now."

He started collecting the magazines. They'd been in date order. Pellegrini was a stickler for tidiness.

"If anyone checks these for prints, mine are going to be all over them."

"Mine will be all over the keys. It shouldn't happen . . . should it?"

She was efficient and quicker than he could have hoped. He'd barely finished replacing the magazines in date order when she said, "Done."

"Mission accomplished?"

She unplugged the cable. "Let's get out before we celebrate. This is the point in the movie when the baddies arrive."

"Our baddy is still on life support."

"Don't count on it."

They locked up and were shortly on the road again.

"What's next?" Ingeborg asked when they were clear of Henrietta Road and into Argyle Street. "Checking all this creepy material, I suppose?"

"Please."

"It won't prove he's a killer, will it?"

"It will be strong corroborative evidence."

"Evidence that he was interested in murder methods, but not that he put any of them into practice."

"Fair point," he said.

"He could be a fantasist."

"There's more to it than that, Inge. A

significant number of people in his circle have died in the last two years."

"Old people," she said.

"Which makes it easier for a murderer to get away with it."

"Why would he do it? There's nothing to suggest he's deranged."

"I'm hoping the computer will give us a lead on that."

She offered to take the hard drive home that evening and make a start. The least he could do after that was drop her off at her flat. Clearly she was sceptical that Pellegrini was a killer, but she'd miss nothing.

He had one more visit to make before getting home. Fortunately the Royal United Hospital was at Combe Park, close to where he lived in Weston. That remark of Ingeborg's — "Don't count on it" — when he'd mentioned Pellegrini was still on life support had made him uneasy. It wasn't that he expected the man to walk in suddenly, but the reverse. He might already be dead.

"You can't stay away, can you?" the caustic sister in charge said when he looked through the open door of her office. He guarded his tongue. He didn't want another verbal punch-up.

"How is he?"

"No change," she said, and then her face softened. "What's the news of Hornby?"

Thank God for Hornby. The virtual cat was the sure way to open a civilised conversation here. "Settling in well, I believe."

"He's not with you, then?"

"People I know and can trust. I'm not at home much. It wouldn't be kind."

"His new owners should keep him indoors for a few days, so that he gets to know who feeds him."

"I expect they've thought of that, but I can pass it on. May I go in?"

"You won't learn anything new." She handed him the pack of sterile protective wear.

"Is it any use talking to him?" he said as he slipped the disposable plastic apron over his head.

"Of course. He'd appreciate that," she said.

"Really? Do you mean that?"

"Absolutely."

"It's a one-way conversation, obviously."

"Not at all. They rub against your legs and purr. That's their way of answering back."

"Actually I meant your patient, not the cat."

"Him?" She raised a smile. "You're welcome to give it a go. We do, quite often.

267

There's a certain amount of evidence from people who emerged from vegetative states that they heard what was being said, even though they couldn't respond in any way. It can't do any harm, as long as you don't say anything upsetting."

"Trust me," he said.

"I don't know if I can. Don't tell him you're from the police. That would upset anyone."

"I won't."

"Keep it friendly."

"I will. I want to see him recover."

Kitted in the mask, hood and apron that he was starting to wear like a seasoned medic, he went in. At least they hadn't switched off the machinery. Technically there was a chance they'd save the patient. Pellegrini's eyes were closed but his chest was moving perceptibly with the action of the ventilator.

Instead of a mask he now had a tube inserted into his nostril and clipped in place, so more of his face was visible.

The face of a killer?

Gaunt, pale, slack-muscled, with a silver beard starting to sprout, a reminder that not everything here was artificially induced.

Diamond stood watching, reflecting on the irony of all the equipment surrounding the bed, the various monitoring devices, the screens, drips, lines and pumps, the catheter, the feeding tube, sustaining life in an individual who may well have systematically deprived others of their existence.

In a long career, the much-tested Peter Diamond had never faced a situation like this where the main suspect was in custody, so to speak, yet couldn't be interviewed. Even the "no comment" every petty crook learned from crime dramas would be better than silence. You found ways of getting past that. Here there was no serious prospect of communication.

No one could know for sure whether a brain was dormant or active.

Better give it a try.

Self-consciously, he took a step closer. His voice was muffled by the mask. "Can you hear me, Ivor? I'm Peter Diamond, the guy who found you after the accident. There's a lot I'd like to ask you about what happened that night."

And other things, too, he might have added.

Not a flicker of comprehension. Even the screens didn't register anything different.

"I live in Weston, not far from here. You'll know it because of Horstman's at Newbridge, where you worked as an engineer."

Horstman's should have been a strong memory but it didn't seem so.

"Everyone is hoping you'll snap out of this, Ivor. Your railway friends in particular. Great Western Railway — does that ring any bells?"

Plainly it didn't.

"*County of Somerset* was your GWR identity, wasn't it? The name-plate over the door of your workshop. I was there this week. Met your cleaner, Mrs. Halliday. And a lady from the church called Elspeth Blake, who turned up with a nice quiche for you. Your domestic life is better sorted than mine. I wouldn't mind a home care package in the shape of Elspeth Blake. But I was asking about your GWR contacts. I spoke to a Captain Jarrow today and he was telling me how a bunch of you broke away from the Bath Railway Society to form your own special interest group. Do you remember Captain Jarrow?"

If he did, he wasn't going to show it.

"Not all your old chums know you're here. We're working on it, all your contacts."

He waited a minute or so in case anything had penetrated the brain.

"If you don't remember people, let's talk about some things you got up to. The night jaunts on your tricycle. That disused sta-

270

tion. What was it called? Now I'm in need of some prompting myself. Got it: Hampton Row Halt. The only reason I'm banging on about all this is to try and trigger a memory."

He was scraping the barrel of his own memories now. What else could he mention that wouldn't bring on a cardiac arrest?

"There are the rabbits digging their holes and covering big distances. We're still a bit mystified about the rabbits. Some sort of joke, were they?"

None of this seemed to have registered. It was difficult avoiding the conclusion that Ivor Pellegrini was brain dead.

Diamond turned his head, just to be certain the sister wasn't behind him. Out of devilment he said in a low voice, "And three gowns in your workshop, made by Fortuny."

Was it wishful thinking, or did one of the delta waves on the nearest screen give the tiniest twitch?

"The Fortuny gowns belonging to Olga Filiput."

This time there was nothing.

As soon as he got home, he called Ingeborg.

"Have you started?"

"Barely," she said. "It's not a quick job, guv."

"Nothing to report, then? I thought you said his computer had loads of memory that hasn't been used."

"I did. He's used about seven gigabytes out of a hundred."

"Is that all?"

"Do you have any idea how many pages of text that represents? Around six million. So don't call me, I'll call you."

12

On arrival at Keynsham next morning, Diamond was asked by the desk sergeant to report to the assistant chief constable as a matter of urgency. He sighed and walked across to the coffee machine. He wasn't going to miss his first caffeine boost of the day.

In the CID room, one of the civilian staff looked up and said, as if she was doing him a favour, "Message for you, Mr. Diamond. The ACC wants to see you as soon as you arrive."

How he yearned for the solid, concealing walls of Manvers Street nick instead of this open-plan layout. He nodded and carried his coffee into the room he called his goldfish bowl. Everyone could watch him through the glass.

Ten minutes later, revived and ready to go, he emerged and was told by Keith Halliwell, "Message from Georgina, guv."

"I got it," he said.

On the stairs, he passed John Wigfull, the PR man who raised a hand. "Thanks," he said before a word was spoken. "I'm on my way."

Georgina had two people in black suits with her — a man and a woman. They didn't get up from their chairs, a sure sign that they outranked him.

"This is Detective Superintendent Diamond, who has been handling the Professional Standards aspect," Georgina said to the suits. And to Diamond she said in a voice almost choking with awe, "Mr. Dragham and Miss Stretch are from the Independent Police Complaints Commission."

Dragham and Stretch. Like a medieval torture.

Georgina had been dreading this for days.

"We were sent a copy of your report," Dragham said. "Nice diagrams but not a lot of beef in the findings."

The diagrams had been Dessie's, the findings Diamond's. He felt an instant antipathy to these people. This wasn't likely to go well.

"I'm a police officer, not a butcher."

Georgina swayed as if avoiding a punch.

" 'Beef' is a term we use," Miss Stretch said. "We need more substance to justify the conclusion you reached."

"Hard to come by when the driver is dead and the accident victim in a coma," Diamond said. "The sergeant in the passenger seat was the only material witness and his statement is there verbatim."

"I saw that, including the ripe language."

"It's what you get from a man in pain."

"We're going to visit him and get a fresh statement ourselves."

"I hope it's more fragrant."

"What do you mean by that?"

"The language. He's improving every day."

Dragham took over from his colleague. "But are there any signs of improvement in the victim?"

"They're all victims," Diamond said, in a stroppy mode he couldn't stop. "If you mean the tricyclist, Mr. Pellegrini, he's still on life support."

"Have you spoken to the hospital staff?"

"Several times. I was there last night. There's been no change since he was brought in."

"We understand he has no family."

"That's my understanding, too. His wife died six months ago."

"So we're not acting on a complaint as such," Dragham said. "A case of a police car injuring or killing a member of the public is referred to us as a matter of course and we decide whether it's appropriate for the local police to conduct their own investigation. If so, it will need to be more thoroughgoing than the one you submitted."

"I was asked to report on professional standards," Diamond said. "There's only so much you can say."

"The way the officers behaved is just one part of our remit," Miss Stretch said.

"So I've saved you some time. Is there anything else you need from me?"

"A little less abrasiveness would be all to the good," Dragham said. "We're not trying to catch you out, Mr. Diamond. We're independent of the police. Do you have a problem with authority?"

Georgina stepped in fast and avoided an eruption. "I can answer that. Superintendent Diamond speaks his mind but he makes a huge contribution to the work of CID and I, for one, wouldn't wish to cramp his style."

Diamond thought he wouldn't mind having that in writing.

Dragham turned to him and made a feeble attempt at humour. "After that glowing endorsement perhaps we should recruit you."

276

"No thanks."

"Getting back to the fatal incident, when were you first aware of it?"

"Soon as I got into work. People were talking about a patrol car crashing and one of our guys being killed."

"What time was this?"

"Nine, or soon after."

"The collision was at six thirty-one," Dragham said. "When did you get there?"

"Nine-forty, give or take."

"More than three hours later."

"I went when I was asked."

"My instruction," Georgina said. "The first response was from uniform, as you would expect. I decided we would need a senior officer to report on the professional standards aspect."

"A lot must have happened already."

"Yes," Diamond said. "They were clearing up when we got there. The police officers had been removed from the wreck and taken to hospital."

"Which is why your report contains no record of what was said by Sergeant Morgan to the paramedics who attended?"

"Makes sense, doesn't it?"

"But you haven't followed up."

"I went to see Lew Morgan myself and got his version of events."

"The next day, when he'd had time to reflect on how much he would tell you."

"It was the first opportunity."

"No, Mr. Diamond," Dragham said, "the first opportunity fell to the paramedics and fire officers who were at the scene shortly after the crash and you haven't taken a statement from them. Crucial things may have been said."

He didn't comment. It was fair criticism. He'd been caught out.

"Which is why a more searching investigation may be necessary."

"To be fair to Superintendent Diamond," Georgina said, "the injured civilian wouldn't have been found were it not for the extra search he made."

"He would have been found at some stage," Diamond said.

"Almost certainly dead," Georgina added.

"We haven't yet visited the scene," Miss Stretch said. "From the report I gather he was out of sight at the top of an embankment."

"With the remains of his tricycle," Diamond said. "No one suspected anyone else was involved."

"What was he doing there?" Miss Stretch asked. "You don't say in the report."

Tricky. He wasn't ready to reveal any of

the information he'd got from inside the workshop, so he gave an obtuse answer. "The force of the impact must have thrown him into the air."

"That isn't what I'm asking. Why was he out on the roads at that hour?"

"Only he can answer that."

"You must have wondered, surely?"

"My job, ma'am, was to check why the police were there, not Mr. Pellegrini."

"They were responding to a call about a naked man. Was it a hoax?"

"No. It was daft but genuine. I found the waste of space who made it. He was the one who witnessed Pellegrini wandering off course as if he wasn't used to riding the tricycle."

"Can he be believed?"

"In my opinion, yes. He's a pain in the bum, but a good observer. In fact, observing things is his main interest in life."

"We'll need to see him."

"He'll be only too pleased to talk. His name is Bellerby and it's the bungalow called Bellerby Lodge with the Union flag in the front garden."

They were sharp, these two, but with any luck Bellerby would keep them busy for the rest of the day.

He left them to it.

■ ■ ■

Ingeborg was in the CID room when he returned there. He noticed she already had the hard disk plugged into the computer on her desk.

"Tell me the story so far."

"You don't want to know, guv," she told him. "It's all about trains — toy trains, real trains, old trains and when it isn't trains, it's tracks. There's masses of stuff here."

"Emails? I couldn't find any when I first tried."

"There aren't any. He must have another computer for them. He uses this one for the Internet and storing documents he downloads or creates himself. It's nicely organised, which I'd expect from an engineer, but I've found zilch of interest to us."

"The discussion about murder methods?"

"Not here."

He almost groaned in frustration. "It *must* be on his computer. He printed it out."

"Direct from the website. He didn't need to keep it on file."

A painful silence followed while he plumbed the shallow depths of his computer know-how.

"Have you been through everything?"

"I've got the overview. I haven't opened every file yet, if that's what you're asking, but I've seen plenty."

"Is there a quick way you can make a search looking for key words?"

"Within a document, I can, and I've tried just in case he's hidden stuff in a long piece about some class of locomotives. I put in Fortuny, for example."

"And . . . ?"

"No joy. I tried other words like the names of his friends. Up to now, it's been a waste of time. I really had hopes that we'd nail him this way."

"Me, too."

"I'll keep going unless you have other plans."

He nodded, trying not to load his disappointment on to Ingeborg. "This one was never going to be simple." He hesitated again before confiding a personal experience. "I was at the hospital yesterday. He's lying there with eyes closed and no movement except what the ventilator is doing, but I got a kind of message — call it telepathy if you like — that he knows who I am and what I'm about and he's well satisfied because he's way ahead of me. Is that possible or is it my insecurity?"

"Funny you should say that," she said. "I

get something like that from working with the computer data. You can't avoid thinking about the brain that set up the system. This is one very smart guy."

"We need to raise our game, Inge."

"But how?"

"We can find out more about how the Filiputs died. There's the friend called Cyril who spoke at the funeral. He ought to be able to give us the inside story."

"Do we know his surname?"

"Neither Dr. Mukherjee nor Mrs. Stratford could tell me, but he used to lecture at the same college in Salisbury that Filiput did. That's how they knew each other. Someone there must remember him. Cyril — it's unusual, isn't it, a bit old-fashioned?"

She smiled. "You could be right. None of my friends are called Cyril."

"You'd remember if you met one?"

"For sure."

First he needed to find the college. He went off to make a search on his own computer. The first to arrive on his screen was Salisbury College of Funeral Sciences. He grinned and scrolled down the choices.

Up came Wiltshire College. Now that he saw the name he remembered passing it often on his way through the city to the A36, a massive white block several stories high with rows and rows of windows.

He found a phone number to call. Eventually he was put through to someone in the science department who had been on the staff long enough to remember. There was only one Cyril he could recall and he'd retired more than twenty years ago. Cyril Hardstaff. He'd lived in a cottage in Little Langford.

This had to be the man. Diamond remembered a signpost to the Langfords not far out of Salisbury on the A36.

He told Ingeborg.

"Are you going there yourself?" she asked with a glance at the car key already in his hand.

"It's not far." In this unsanctioned investigation he couldn't ask Wiltshire police to check the address for him. Besides, he had a gut feeling it would go wrong if he didn't make the trip himself. The gods had not been charitable lately.

"Do you want company?" she asked.

"You're better employed on the computer."

She rolled her eyes upwards. "Thanks."

"We went to a lot of trouble to copy the disk. I'm not giving up."

"*You're* not giving up?"

He got out fast.

283

Driving away from Keynsham, he felt some sympathy for Ingeborg, but this, surely, was the best use of his small team. At some point he expected to elevate the enquiry into a full-scale murder investigation with the whole of CID actively involved, but until strong suspicion turned to certainty, it wasn't on. Convincing Georgina and Headquarters was a challenge yet to be faced.

There was still a chance, wasn't there, that Pellegrini was innocent?

The day was clear, the road not too cluttered with commercial traffic and the vast open spaces of the Wiltshire countryside were a joy to drive through. He passed Warminster inside fifty minutes and started looking for the Langfords. Great and Little, Upper and Lower, they liked subdividing villages in this county. It turned out, when he came to the sign he remembered and took the right turn, that there was a Steeple Langford leading to a junction that offered Hanging Langford and Little Langford. Good to avoid Hanging Langford, he told himself. The lane became more narrow and the signs of habitation fewer as he entered Cyril Hardstaff's home territory. Little Langford was a place of scattered buildings, including a church of its own.

He reached a farmyard and stopped to ask for directions. The young lad he met listened carefully but said nothing. He simply pointed up the lane.

"Is it far?" Diamond asked, hoping for at least a word or two.

The boy shook his head and walked off.

About two hundred yards further on was a slate roof. Trees and bushes obscured the view. As he got closer he saw this stone cottage in a neglected, overgrown garden. A white van was outside and someone's legs were visible below the open rear doors.

Diamond stopped and got out.

"Morning."

A woman in her sixties stepped back and looked him up and down. Men in suits are not often seen in villages. She was wearing a tank-top and jeans. Her tanned arms were well muscled.

"I'm looking for a gentleman called Cyril Hardstaff, a retired lecturer. I was told he has a cottage here."

She nodded as if to confirm it. "What's it about?"

Nosy, he thought. Village life was like that. "I'm saving my news for him. Can you tell me where he lives?"

"I'm his niece Hilary," she said.

"Well, that's a bit of luck." But he still didn't plan to share anything with Hilary about Cyril's links to a murder plot.

She seemed to be reading his thoughts. "Anything you want to know, you'll have to ask me. I'm clearing out the place by stages. This old heap was where my uncle used to live."

"Used to live?"

"He died six weeks ago."

He played the words over, mentally reeling.

"I had no idea." All the optimism built on the journey had just vanished like hot breath on a mirror. "You have my sympathy."

She shrugged as if to show she was past needing sympathy. "He had a long life. He was over ninety."

Diamond couldn't be so philosophical. Another death. Another old person. It was too mind-blowing to take in properly.

"What did he die of?"

"Old age. He went peacefully."

That word again.

"Here? At home?"

"In his sleep, the doctor said. Heart. He'd treated him for years."

"Six weeks ago was February."

"February seventeenth. I had to register the death."

"Who was it who found him, then?"

"The housekeeper, Jessie."

"Is she about?"

A shake of the head. "She packed her things and left the same day. She had no reason to stay. She'd lost her job, hadn't she? I'm his closest relative, so it fell to me to make the arrangements. It's been non-stop."

"Did he own the cottage?"

"He left it to me. He left everything and it's more trouble than it's worth. No use to me, most of it. Goods and chattels, the lawyers call it. I spend more in petrol carting goods and chattels to the council tip every day than I'll ever inherit."

"I'm shocked. He spoke at a funeral less than a year ago. He seemed to be in fine form then, made a witty speech, I was told."

"That's Uncle Cyril for you," she said. "He was a charming man as any round here will testify and there was nothing wrong with his brain. His passing was very sudden. There didn't seem to be anything amiss. His body gave up, I reckon. Bound to, if you live long enough, isn't that the truth of it?"

The logic was inescapable. "I'd like to speak to the housekeeper. Where is she now?"

"I couldn't tell you."

"No forwarding address?"

"If you ask me, she didn't know where she would end up next."

"Didn't she even leave a contact number?"

A shake of the head. "She'll be in another job by now. There's no call for her sort of work in the Langfords."

He couldn't allow Jessie the housekeeper to go off the radar. She'd been at Massimo Filiput's funeral. Maybe the lawyers would have her new address.

"Did she receive a legacy?"

"No, it all came to me — and I wish to God it hadn't. Who exactly are you, asking all these questions?"

If he said he was police, all communication would cease. "I'm Peter Diamond from Bath. There was an accident there a few days ago and a man is in hospital in a coma. We're trying to trace people who might know him. Your uncle Cyril was a possibility."

"How come?"

"They both used to visit a house in Cavendish Crescent."

"Is that so?"

It was hard to tell whether Hilary was holding back information or treating him with the suspicion many country people had

288

for townies.

"He never mentioned them?"

"I didn't see much of Uncle Cyril. I live on the other side of Warminster."

"I suppose you had to arrange his funeral."

"It wasn't much. A short service at the crematorium in Sarum. Being so old, he'd outlived most of his friends. A few folk from the village came out of respect." This was better: freely given.

"Nobody from Bath?"

She shook her head. "His old friend Max passed over last year."

"Max was the person I mentioned, the one he used to visit in Bath. Max Filiput. They played Scrabble once a week."

"Did they indeed? Crafty old bugger," she said, eyes lighting up in amusement.

"You mean Cyril? Why do you say that?"

"He had the Scrabble dictionary with words you'd never know unless you had one yourself. It's on the shelf over there. Does that count as cheating? They will have played for money, that's for sure. He'd bet on anything, would Uncle Cyril. I threw out his box of Scrabble yesterday. No use to me and I couldn't be bothered checking if all the grubby little tiles were still in the box."

"Is there much else to sort out?"

"I'm hoping to finish tomorrow and put

the place up for sale."

"What happened to the car?"

"Which car was that?"

"He used to be driven to Bath when he visited Max."

"Jessie had a little runabout of her own. I expect they used that. Uncle Cyril had a rusty old Volvo at one time that he serviced himself, but he got rid of it after he gave up driving. Most likely it went for scrap. He wouldn't have got much for it."

There was more to extract from her, he was confident. "Now that I'm here, can I help you move anything out of the cottage?" If nothing else, he'd get a look inside.

She glanced at his suit. "You're not dressed for work."

"I'll take off my jacket."

"If you mean it, you could help shift a couple of beds from upstairs."

A couple of beds? He'd been thinking of something more portable, like a laptop or some box files.

She stepped back to allow him inside. The living room was bare except for some half-filled cartons and a bookcase. He could tell by the marks on the carpet where other furniture had stood. After removing his jacket and tie he followed her upstairs, where there were two bedrooms divided by a bathroom.

"This was his. Can you take the bed to bits?"

"Let's give it a go." He was better at dismantling things than assembling them.

They were in a small room with little else except a fitted wardrobe and a chest of drawers.

He shifted the double mattress from the wooden bed frame and propped it against the nearest wall, and knocked off a picture as he did so. The Laughing Cavalier didn't enjoy the joke as he hit the floor hard and his glass smashed.

"Oh Christ. I was born clumsy."

"Doesn't matter," she said. "Leave it."

The least he could do was stand the frame upright and push the broken glass with his foot into a tidy heap in the corner. He'd just about finished when he noticed at one end of the mattress the manufacturer's label with information about the features, notably a thousand sprung pockets that ensured comfort, elegance and value.

"What have we got here?"

The label appeared to be one more pocket, bulging oddly, but Diamond had noticed it was unstitched on three sides. He tugged at the edge and heard the sound of Velcro separating. Underneath was a small cavity.

Something black had been stuffed inside. He drew it out carefully.

A velvet bag.

"Hey ho."

Light in weight, it definitely contained some small object.

He loosened the drawstring and brought out a gold necklace that was clearly antique, the pendant in the shape of an engraved serpent's head, with five inset diamonds and blue enamel for the eyes.

He draped the piece across his palm and held it out to Hilary. "What do you reckon?"

"Where in the name of heaven did the old rogue get this from?" she said, looking but making no move to handle it.

Diamond had a good idea but didn't say. "Want to try it on?"

She shook her head. "Not my thing at all."

"The label says comfort, elegance and value. I'd say this has got elegance and value even if you're not comfortable with it."

"My flesh creeps just looking at it. I hate snakes."

"A popular design at one time."

She put her hand to her mouth. "Is it stolen goods, do you think?"

"He was too old for smash-and-grab raids or break-ins."

"Well, I can't think what he was doing

with it. What am I going to do with the bloody thing? I was taking the mattress to the council tip."

He'd been making a rapid review of his options. He didn't want to reveal that he was from the police, but there was no other way he could reasonably take possession of the bag and its contents. He already had a fair idea where it came from. He could suggest Hilary took it to the lawyers handling Cyril's estate, but they'd be obliged to inform the police, and if Wiltshire CID got involved one of the first things they'd ask was who had found it.

"Actually," he said, "I ought to have shown you this before." He produced his warrant card.

She nodded as if to confirm she'd known all along. "Why the heck didn't you say you're a cop?"

"A plain-clothes cop. The general idea is that we don't go round introducing ourselves to people."

"And now you think you ought to come clean?"

"So as to hand this in. I'll write you a receipt. It's yours by rights if it isn't stolen."

"Take it, and welcome," she said. "What are you really here for? Was he in trouble with the police?"

"As I told you at the start, this is about the man in a coma. I thought your uncle Cyril was alive and might help us identify him."

"You've got another mystery now." Unexpectedly, she was reconciled to the police presence.

He made a point of writing a form of receipt on the reverse of one of his official cards. Then he pocketed the bag containing the necklace.

"You spoke of betting before we found this. Uncle Cyril liked a flutter, then?"

"He was addicted. It's why there's nothing left that's worth having, apart from . . ." Her voice trailed off. "Wicked old blighter. Any money I get from the sale of the cottage will go to paying off his debts."

"That's tough, really tough. I didn't know."

"You said something about him playing Scrabble with Max. That wouldn't have been for matchsticks, he'll have made sure of that. You get points for making words, don't you?"

"I believe you do."

"He'd lay money on anything. Horses, football, poker. He had a few good wins, but of course in the long run he lost, big time. He ran up massive debts and had some nasty people coming to collect from time to time."

"Who were they — do you know?"

"He never said. I heard about it from Jessie one time. She was shocked. She said they acted like bailiffs, seizing his electrical goods, his TV, his laptop, even his power tools. She told him to report them but he wouldn't. He was so worried, he was taking Temazepam to get any sleep at all. Are you still going to help me with this job?"

"Of course. We started and we'll finish."

"What we need is an Allen key," she told him after examining the bolts on the bed frame.

"Definitely," he said, trying to sound competent. He was not a handyman. He wouldn't have known an Allen key from a pineapple.

"There's one downstairs."

While she was fetching it, he weighed the new information. If Cyril Hardstaff had been in hock to some loan shark he must have felt insecure, to say the least. Unsurprising that he'd have a hiding place for anything of value. Presumably it had been waiting there to be pawned or sold. A man of charm and wit on the surface, at desperation point underneath. These old men and their personal failings were bringing extra

295

layers of deception to the case.

He was relieved to find that the Allen key was nothing more complicated than an L-shaped spanner you used like a key. While loosening the bolts, he asked Hilary whether Cyril had ever been married.

"He was, yes, to my aunt Winnie. She died of a brain tumour seven or eight years ago. A tough lady and very successful. She started a secretarial agency in the days when every business wanted typing staff and it got to be one of the biggest in London, worth millions. She kept Uncle Cyril well under her thumb. He didn't do much of his gambling while she was alive. We were all a bit scared of Aunt Winnie."

"I was wondering if the necklace could have been hers."

"No chance. She went in for fashion jewellery. Showy modern stuff. We'd better turn the bed on its side. It's going to collapse if you loosen the other bolt."

"Good thinking," he said. "I was on the point of doing it."

In a short time he had the headboard and footboard separated from the frame.

"Did Cyril inherit the fortune his wife earned?"

A smile and a shake of the head. "She was smart. When she wrote her will, she put all her money in trust. He was allowed an annuity of fifty thousand but he couldn't get his hands on the rest, except a salary was set aside for a housekeeper — because she knew he wasn't capable of managing on his own. He's had a string of housekeepers, has Uncle Cyril. He's not easy to manage. The house in a posh part of London went to him, but he sold it to get more cash to gamble with. I think he bought a smaller place and then sold that, and so on, until he ended up in this dump. Prop them against the wall and you can unscrew the other bed," she said. She was definitely the foreman of this team.

"If Aunt Winnie was as wealthy as you say, some of her fortune must be left over."

"I won't see a brass penny of it. It's all going to War on Want."

"Rather that than the bookmakers."

"True."

The second room had been the housekeeper's. Nothing personal remained but it had a fresher look to it than Cyril's room and the bed was a divan with a padded headboard. He succeeded in shifting the mattress without damaging anything — except one of his lower vertebrae.

He'd never been kicked by a shire horse but he now had some idea how it felt.

He roared.

"What's up?" Hilary asked.

He slumped on to the sprung bedstead. "Give me a moment."

"Your back, is it?"

He rubbed it, trying not to swear.

"You know what they say," she said. "No good deed ever goes unpunished."

"Do they?"

He was in too much agony to trade smart talk.

"There's a medicine cabinet in the bathroom where he kept his sleeping tablets," she said. "There must be painkillers of some sort."

"I don't want his stuff."

"I can see if there's anything you can rub on it. I don't mind doing it for you."

"No thanks." She might not mind but he did. He braced himself and succeeded in standing up. "Let's see if we can unscrew the legs from this thing."

"You're tougher than you look," Hilary told him.

"I played rugby when I was younger," he said. "The idea is to get straight back into the game."

Presently he'd recovered enough to slide the mattress out to the landing on its side and let it shoot downstairs. They dealt with the other one the same way. Then without actually needing to lift them, they manoeuvred them into the van.

She offered to leave the bedsteads for another day, but he insisted he would be all right and they returned upstairs to finish the job. He really believed there was some benefit in soldiering on rather than collapsing and letting the injury stiffen up.

When they shifted the second bed he saw something gleaming on the floor that turned out to be a cheap plastic hairbrush. Pink, with white nylon bristles.

"Jessie's," Hilary said, picking it up. "She didn't leave anything else behind."

"She won't be coming back for it," he said. "Can I see?"

"Keep it if you want."

"I will." No detective worthy of the name turns down an offer like that. He wrapped the brush in the folded papers in his jacket pocket. A few blonde hairs were enmeshed between the bristles.

Hilary offered black coffee — there was no milk in the small kitchen — and he drank it standing up.

"All you got for helping me was a sore back and an old hairbrush," Hilary said. "This hasn't helped your friend in hospital."

In his present state of discomfort, he had

299

to think who his friend in hospital was. Pellegrini and friendship went together like fire and water.

A lot has happened since I last put anything in the diary. How events move on. Memo to myself: must do better in keeping the record updated. If I leave it too late, there's no point really.

What can I say about the last one? He was an overdue train that needed taking into the terminus (he'd appreciate that). After his wife went, he found life increasingly difficult. He had vague suspicions certain people were taking advantage, but he was in no condition to stop them. I did him a service, ending his journey.

13

The drive back was a blur. He made a short stop at work to bag up the hairbrush for forensics and then went straight home, needing to get horizontal. The pain in his lower back wasn't going to go away quickly. He let himself in, swallowed some painkillers and dropped like wet washing on the sofa in the front room.

He hardly stirred until he felt something soft nudging his face.

Raffles, wanting to be fed.

He checked the time. Four hours had gone by.

Four hours?

Without thinking why he was there he swung his legs off the sofa and was sharply reminded by his lumbar region. He swore so loudly that Raffles shot upstairs.

After more groaning, mainly at his own folly as he recalled what had happened, Diamond eased himself up, shuffled to the kitchen and opened a tin of cat food. Raffles reappeared as quickly as he had gone.

In CID they would be wondering where the boss was. Better let them know.

He called Halliwell.

"Keith, it's me."

"Okay."

The slightly bored response wasn't the fanfare of relief he'd been expecting. "What do you mean — okay? I've been out of the office since midday. Didn't anyone notice?"

"You were going to the Langfords. We didn't expect you back in a hurry."

"Nearly seven hours?"

"Was it as long as that?"

"Forget it. What's been happening?"

"Some progress. A bit of a breakthrough, in fact. Hold on. I'll pass the phone to Inge."

"Guv," Ingeborg's voice took over. "Did you meet Cyril?"

"No. He died."

There was a sharp intake of breath. "Another one?"

"My reaction, too, but I can't see how his death could have been caused by you-know-who. He went peacefully at home in his own bed."

"So did the others. The men, at any rate. And was he rich, like Filiput?"

"He may have been at one time. By the

303

end he was up to his ears in debt. I met his niece who is the sole heir and she's come into nothing except a load of trouble."

"So was it recent, his death?"

"Six weeks." He told her about Cyril's gambling addiction and the special provisions of his wife Winnie's will. "She made sure her life's savings didn't all go to the loan sharks and bookies."

"I'm warming to this woman," Ingeborg said. "She must have cared about him to arrange the annuity."

"He still managed to get through a lot, including the profit from selling their house in London. The cottage is just a two-up, two-down place unlikely to cover the debts. Even the Scrabble sessions at Cavendish Crescent seem to have been for money."

"How do you play Scrabble for money?"

"Like any other game. There's a winner, isn't there? Or it could be a pound a point. Two people playing will score more than five hundred points between them, easily."

"Are you a player, guv?"

"I used to have the occasional game with Steph, but not for money." He went silent for a moment, remembering. Then he snapped out of it and told her about the necklace he'd found.

"What was he doing with a gold necklace?" she said.

"An antique gold necklace. I'm wondering if it belonged originally to Olga Filiput. She had some valuable things, I was told by Dr. Mukherjee, antiques and jewellery as well as those Fortuny gowns. Max inherited them and got worried because he couldn't keep track of them all. He suspected some went missing — and we know where the gowns ended up."

"Cyril nicked the necklace?"

"There was quite a free-for-all at the funeral."

"I thought that was about Filiput's railway collection."

"Right, but railway items didn't interest Cyril. He was the Scrabble partner, nothing to do with the GWR lot. He was under pressure from people he'd borrowed from. I'm wondering if he took his chance to look for something really worth taking while the others were fighting over the photographs and posters."

"Wow. It's possible."

"What's your news?" he asked her. "Keith said something about a breakthrough."

She laughed. "That's putting it strongly. I may have solved a small mystery. How would you like a midnight adventure with Keith and me?"

"Tonight?"

"That's what we have in mind."

"Doing what?"

"What Ivor Pellegrini does — a jaunt in the country to see if we can find them digging their holes."

"The rabbits? Oh, for Christ's sake, Inge."

She laughed again. "I can pick you up from your house about eleven-thirty if you're game."

He was game but he wasn't sure if his back was. "Are you sure this won't be a waste of time?"

"Trust me. I've done my research. It's going to be a revelation. Come on, guv. You'll miss a few hours' sleep but so what?"

Loss of sleep wasn't the problem. He'd just had four hours. "All right. I'm on board." He ended the call and went off to look for more painkillers.

He'd had a bath by the time they arrived but he couldn't pretend he was fit.

Before they even got to the car, Halliwell asked, "What happened, boss? You look terrible."

"It'll pass."

"You're not walking right."

"If you really want to know, I was helping a lady with a bed."

Ingeborg was quick to warn Halliwell, "Don't go there." She opened the car door. "Are you able to get in, guv?"

"In, yes. I might need help to get out."

The roads were almost empty but Ingeborg still observed the limit, mindful that at this hour any vehicle would be obvious to a police patrol. "We'll go past Pellegrini's house and follow the route he took the night of the crash," she said.

"Do we know it?" Diamond asked.

"We do now."

"How did you work this out?"

"What he was really up to? From his computer data. I spent hours searching for the download of the stuff he'd printed out — those murder notes — until steam was coming out of my ears. Then I had the idea of making a different search trying some of the crazy stuff he said when he was stopped by our guys. I used the search function, working with the most recent documents, which all seemed to be just boring railway stuff, and suddenly there it was staring back at me from the screen."

"The crazy talk?"

"The meaning of it all."

"Get away."

"I'm serious."

"Which word did it — rabbits?"

307

"No. If you look at the notes you made after your second visit to Lew Morgan, he was careful to point out to you that Pellegrini didn't actually mention rabbits. That was Lew, trying to make sense of it."

"As anyone would. As we did, in fact."

"Pellegrini said he heard them digging their holes, right?"

"Supposedly. And heading for Bath."

"Using hops."

"Are we dealing with some other creatures, then?"

"You'll see. It was the word 'hops' that cracked it for me." She left that to sink in. "Henrietta Road is coming up shortly. Ideally we should be switching to tricycles to reconstruct his journey properly. We'll have to imagine him packing his supplies in the saddlebag and pedalling off on his nightly jaunt."

"A right bunch of idiots we'd look on trikes," Halliwell said.

"There's Pellegrini's workshop, anyway," Diamond said, looking left at the white building in front of the large house. "From now on we're following in his tyre tracks." He didn't trouble Ingeborg any more for explanations. She'd made it plain that the whole purpose of the trip was to show, not tell.

They turned right at Henrietta Road and, shortly after, crossed the canal by way of Sydney Road.

"I'm going to cheat a bit now," Ingeborg said. "He used the back roads but it's simpler for us to nip along the A36. We'll rejoin him at Bathampton."

"Is that rain I see on the windscreen?" Diamond said.

"Doesn't matter."

"Are they just as active in the wet, then?"

"It won't stop them." She steered the conversation away from the rabbits — or whatever she was saving for later. "With Cyril dead, that makes two men and two women in a year and a half: Olga and Max Filiput, Trixie Pellegrini and Cyril. Pellegrini is dangerous to know."

"Tell me about it."

"Plus three others from the railway club, Seaton, Carnforth and Marshall-Tomkin," she went on. "Okay, they passed away a year or so earlier, but it's a frightening tally."

Diamond tried to turn in the seat and speak to Halliwell. A stab of pain in his back made him yell so suddenly that Ingeborg's steering wobbled. He apologised before saying, "Keith, you were going to find out how they died."

There was a long silence from behind him.

Finally Halliwell said, "I don't know if you want to hear this. Copies of the death certificates arrived this morning."

"And?"

"If you remember, Carnforth was the one who died after a short illness, according to the paper. It was the flu."

Another silence followed, this time of Diamond's making. He'd just lost one of the potential serial-murder victims. He ought not to complain. "That's certain?"

"It's given as the cause of death."

He gritted his teeth. "Can't argue with that, then. How about the other two?"

"Edmund Seaton had bronchial pneumonia and Jeremy Marshall-Tomkin an aneurysm."

"Is that peaceful?"

"It's quick. Doctors certified these deaths and they sound like genuine medical conditions you wouldn't confuse with murder."

Two more gone.

"I don't think we can blame Pellegrini," Halliwell continued. "My reading of it is that none of those three was murdered. They agreed among themselves that they wanted their ashes scattered on the railway when their time came and whoever survived the others would perform this last duty for his fellow members. It had to be done secretly at night because Network Rail wouldn't permit it."

"Sounds right to me," Ingeborg said. "He kept the urns as a kind of memorial."

"We can all agree on that, then," Diamond said with no pleasure at all. Poleaxed wasn't enough to describe his state. "Instead of seven possible victims, we're down to four, maximum. And I can't honestly see why he would have wanted to murder Cyril."

"Which brings the tally down to three," Halliwell said. "Trixie, Olga and Max."

"So whose ashes was he carrying on the night of the collision?" Ingeborg said.

"The urn was empty," Halliwell said.

"When it was found, it was. By then he'd scattered them somewhere along the track. He was on his way back when the patrol car hit him."

"Had to be Max," Halliwell said. "He was the last of the railway club to die."

"Last summer. Quite some time ago."

"Yes, but you can keep ashes indefinitely. There's no urgency."

They were fast approaching the Bathampton Lane turn. Diamond was silent, still wrestling with the news that three of the deaths had *not* been caused by Pellegrini.

"How are we doing?" Halliwell asked.

"We're good," Ingeborg said. "The track

is somewhere on our left. We'll go on a bit and then do what Pellegrini is supposed to have done."

"Except we don't have any ashes to scatter," Halliwell said.

"I'm talking about his cover story."

"The rabbits?" Diamond said, making a huge effort to pay attention.

"The hops."

"You're calling it a cover story. Are you sure?"

"I am now. His real objective was dealing with the ashes."

"And he had this other story ready in case anyone stopped him and asked what he was doing? He'd say he was studying wildlife?"

"He didn't say that. This is where we got him wrong. He's an engineer used to dealing in facts, not fantasy. He picked something real as his cover. Anyone could verify that it was true, as I will demonstrate shortly."

"And it's on his computer?"

"That's how I know it happens each night while we're sleeping."

They bridged the canal, the railway, the A4 and the Avon at Bathampton and followed London Road East to link up with the A4.

"For an old guy he's a strong cyclist if he

came this far," Halliwell said.

"Come on," Ingeborg said. "The bike was motorised."

"He didn't need to," Diamond said. He'd got the sense of what Ingeborg had said earlier. "This was only his cover story."

"The railway is now on our right," Ingeborg said.

"All the way to Box," Halliwell said. "Are we going as far as that?"

"We may not need to. If I've got it right, they'll be this side of the tunnel."

Box Tunnel was dug through Box Hill at the start of the Victorian era to bring the railway to Bath and Bristol. Almost two miles in length, it was one of the great engineering projects undertaken by Isambard Kingdom Brunel.

"We'll stop in the next layby," Ingeborg said. "Don't want to drive straight past them without realising."

"God, no. They're good movers, not easy to catch," Halliwell said in amusement. "They cover up to a mile a night."

"We're not trying to catch anything."

Ingeborg pulled over at the top of the next rise, switched off the engine and got out. She told Diamond, "You don't have to move yet, guv. I'm checking how close we are, that's all."

After midnight not much else was on the road. There were intervals between the sets of headlights. The light rain hadn't gone away.

Still in the car, Diamond asked Halliwell, seated in the back. "Can you see anything?"

"I don't know what we're looking for any more."

Ingeborg had walked a short distance from the car and was standing with arms folded, apparently alert to something.

"She can't see a bloody thing," Halliwell said. "She's having us on."

"I'll have her guts for garters if she is."

She returned. "We're in luck," she said as she got in. "They're not far off."

"Did you hear them digging their holes?" Halliwell said with sarcasm.

"Actually, I did, but you can't see them from here."

The silence from the back seat said it all.

They started up and turned right at a side road a short way on. Ingeborg explained that they would get a better view this way. Neither of her passengers commented.

"I'm stopping again," she said presently. "A lot of this is guesswork now."

Halliwell couldn't resist saying, "Can't you pick them up on your satnav?"

She opened her door and stepped out.

"Listen. Open your window and listen."

Diamond opened his door.

No argument: there was definitely a rhythmic sound coming from not far off, but it was more mechanical than natural.

"Is that them?"

"We can get closer," she said. And they were off again.

After two more turns they had a view across the fields to the railway and an extraordinary floodlit spectacle, a stationary train made up of at least a dozen units in bright yellow.

A train?

Diamond was so confused that he got out of the car unaided and felt no pain. He stood with hands on hips taking it all in.

The sound they had heard was coming from a carriage that was, in effect, a piling rig driving a huge tubular pile into the ground attended by a team of workmen in hard hats and high-visibility jackets. Other rolling stock was made up of excavators, flat-bed wagons loaded with more of the piles, tanks that presumably held cement and water and a concrete mixer.

"It's a bloody factory on wheels," Halliwell said.

"Officially known as the High Output Plant System," Ingeborg said, and waited a moment to deliver her punchline. "HOPS."

A pause followed.

"HOPS, right," Halliwell eventually said, grinning sheepishly. "Digging their holes. Pellegrini isn't such a dumbo as we thought."

Diamond was shaking his head. "Speaking of dumbos, I should have thought of this. The electrification of the Great Western main line. The booking clerk at the station talked to me about this and I didn't cotton on that it was the thing Pellegrini was on about."

"He's got several long pieces about it on his computer," Ingeborg said. "When I put in the word 'hops' I had scores of hits. They're working six nights a week, sinking 16,000 piles between Maidenhead and Swansea. That's 235 miles and they can do between 1,200 and 1,500 metres in a night."

"You're really into this," Halliwell said.

"They follow up with the masts and portal booms and string the overhead cables as they go. Do you want to know about the HOOB?"

"The what?" Diamond said.

"The High Output Operations Base. It's a place near Swindon where the HOPS can lie up by day ready to roll into action the next night. Then there's the Hobbit."

"What's that?"

"A little guy with pointy ears."

Another pause for thought before Halliwell said, "Ha bloody ha."

"Sergeant Smith," Diamond said, "you're in serious danger of losing all the credit you just built up."

They stood watching the pile-driving for ten minutes more, until the rain forced them back to the car.

Fatigue set in as they drove back to Bath, but Diamond still found the energy to say, "We seriously underestimated this guy, calling him a nutter. He may be helpless in hospital but he's having a bloody good laugh at us."

14

Was the case against Pellegrini in any way undermined?

Diamond was in a defiant frame of mind. For days suspicion had mounted inexorably to the point where it was no longer tenable to believe the man was anything else but a serial killer. It had been hell to admit. The sense of loyalty, kinship, almost brotherly love, engendered by the lifesaving episode had set up a conflict that seemed irreconcilable. But he'd passed the tipping point. His responsibility as a detective overrode everything else.

He'd made up his mind, hardened his heart, and then what? The death certificates showed three of the presumed victims died naturally.

Would he go into reverse?

Not now.

There was evidence of theft, of a demonstrable interest in murder methods and there were other suspicious deaths — to which Cyril Hardstaff's might now be added.

He gave serious thought to the matter over a later-than-usual breakfast next morning. He felt better than expected after not much sleep, so he treated himself to bacon and eggs and a generous assortment of extras. Dr. Mukherjee's concerns about his health weren't going to stop him. He needed nourishing. His brain worked better when he ate well.

On the face of it, Cyril had died naturally, in his own bed. No doubts had been raised at the time.

A pathetic old man up to his ears in debt. Who'd *want* to kill him?

And why?

Pellegrini was a man with a proven interest in killing. He appeared to have found a clever way to take the life of his so-called friend, Massimo Filiput.

Clever and calculated.

He hadn't done it under pressure, in a hurry or a panic. First he'd committed theft. The three Fortuny gowns had been stolen some time before Filiput died.

Then murder.

And then Filiput's friend Cyril had died.

Similar situation: at home, in bed, apparently of natural causes.

Both were old men whose wives had died. Both had once worked together. Both met regularly for a game of Scrabble. But their personal fortunes couldn't have been more different. Filiput had died a millionaire whereas Cyril had gambled away all the money he could lay his hands on.

Puzzling.

Diamond poured himself another coffee.

Think of it in terms of the old trinity every prosecution has to address: motive, means and opportunity.

Finding a motive that fitted both victims would not be easy.

If it wasn't financial gain, what else could it be? This hadn't been spur-of-the-moment violence. It was coolly planned and cleverly carried out.

Had it been done to settle old scores? These were elderly men, all three. Had there been issues at some earlier stage of their lives? If so, the truth would take some unravelling, with two dead and the other insensible.

The motive he'd thought up already while watching the boules-players in Queen Square still appealed to him — that the killing had been done out of conceit, just for the ego trip of carrying out a perfect murder. Or a series of perfect murders. He wasn't ready yet to share this startling theory with Keith and Ingeborg, but the possibility remained.

Motive, means and opportunity.

Means.

You name it, Diamond told himself as he recalled the pages from the online forum. Ingenious poisons, icicles, air in the bloodstream. Umpteen suggestions to work with. Detecting them would be the problem. Both men had been cremated.

"And so, ladies and gentlemen of the jury," he said to no other audience than his cat, Raffles, who didn't even look up from the food dish, "we come to the third element — opportunity."

Filiput had died at home in Cavendish Crescent, apparently alone. His body had been discovered in the morning by his cleaner. It wasn't a locked-room mystery because he kept a spare key behind the drainpipe outside the front door. Mrs. Stratford knew about the key and so, in all probability, did others.

Simple.

Cyril, too, had died at home, but his situation was more problematical. He lived an hour's drive from Bath. Getting there might be difficult. Did Pellegrini drive, or did he only get about on his tricycle? And how would he gain access to the cottage? They weren't insurmountable questions, but they needed to be asked.

Cyril Hardstaff's death warranted urgent investigation. His life, too.

At work, he walked straight into an ambush. The IPCC duo were standing beside Keith Halliwell's desk. What were they called — Grabham and Slice? Keith looked as if he'd already been dragged and stretched, and that aided the memory.

"There you are, Mr. Diamond," Dragham called across the room. "Was the traffic extra heavy this morning? I thought by now the Bath rush-hour would be over."

He let the sarcasm roll off. He wouldn't be telling them about the night excursion and he hoped Keith hadn't.

Miss Stretch said, "We're following up on our visit yesterday to Mr. Bellerby, the gentleman who made the emergency call. We weren't aware that you took two colleagues with you until he informed us."

"Is that a problem?"

"It was for Mr. Bellerby. He complained about police, in his words, 'crawling all over' his bungalow."

"Ridiculous."

"DI Halliwell admits to handling a pair of binoculars without the permission of the owner."

"Is that crawling all over the bungalow? As I recall, he was testing what you could see through them. Isn't that so, Keith?"

Halliwell nodded. "Absolutely."

Miss Stretch switched from Keith's failings to Diamond's. "Mr. Bellerby didn't like the tone of your questioning. He called it a Gestapo-style interrogation."

"For crying out loud, he's the little Hitler, not me."

"He hasn't registered an official complaint yet, but I'd better warn you. If he does, we'll need to investigate."

This was becoming farcical. "Couldn't you see for yourselves what he's like? The man's got an agenda. He objects to the restoration of the lido he can see from the back of his bungalow."

"He didn't say anything about a lido to us."

"Did you go into the back bedroom where he keeps his spying equipment?"

They looked blank.

"I thought not. We have the advantage of local knowledge."

"You'd better tell us," Miss Stretch said.

He took on a confiding, almost sympa-

323

thetic role. "The lido is well known, a site of historic interest. Cleveland Pools is the only surviving Georgian lido in Great Britain. It was used from 1815 until the 1980s and then went into disrepair. The people who run the trust have done well. They've got lottery funding and they're putting on events to raise more money. Bellerby doesn't approve."

"Why?" Miss Stretch asked. "What's his objection?"

"He thinks he's going to be kept awake by late-night revellers walking up the footpath and he's looking for any opportunity to dish the dirt. He spotted some health freak having a skinny-dip at dawn, so he called 999. That's the kind of tosser he is. If he hadn't made the call, Aaron Green would still be alive and the others wouldn't have ended up in intensive care."

"You're getting rather worked up yourself, Mr. Diamond. We can't turn back the clock. As it happens, Mr. Bellerby is rather important to us. He has provided the only eyewitness account of Mr. Pellegrini on his tricycle a few minutes before the collision."

"It's all in my report. He was wandering off course, as if he wasn't used to riding the thing. Bellerby's words, not mine."

"If those really were his words, he wasn't

so explicit under questioning from us. He said the tricyclist was slightly unsteady."

"You can't be unsteady on a trike unless your steering is off. It's not like being on two wheels."

"We're aware of that," Dragham said. "His control or lack of it is, of course, crucial to our enquiry. Do you have an opinion why he should have been unsteady?"

"Drink, I suppose. That's the first thing that springs to mind."

"Inebriation? How would you account for that?"

"He could have brought a hip flask with him. It was a cool night."

"There was no hip flask found."

"A bottle, then. He may have slung it away. I'm guessing here. You asked me for a suggestion. If it wasn't drink, it could have been drugs. I don't suppose we'll ever know."

"We may," Miss Stretch said. "The hospital informed us that they took a blood sample for their own information soon after he was admitted."

This was news to Diamond. He'd thought Pellegrini had been too far gone. "Brilliant. It should show up, then. Have they tested for alcohol?"

"Unfortunately there's a catch. Firstly, the

sample belongs to the hospital. We have no power to take and test blood specimens used in the treatment of hospital patients, and neither do you, the police. Secondly, even if it was offered to you, the patient has to give consent."

"But the patient is unconscious."

"And therefore the sample must be kept until he is able to decide on consent. That's the law of the land."

"Murphy's law."

"I don't follow you."

"Also known as sod's law. If anything can go wrong, it will."

But in reality, Diamond didn't think Pellegrini had been drunk or drugged. The man was too smart for that. Either he'd been unwell or exhausted or there was a fault with the tricycle.

"However, the blood sample taken at the postmortem on the police driver, PC Green, was negative for alcohol," Miss Stretch said.

"As we all knew it would be."

"Everything must be double-checked. Today we're visiting the hospital to get Sergeant Morgan's account of the crash."

"That'll really make his day."

Dragham frowned. "What do you mean by that?"

"Visitors. He hasn't had many."

326

"And how will you be spending your day, superintendent?"

A low punch. He backed off fast. "There's always plenty going on in CID."

"Have you traced the first responders yet?"

"Who?"

"We spoke about this yesterday. The fire officers and paramedics who must have spoken to Sergeant Morgan at the scene. I thought you were on to this."

"Top of my list but no joy so far."

After they'd gone, he checked with Halliwell that nothing had been said about the midnight visit to the HOPS.

"They wouldn't know about any of that stuff, guv."

"They may after they see Lew Morgan. A lot depends on what he chooses to say. If, like me, he takes an immediate dislike, he may not tell them anything."

"They'll question him."

"Doesn't mean they'll get answers. Lew is one of the old school of police sergeants. But if he chooses to open up with them about the rabbits, they'll be wondering who's the more crazy, Pellegrini or Lew himself."

"I hope he doesn't talk himself into trouble."

"After losing his leg he won't care a toss. I wouldn't. The main thing is that Aaron the driver was negative for alcohol. They could still say he drove dangerously in some way, but it's more than likely they'll decide Pellegrini was responsible." He looked around the CID room. "Where's Ingeborg this morning?"

"She may have gone for a coffee. She sometimes goes there for peace and quiet to work on her laptop."

"We seem to have drawn a blank with the hard disk. We have to find another way into Pellegrini's secret life. There's something you can do, Keith. It occurred to me as I was coming in this morning. When I first went to the house in Henrietta Road, I asked the woman who was cleaning, Mrs. Halliday, if Pellegrini drove a car as well as getting about on the trike. She said he didn't. He has an account with a taxi firm."

"You want me to phone around?"

"Would you? They keep a log of their journeys. I'm interested to discover if he ever took a trip to Little Langford."

"To Cyril Hardstaff?" Halliwell's interest quickened and he asked, "Did those two know each other?"

"They met at Filiput's funeral."

"Only once."

"Apparently."

"Hardly a reason for murder."

"It only wanted one taxi ride."

"But why? What had he got against Cyril?"

"Let's cross that hurdle when we come to it. For the present I just want to know if it was possible."

His next challenge was a phone call to the formidable solicitor, Miss Hill. She was busy, of course. He didn't expect to get through without an effort. The receptionist said she would ask Miss Hill to call him back.

"That's no use to me," he said. "I need to speak to her now."

"She's in a meeting."

"They always are. Remind her I'm from the police and tell her it's an extreme emergency."

Presently he was rewarded with Miss Hill's stonewalling voice. "Why can't you make an appointment like anyone else?"

"Because I'm not anyone else," he said. "I'm a professional like you, and just as busy."

She seemed to take that as a peace offering. "Then you can understand."

"However," he said.

"However what?"

"This is a matter of life and death."

"What is?"

"You'll need your files on the estates of Olga and Massimo Filiput. Do you have them nearby?"

At the other end of the line there was some conversation he didn't pick up. This was encouraging, because it probably meant she had some personal assistant with her. There was the pleasing rasp of a filing cabinet being opened.

"What now?" Miss Hill asked.

"Do you also have a scanner in your office?"

After a gasp of horror, she said, "I'm not copying confidential material for you, if that's what you're suggesting."

"I wouldn't think of asking you," he said, "but you and I know that wills become public documents after the testators die, so it isn't confidential at all. I could get copies from the probate registry, but I need them urgently, and you know what bureaucracy is. For you, I'll make it easy. All I need is the inventory of Olga's assets, the antiques and jewellery. And for comparison, I want the corresponding document for Massimo."

"We went through this before, in my office."

"I know, Miss Hill. It's a pain, but this is

a fresh enquiry. Something else came up. I'll give you my email address and you can send them through directly."

"You said it was a life and death matter."

"Isn't that the definition of a will?"

His own filing system was more individual than Miss Hill's. For days he'd been walking about with some sheets of paper stuffed in his jacket pocket: the Internet discussion forum about murder methods. He took them out and unfolded them.

He should have been treating them with more respect, he realised. Normally printouts were insignificant, easily replaceable. But these, it had become clear, weren't saved as files in Pellegrini's computer. They were the only record of the man's interest in ingenious ways of killing. They ought to be kept in an evidence bag.

Some of the so-called methods were pretty absurd. The icicle through the heart. The poisoned toothpaste. The air bubble in the bloodstream. They might impress in an old-fashioned detective story, but putting them into practice in reality would be so difficult and risky that no intelligent killer would bother with them.

And yet Diamond knew of real crimes that were scarcely less ingenious. Who would have thought of an umbrella as a murder weapon? In 1978 a Bulgarian defector called Georgi Markov was queuing for a bus on Waterloo Bridge when he felt a sharp pain in his thigh and turned to see a man picking up an umbrella. Three days later Markov died, poisoned by a small platinum pellet containing the deadly poison ricin, apparently fired from the umbrella. Of course, this theory relied on Markov's memory of the shooting. It might have been dismissed as fanciful were it not for the discovery of the pellet when the muscle tissue was forensically examined. It then emerged that only ten days earlier another Bulgarian called Kostov waiting at a station in the Paris Metro had been shot with a pellet fired from a shopping bag.

Pellegrini, an inventive man, an engineer, was not incapable of devising a method all his own. He'd researched other original murders, as he would, being methodical. But he aspired to perfection, the undetectable crime.

Poison?

The victims had died at home, in bed, apparently of natural causes. Had he found some substance that acted efficiently and left no trace? Poisoners had long looked for the colourless, odourless deadly dose. Even if he'd found such a thing, how was it administered? He was known to go out at night. Had he visited the old men and made sure they took their toxic nightcaps? It didn't seem likely. The risks were too high.

And Pellegrini was an engineer, not a chemist. Poisons unknown to science weren't his stock-in-trade.

The answer had to be different, clever and foolproof.

Well, Diamond told himself, I'm no fool.

Even so, he tucked the printouts into an evidence bag.

Keith Halliwell had been on the phone some time, trying to find whether Pellegrini had an account with a local taxi company.

"Any joy?" Diamond asked.

Joy wasn't in the look he got back. "Got it straight away. He's used Abbey Taxis for years."

"And . . . ?"

"They've never taken him to Little Langford. Even as I was speaking to them I was thinking how bloody silly it was," Halliwell said. "An intelligent killer wouldn't do this. He'd go to a different firm."

"You tried them all?"

"All the ones in Yellow Pages. And I thought of something else." Halliwell was frayed at the edges this morning, proving he, too, was tired from last night.

"Tell me, then."

"He wouldn't use his own name."

"Ah, but he'd still have to give them the address."

"Come on, guv, get real. He could ask them to pick him up outside the nearest pub if he wanted. Anywhere, really."

Diamond was forced to agree. His long-term deputy was ahead of him over this task. "Should have thought of it before I asked you."

And now Halliwell looked down and re-arranged the pens on his desk as if he was uncomfortable about what he was going to say. "You're just as confident as ever, are you?"

"Confident of what? His guilt?"

"Not that exactly. Don't get me wrong, guv. You've got my full support. The thing is . . . can we be certain these deaths are suspicious?"

Diamond could have erupted, but he didn't. He summoned a smile. "Of course they're suspicious or we wouldn't be beating ourselves up to get at the truth. All the suspicion is on our side — or mine, if you like. So, yes, they're suspicious deaths as long as we have our doubts about them. The question you meant to ask is can we be certain these deaths are murders, and of course we can't. They were certified as natural and the bodies were cremated."

Halliwell eased a finger around his collar. After this admission, he really had to press the big man harder. "We wouldn't be questioning them at all if it wasn't for what we know about Pellegrini."

"True. He almost got away with it."

"We're pinning everything on him?"

"Is there anyone else?"

"But there's nothing definite."

"This is normal, Keith. We're not going to find a smoking gun. We do the groundwork and build up a case. It's why Inge has been slogging over the computer and you're phoning taxi firms."

"I understand that." He cleared his throat. "I was awake most of the night asking myself how it was we came to cast him as a killer in the first place."

"That's down to what I found in his workshop."

"The Internet material?"

"And the stolen gowns." Some irritation crept into his voice. He, too, was well down on sleep. "I thought you were up to speed on all this. Max Filiput was suspicious that valuable items like the gowns were disappearing from the house. He talked to Dr. Mukherjee about it."

"It makes Pellegrini a thief, but does it make him a killer?"

"It gives him a motive for murder, covering up the crime. The timing is significant, too. Filiput dies pretty soon after. You still don't look happy with this. Have I missed something?"

Halliwell rubbed the side of his face, deeply ill at ease. "Until yesterday we were thinking those old men in the railway club were earlier murder victims, but we changed our minds because of the death certificates. They didn't die mysteriously in their sleep. They were ill, seriously ill. Flu, bronchial pneumonia, an aneurysm. The reason Pellegrini had their cremation urns was to scatter the ashes secretly along the railway as they'd requested."

"Agreed."

"Murder was in our minds," Halliwell went on in the same dissenting tone but almost apologetic. "Serial murder. But now we have to rein back."

"Okay," Diamond said, testy from fatigue. "Three names come off the victim list."

"Who's left? What about the wives? We thought he may have killed Trixie and Olga but that's far from certain."

"We know he was present when they died, both of them," Diamond said. "Up to now we concentrated on the others. We've yet to investigate what really happened. There's only so much three of us can do."

"The women are long shots if we're honest, guv. Olga falling down the stairs doesn't square with any of the other deaths."

"So what are you telling me? None of it happened?"

"It's not the case it was shaping up to be. We're down to Max and possibly Cyril, and they were signed off by their doctors as dying naturally."

"Naturally — but suddenly."

"They were both old men over ninety. What I'm trying to say is are we clinging to the idea of murder on not much evidence?"

Diamond put a good face on it but he was shaken. He understood the effort it had taken for Halliwell to voice his concerns. The team was losing confidence, and it had to be addressed. "Personally, I don't share your doubts, but maybe that's because I'm closer to the man than you are. I've spoken to some of the people who knew him and I've seen inside his house and his workshop and sat beside his bed in hospital. I gave him the kiss of life, for Christ's sake. I'm not going to say I have a hunch about him.

337

I don't work on the basis of hunches, as you know. But I'm not giving up on him. It's your choice whether you go along with me. It's not part of your job description, right?"

"I'm not quitting, guv. It needed to be said, that's all."

He tried to make light of it. "In case we're up shit creek and I haven't noticed? Wouldn't be the first time."

Halliwell grinned back. "I'll have another crack at the taxis."

"What does Inge think?"

"Don't know. Haven't seen her all morning."

"I hope *she*'s still on board. Shit creek isn't the ideal place to jump ship."

Back in his office he stood in thought.

There's always a low point.

He stared through the glass at everyone busy on official duties.

Get on with it, you great lummock, he told himself. You can only go upwards from here. Stepped round his desk, rolled out the chair, lowered himself into it and screamed like a seagull at the spasm of pain that hit him. Yesterday's injury hadn't gone away. He'd forgotten the low point in his own spine.

When the agony had subsided to mere soreness he checked his inbox and found one from Miss Hill with two attachments: the documents he'd asked for.

Olga's collection of jewellery wouldn't have disgraced a queen. The inventory ran to six pages: necklaces, bracelets, bangles, rings, brooches, lockets, earrings and even two tiaras. Almost all were listed as antique and many were Austro-Hungarian or Russian. Some of the valuations in the right-hand column made him blink and look twice.

The serpent's head necklace of 18 carat gold with five inset diamonds and blue enamel was listed on page 3 and valued at £2,600.

The real thing in its velvet bag was tucked away in the bottom drawer of his desk. Normally he would have handed it to the exhibits officer who stored every item of evidence, but this wasn't an official investigation.

He'd lock the drawer in future.

He turned to Max's assets and found what he expected: some notable omissions.

No mention of the serpent's head necklace.

He spent the next hour checking one list against the other, item by item, and several other pieces hadn't made it to Max's inventory: a gold bangle with appliquéd decoration, a gold and enamel brooch set with a star sapphire, a gold and carnelian signet ring, an art deco sapphire and diamond pendant on a gold chain, a diamond and amethyst necklace. Altogether, they were valued at more than twenty thousand pounds. Of course, you'd get a fraction of that if you fenced them, yet it was still a sizeable haul.

They'd been cherry-picked, by the look of it.

There was a crime here for sure. Max wouldn't have sold them himself. He hadn't needed the money.

Max was doddery but he'd sensed that things were disappearing.

Look no further for a motive.

Diamond called Miss Hill again. She was shocked to hear of the missing items and swift to make clear it wasn't her job to compare one list of assets with another. He asked whether photos had been taken at valuation. She said it was standard practice. He told her he would immediately email a list of the missing items and she agreed to reply with jpegs of each of them. He could rely on her discretion, she said. Nothing of this would be revealed to her colleagues or anyone else. He believed her.

15

It was obvious Halliwell had got a result at last.

"This time, instead of asking about Pellegrini, I phoned around to see if any driver had made a trip to Little Langford in the past six months. Small place, large fare, so they'd remember, see?"

"One of them did?"

"None of the big companies had any record of it, but I struck lucky with a small firm called Rex Cabs."

"No surprise it's small with a name like that."

"Yeah?" Halliwell looked vacant.

"Come on," Diamond said. "Wrecks cabs. Geddit?"

"Oh yeah. Well, I spoke to Rex himself and he definitely drove someone there on a Monday evening six weeks ago."

"About the time Cyril died." Diamond cut the jokey stuff. "We must talk to Rex.

Where is he?"

"Right now? In the rank at the station, waiting to meet the next London train."

"Call him and ask him to drive out here. No, better not. On second thoughts, we'll meet him at Verona."

"Verona?"

"The coffee shop. Get with it."

Rex looked about eighteen, bucktoothed and chewing. He wore a red jacket with an emblem of a robin perched on a football. Either the robin or the football was out of proportion. His baseball cap had the same design. Tufts of bleached-blond hair stuck out under the sides and back.

Diamond offered coffee.

Rex said he'd prefer a Coke.

"Good of you to come," Diamond said. "We'll reimburse the fare right away. Will twenty cover it?"

"No problem," Rex said and pocketed the note.

"You heard what interests us — the fare you took to Little Langford some six weeks ago."

"No problem," Rex said again.

"Do you remember who it was and where you picked him up?"

Two questions together seemed to be

more than Rex could handle. He chewed hard and looked up at the ceiling.

"The fare. Was it a man?"

Rex nodded.

This was hard work.

"About what age?"

He shrugged. "Dunno."

"Try. It's important."

"An old guy."

"That's better."

"No problem."

The two words were marginally preferable to "no comment," but they didn't make for a connected conversation. If it hadn't mattered so much, this would have been a parlour game, trying to steer Rex away from his favourite catchphrase. Diamond tried again. "Where did you pick him up?"

"City centre."

"Where exactly?"

"Orange Grove."

"Right. The rank at Orange Grove. We're getting somewhere."

"No problem."

"Can you tell me how he was dressed? I'm trying to work out whether we're talking about the same guy."

This, it seemed, *was* a problem. Rex chewed some more and said nothing.

Fortunately Diamond had brought the

group photo of the Bath Railway Society. He unfolded it. "Is he one of these?"

A nicotine-stained finger went straight to the likeness of Pellegrini.

Every pulse in Diamond's body zinged.

"You're a star," he said. "An absolute star." And before Rex opened his mouth, he added, "So this old gentleman asked you to drive him to Little Langford?"

A nod.

"Tell me, Rex, did he have anything to say on the journey?"

This got a frown and a moment's thought, followed by a shrug.

"You don't remember? Did he know the way? Did he tell you when the turn for the Langfords came up?"

Rex chewed some more and said, "Sat-nav."

"Right."

"No problem."

"When you dropped him off did he ask you to wait?"

But the young man lapsed into silence again. It was a straightforward question he didn't seem capable of answering.

"It's a simple question," Diamond said. "What's the problem?"

No answer.

Keith Halliwell had said nothing yet, sipping his coffee while Diamond was trying all he knew to prise out information. Now, out of nowhere, Keith put in a comment of his own. "That was a goal on Saturday, wasn't it?"

Rex's face lit up like a breaking cloud. "Did you see the replay? It's obvious it crossed the line. The ref was nowhere near. It was criminal. He's done it to us before, that ref. Was you there then?"

"I caught it on *Points West,*" Halliwell said. "I can't always get to the games. They should be using goal-line technology, in my opinion."

"Dead right, mate. It's a no-brainer," Rex said.

"So you don't work when there's a home game at Ashton Gate?"

"I'm self-employed, aren't I? I put in the hours all week, so why shouldn't I watch football?"

Halliwell smiled. "I wish it worked like that for me. Mr. Diamond here is a rugby fan. He doesn't know what we're talking about. He gets to most of the Bath games and I have to stand in for him at work." Without pause, he said, "Is there anything else you can tell us about the fare you took to Little Langford?"

The football talk had worked a miracle.

"What do you want to know?" Rex said, as if the topic had only just been raised. "He was a good tipper. Gave me twenty extra at the end of the evening. I told him I do cards, but he paid cash."

"You charged for the waiting time?"

"Yeah, it was on the meter. He was under the half-hour, if that. He said he wouldn't be long and he wasn't."

"Where did you wait? In the lane?"

"There was this yard, so I parked there."

"No sign of any other car at the cottage?"

"Not when we drove up. There was just me. I got out and had a smoke. It wasn't raining or anything."

Halliwell was doing the job, so Diamond let him carry on.

"About what time was this?"

"Nine-thirty, I'd say. No, I tell a lie. It was ten. When I got back in the cab, I turned on the radio and caught the news. I was listening for the Chelsea result. They were playing an evening match. Spurs. Three one."

The football talk had paid another dividend. They could fix the date from this.

"I just about caught the result when there's someone knocking on my window."

"He was back?"

"No, it was the lady of the house."

"Who?"

"Jessie the housekeeper," Diamond put in for Halliwell's benefit.

"She'd driven up in a Fiat, one of them two-seater jobs, and I hadn't even noticed. I put my window down, thinking I must be blocking her, but it was okay. She only wanted to know who my fare was."

"Did you tell her?"

"I couldn't, could I? He never told me his name. She goes, is he from Bath, and I'm like, yes, and she goes, is he alone? Then she wants to know if I've heard of Larry Lincoln. Jesus Christ, she only thinks I had Larry bloody Lincoln in my cab, one of the hardest men in Bath."

Hearing this, Diamond slopped some coffee on the table. "She was expecting Larry Lincoln?"

"You know the evil bastard. You must," Rex said.

Any police officer who said he didn't know Lincoln would be a liar. "One of the hardest men in Bath" was no exaggeration. This thug had done long stretches for various forms of assault. He was a walking affront to the effectiveness of the prison system. If Cyril had been expecting a visit from Lincoln that night, he was really in deep.

"Do I know what Lincoln looks like, she

asks me, and she's dead worried, just about wetting herself. Lady, I goes, the geezer I brought is old enough to be Larry's dad."

"Did that calm her down?"

"A bit. She goes into the cottage then. Not long after, my old fellow comes out and tells me he's ready to roll again."

"How did he seem? Keen to be off?"

"He didn't say much. He wasn't sitting beside me. He rode in the back, which I take to mean they don't want to chat. I just checked he wanted to go straight back to Bath, and he did."

"Nothing more was said?"

"Not for some time. About twenty miles down the road he asks me if the woman spoke to me and I said she wanted to know who my passenger was and I wasn't able to tell her. I didn't say she thought he might be Larry Lincoln. Some people might think that was a laugh, but you never know how anyone's going to take stuff like that. Personally I wouldn't be happy with it. So I kept it to myself."

"Probably a good decision. Have you met Lincoln?"

"I seen him a few times, mostly in pubs. I stay well clear."

"Good thinking."

"No problem."

"Was that all that was said in the cab?"

"Just about. When we was near Bath I asked if he wanted me to drive him to his house and he said I could put him down at the rank and that's what I did. Like I said, he paid cash and give me a good tip. I still can't tell you his name."

The two detectives made their way through the Ashmead Road industrial estate towards the glazed monolith that was their temporary (they hoped) place of work.

Halliwell was using his iPhone as they walked, much to Diamond's irritation.

"What's so important? Can't it wait till we get there?"

"It's a football app. It shows all the fixtures. I'm checking the date of that Chelsea–Spurs game. An evening match, he said. We can find out when it was Pellegrini called on Cyril. February, should be."

Diamond stopped complaining and presently had it confirmed that the date of the taxi journey must have been Monday, February the sixteenth. "Spot on," Halliwell told him. "The night before Cyril was found dead."

"Was that Bristol City football club you and he were talking about?"

"The Robins, yep."

"I should have guessed from the badge."

"I saw a lot of them at one time when I had the flat near Ashton Gate."

"You did well, loosening him up. By the end, he was almost volunteering things, but I wouldn't risk him in the witness box."

"What is it with the Larry Lincoln stuff?" Halliwell said. "Do you really think a sad old gambler like Cyril was expecting a visit from the likes of Lincoln?"

"My guess is that it was scare tactics."

"From whoever he was owing money to?"

"Right, Lincoln's reputation as an enforcer is enough to make anyone stump up."

"He must have told Jessie. She swallowed it."

"We need to trace her," Diamond said. "I wonder if she came from an agency. Is that how housekeepers find jobs?"

"They call them carers these days, guv."

"Housekeeper is how it was put to me," he said with irritation. "If you want to call her a carer, fine."

"I'm only saying the agency would be a care agency."

"As you're so well informed, get on to it, would you? All the local care agencies. She could be our key witness."

"Do we know her surname?"

"Oh Christ."

"No problem."

"Don't mess with me," Diamond said, at the limit of his patience. "I've had it up to here with no problems."

"I'm telling you I'll go at it the other way, like I did with the taxi companies — give them Cyril Hardstaff's name and ask if he was their client."

"Fine." He felt a twinge of conscience for snapping at his deputy. "If I didn't know better, I'd call you a genius."

Back in his office Diamond's mood improved on finding that Miss Hill had sent through the valuation photos he'd requested of the missing jewellery. He spread the sheets across the floor.

Twenty grand's worth of bling. Had Cyril swiped the lot or had Pellegrini taken some, along with the gowns?

He unlocked his desk drawer and took out the serpent necklace and compared it with one of the pictures.

No argument. It matched.

Any uncertainty over motive stopped here. Olga's collection of jewellery and antiques had been there for the taking after she died. Dozy old Max wasn't capable of managing it. The vultures had swooped — or at least one vulture had.

For Diamond, this should have been decision time. He had enough information to go public and order a full-scale investigation into the theft. The question whether murders had also been committed would follow on as part of the operation. He'd be able to use the full resources of CID and forensics.

But there was a catch.

He was sure to be asked about the source of his intelligence. Entering and searching a building without a warrant and seizing property was a no-no. He'd gone in twice and taken Ingeborg with him the second time to obtain the computer data, all based on suspicion he couldn't yet substantiate.

Imagine what Dragham and Stretch would make of his conduct.

Then there was the added pressure of Pellegrini being comatose and on the brink of death. Anyone with compassion was going to be sympathetic. Labelling a helpless man a killer was high risk.

Even Halliwell had doubts. *"Are we clinging to the idea of murder on not much evidence?"*

The only strategy open to Diamond was to prove beyond doubt that his suspicion was right and murder had been committed.

But how?

It was just that: suspicion.

For the first time he feared that the murder case was unravelling.

16

One thing Diamond had learned in life was not to feel sorry for himself. Rage against the gods by all means, but don't have anything to do with self-pity. It's toxic. His back was sore, he hated the new office, the IPCC people were on the prowl and his own deputy was losing confidence in him, but would he let it drag him down?

He was too busy for that.

The funeral bash — as he thought of it — in Cavendish Crescent in May 2014 had become a pivotal event in this case. Max's cleaner, Mrs. Stratford, had talked of mayhem and insanity when the mourners were given the green light to help themselves to the railway items. Some exaggeration, there. Coffee had been spilt, Jessie's skirt stained. But it had created a distraction. Maybe an opportunity for Cyril — who wasn't interested in railways — to go looking for more valuable items.

Miss Hill, the solicitor, had presided over the funeral.

He called her on her direct line.

"Thanks for the valuation photos. You've been a splendid help already."

"What do you mean — already?" she said. "I do have other matters to attend to."

"And I won't delay you long. You made the arrangements for Massimo Filiput's funeral, you told me."

"He had no family. We have a duty of care for our clients, even after death."

"Admirable — and I understand you attended in person, not just the funeral but the reception afterwards."

"How do you know that?"

"I spoke to someone who was there, his home help, Mrs. Stratford."

The name worked like a bunch of flowers. "A bright young woman. She gave me considerable assistance before and after the funeral. She knew where things were in the house."

"Did she help you contact people?"

"She found his address book. I sent the details to just about everyone in it, but only a handful turned up, mostly elderly men."

"The railway enthusiasts. This is what I was coming to. I'd like to meet them, those who are still alive."

"You might be disappointed. They don't have much conversation apart from steam trains."

"I'm prepared for that."

"This may be unkind, but I believe the only reason most of them came was to find out what would happen to his collection. I said I needed to dispose of a stack of worthless posters and magazines and they cleared the lot like locusts."

"One of the mourners — Cyril Hardstaff — wasn't part of that lot."

"Yes, an old teaching colleague from Wiltshire College. Much more balanced. He spoke so warmly on the phone of Mr. Filiput that I invited him to give the eulogy and I'm glad I did. He was excellent. You should meet him."

"Too late," Diamond said. "He died suddenly six weeks ago."

"Oh my word. I'm sorry to hear that."

"I wanted to check with you whether Mr. Filiput made any provision in his will for Cyril."

"No. Everything was put up for sale and the entire proceeds went to the railway museum. I thought I told you this."

"I needed to be certain. Between ourselves, Miss Hill, I was at Cyril's cottage yesterday and I gave some assistance to his niece, who was clearing the place. We found a gold necklace that formerly belonged to Olga Filiput, the serpent necklace from those probate pictures I requested from you."

He heard a sharp intake of breath.

"That's difficult to believe."

"I'm sorry. I promise you it's true. It was in a velvet bag, hidden in a mattress. I suspect he stole it. I'm telling you this in confidence because I know I can rely on you."

"I took him for a gentleman, an absolute gentleman."

"Also a compulsive gambler under pressure to repay large debts. You wouldn't know about that."

"Oh my word." An expression that in Miss Hill's scale of shocks wasn't far short of a major earthquake.

"If he saw something as valuable as the necklace, the temptation would be too much."

"This is so unexpected."

"Yes. Do you know where the jewel collection was kept?"

"Upstairs in the bedroom that was originally Olga's."

"In a safe?"

"In an antique tallboy."

"With locking drawers?"

"No."

"Could Cyril have gone up there while the reception was in full swing?"

"There was nothing to stop him or anyone else. I didn't think security was necessary at a post-funeral gathering."

"He may have sneaked out while the railway people were scrambling for the posters."

"Mr. Diamond, this is so unlikely. He was the most charming man you could wish to meet."

"I heard exactly those words from two other ladies."

"Is it possible Max made him a present of the necklace while he was still alive?"

"A generous thought," he said, "but why should he? I wouldn't give away items that belonged to my late wife. Handing them to another man you play Scrabble with? It's unlikely."

She was still grappling with what he'd told her. "Are you suggesting he stole the other pieces of jewellery as well?"

"Very likely. He may not have taken everything at once. Remember he was a regular visitor, and even Max had a vague idea that things were missing."

"But how could anyone give such a wonderful eulogy in the knowledge that he'd behaved as badly as that?"

"There's an old saying: debtors are liars."

"Oh dear, you make it sound all too possible. We'll need to inform the sole legatee, the railway museum."

"Not yet," he said quickly. "Not while we're still investigating. We'll see what else we can recover."

"There are legal issues, now I think about it."

"Take your time over the fine points of law, Miss Hill. The museum can afford to wait. And there is another favour I must ask."

"What's that?" Her voice was an octave higher.

"Just a formality. I need the names and contact details of everyone who attended the funeral."

"I can see to that. But you will be discreet?"

"Never more so. This is strictly *sub judice* as far as I'm concerned. It's all conjecture, isn't it?"

The official work of CID demanded his attention for the rest of the morning. John Leaman had been interviewing the church-roof robbers and now wanted to extend the enquiry by pulling in the scrap-metal merchant they did business with. Paul Gilbert was dealing with a poison-pen case, local councillors complaining about obscene letters. Both Leaman and Gilbert made clear in their different ways that they were feeling sidelined. He'd never been one for nurse-maiding his team, but they had a point. His priorities were elsewhere and it was all too obvious. He sat down with them both and forced himself to show more interest.

By lunchtime, Halliwell had the glazed expression of an election teller after an all-night count.

"No success with the care agencies?" Diamond said.

"Do you know how many there are, because I don't and I'm only up to the letter C. Comfort Care, Candlelight, Calm and Caring, Care Matters, Call Us, Clearway, Coming to You, Come What May, Cat's Whiskers —"

"Is that a care home? Sounds more like a cattery."

"I don't know. I don't know anything. I'm in need of care myself."

"Let's get lunch."

Ingeborg had phoned in and made her

peace with Diamond. She was working from home.

"Unlike her," Halliwell said. "She likes the buzz of the office."

"She's still hoping to find something from Pellegrini's computer," Diamond told him. "She can concentrate better."

"I would have given up by now."

"You're not a quitter, Keith. I have every confidence you'll reach D for Day Care before you draw your pension."

They were in the Lock Keeper, one of the two Keynsham pubs they'd decided was worth the short drive. In the summer, the beer garden overlooking the Avon would be good, but today in a north wind and with sleet pinging against the windows, everyone was inside except a couple of desperate smokers.

Diamond picked up the previous conversation while waiting for his burger and chips. "The good thing about modern technology is that you can do more than one thing at a time."

"Such as?" Halliwell asked, frowning. He'd known his boss long enough to suspect something lay behind the statement.

"Your research into care agencies. You can do it on a laptop anywhere you like."

"If you have wifi."

"This afternoon you'll be joining me on a mission to Frome. Nothing to stop you using the laptop in idle moments."

"Frome? What for?"

"Miss Hill sent me the guest list for Max's funeral. There are two members of the GWR group we haven't caught up with — the only two who aren't dead or brain dead. Jake and Simon Pool."

"Brothers?"

"No. They're married and they live in a signal box."

The driving rain and sleet kept the wipers working at double speed most of the way down the A30 and Diamond was repeatedly telling Halliwell to slow down.

"Do you know where this signal box is?"

"Beside the railway."

"I can work that out for myself," Halliwell said, under stress. "Which side of the town?"

"I phoned ahead to find out."

"So do I head left or right?"

"It's not simple. I was given a potted history. Originally there were four boxes. It was a busy junction, with trains serving the Somerset coalfield as well as the passenger routes. This one is known as Frome Middle."

"Yes, guv, but where is it?"

"We'd better ask at the station."

No one at the station seemed to have heard of the place, but when Diamond mentioned it was in use as a house occupied by a gay couple, everyone knew. It was a reconstructed signal box a mile out of town.

They found it without more difficulty along a stretch of disused track, a smart, two-storey building with red bricks to halfway and a wooden superstructure painted in the chocolate and cream colours of the GWR, all topped with a pitched, tiled roof and chimney. The name was displayed in brown lettering. Above this, a long row of brave, buffeted daffodils in window boxes made a stirring sight on this dismal day. End-to-end windows upstairs are a necessary feature of a signal box home.

The small garden had more daffodils and some late snowdrops. Railway sleepers had been used to make the raised flowerbeds.

Halliwell parked beside a Toyota on the gravel.

The door at ground level didn't look like the official entrance, so they went up the stairs and were greeted by an open door and a booming, "Come in, whoever you are. Heard you coming."

A large man, rather too large for a signal-box existence, showed them inside. Prob-

363

ably not much older than Diamond, he was positively youthful by comparison with the rest of Pellegrini's friends. He was in a T-shirt, jeans and carpet slippers. The room was invitingly warm. "I'm Jake Pool and my other half, Simon, is downstairs making tea. You *are* the police, I take it?"

Diamond explained who they were. "I expect everyone asks you: did you build this yourselves?"

"Yes, it's a cheat, I'm afraid, only a replica. The 1875 building was demolished in 1933 when they made major changes and opened a new line between the junctions at Clink Road and Blatchbridge so that the expresses and much of the goods traffic could bypass dear old Frome Station. If you want to see a genuine version, go to Didcot Railway Centre. In 1983, when we were rather more spry than we are now, we helped remove the box at Frome Mineral Junction and rebuild it there with the original materials. And already I see your eyes glazing over, so I'll spare you further suffering."

Difficult to follow up a remark like that. "I don't know about you," Diamond said to Halliwell for politeness's sake, "but I've never been in a signal box before."

"It's an experience," Halliwell said.

"We're juvenile enough to like it," Jake

364

Pool said. "Everything you see in here except the sofa beds is ex-railway. We didn't have room for the signalling equipment, more's the pity. The kitchen, shower and loo are downstairs, which originally would have housed the interlocking mechanism, the signal-wire wheels and the point-drive cranks. Speaking of cranks, I've been called one myself for going on about railway engineering. I'd better shut up. Please take a seat on the first-class upholstery from the Cornish Riviera express."

"There's someone at the door."

"That'll be Simon with the tea. We keep saying we should have built interior stairs. It's no fun having to go outside in weather like this. Would you mind letting him in?"

Halliwell opened the door to a small windswept man holding a tray of tea things.

"Has he been boring you?" Simon asked. "Relief is at hand." He set the tray on a polished table that was probably from some Pullman dining car. Neither visitor enquired.

"The crockery is genuine GWR from the 1940s," Jake said, "now becoming rare."

"But the tea is Lipton's English Breakfast," Simon said. "I'm not sure which brand they used on trains in those days. And the scones aren't 1940s either. I made them

365

myself this morning. I must have had a premonition we'd have visitors."

"Or that the law would catch up with us eventually," Jake said with a grin. "Do make yourselves comfortable, gentlemen."

Cream tea in a signal box. Policing is never predictable.

"You must have heard about Ivor Pellegrini's accident," Diamond said when the cups were filled. "We're following up. He's still in a coma unfortunately, so he can't tell us what he was doing out so early on his tricycle."

"Poor fellow, yes," Jake said. "We were shocked when we heard. Our little branch of the Great Western Society has suffered terribly over the past two years."

"We're the only members still standing," Simon added. "There were seven of us at one stage. I know we're getting on in years, but four deaths and an accident is a bad run, to say the least."

"You meet in each other's houses and discuss the great days of steam, we were told."

"And there's the occasional excursion. It's as harmless as the girl guides. I can't think why the gods decided to inflict such losses on us."

"The deaths were natural, weren't they?"

"Yes, but so many. The latest was only last May."

"Max Filiput?"

"I can see him sitting in that chair where you are now, a grand old boy, over ninety," Jake said. "He looked forward to coming here when it was our turn to host the meeting. It was the experience he came for."

"And my sausage rolls," Simon said.

"You went to his funeral," Diamond prompted them.

"As fine a send-off as I can remember. Good hymns, nice music and the man who gave the eulogy really had done his homework and yet managed to work in some amusing asides. He wasn't a railway buff either."

"He and Max once taught together at that big college in Salisbury," Jake said.

"I know who you mean. His name was Cyril," Diamond said. "Cyril Hardstaff. I learned this week that he, too, has died."

They almost dropped their precious teacups.

"I find that incredible," Jake said.

"Extraordinary," Simon said.

Jake shook his head. "He was in sparkling form at the funeral, regaling us all with his stories. Witty, fully in command, unlike poor old Max."

"You can't be witty from inside a coffin," Simon said.

"That isn't what I meant. Max was definitely losing it towards the end."

"But he still hosted the meetings. I wouldn't call him senile, just absent-minded at times, and that's understandable at the end of a long life. Do you want more cream on that scone, officer?"

"It is rather good." Diamond scooped up some more. "Getting back to the funeral, I believe the solicitor, Miss Hill, made some kind of announcement when you all went back to the house."

"She indicated, without precisely saying so, that no one present stood to benefit from Max's will and it later emerged that he'd left everything to the National Railway Museum."

"Is that Didcot?"

"No, York. And then she told us there was a stack of paper items of no great value that Max had stipulated could be shared among his railway chums. We were welcome to help ourselves to any of them if we desired. *If we desired?* When you issue an invitation like that to a group of fanatics like us, you'd better stand back. The next half-hour was not dignified."

"Did you find anything?" Halliwell asked.

"Several fascinating items."

"And who was involved?" Diamond asked. "Both of you, obviously, and Ivor Pellegrini. Was he in the thick of it?"

"Naturally," Jake said. "Ivor is as keen as we are. He was so eager that he elbowed some lady and tipped coffee over her skirt. I'm sure he made an apology, but he wasn't distracted for long."

"If you were sifting through the papers, I don't suppose you noticed what the others were up to — the people who weren't collectors."

Simon laughed. "It's just a blur."

"You can't tell me if anyone left the room?"

"I can tell you two of the ladies went off to the kitchen to see what they could do about the coffee stain."

"I don't know why you're asking," Jake said. "Any of us could have slipped out and probably did. The bathroom is upstairs. We know, because we've been to the house often enough for our meetings."

"The meetings, yes," Diamond said, willing to shift direction. "And you've also been to Mr. Pellegrini's house?"

"That's the arrangement. We take it in turns."

"Where does he play host — in his work-shop?"

"Have you seen inside?" Simon asked.

Diamond didn't exactly tell a lie. "I can't say I have."

"We're green with envy."

"Was he the founder of your club?"

"It's not really a club," Jake said. "Just a gathering of like-minded people. We're an unofficial branch of the Great Western Society, not affiliated in the way some of the bigger branches are. We don't have the numbers."

"We were never enough to form a branch," Simon added.

"More like a twig," Jake said, "and a thin twig at that."

"Who started it?"

"We're an offshoot of the Bath Railway Society. That's how we met. They're interested in railways generally and some of us were looking for a more focused approach."

"Focused on the GWR?"

"We're anoraks and proud of it," Simon said. "Jake and I first met as teenagers collecting train numbers on Paddington Station. Did you know that the term 'anoraks' was first used about train-spotters? The anorak is the perfect garment for standing on the most exposed bits of draughty sta-

370

tion platforms, your large pockets filled with notebooks, your ABC of locomotives and, of course, your sandwiches. So that's us, glad to be gay, ardent to be anoraks."

Jake smiled. "But the rest of the world thinks we're barmy."

"Not by my reckoning." Diamond was trying to find a way of asking about the cremation urns without revealing that he'd seen them himself. "Mind you, we had our doubts about your friend Ivor."

"Why was that?" Jake said. "He's the sane one. You don't want to be put off by the clothes he wears."

"It wasn't the clothes. It was a remark he made about hops when he was stopped by a police car."

"HOPS — the electrification project?"

"We didn't know that at the time."

"He was probably on his way to watch them at work with their special factory train."

"That wasn't the only strange thing he said. He had a plastic pot in his saddlebag that he claimed contained the ashes of his late wife, Trixie."

"Is that so?" Jake's attention switched to Simon. "Have you topped up the teapot?"

A clear attempt to get over an awkward moment.

Diamond didn't hold back this time. "To cut to the chase, gentlemen, we've done our research. His wife wasn't cremated. She was buried. The urn must have contained the ashes of someone else. Your friend Ivor was on his way to scatter them secretly somewhere along the railway."

Neither of their hosts said anything.

"It's not a criminal offence," Diamond added, "but Network Rail wouldn't look kindly on it. Was such a thing ever discussed at your meetings?"

"I'd better boil some more water downstairs," Simon said.

"No you don't," Diamond said, gesturing to him to sit down. "I want an answer from you."

"About the scattering of ashes?" Simon said, as if he hadn't understood. He turned to Jake. "Do you have any memory of this?"

"We're not the transport police," Diamond said. "No one's in trouble. I'm only trying to confirm what Ivor was doing that night."

Jake had been staring into his cup as if he wished he could dive in. Now he looked up. "There is an understanding between us that when our time comes and we are cremated, someone will unite our remains with the railway we love. Up to now, this service has been performed by Ivor. I expect the ashes

372

were those of Max. While HOPS is in progress it's not unreasonable for a railway enthusiast to be out and about at night."

"Ivor did the same for the three who died previously?"

"He did."

"That's what I wanted to know. It's clear you put a lot of trust in him."

"He's a great guy, the mainstay of the group. This accident is catastrophic."

"I'm getting the picture of a group of people sharing an interest so strongly that you thought nothing of inviting them all to your homes. It's all very cosy. But in any group there are going to be differences of opinion, misunderstandings, even the occasional flare-up. I don't suppose your lot were any different."

"What are you getting at now?" Jake asked.

"You spoke about Max losing it towards the end. He had some fine antiques and jewellery in that house in Cavendish Crescent. Was there ever any talk of things disappearing?"

"Hold on a minute," Jake said, colouring noticeably. "Don't get me wrong. Losing his concentration, not his property."

"Some items did go missing," Diamond said.

"Railway items?"

"Pieces of his late wife's collection of antiques and jewellery."

Jake swung to Simon in surprise. "Did you ever hear him speak of this while we were there?"

Simon shook his head. "I'm appalled if it's true."

"I'm afraid it is," Diamond said, "and Max was troubled enough to mention it to his doctor."

"Did he suspect any of us?"

"He didn't name anyone."

"And are you suggesting things were taken at the funeral?"

"It was the last opportunity the thief would have."

"But there were other people present. Neighbours, his cleaning lady, the solicitor."

"His old friend Cyril," Jake said. "And the woman who came with him. Don't just point the finger at us railway buffs. If we wanted to steal anything, it wouldn't be jewellery. It would be a locomotive nameplate."

Diamond believed him.

17

"Why exactly am I doing this?" Keith Halli-well asked nobody in particular towards the end of the day. He hadn't struck gold with any of the local care agencies. He hadn't struck anything at all, but he soon would, the way he felt. He was still trying to trace Jessie the housekeeper, giving Cyril's name and address, and getting more frustrated with each call.

Then he spoke to someone who put yet another doubt in his head. "The person you're looking for may not have gone through an agency. She could have been freelance."

He stepped into Diamond's office.

"Guv, I'm wondering if there's an easier way."

"What's that?"

"Going back to the village and knocking on doors."

"You're serious?"

"All the hours I've spent on this already, I could have driven to Little Langford and back several times over. Cyril was an outgoing guy. The locals must have known him and they probably knew Jessie as well."

Diamond saw the sense in what his deputy was saying. He, too, doubted whether it was worth spreading the net any wider. Local knowledge might be the key. "You'll be on your own, I'm afraid. When will you go — tomorrow morning?"

"That's my plan."

"Right. Get the local map on your screen," he said, to demonstrate his computer know-how. "I'll show you where the cottage is."

Halliwell grinned. "No need. I can use the satnav."

"Okay — be like that."

"If I see Cyril's niece Hilary is it any use asking her?"

Diamond shook his head. "She's not local and she doesn't know Jessie's surname. Talk to her by all means, but take my advice and don't offer to move the furniture."

That evening, Paloma came to the house and gave him a back massage.

"You may need to see a chiropractor," she said.

"I don't hold with that sort of thing."

"You don't have to do the holding. They hold you. It's your spine that's hurting, isn't it? That's their speciality. What I'm doing is superficial. It has no lasting effect."

"Wrong. I'm feeling better by the second."

"Until you try and sit up. What have you got against chiropractors? Don't tell me you'd rather suffer than get help."

"The body cures itself eventually."

"Why ask me for a massage, then?"

"That's different. You take away all the stresses of the day. Magic hands. Shall I turn over now?"

"I'm working on your lower back. If you're looking for some other kind of massage, go to someone else and pay for it." Her tone softened. "Are you really under stress?"

"Remember the Fortuny gown?"

"How could I forget? *That's* my idea of magic. Have you solved the mystery yet?"

"I thought I had."

"But something isn't right? Hence the stress?"

"You've got it. I'm struggling. Most of my theories are falling apart. I realise I've done too much theorising and not enough solid detective work. But it's like no case I've ever worked on. For one thing it's unofficial. Keith and Ingeborg are helping, but no one else knows what's going on. And the main

377

suspect is on life support and there's a shortage of witnesses."

"Can't you make it official?"

"Georgina would go spare. The Independent Police Complaints Commission are with us trying to work out whether Pellegrini — he's my suspect — was injured through a driver error or some other mistake on our part. He's painted as the victim, you see."

"If he's as badly injured as you say, he *is* a victim."

"Yes and deserving of all our sympathy — which makes me a right shit for even thinking he's a killer."

"I wouldn't call you that."

"Plenty of others would. I can't possibly go public."

"I can see the difficulty. And you say there are problems with your original theory?"

"Large holes."

"Do you want to tell me — strictly in confidence?"

He hesitated. He'd often discussed cases with his late wife, Steph, and she'd sometimes pointed him in a fresh direction that made all the difference. By mutual consent, his relationship with Paloma was not so close, leaving space for them to lead independent lives. It came down to trust. She'd already helped with her expert advice about the Fortuny gowns. She'd said "strictly in confidence" — volunteered it — and he believed she meant it.

"It would help to go back to what I know for sure. Thanks to you, I know where the three gowns came from."

"The house in Cavendish Crescent?"

"Right. And of course I know where they ended up."

"In your suspect's workshop? You told me that much."

"Did I tell you what else I found in that workshop?"

"More garments?" Her fingertips pressed into his flesh at the thought.

"A printout from some online forum on the subject of murder methods." He felt her interest lessen. "All sorts of so-called clever ways of committing the perfect murder. I wouldn't have thought much of it, but people around him were dying, too many to be normal. On the face of it they were natural deaths, none of them queried by the coroner. Four elderly men he knew because they shared his interest in railways, his own wife and the wife of one of the others — who originally owned the Fortuny gowns. And since then, I've learned of yet another. This was a man who used to visit Cavendish Crescent to play Scrabble. That's seven in a little over two years."

"That's a lot, I agree."

"Too many. But the death certificates tell a different story. One dies of flu, another of an aneurysm, pneumonia, narrowing of the arteries, one has a fall. There's no pattern. Finding this out has rocked my confidence. Some of them may be innocent deaths. All of them, even. They're all old people anyway."

"You're not convinced?"

"He's an engineer by training, a clever man. Has he worked out his own way of fooling everyone?"

"Why? Why would he want to kill all these people?"

"I've thought long and hard about motive. The theft of the gowns suggests murder for gain, but what did he plan to do with the gowns? Sell them on? I don't think so."

"Neither do I," Paloma said. "They're works of art, like a Rembrandt or a Van Gogh. Put them on sale and keenos like me will want to know their provenance."

"Just what I'm thinking. Anyway, he's not short of money. I suspect they're trophies, proof of his success. He gets his kicks from killing in some brilliant way he thinks is undetectable. When each death is registered as different from any of the others he's not going to get found out."

"What about the doctors?" she asked.

"What do you mean?"

"The doctors named on the death certificates. Is one medic signing them all, by any chance?"

"Good thinking," he said. "But no, each one is different."

Paloma was using some kind of oil. She poured more into the palm of her hand. "If this is killing for the sense of achievement, I don't understand why he takes the risk of stealing things as well. That's not smart."

"He's a collector. I don't know if I told you his workshop is filled with bits of railway junk that he's acquired over the years. That's his hobby — although I'd call it a compulsion really."

"And you think he's collecting murders?"

"Possibly. And for each successful killing he keeps a trophy of some kind. It started with cremation urns. He has three of them lined up on a shelf. They're decorated with pictures of steam engines and the names of the victims."

"It sounds more like a shrine than a trophy shelf. How did he acquire the pots?"

"I'm not telling it right. His railway club had an arrangement that when each one

died his ashes would be scattered somewhere along the track. My suspect took on
the job and that's how he finished up with
the empty pots."

"Doesn't necessarily mean he murdered
them, does it?"

"You're right," he said. "Keith Halliwell
agrees with you. I've got doubts myself since
we discovered they were signed off as dying
naturally and from all these different causes.
Have I constructed a murder theory out of
nothing? But there's another twist."

"What's that?"

"The latest death."

"The Scrabble player?"

"Yes. Cyril isn't from Bath. He lived in a
village near Salisbury and his body was
found there six weeks ago. Died in his
sleep . . . apparently. He was over ninety,
but a lively ninety. He gave a very good
tribute speech at Filiput's funeral last year.
I drove to his cottage the day before yesterday expecting to meet him. Instead I met
his niece, who was clearing the rooms.
That's how I did my back, trying to give
her a hand."

"And root out more information, no
doubt."

"Well, yes. What I got was several shocks.
This charming old man had been a compul-

sive gambler, deep in debt. And a thief. We found an antique necklace hidden in a mattress and I've since confirmed it was one of a number of pieces of jewellery stolen from Filiput's house. Originally they belonged to Olga, the owner of the Fortuny gowns."

"This Cyril was stealing to fund his gambling?"

"Or to pay off debts. Some very unpleasant people were asking him to settle."

"Poor old man. He must have been desperate. At his age, pressure like that would be enough to bring on a heart attack."

Diamond tried turning his head to see if she was teasing, but he couldn't twist enough to tell. "Maybe."

"You didn't say that with any conviction. Is there something else I should be told?"

"Only this: shortly before his death, Cyril had a visitor. Pellegrini took a taxi all the way from Bath, stayed under half an hour and left without saying much at all."

"No," she said, making the short word long by rolling it in her throat before adding, "You're not serious?"

"It's true."

"How do you know this?"

"You've got to appreciate that I'm out to nail this man. I figured that if he murdered Cyril, he must have needed transport. We traced the driver who made a trip from Bath to Little Langford that night."

"Top marks. Did Pellegrini give his name and address?"

"He's too smart for that. He picked a cab from the rank at Orange Grove outside the Abbey rather than having it fetch him from his house. At the end of the evening, he asked to be put down in the same place and he paid in cash. He has an account with one of the big taxi fleets but that night he didn't use them."

"How can you be sure this man was Pellegrini?"

"The driver picked him out from a group photo."

Silence filled the next few seconds while Paloma continued to work on his back, weighing the significance of all he'd told her. "You've got a strong case. Are you suggesting this was the night Cyril died?"

"It was. We confirmed it."

"This is your smoking gun, Peter."

"Not quite. There are problems with it. While the driver was waiting outside the cottage, another car drove up and a woman got out: Jessie, the housekeeper."

"Cyril had a housekeeper?" she said with surprise. "How could he afford her?"

"Thanks to his late wife, Winnie. She was

384

a smart lady with a secretarial business in London worth millions. When she made her will she set up a trust and one of its provisions was a salary for a housekeeper for the rest of Cyril's life. She must have known he was hopeless with money."

"Enter Jessie."

"She wasn't the first. She was the latest in a long line of carers. She lived in and did her best to look after him — the shopping and the cooking, driving him about and so forth."

"And trying to discourage the gambling? Tough call."

"It would be."

"You said she returned to the cottage while Pellegrini was inside with Cyril?"

"That's my first problem. If Pellegrini was there to murder Cyril, Jessie walked straight in on them."

"Could he have murdered them both?"

"No chance. She was a reasonably fit, middle-aged woman. Besides, the only corpse found in the cottage was Cyril's. And there's the question of her car. If she was dead, it would have remained outside."

"Did Pellegrini know of Jessie's existence?"

"Certainly. They met at the funeral."

"So if he made that trip to Little Langford with the purpose of putting an end to Cyril's life, he must have factored in Jessie?"

"I'm sure of it. He's a meticulous planner. He may have spoken to Cyril on the phone and said he wanted to see him alone. Jessie went out but returned early."

"You need to interview this woman."

"Problem two," he said. "Jessie has vanished. She hasn't been seen since Cyril died."

"When you say 'vanished' . . . ?"

"I'm being melodramatic. We haven't been able to trace her."

"Have you made a TV appeal?"

"I can't. It's not an official investigation. It's just Ingeborg, Keith and me working our butts off."

"From what I can see from here," Paloma said, "you don't have to worry about that."

"Cruel!"

"But you do need to find Jessie."

"Tell me about it. Keith spent most of today phoning round the care agencies. First thing tomorrow he's off to Little Langford to question the neighbours."

"This is a mystery in itself," she said. "What do you think happened inside the cottage when she walked in?"

"Nothing dramatic. Cyril was still alive. He died later in bed, apparently of a heart attack. This was the MO — the modus operandi. Each of the victims dies in bed. My best guess is that Pellegrini used some form of drug with a delayed reaction of an hour or so. The two old men had a drink together. Have you heard of a Mickey Finn?"

"Some kind of knock-out pill?"

"A century ago when the term was invented they used chloral hydrate, but there are modern sleepers that are more effective and more lethal. Temazepam is the best known. After half an hour or so he'd feel drowsy and if he was given enough he wouldn't wake up."

"Wouldn't it show in the blood?"

"Who's going to order a postmortem? These are elderly people dying in their sleep. This is my current thinking, anyway. To come back to what happened, Cyril has his doctored drink and is ready for bed when Jessie comes in. Pellegrini helps rinse the glasses and leaves. Next morning Cyril doesn't get up."

"You make it sound terrifyingly simple."

"The clever murders are."

"So Pellegrini got into his taxi and left them to it?"

"Job done."

The skin she had massaged was glowing

387

pleasantly. He was getting drowsy himself. Paloma covered him with a quilt and went to wash her hands.

He wasn't sure how much time had gone by when he heard her making coffee.

"Any improvement?" she asked when she arrived with the tray.

"Vast."

"Don't sit up suddenly. Easy does it."

When he was propped against the pillows, she said, "Your Mickey Finn theory is persuasive but there's one thing you didn't explain."

"What's that?"

"Why he did it."

He added sugar to his coffee. "The best I can think of is this: Cyril and Pellegrini were both taking advantage of their mutual friend Max, stealing valuable items from the house. And I know from Max's doctor that the old man had some suspicion this was going on. He was becoming confused towards the end of his life and he may have thought he'd put things away in places he'd forgotten, but it worried him enough to speak to the doctor. Are you with me?"

Paloma nodded.

"Now Cyril was his oldest friend and they spent afternoons together playing Scrabble. It's not unlikely that Max confided the same

388

worries to Cyril, not realising he was talking to one of the thieves. And he may have gone so far as to say the Fortuny gowns weren't stored in the place he remembered putting them and he wondered if someone had taken them. Cyril would surely ask who he suspected and Max would say it was one of his railway friends called Ivor."

"I can see where this is going," Paloma said. "Cyril would seize on the chance of blackmail. He meets Pellegrini at the funeral and decides he'll put the screws on him — not realising he's dealing with a killer."

Not for the first time, Diamond was impressed by her clarity of thought. "The events dovetail neatly. The funeral marks the end of Cyril's stealing. Everything is taken over by the executors, listed and locked away. One steady source of income has dried up, but blackmailing Pellegrini is a new opportunity."

"Wicked old man."

"It didn't help him, did it? He was up against a master criminal."

"I don't know why you're so uneasy about it all," she said. "You seem to have it buttoned up."

He shook his head. "None of this will stand up in court. I need evidence and witnesses."

"You've got the gown."

"I returned it to the workshop."

"Well, you know where it is. You can go there any time. Have you still got the stolen necklace?"

"I have, but it incriminates Cyril, not Pellegrini. And Cyril is dead."

"What about the printout from the workshop — the murder forum? You have that still?"

"I do. But it proves nothing, except an interest in criminology, as any lawyer would point out in court."

"A morbid interest."

"Plenty of people like to read about such things."

"I know," she said. "I've looked along your bookshelves. But you're a professional. You need to know about this stuff. A retired engineer doesn't."

"You can't convict on people's interests," he said. "Pellegrini is no more culpable than all the people who contributed to the forum. Less so, if he simply reads the stuff and doesn't join in. We can't even prove it was downloaded to his computer."

"When he comes out of the coma, he'll have plenty of questions to answer."

"*If* he comes out of the coma."

"That's defeatist talk I don't expect to

hear from you, Peter Diamond."

His mobile phone rang. He'd left it in the hall by the front door.

"Do you want me to get it?" Paloma asked.

"Don't bother. It'll be some cold call."

"Do you get them this late? I don't."

"Not usually, but I've known it to happen."

"Could be an urgent call from the police."

"Yes, and I could be out walking the dog."

"You don't have a dog."

"The neighbour's dog, then. If it's important, they'll try again."

The ringing stopped.

"Where were we?" Paloma asked.

"Defeatist talk."

"Yes, you were saying Pellegrini might never come out of the coma, but even if that's the case, the truth about his crimes needs exposing."

"Sorry to disillusion you," he said, "but we drop the investigation when there's no one to prosecute."

She frowned. "You mean they're the winners if they die first?"

"In a sense they are. We can't collar Cyril for stealing the jewellery. He gets away with it. All we do is make a note on file that he was the main suspect."

"And what if he was the killer? Is that the end of all interest as far as the police are concerned?"

"Cyril the killer? That's a new angle."

"For argument's sake, I mean."

But Diamond was already running with this fresh idea. "He was desperate enough to kill. Bath's lowlife were issuing threats. But I can't see how it would help him to have Max dead. That's killing the goose that lays the golden eggs."

"I wasn't serious."

"I am. We can't rule out anything. Let's not forget Max was getting suspicious about the jewellery disappearing. How do we know he didn't confront Cyril and accuse him of being the thief?"

"Max died in bed," Paloma said.

"I'm not suggesting they came to blows. It's the same MO, some slow-acting knock-out drug. Cyril was on Temazepam for his insomnia. He was already out of his mind with worry about Larry Lincoln demanding payment."

Seeing it now, she took over. "To cap it all, Max — pathetic old scatterbrain that he is — works out what's happening and threatens to blow the whistle on him. The thieving has to stop."

"Exactly. What do you do with a goose

that stops laying? You kill it.'"

"So you're stymied," she said.

"Why?"

"If Cyril is the killer and he's dead there's no one to prosecute. Case closed."

The phone rang again, except this time it was the landline beside his bed. If this was the same caller, they had to be someone who knew him well.

"What time is it?"

"Almost ten," Paloma said. "You'd better pick it up."

"Guv?" The voice was Ingeborg's and she sounded excited. "Sorry to trouble you this late. I thought you might like to know I found something tonight on Pellegrini's hard disk."

"Great!"

"I've been checking his files all day. It's why I wasn't in. You got my message, I hope? I needed to work alone."

"What have you found, Inge?"

The words came in a torrent. "A file in a place where you wouldn't go looking for it, among the administrative tools. It's clearly been put there for a reason. It doesn't even have a name, just a number, and it's been stored among about ten others with numbers, but they must be a distraction for this one to hide among. They're mostly empty or have a jumble of letters and numbers that he's typed in at random."

"You're talking to a computer dummy, Inge."

"I'm trying to use simple language, guv."

"Just tell me what's on the file."

"I can't. It's encrypted."

"Great." This time he spoke the word ironically.

"But I can tell it's nothing like the extraneous stuff. There's something there for sure. Solid information that he's gone to a lot of trouble to hide using an encryption tool that employs algorithms."

"Can you decrypt it — if that's the word?"

"It's well beyond my level of competence but the data forensics unit could surely crack it."

He sighed. "I can't use police people, Inge. I'd have to explain what it was for and Georgina would be on my back straight away."

"That's a pain. Wouldn't one of them do it unofficially?"

"I don't know any of them well enough to ask a favour. They're not my choice of drinking companions. We soon run out of things to talk about. They might respond to you, the blokes, I mean. In fact, I'm certain they would."

Mistake.

"Don't start me off," she warned him. "You ought to know by now I'm not going down that route."

He felt the sting of her disapproval down the phone line.

Rapid rethink. "Before computers took over the world we used to have a young guy called Alex who dealt with the queries. This would have been before your time. He was red-hot, and he was at least nine parts human."

"Did he give up?"

"He was transferred to another station and I heard later he couldn't take any more, so he left."

"A personality clash?"

"The nature of the work. Not many last long as police geeks these days. They're forced to spend most of their time trawling through sickening footage of child porn, rape and every kind of extreme sexual behaviour and if they can't stand that they find themselves doing counter-terrorism — torture and beheadings. Alex jacked it in for some kind of job outside the police. Industrial espionage, I think. But I'm sure I can track him down and see if this interests him. He's discreet."

"He'll want a fee, no doubt."

"I'll deal with that. Bring in the box of tricks tomorrow and we can see if we get lucky."

Paloma had stepped out of the room while the call was going on. She returned wearing her jacket. "Was it a call worth taking?"

"It was. We could be on the verge of a breakthrough."

"Don't get carried away," she said. "Normal life goes on. I just opened a tin for Raffles. He was hungry."

"He was fooling you. He had his supper two hours ago. He'll get overweight."

"Look who's talking." She zipped up her jacket.

"Aren't you staying the night?" he asked.

"With a back patient? You're joking."

Today I'm rather pleased with myself. A situation has arisen giving me the chance to insure my secrets against discovery. It's the conjuror's trick of misdirection, simple, but effective. The nice thing is that I am uniquely placed to pull this off. I've baited the trap and we'll see if it works. No worry if it doesn't.

18

Eight-fifteen next morning found Diamond at the Guildhall in Bath High Street attending something he wouldn't normally have dreamed of going near, a gathering of geeks called the Techie Brekkie. He was on the trail of Alex, the one-time IT problem-solver for Bath Police. Early morning enquiries through a website called BathSpark had suggested this was where Alex was likely to be.

It was a good thing Ingeborg had come too. Mingling with this lot would be next to impossible for him. Aside from the fact that he was the only man in a suit and their average age was about twenty-five, he wasn't likely to hold up well in conversation. Plenty was going on, serious networking. This was a quarterly opportunity for computer slaves to emerge from behind their screens for a brief respite with fellow sufferers — the chance to meet real people. They had embraced it in numbers.

"Fancy a bacon butty?" Ingeborg said.

"Better not. I'll need to shake hands with Alex when I spot him."

"They won't do handshakes," she said. "High fives, more like."

"Not with a bacon butty."

"What does he look like?" she asked.

"Average height. Dark, shoulder-length hair in those days. This lot seem to shave their heads."

"The name badges might help." Everyone including themselves had a blue ID on a cord. Diamond's just said Pete. They'd asked if he belonged to an organisation and he thought Bath Police might be off-putting.

"We'd better move in and start looking," Ingeborg said. "They start their discussion soon."

"Jesus Christ, I want to be out before then."

Alex was one of the last to arrive and he spotted Diamond first. He'd changed his image, clipped the hair from the sides of his head and grown a mohawk on top. He was wearing shades. "I had to look twice," he said.

He had to look twice?

"No disrespect, Mr. Diamond, but I

wouldn't have placed you here in a million years."

All three slipped away from the brekkie through a door marked THE NEVER BORED ROOM. There wasn't much time for catching up on the last ten years or however long it had been. Alex soon understood why they'd come looking for him. He agreed straight away to see if he could help. He gave them a card with his contact details and Ingeborg passed him the "box of tricks," as Diamond had called it: a USB flash drive containing the encrypted file.

"We can't pay you anything up front," Diamond said.

Alex flashed his teeth. "So what's new?"

The aroma of bacon in the Techie Brekkie had got Diamond's juices going.

"A lot has happened since yesterday morning," he told Ingeborg. "We need to touch base."

The nearest base was Café Retro, on the corner of York Street. He ordered the Big Bath special, she the granola and yoghurt.

"Don't stand on ceremony," he said when hers arrived first. "Get stuck in."

There was plenty to tell. She hadn't even heard about Pellegrini's taxi ride to Little Langford on the evening of Cyril's death.

400

"That's the clincher, guv," she said. "Got to be."

She understood right away why it was so vital to speak to Jessie the housekeeper. "When she walked in he must have had the shock of his life. Do you think he murdered her as well?"

"No," he said. "She was there next morning. She found Cyril dead in bed and called the doctor."

"She's the only witness, then."

"Right. And she won't even know he was murdered."

"Can we be certain he was?"

"Why else did Pellegrini go there? It's like the other cases. An old man dies in his own bed and it gets put down as natural. My best guess is that they had a drink and he popped something in Cyril's glass."

"Poison?"

"Sleeping tablets of some sort."

"Would that be enough?"

"Mix them with alcohol and they can be lethal. Cyril would have gone to bed feeling drowsy and never woken up."

"But Jessie coming back early wasn't in the script." Ingeborg's hand went to her mouth. "Guv, I have a horrible feeling about this. How long ago was it? Six weeks?"

"More like seven now."

"Time enough for him to have caught up with her and killed her. Don't we have any idea where she went after Cyril's death?"

"Keith spent most of yesterday trying to trace her through the care agencies. Difficult, without a surname. We got nowhere."

"Maybe she got the job independently."

"Possibly. We haven't given up. He's at Little Langford knocking on doors as we speak." He paused as the Big Bath special was put in front of him. "This is what I call a breakfast."

"She'll have left the village, won't she?" Ingeborg said.

"I'm sure of that, but someone may be able to tell us more. Her surname or what she was planning to do next."

"Did she have a phone?"

"I expect so. But she took it with her."

"I'm thinking Cyril must have stored her number on his own phone."

"If he did, his niece Hilary slung it out with all the other junk. She was doing a house clearance, a wholesale clearance. Hilary is a force of nature, a whirlwind. The place was bare except for the heaviest furniture when I got there. The only personal item left was a plastic hairbrush we found under Jessie's bed. And I know what you're about to ask me."

"DNA?"

"There were a few blonde hairs caught in the bristles. I already sent the brush to be analysed. It must have been under that bed at least six weeks. I don't know how long DNA survives."

Ingeborg was better informed. "The best results come if the follicle is still attached. That's where the living cells are found. There's still a chance of getting mitochondrial DNA from the shaft of a hair."

"Dyed hair?"

"No difference."

"Anyway, the result isn't back yet."

"Let's be positive," she said.

"I'd rather have a name to work with. A DNA profile is bugger all use unless we can compare it with another."

"She could be on the national database."

"We're talking about a carer here, Inge. If Jessie had a criminal record she wouldn't be in the job."

"Got to be checked, though. It's vital that we trace her."

"No argument about that."

When Ingeborg drove back to Keynsham to catch up on her CID duties, Diamond remained in Bath. "If Georgina asks for me, tell her I'm having another look at the accident site," he'd told her.

"Is that what you're really up to?"

"It's what you tell Georgina, okay?"

Left alone, he made his way on foot to Green Park Station, a place no longer of interest to railway buffs except for its ironwork architecture. The last train was seen there half a century ago. The Beeching cuts brought quietus and for years the site was a soot-stained, decaying embarrassment. Regeneration came in 1982–4, courtesy of Sainsbury's, who built their supermarket, cleaned the entire Victorian terminus and installed shops, a car park and a farmers' market where the locomotives had once steamed in.

Diamond wasn't there for the railway history but to look up one of Bath's characters: the watercress man. Garth Ogle sold nothing but watercress and watercress products from a market stall. The cress came fresh in bunches or processed and packaged in a variety of forms, as soup, pesto, oil, sausages, ice cream, a range of cosmetics and even gin infused with the stuff. Some of the sausages were being cooked on a Primus and smelt good, but even a man of Diamond's capacity couldn't face one after the Big Bath special.

Few of Garth's ritzy customers knew what

Diamond knew: that the watercress man had once been a guest of Her Majesty and had drawn up his business plan in Erlestoke Prison while doing time for armed robbery. All credit to him for turning his life around. And even more for remaining loyal. Since going straight he had stayed in touch with his former associates.

Diamond caught Garth's eye over the head of a little old lady buying soup. There was a swift glance left and right to see if any other police were about. The customer said something about the scarcity of watercress soup in all the other shops and then it was Diamond's turn.

"Good to see you doing so well, Garth."

"It's ticking over, Mr. D." For brand identity, the watercress man dressed entirely in green, which happened to be no different from his last prison uniform. "What will you have today?"

"I might sample the ice cream, but I'd also like some help."

"Have you ever tried it?"

"Your help?"

"The ice cream. You'll like it."

"No, that's new to me. How much?"

"A small tub? To you, one fifty."

"I'll take one. And a small tub of help."

"That'll cost you more, depending what

405

you want."

"I want to find Larry Lincoln."

Garth's face creased as if he'd been struck. "You surprise me."

"Why?"

"No one goes looking for Larry. He comes looking for them."

"Where does he hang out these days?"

Garth indulged in some displacement activity, rearranging the day lotions and face cleansers.

"Larry Lincoln," Diamond said, to get his attention again.

"Keep your voice down, Mr. D. You never know who might be listening."

"Would you rather I talked about liver fluke disease and how you get it?"

"Oh Christ." Garth slid aside the glass lid of his small fridge and took out a tub. "All of mine is cultivated cress, guaranteed clean, not wild. He's not in trouble, is he? I wouldn't want him to get the idea I shopped him."

"It's a routine enquiry."

"Like you always say."

"The main man is someone else," Diamond said. "Larry is just a bit player. I wouldn't worry if I were you, but this may ease your mind." He placed two twenty-pound notes on the counter.

Garth eyed them as if they were liver fluke worms invading his stall.

"And here's another to pay for the ice cream."

Garth took it and picked up the others. "If I were you, I'd go for a drink in the Shot Fox about eleven."

Diamond nodded his thanks. "Do you by any chance have a plastic spoon to go with this?"

He took it to one of the benches in Kingsmead Square and decided he'd made a mistake. The soup would have been a better choice on this raw April morning. The bench was metal and was rapidly lowering his body temperature before he even started on the ice cream. He took out his mobile and pressed a number.

"Me."

Keith Halliwell's voice said, "I know it's you, guv. You came up on the display."

"Is this a good moment?"

"Good as any. I'm between houses."

"Anything to report?"

"It's freezing here."

"I know that."

"Some of the neighbours spoke to her occasionally, called her Jess or Jessie without finding out her full name. She'd been there over a year. She was just the latest in a long line of housekeepers. They didn't last long, most of them. The situation wasn't what they were used to, being so isolated, and Cyril was always on the scrounge. They liked him at first but it wore off when he asked for money; I suppose to fund his betting. He wasn't their paymaster, you see. Their wage was paid by the trust."

"Have you been to the cottage?"

"I had a look through the windows. It's empty now. Hilary must have finished. There are signs of a bonfire in the garden, just ashes."

"Not human, I hope."

The Shot Fox was a shabby pub in a side street off the Upper Bristol Road, near the river. Diamond had last been in there when it was called something else. To his knowledge it had changed names twice since then. The new identity might not last long. The board outside, with its image of a dead fox hanging from a wire by its rear legs, wasn't much of an invitation to go in.

Diamond thought at first he was the only living soul inside. He stood for some minutes before a youthful barman rose by stages behind the bar: head, shoulders, then full torso.

"Sorry, mate. I was down the cellar changing a keg. What'll you have?"

"Actually I'm working." He showed his warrant card. "Does Larry Lincoln come in at all these days?"

The barman tensed at the name and then said, "I wouldn't know."

"You mean you know but you wouldn't care to say."

"I do three days a week, that's all."

"I wasn't asking about your employment, but as you've brought it up I hope you're fully taxed and insured. What's your name?"

"Steve. I don't know every customer that comes in, that's all I'm saying."

"You said a lot more with your body language when I spoke Larry's name. It's obvious you know who he is, so stop wriggling and give me a straight answer. He drinks here lunchtimes, right?"

"Not every day," Steve — if that was his real name — said.

Diamond pulled out a stool and perched on it. "I'll wait for him. What bitters do you have? Draw me a half of Directors. And then I'll be watching you, just so you aren't tempted to use a phone."

The trail had better not go cold here. Cyril Hardstaff had become central to the crimes under investigation and if he was really being pursued by Larry Lincoln, his situation

409

had been desperate enough to fuel a major crime.

Steve the barman had filled the glass and taken the money and was a picture of unease, biting his thumbnail. When someone else came in, he twitched like a horse under attack from flies.

The newcomer wasn't Lincoln. He didn't buy a drink or say anything. He was carrying a metal case the size and shape of a rifle. Without as much as a glance, he crossed the bar, opened a door and was heard mounting a staircase.

"What's upstairs?" Diamond asked.

"Function room," Steve said.

"Has someone booked it?"

"Dunno."

"Yes, you do. Is that where Larry is?"

Steve didn't answer. Voices were already coming from the room above.

Diamond moved at speed towards the stairs and mounted them. Two men were inside. The one who had just arrived had removed his leather jacket and revealed forearms so tattooed that they looked like sleeves. He had opened his case and taken a polished wooden shaft from it. The other was bending over a snooker table, practising shots.

Diamond said, "Larry?"

Without straightening up, the man at the table said, "If you need to ask, you shouldn't be here. This is a private room."

"Turn round, Larry. You're helping the police."

"Fuck that," Larry said, but he did make a slow turn to face Diamond and scrutinise him through eyes that had less expression than the cue ball. "I know your face. CID, isn't it?"

"It is."

"You got nothing on me. I'm clean."

"It's not about you," Diamond said.

Larry turned to the tattooed man. "Why don't you get yourself a sandwich, Jules? We won't be long."

Jules left the room to do as he was told.

Diamond said, "I'm interested in an elderly man called Cyril Hardstaff."

"What of him?"

"He got into difficulties. Owed a lot of money."

"Familiar story," Larry said.

"I'm sure it is, to you. Cyril had a gambling habit. Couldn't stop. Each bet was going to get him the big win that solved his problem and of course it didn't happen. He ended up with the loan sharks."

"My heart bleeds." He went back to practising his shots.

411

"Did he borrow anything from you?"

"Do I look like a man who lends money?"

"He seemed to think he had to pay you back."

"That's another matter," Larry said. "Some people need reminding. I've been known to knock on doors on behalf of my friends."

"As an enforcer."

He struck the ball with such force that it hit the far cushion and ricocheted around the table. "That's not a word I recognise."

"What do you call yourself, then?"

"I don't like labels. I'm more of a financial adviser than anything else."

"Advising them to pay up or else?"

"Helping slow payers face up to their obligations, that's all. You wouldn't believe how disorganised some of them are."

Larry Lincoln's black humour wasn't lost on Diamond, but it would have been unwise to show any amusement. "Did you visit Cyril?"

"Who is this Cyril?"

"I just gave you his name — Hardstaff. An old guy living in Little Langford."

"He died," Larry said, and added after a pause, "of old age."

"So you know who he was. We're getting somewhere."

"All I know is I wrote off the debt. That's the risk you take with old people."

"His housekeeper seemed to think you would turn up any time, so you must have had dealings."

"I may have held a paper on him, that's all."

"You don't lend money, but you collect?"

The red missed the pocket.

Larry said, "You're putting me off my game."

"I want an answer."

"Hardstaff was small fry, just a name to me."

Diamond wasn't letting him off so easily. "You can do better than that, Larry. Financial advisers keep tabs on everything or they soon go out of business."

"So I'll have to consult my records, won't I?"

"I can do that for you," Diamond said, trading some sarcasm of his own. "I can send a vanload of coppers to your nice house on Lansdown tomorrow morning and batter your door down."

Larry appeared to be untroubled. "You'll need a warrant," he said, straightening up and chalking the tip of his cue. "This was legal, so you can't touch me. The business came my way after a mate of mine dropped

413

off the perch. I took on his paperwork as collateral for some favours he owed me. It brought nothing but death and disappointment, and I'm glad to be shot of it."

"Which mate was that?"

"Bob Sabin. Lovely guy." He leaned over the table again and lined up his next shot. "Lend you his last penny, he would — and demand it back with interest."

Delighted to have got the name so easily, Diamond said, "I remember Bob Sabin. Didn't he have a grand funeral at the Abbey three or four years back, with a horse-drawn hearse? Black plumes on the horses' heads?"

"Of course you bloody remember. You were there. Every copper in Bath was there, catching it all on video. The biggest gathering of the firm I can remember. They came from all over to pay their respects. Some of those wreaths were bigger than I am. 'Bob's Your Uncle' one of them said and another was 'Bob a Job.' He would have liked that. He did a few jobs in his time."

"Bank jobs?"

"Contract jobs, bucket jobs, container jobs, you name it."

"What's a container job?"

"Illegals."

"Got you. Trafficking."

"Personally, I wouldn't touch it. Big

414

returns, but when things go wrong it can be messy, real messy."

He didn't need to say more. Diamond knew of two men and a woman believed to be illegal immigrants found dead in the canal over the last year. For all the ironies, some significant truths were emerging in this conversation.

"Did you inherit Bob Sabin's empire, then?"

Lincoln laughed enough to shake the bottles downstairs. "No chance. All I got was a small list of names. The plums went to his nearest and dearest and I don't mean his wife, Dilly. There's no sentiment in our business. She ended up with the Rottweilers and not much else."

"I don't remember Dilly. Was she a token wife?"

"You mean some airhead model? No, she was the real deal. They were together a few years. No kids. She liked her holidays and her parties and the indoor pool. She should have looked out for number one. She was given the double-shuffle."

"Who were his nearest and dearest, as you put it?"

"His trusties. I'm not naming anyone. You work it out."

"You made sure you got your share."

"Like I said, he owed me."

"You took on the debts of Cyril Hardstaff and some others who were in hock to Sabin. How much did Hardstaff owe?"

"Peanuts."

"Five figures?"

"Not much over."

"He came up with some of it before he died, didn't he?"

"Dribs and drabs. Nothing to speak of."

"How was it paid? In cash, but not in person, I take it?" Enforcers like Larry had risk-free arrangements.

"Yep."

"Did you know where it was coming from?"

"Not my problem."

"But there was still plenty owing when he died — plenty by his standards, I mean?"

"Like I said, I took a hit. Shit happens."

In the business of police interrogation, you soon spot the deception and obfuscation. All in all, Larry had been more candid than Diamond expected. This was because he was confident he was untouchable.

"Just to be clear. You didn't ever visit Cyril?"

A shake of the head.

"Bob Sabin would have met him?"

"Before my time."

"Remind me, Larry. What did Sabin die of?"

"I'm not his fucking doctor. All I know is he went peacefully."

19

There was a voicemail on Diamond's phone.
Unusual.

He never encouraged the team to call him and Paloma was the only other person who had his number — or so he believed.

This was Georgina. "Peter, it would help if you kept me informed where you are when you're out of the building. Contact me as a matter of urgency."

Every summons from the ACC was a matter of urgency. One day she would ask him to call her in his own good time and he would be so shocked he'd be on the line at once. He deleted the message and then noticed there was another.

Georgina again, but speaking through clenched teeth by the sound of it. "Didn't you get my earlier message? It's vital that you get in touch immediately."

It had been a demanding day so far. He'd diverted to Kingsmead Square and treated himself to coffee and lemon drizzle cake in the Boston Tea Party. Immediately? Immediately after he'd finished his cappuccino.

"Where have you been?" she demanded when he finally got through. "I almost sent out a search party."

"The Techie Brekkie."

"The *what*?"

He repeated it and added archly, "Networking with some of my IT contacts. How can I help?"

She was muttering inaudible things. When she became coherent she said, "We heard from the hospital early this morning. Mr. Pellegrini, the accident victim, opened his eyes."

"Get away!"

A real matter of urgency.

"One of the night nurses reported it. They're thrilled. It's the first sign of life that hasn't been induced. He closed the eyes again almost at once, but there are now grounds for hope that he'll emerge from the coma."

"Great." His mind was racing.

"It is and it isn't," Georgina said. "Marvellous that he seems to have survived, but what will he have to say to the IPCC people?

I'm worried that he may be critical of our driver."

"He may not remember much. Do Drawham and Quarter know about this?"

"Who?"

"The IPCC."

She clicked her tongue. "Really. Mr. Dragham and Miss Stretch. No, they weren't in this morning when the hospital got in touch, but they could arrive any time. Peter, stop whatever you're doing and get to the RUH as soon as possible. I'm not suggesting you bring any influence to bear on Mr. Pellegrini if he's able to talk."

But you are, Diamond thought. That's exactly what you're suggesting. "I'm on my way."

In the car he reminded himself how little Georgina knew about Pellegrini. There was so much else to be clarified than the minor matter of whether Aaron Green had been driving without due care and attention.

His ally, the Critical Care sister, was in her office entering something on the computer.

"I would have put money on them sending you," she said. "Couldn't you have got here earlier?"

"I was only just informed. Do you have a kit for me?"

"Kit?"

"The sterile clothing."

"There's a stack outside the door. I thought for a moment you were speaking of kitties." No prize for guessing her next question. "How is he getting on?"

Until he'd met this woman he'd believed himself to be the world's least convincing liar. He was getting a conscience about Hornby, but owning up wasn't an option.

"The last I heard was good." He moved to the more realistic matter. "What's happening here? It sounds promising."

"We're encouraged, but don't expect him to sit up and talk. They don't snap out of a coma just like that."

"Any more signs of improvement?"

"He opened his eyes again briefly twenty minutes ago. There's also some flexing of the limbs. He's still in a vegetative state and it's quite usual for the eyes to open. He may soon begin responding to sounds. Try talking to him when you go in, simple, undemanding stuff. Hold his hand and see if he responds, but don't distress him."

In the private room where Pellegrini was, a nurse was changing one of the bags of fluid hanging from a drip stand. "Are you family?"

He shook his head. "He doesn't have any left."

"Poor old Ivor. Good thing he's got friends."

Friends?

He didn't go into why he was really there. It was obvious from the mask, tabard and gloves that he was an approved visitor. "Was it you who first saw him open his eyes?"

"That was the night nurse some hours ago. It's in his notes. I was here when it happened the second time. He didn't move his head or focus or anything, but it shows there's life in him."

Anyone could be forgiven for thinking the opposite. The patient looked ready for the undertaker.

Diamond found the chair he'd used before and moved it closer to the bed. He could see how much the facial hair had grown since his last visit, already more like the start of a beard than five o'clock shadow.

"Talk to him if you want," the nurse said. "Don't mind me. I'll be out of here in a minute."

His previous one-sided conversation with Pellegrini hadn't made much difference. "I'll have to think what to say."

"The first thing that comes into your head. We do." She laughed. "It's funny. You

422

can find yourself saying really personal, intimate things to patients in comas because you know they won't answer back, and then when they recover you feel really embarrassed and wonder if any of it sank in."

"I'm shy. I won't be telling my secrets."

She laughed. "Who are you kidding?"

"Not to him, anyway, and not you."

"Shame. Hold his hand and talk to him about old times, then, things you have in common, and be sure to keep on using his name. That's the main buzzword: Ivor." She picked up a bag she'd been filling with discarded items. "I'll leave you to it. Press the button if you need me."

Tentatively he reached for Pellegrini's left hand, palm down on the bed, and slipped his own underneath.

Clammy. Limp. Swollen joints. Not easy to touch.

"Me again, Ivor," he said. "The same bloke who found you. Hope you understand some of this, even if you can't say so. You're showing definite signs of improvement, and we're hoping for more. There's a lot I'd like to ask you, but let's just try the word game. How about locomotive?"

No reaction.

"Squeeze my hand if I'm getting through to you. I know the things that interest you.

423

Like steam engines."

The hand remained inert.

"Great Western Railway."

Above the bed, the delta waves patterned the screen in the same regular formation.

"You wouldn't believe how much of this I've had to mug up on. Your personal name-plate, County of Somerset."

Personal it may have been, but it made no impact on Pellegrini's brain or heart rate. A monitor on Diamond's own would have shown big fluctuations. He'd never been a patient man. How did I come to this, he asked himself, pandering to a serial killer?

"A place you visited recently: Hampton Row Halt."

The hand resting on his could have been an uncooked fillet of cod.

"Did you get that, Ivor? I hope you're listening. The one-time railway station. Hampton Row Halt."

Pause for inspiration. There's only so much you can say that's simple and unde-manding. After some time he tried a fresh approach, letting the words flow more, as the nurse had suggested.

"I was there myself, standing on the iron bridge looking along the track where the HOPS are coming. Yes, it took some work-ing out, but I know all about the HOPS now. Saw them for myself only the other night." He'd scarcely begun before he ground to another halt. Aimless chat didn't come naturally to him.

He looked up at the screens and stands and tubes, all functioning efficiently while he was failing lamentably to make any difference.

"You know what they should do?" he told Ivor when he started up again. "Fix you up with earphones, put on a tape of steam railway sounds and see what that does for you. I'm sure there are plenty of recordings. Then you wouldn't need idiots like me talking about it. They play music to coma patients. I've heard of miracle cures with Beethoven and Brahms, so why not the *Flying Scotsman*? Oops, that would never do. Got to go GWR, not north. The Cornish Riviera Express, London to Penzance. About six hours' worth of clackety-clack. Cure anyone, that would."

The only good thing about the lack of any response was that Dragham and Stretch were going to have to wait just as long as he was for the victim's account of the collision. There would be no sudden breakthrough. They don't snap out of a coma, the sister had said.

"Okay. The railway stuff leaves you cold.

I'm going to try some names, like your cleaning lady, Mrs. Halliday."

He waited.

"She doesn't do anything for you? There's a woman from the church who brings you meals on wheels and I'm trying to recall her name. She arrived with a quiche when I was at your house asking about you and I thought I'd got lucky, but she insisted on saving it for someone more needy than I was. Blake. Elspeth Blake."

He might as well have named William Blake, or *Blake's 7*.

He knew of other names more likely to trigger brain activity, but that would be crossing a line. The sister had said not to distress the patient.

Bugger that, he told himself. The sister doesn't know she has a killer in her care.

Go for broke.

"Max Filiput? Your friend Max?"

Friend or foe, it made no difference.

"Cyril Hardstaff?"

He might as well have said Joe Bloggs.

"Your late wife, Trixie?"

One of Pellegrini's fingertips tensed and pressed against Diamond's palm. Unmistakably. Trixie's name had worked.

A miracle.

The touch was soft, but to Peter Diamond

426

it felt like a thousand volts.

Fizzing with the force of it, he squeezed back. "Good man. We got there, thanks to Trixie."

Another twitch confirmed it.

Communication at last.

A small but sensational triumph.

Nothing else happened. Pellegrini didn't open his eyes and say, "You've got me bang to rights, officer, I'm ready to confess." Something may have registered in the vital signs but Diamond missed it, too surprised to look up at the monitor.

He was thrilled beyond description.

Impossible to overestimate his sense of relief. The raw emotions of that morning on the embankment came flooding back: fear that he would get the compressions wrong and destroy a life he could have saved, revulsion at the mouth-to-mouth, exasperation with the discipline of counting, but above all the will to succeed — and all brought to a halt by the anti-climax of the paramedics taking over. From that moment until now, any hope had been put on hold.

The immediate effect on Diamond was dramatic.

The drip, drip of suspicion accumulated over the past week drained away. None of it had any part in this moment. He felt only the closeness of a shared experience, an irresistible warmth towards the helpless man who had freed him from uncertainty with no more than a touch.

He had to tell someone and he'd taken Paloma for an evening meal at one of their regular haunts, the White Hart at the bottom of Widcombe Hill. Church pew seats, but cushioned, white walls and wood floors. Real ale, too.

"It was uncanny," he said, after a long first gulp. "I almost gave up, and then this. He may be a thief and a murderer. God knows I've found enough evidence to arrest him, but when I felt that tiny movement of his finger and knew he'd understood me, I melted. We were sharing in something intensely personal. If there hadn't been so many tubes and wires I'd have hugged him. It's unprofessional. It's all about some primitive drive to connect."

"That's understandable," Paloma said. "You saved his life. You have a stake in his future."

"It goes deeper than that. I'm doing something a cop should never do — taking sides. In the face of all the evidence I'm now trying to think of reasons why he might be innocent."

"He has a right to be understood, whatever he's done."

"My heart is ruling my head."

"It's allowed," she said.

"Not in my job."

"Perhaps he is innocent. You said all the deaths were signed off by doctors as natural. The doctors may be right."

"How I wish!"

"Well, you haven't explained to me how the doctors could be mistaken."

"Actually, there's a long history of doctors getting it wrong. They're not trained to spot the signs of criminality. Some killers are so confident they call in their GP to examine the corpse and certify death."

"Confident of fooling them?"

"The stuff he downloaded from the Internet was nothing else but clever ways of killing people."

"Doesn't mean he put it into practice."

"That's my hope."

She sat back and took a sip of wine. "You'll know before long, so why agonise over it? He'll get his head straight and you'll be able to question him."

"That's if he makes a full recovery. It's not guaranteed. Parts of his brain may have been permanently damaged. He reacted to his wife's name, and that's a positive sign."

Paloma smiled. "A lot more positive than reacting to a steam train. There's hope for him, whatever he's guilty of. If I were you I'd soft-pedal until he's well enough to give his own account."

Good advice, he decided.

"How's your back now?" she asked.

"Much improved. Another massage might see it right."

She gave him a wide-eyed look that didn't commit to anything.

"Your place or mine?" he asked.

"Well, I don't think they'd welcome it here."

The best-laid plans . . . I made my preparations and knew what ought to work, but the
current one behaved out of character. People,
being people, have minds of their own. I
mustn't let it get to me. I can't bail out this
time, because this one knows far too much
and he has to go. Knows I'm coming? Possibly. It's a new challenge for me. I simply
have to be equal to it.

Cool is the rule.

20

The soft-pedalling came to a stop as soon as the next morning when Diamond arrived at Keynsham. A note was on his desk asking him to call someone called Frankie on a Bristol number.

Frankie turned out to be female and a forensics officer.

He reached for pencil and paper. The science would go over his head if he didn't jot down the salient points.

"You recently sent us a pink plastic brush with some hair samples for testing." Frankie spoke in a tone of disapproval, as if it had been a letter bomb.

Jessie the housekeeper's dyed hair ought not to have upset them. "The day before yesterday. Did you get anything from it?"

Frankie wasn't ready to say. She had questions of her own. "You found the brush at an address in Wiltshire, according to the information you supplied. Is that right?"

"A cottage in Little Langford, not far from Salisbury."

"Was that you personally?"

"Yes, it was."

"And is there an unbroken chain of custody?"

This was something Forensics were hot on. You had to keep a written record of the whereabouts of every piece of evidence to show it wasn't corrupted, but it was a bit insulting to be asked. "I wasn't born yesterday. Did you manage to get some DNA off it?"

"We did, both nuclear, from the follicle cells, and mitochondrial, from a hair shaft, which is more difficult to extract. So we have a result. But you didn't provide the name of the individual whose hair it is. Was there a reason for that?"

He was writing and speaking at the same time. "We don't have a surname. She's known as Jessie."

"And you're absolutely sure the brush belongs to her?"

"I found it under her bed."

"The hair is definitely female and originally brown in colour, tinted blonde," Frankie said.

"That all ties in," he said. "Jessie has blonde streaks."

"Fortunately the chemicals used in tinting hair don't degrade the DNA. We checked the national database. Currently it stands at six million DNA profiles."

"Don't tell me you found a match," he said, more in hope than expectation.

"We did."

"Frankie, you're a star."

She gave a grunt like a boxer taking a punch. Accepting a compliment was clearly difficult for her.

"So what's her surname?" He was ready with the pencil.

"I can't tell you."

The pencil broke. "What?"

"The match is with an unknown woman."

"Unknown? How can that be? If it's a database it has names."

"Not in her case. This individual was found dead in the River Avon two weeks ago."

He needed a moment to take it in. "That's awful. Did she drown?"

"The postmortem was inconclusive. Any pathologist will tell you drowning is difficult to be sure about."

Thoughts flapped around his head like trapped birds. Jessie dead? He'd counted on her as his key witness. She'd been at Max's funeral. She'd been in the cottage when

434

Cyril died. She'd spoken to Rex, the taxi driver. She must have had words with Pellegrini that night. Soon after that, she'd gone missing, but the possibility that she'd died hadn't seriously crossed his mind.

"Could there be a mistake?"

Stupid bloody question.

Frankie said after a couple of beats to register disapproval, "No two people have ever been found to have shared the same DNA, other than identical twins. I wouldn't be speaking to you if there was any doubt."

"Let me get this straight," he said. "A woman's body was found in the river. Where exactly?"

"A few miles west of Bath, near Swineford."

"That's a long way from Little Langford."

"It's not my job to explain how she got there," Frankie said. "You asked for the location and that's it. Your own police authority must have dealt with it."

His own station.

He was looking at the map on his office wall and Swineford was barely two miles from Keynsham.

"I wasn't informed. I'll take it up with them. Will you be emailing your findings?"

"All you need to know."

"Please make sure it reaches me person-

435

ally. And, Frankie . . ."

"Yes?"

"I wasn't really casting doubt. You knocked me for six."

After ending the call, he went straight to the most senior uniformed officer on duty, Chief Inspector Richard Palmer.

"Was there a body fished out of the Avon recently?"

Palmer knew straight away. "Woman in her thirties, about two weeks ago. She hasn't been named yet. Doesn't match anyone reported missing."

"We weren't told about this in CID."

"Get off your high horse, Peter. We're dealing with it. If we gave you every death that got reported you wouldn't be too thrilled. Accident or suicide, we believe. There's no evidence of anything else."

"It could tie in with a case we're working on. I should have been informed."

"It's no secret. Been on the website all week. Don't you look at it?"

A low blow that he ignored. "Show me."

"Be my guest." Richard Palmer found the Avon & Somerset Police website, clicked on "newsroom" and had the appeal on screen straight away:

UNIDENTIFIED WOMAN — CAN YOU HELP?

The left side of the screen was filled with a photo of a blonde white woman you wouldn't have known was dead unless you read the information. The eyes were open, as if looking at the camera. She had neatly shaped eyebrows, high cheekbones, a straight, small nose, fine, narrow lips and a dimpled chin. A good-looking woman probably in her late thirties.

The text at the side read:

A woman's body was recovered from the River Avon, near the Avon Valley Country Park, Swineford, at 11 A.M. on Sunday, 29 March, and we are appealing for assistance from the public in identifying her. She is white, aged about 30–40, with tinted blonde hair and hazel eyes, of slim build and about 5ft 5in in height. She was wearing a light blue hip-length padded jacket made in China, white sweater size 10 from BHS and blue Chino style jeans and white socks with pink heels and toes. Her underwear was also from BHS, white, 34D bra and knickers. She was not wearing shoes or any form of jewellery. She is believed to have been in the water for up to twelve hours.

If you were in the vicinity of the country park on Saturday 28 or Sunday 29 March and remember seeing a woman of this description alone or in company or if you recognise her picture, please contact us on 101 and quote the reference number 7773250.

"Has anyone got in touch yet?" Diamond asked.

"No one useful. We still don't have a clue who she is."

"Has it got in the local press?"

"Not yet. It will soon."

"And no signs of violence? What's the thinking about her?"

"She could be an immigrant. To me, the shape of the face looks Slavic. The eyes, the cheekbones. I sent the DNA profile to Interpol in case she fits one of their mispers."

"I meant, what's the thinking about how she ended up in the river?"

"Accident, probably. Saturday-night drinking."

"Round here, you mean?"

"Some of them are legless by the end of the evening, and not only the men. It's either that or suicide."

"Is there a pub at Swineford?"

"Nice one. The Swan."

"I suppose you sent someone to ask?"

Palmer grinned. "Thinking of volunteering, Peter? Hard cheese. It's been done. Actually the body was about a mile downstream from the Swan. It could have carried from there. Swineford weir gives a boost to the flow."

"Was she checked for alcohol?"

"Negative, but it could have metabolized in the time she was in the water. Basically, we're at a loss."

Diamond decided he'd better share some of what he knew. "I may have some information for you, going by DNA evidence, but it won't answer all the questions." He told Palmer the little he knew about Jessie the housekeeper's history, but he didn't go into the case against Ivor Pellegrini. His feelings about the eccentric engineer had undergone another step change.

"Isn't it likely someone in Little Langford knows this woman's name?" Palmer asked.

Diamond shook his head. "I had a man doing door-to-door yesterday. If anything new turns up, I'll let you know."

"Likewise," Palmer said.

"So how did he do it?" Ingeborg was quick to ask when Diamond told his small team how Jessie's life had ended.

"Who are we talking about here?" he said.

439

Ingeborg and Halliwell exchanged startled looks.

"Come on, guv. Pellegrini, of course. It's obvious Jessie knew too much and had to be silenced. She came back to the cottage that night and if she didn't catch him red-handed murdering Cyril she was left in no doubt who was responsible. The only question is how an old guy in his eighties or whatever age he is succeeds in killing a fit woman forty years younger."

"Seventy," Halliwell said.

"What?"

"His age. He's seventy. He may look older in his present state of health, but that's his age."

She swung round to face him. "How do you know that?"

"Because of that name-plate in his workshop. *County of Somerset.* The locomotive was built in 1945 and got its name the next year. I thought we'd all agreed they linked themselves to trains built in their birth years."

"Did we?" She turned to Diamond.

The big man's thoughts were elsewhere. "I've changed my mind about Pellegrini."

"You don't mean that," she said, appalled.

"We assumed from the start that he was a

440

murderer because of his wayward behaviour."

"Wayward? I'd call it guilty."

"Hold on, Inge. Highly suspicious, anyway, the night excursion, the cremation urns, the valuable gowns found in his workshop and the Internet material about perfect murders. We soon had him down as a serial killer, but we were forced to modify that when the death certificates came in and we found his railway friends died from things like flu and an aneurysm." He could tell they were both on the point of interrupting again, so he raised his hand. "I know what you're going to say, there were other deaths, Max's and Cyril's, and we found solid reasons why he might have wanted those two dead, basically to cover up the theft of the gowns. But Max and Cyril died in bed, like the others, and their doctors signed them off as natural deaths. No sign of a struggle, no marks. If he'd murdered them, we'd have found out by now."

Ingeborg couldn't contain herself. "I can't believe what I'm hearing. Isn't this the whole point, that he was researching murder methods? There's a load of circumstantial evidence. We can place him at each scene shortly before the deaths. We just have to work out how he did it. We know why, basically — because his friends got wise to his thieving."

And now Halliwell chimed in. "Let's not forget the deaths of Trixie Pellegrini and Olga Filiput."

Diamond shook his head. "They weren't murders. Olga had a fall, which would be a crude and unreliable method for a man supposedly carrying out perfect murders. And there's no reason for him to kill her."

"Same motive," Halliwell said. "She owned this stack of jewellery and antiques and he figured Max was easy prey once Olga was dead."

"And his wife, Trixie? He didn't murder her."

"She probably found out she'd married a kleptomaniac and challenged him with it."

"After a lifetime together? She would have found out sooner than that."

"Okay, it was a long-term problem and she finally got sick of it and threatened to call the police."

"I said he didn't murder her and I'll tell you why." He shared with them yesterday's experience in the hospital and the first thrilling sign of life from Pellegrini, the response to Trixie's name. "He loved her. When his finger pressed into my hand like that, I don't mind telling you I was moved. By then I'd gone through what I thought was a list of buzzwords and names, but it was Trixie who was the spark. It's hard to explain. No one's more hard-bitten and cynical than I am. This time there was communication, like some form of telepathy. He was telling me she was more important to him than all the railway stuff I'd been going through, all his friends and carers. He was coming alive for Trixie and her alone."

The silence that followed told Diamond he hadn't done a good job of explaining the extraordinary revelation Pellegrini's touch had been for him.

The team looked embarrassed.

It was Ingeborg who finally spoke. "This is difficult to say, guv. Is it possible you were influenced by personal experience?"

"I don't know what you're on about."

"Him responding when his dead wife's name was spoken."

"You mean . . . ?" He couldn't complete the sentence, couldn't even say Steph's name without getting a lump in his throat. "I don't think so, don't think so at all." He forced himself to get a grip. "It's not obvious to me, anyway." But inside, he knew Inge could be right.

She now made an effort to cover the raw

wound she'd exposed. "It doesn't affect the point you're making. You're saying we may have misjudged him?"

But Halliwell wasn't having any of that. "It's too much to believe all these deaths are natural. Something very weird is going on, that's for sure, and Pellegrini is the common factor. And now we can throw another killing into the mix. Do either of you seriously believe Jessie fell into the river by accident?"

"There was no evidence of violence," Ingeborg said, back-pedalling out of consideration for Diamond's feelings.

Halliwell wasn't stopping now. "So she wasn't shot or stabbed or knocked on the head, but she could have been pushed in or held under. Or drugged and dropped in the river unconscious. Or given so much drink she was incapable of saving herself. She knew what happened that night in the cottage and she had to die. And who was there with her? Pellegrini."

"A double murder?" Ingeborg said on a rising note, all tact abandoned. "You think he killed them both?"

"Not the same night," Halliwell said. "It was Jessie who reported Cyril's death next morning. But she went missing soon after. He will have set a trap, lured her to Swineford on some pretext. He may have offered her hush money. It's out in the country, quiet there most times. They meet somewhere — let's say the Swan — and then do a bit of the Avon River Trail along the bank. He'll have come prepared. He wouldn't simply push her in and hope she'd drown. He could have used chloroform."

"Not easy to obtain," Ingeborg said.

"Unless you're a scientist," Halliwell said at once. "He was well capable of passing himself off as one. If it wasn't chloroform it was some other knockout drug. He could have put something in her drink. We can work out the method later. His party trick is rendering people senseless and he used it on Jessie and dumped her in the river. With Jessie dead, he thought he was in the clear. No one could finger him for Cyril's murder."

"Except Rex the taxi driver."

"He thought he'd covered that. He made sure Rex didn't know his name or address. Have I made the case?"

Halliwell looked for a response from each of the others. Diamond was subdued, playing the scenario over in his torn mind. Ingeborg too was pensive, fingering her blonde hair.

Then she spoke. "There's another way to

look at it, isn't there?"

"What's that?"

"From Jessie's point of view. She seemed to be coping well with Cyril, an old man with serious money worries. It was a job with a guaranteed wage because it was paid by the trust. A nice little earner — if she could stand being stuck in that cottage out in the country with just a ninety-year-old for company."

"Her choice," Halliwell said. "Caring was her job."

"True. But when he dies suddenly she's jobless. She has to think about her future. Seems to me she'll look around urgently for a new employer."

"Pellegrini, you mean?"

Ingeborg nodded. "She'll have given him the once-over and decided he isn't short of cash. His wife is dead and he's getting on in years, so he might be glad of a live-in housekeeper. How will she approach him? Better do it fast. A meeting is set up."

"At Swineford?"

"First she may have gone to the house and the next time —"

"Before you go any further," Diamond interrupted her, "Pellegrini didn't need a housekeeper. He was organised with a cleaner, Mrs. Halliday. I met her and she

446

was doing the job nicely. He had someone from the church bringing him meals on wheels. I can't see him wanting anyone extra."

"That's immaterial," Ingeborg said. "I asked you to look at it from Jessie's point of view. She'd make a pitch without knowing his arrangements."

Fair point. Diamond wished he hadn't spoken. It was increasingly obvious he was on a different wavelength.

"The upshot is the same," Halliwell said. "She ends up dead in the river and there's only one possible killer."

Diamond wasn't willing to listen to any more. He'd told them his current thinking and it pained him to have it disbelieved. Their arguments were rational, his intuitive, and it wasn't the way he liked to work. "I'm out of here."

"Are you okay, guv?" Ingeborg asked.

"Perfectly."

"Something I said?" Halliwell asked.

"Leave it," Ingeborg told him.

When the two were left alone, Ingeborg said, "Did you see his eyes?"

"What do you mean?"

"Kind of troubled, tortured almost. I've never seen him like that. Is he losing it, do you think?"

"I hadn't noticed," Halliwell said. "Over-work, do you think?"

She shook her head. "It's got personal for him, this investigation, and he's not used to that. Something seismic happened at the hospital yesterday. We know Pellegrini may be starting to come out of the coma, but it's more than that. It goes really deep and I'm not sure what it's about."

"Holding his hand?"

"Maybe. I wish I hadn't mentioned his own wife when he was telling us about Trixie being the name that triggered the result. That was tactless of me."

"He doesn't often talk about Steph," Halliwell said, "but she's in his thoughts still. They were very close."

"Too painful to share with anyone?"

"Probably," he said, tilting his head as if listening to some distant sound. "I'm forgetting this was before you joined CID. I was first at the scene that morning when we got the shout that a woman had been shot in Victoria Park. Neither of us had the slightest idea it would be Steph."

"The shock," Ingeborg said, crinkling her eyes. "I can't imagine."

"It was as bad as it gets. For fifteen, twenty minutes, maybe longer, he was on his knees beside her. It was obvious she was dead. I went to see if I could offer sympathy or support and he told me to back off. He wouldn't let the police photographer near, the SOCOs. Anyone. All this time he was holding her hand, kind of cradling it."

Ingeborg dragged her fingers through her hair. "Oh my God. I didn't mean to hurt him. I really have messed up."

Diamond walked steadily in the direction of the river — but not to throw himself in. Needing to get his thinking straight, he'd decided to visit the place where Jessie had been found. It was barely half a mile from the Keynsham police centre and the most direct route was up Pixash Lane over the London to Bristol railway and through an eighty-acre kids' attraction known as the Avon Valley Adventure and Wildlife Park. From Brunel's stone bridge he glanced down at the long stretch of track and gave a thought to Pellegrini. This might well have become a vantage point for a night visit after the HOPS moved on from Bath Spa station.

He showed his warrant at the park entrance and got a wary look, but didn't explain the purpose of his visit.

Incongruously, on his way to a possible

crime scene, he found himself among small, noisy people and their young mothers pushing strollers. Donkeys, goats, lambs and ducks were penned at either side and rides were offered on tractors and go-karts. Most of the kids, he suspected on this cool April day, were heading for the shelter of the play barn. One shrill voice said, "Let me go on the death slide, Mummy."

Diamond left all that behind and approached the tree-lined riverbank.

He stood for a few minutes, imagining the scene. The water was flowing at a good rate. Although the body had been found along this stretch it didn't follow she had got into the water here. About a mile upriver was Swineford weir and she may well have floated with the current from just below there and finally lodged against some obstruction. Behind him were moorings for narrow boats but the body had been found before reaching there. As so often happens, a person walking his dog had made the discovery. The immediate area would have been combed for her shoes, a bag or a suicide note, but by CID standards the search may not have lasted long.

Might as well keep a lookout along the bank in case some item had been missed by the search team.

Too much to hope?

On this bleak day, yes.

He understood the mystification — to put it mildly — of his two colleagues when he'd changed his mind about Pellegrini. After days of insisting they were dealing with a serial killer, he'd let them down with a bump and made a poor job of trying to explain why. How do you explain a gut feeling?

That Damascus Road moment in Critical Care was impossible to convey to anyone else, but from his new perspective he could see how flaky the whole case was. When suspicion alone is driving an investigation you're on dangerous ground. You need evidence and it's easy to kid yourself you've got it.

Evidence?

The urns had not been sinister after all. The night excursions on the trike were either to scatter ashes or visit the HOPS. The Internet forum was just that, an exchange of information on computer. The Fortuny gowns looked like stolen property, but may have been a gift. The visit to Little Langford could have been by invitation. Unless it could be proved that one or more of the unusually large number of deaths had

451

been induced, there truly was no case to answer.

There had only ever been one suspect. Cyril was almost certainly a thief but there was no suggestion he'd murdered anyone. Max's death hadn't benefited him. On the contrary, it had closed down his thieving possibilities.

He kicked at a stone and watched it splash. Some ducks took flight.

It had been an investigation like no other in his experience. The crimes may not have been crimes at all. The only suspect couldn't be questioned. The witnesses were dead — all the principal ones, anyway. The scenes weren't accessible without a warrant and he wouldn't get that. The evidence was no more solid than a sandcastle.

What had induced him to start on this? Suspicion.

You sow a seed and it grows. Water it and it thrives. Throw on some feed and it spreads all over. But watch out for what you get. It may be a monstrous weed.

Here he was, angry with himself and unable to face his own team. He'd never invested so much for such a poor return.

Ahead he could see a beam bridge spanning the river, a solid-looking, dead-straight construction of metal and concrete supported at the centre by twin piers. Not the most beautiful of the bridges over the Avon, he reflected as he walked towards it, but sturdy enough to carry heavy traffic, conceivably even a train.

Out here in the middle of nowhere? Unlikely. The main line to Bristol was half a mile south of here, running parallel to the Bath Road. This pointed in another direction, north-west along the valley.

Yet it had the look of a railway bridge.

Death and the railway: the two constants.

Out of curiosity he climbed the embankment for a closer look and sure enough he found a single rail track heading north-west to only God knew where. A path for pedestrians and cyclists ran beside it.

Memories were stirring. He'd heard of the privatised Avon Valley Railway without ever having had reason to visit. Volunteers had been working for years to restore some abandoned branch line near Keynsham and this was obviously it. The southern end couldn't be far off or it would run straight through Swineford.

Wouldn't hurt to check, he thought. So he followed the track for a short distance. Presently the single rail became double, operated by a point, and a short way further on were twin platforms. A little station with its own name: Avon Riverside. Beyond were more points and a loop arrangement of the track to enable an engine to move from one end of the train to the other.

All local railway enthusiasts must have known about this.

Shaking his head, forced to accept another possible link between Pellegrini and Jessie's death, Diamond returned to the bridge, leaned on the railing, peered over the edge and saw the reflection of his head and shoulders fragmenting in the shifting water. Summed up the way he'd felt all morning.

He'd never considered suicide, even in his darkest moments, and he wasn't planning it now, but he could feel an inexplicable pull from the swirling water below. Could Jessie have stood here and looked over?

Or had she been brought here by her killer?

21

His bad day was about to get worse, but he didn't know it when he first returned to the office.

Alex the techie had left a voicemail message asking him to get in touch.

"I thought I'd ask for you in person," Alex said. "It's about that file in ciphertext you asked me to work on."

"Did you crack it?" Diamond asked.

"Sure. It wasn't all that difficult. Pretty basic, really. A programme they were using ten years ago. I didn't expect to come across it again in my lifetime."

"The person using it is quite elderly."

"That figures. Well, I have it in plaintext for you."

"Makes good sense, does it?"

"Sense, sure. Good, I'm less sure."

Diamond didn't pick up on that. He wanted to make up his own mind about the merits of the thing. It might be nothing to do with Pellegrini's secret life, just some treatise on engineering. "Where can I pick it up?"

"This is what I was about to ask. Emailing may not suit you. And I got the impression you didn't want me calling at the police station."

"Understood. Where are you now? Can we meet?"

"In the Internet café in Manvers Street. Do you know it?"

"I know Manvers Street. I ought to, after working there almost twenty years." Diamond had a troubling thought. "You didn't print this out in a café?"

"What do you take me for, Mr. D? I like the coffee here, that's all."

"I can be with you in half an hour. As you say, a personal handover would be best."

Fully two hours later, one poleaxed policeman remained in the Internet café with his third cup of coffee. Alex had long since left, duly rewarded for his expert help. He'd handed across a printout of the decrypted computer file and it was devastating.

Diamond had needed to read the thing in stages, forced to break off many times to get his head straight. Once through, he'd made himself start again. The shocks were just as jarring at the second reading. The pages shook in his hands. There was no way he could face his colleagues yet. Face them he must, but not in the blitzed state he was in after going through this material.

No wonder the file had been encrypted.

It was in the form of a journal. Not so much a diary as an outpouring of arrogance that left no doubt that the writer had committed a series of murders.

To think that by this morning, Pellegrini had been absolved of all guilt — at least, in Diamond's estimation. That heartwarming touch of fingers at the bedside, linking the two men in their grief as widowers, was now exposed as a cruel con.

The big detective was close to tears. Tears of rage more than regret.

Needing yet more time to collect himself, he finally left the café and moved like a sleepwalker up Manvers Street and across the square to Abbey Churchyard, the place where he'd found consolation before at critical moments of his life. He wasn't drawn there by religion, but the need for some kind of therapy.

On the west front of the Abbey were carved a number of figures attached to twin stone ladders. The founder from five hundred years ago, Bishop Oliver King, had dreamed of angels ascending to heaven and his vision had been immortalised this way. An assorted host by any criteria, the angels had been sculpted in different centuries, the lowest and most dilapidated in the sixteenth century, the next pair as recently as 1960 and the top ones from 1900. But the replacements were based on the originals. And as sometimes happened in medieval church architecture, a touch of humour had crept in. At odds with the iconography, certain of the angels were clearly descending the ladders head first.

Diamond's sympathies were wholly with these misfits trying to come down against the flow. How they would pass the aspiring ones just below them was anyone's guess. Maybe before they bumped heads they would be persuaded to turn and resume the climb. Or would they tell the high-flyers that heaven wasn't all it was cracked up to be, and the only way was down?

The dilemma spoke to his troubled brain in times of personal crisis and never failed to lift his spirits.

Sure, the latest twist in the investigation had wrong-footed him, but he was still clinging to the ladder. He'd find a way to move on. He always did.

Back in the CID office, he didn't immediately speak to Ingeborg and Keith. Bath's criminal fraternity provided unending challenges. They stole cars and burgled and dealt drugs every day of the year. Enquiring into serious crimes ought not to be thought of as a displacement activity, but that was how it worked for him today. He had earnest discussions with John Leaman and Paul Gilbert about their caseloads. Another hour passed before he asked his two closest colleagues to step into his office.

"I owe you both an apology," he said after making sure the door was closed. "You said this morning there was only one possible killer and I disagreed. I doubted if murder had been done at all. How wrong I was." He slapped down the sheets he'd collected from Alex. "Take a look. This is the decrypted version of the file you found on Pellegrini's hard disk, Inge. It's chilling."

Ingeborg picked up the first page.

Another one goes tonight.

This time I'm ahead of myself so this isn't a to-do list. Everything is in place, as they say. But being methodical I want something on record to look at when it's all over. You're on your own in this game, so any debriefing is with myself.

The only thing left is to make sure I get the timing right. I'm going for 2 A.M. when he'll be sleeping soundly, guaranteed. Get gloved up, let myself in, do the necessary and get out without leaving any trace. The police have no idea and I'm not doing them any favours.

He'll rest in peace and so will I, with the difference that I'll wake up tomorrow morning.

She looked up with eyes that had stared into the abyss.

Halliwell had been sitting close enough to Ingeborg to have read it at the same time. "The calculation behind it. You said it, guv. It's chilling."

"How much more is there?" Ingeborg asked.

"Pages and pages," Diamond told her.

"Why has he written it down?"

"He addresses that later." He sifted through and handed her another page.

This isn't a compulsion. I'm not psychotic. I can stop at any time. And when I do, the world won't be any the wiser, which will be a personal success. I keep this record of my ordered state of mind at every stage so I can look back at each episode and recall exactly why it was necessary to put an end to a life and how I dealt with it. Of course there are glitches sometimes. I think back to the first and cringe at how naïve I was. Fortunately no one noticed except me.

Right now I'm thinking another one may be beckoning, but not in the near future, not before I've taken time to make all the arrangements. Good preparation is the key.

"What an ego. Is there any pity at all for his victims?"

"None that I've seen." He reached for the pages and leafed through them. "The nearest he comes to it is this, but it's hardly pity." He handed over another sheet.

I was thinking today about the first two. I'm not stony-hearted but I've made it a rule never to mention names or dates in these occasional jottings. I'm not going to forget who I helped on their way. If I ever DO forget, it will be time to stop. No, I remember every one, some with more regret than others.

There are times when I wish I could share my experience with someone else, but it can't happen. If ever I'm feeling isolated, I can glance through these notes and take stock of myself and how I handled matters. It's not as if I'm lonely. There's this area of my life that is private, that's all.

"Bloody hypocrite," she said, "talking about regret."

"It's all about self-congratulation," Halliwell said. He'd looked higher up the sheet and read aloud:

Today I'm rather pleased with myself. A situation has arisen giving me the chance to insure my secrets against discovery. It's the conjuror's trick of misdirection, simple, but effective. The nice thing is that I am uniquely placed to pull this off. I've baited the trap and we'll see if it works. No worry if it doesn't.

"Do you think he wanted this to be found?" Ingeborg said.

"Not while he was alive," Diamond said. "It's meant to be a voice from the grave. If there's a theme running through all this, it's the knowledge that he wants recognition for his brilliance and knows he can't get it in his lifetime."

"Give me a break," Ingeborg said.

"But in all his careful planning he didn't expect to become an accident victim on life support. That undermined him."

"No, guv," she said. "He could have had the accident and got away with it. What undermined him was you illegally entering his workshop and finding the printout of the Internet forum on murder."

He summoned the faintest of smiles. "True, I suppose."

Ingeborg was already thinking ahead. "When he comes out of the coma, he won't expect us to know any of this. If we handle it right, we'll get a proper confession. This stuff is hot, but it doesn't name any names, unless there's something I haven't seen yet."

"He comes close to it here." He pointed to another section:

A lot has happened since I last put anything in the diary. How events move on. Memo to myself: must do better in keeping the record updated. If I leave it too late, there's no point really.

What can I say about the last one? He was an overdue train that needed taking into the terminus (he'd appreciate that). After his wife went, he found life increas-

463

ingly difficult. He had vague suspicions certain people were taking advantage, but he was in no condition to stop them. I did him a service, ending his journey.

"That's got to be Max," Ingeborg said.

"I agree," he said, "but we still don't know for sure who all the victims are."

"Max, Cyril and Jessie."

Diamond clasped the back of his head with locked fingers. "I wish it were so simple. Take a look at this entry. I've been trying to relate it to what we know, and I can't."

The best-laid plans . . . I made my preparations and knew what ought to work, but the current one behaved out of character. People, being people, have minds of their own. I mustn't let it get to me. I can't bail out this time, because this one knows far too much and has to go. Knows I'm coming? Possibly. It's a new challenge for me. I simply have to be equal to it.

Cool is the rule.

"Something went wrong," Ingeborg said. "The intended victim ducked out in some way and it really upset him."

"Who does he mean?" Halliwell said.

"Who was it?"

"That's what I'm asking you," Diamond said.

"Jessie, obviously," Ingeborg said. "He's had to change his method. She doesn't die at home like the others. She's younger and more mobile. He has to take extra risks with her, but she knows too much about Cyril's death, so there's no choice but to kill her. She ends up in the river, apparently drowned. Major change in the modus operandi."

"I wish I could feel so confident," Diamond said.

"What's your problem with it, guv?"

"I thought of Jessie when I read it first time, just as you did. But what if it referred to somebody else who knew far too much for Pellegrini's liking?"

"Another victim?"

"That's my worry. He talks about the conjuror's trick of misdirection."

" 'I've baited the trap and we'll see if it works.' "

"Exactly. Are we walking into his trap? I've got the advantage of having read this thing right through more than once and it's clear to me they aren't the only killings. There's a history of homicide here."

"The railway friends?"

465

"Maybe them, maybe not. It's tempting to lay every death at his door, but we've already looked into this and some of them may be from natural causes. There must be others. I get the impression it goes back years."

"Nobody who ever met him was safe," Halliwell said.

"They said that about Graham Young," Diamond said.

"Who's he?"

"Who *was* he? A poisoner who came to trial in the early 1970s. Most people haven't heard of him. He's not up there in the top ten with Nilsen and Shipman and murderers like that, but he ought to be."

"I sense a story coming on," Ingeborg said, knowing of Diamond's reading habits. "Is it X-rated?"

"I'll tell you about him because there are parallels. He was just a bright teenager when he started, fourteen, I think. A grammarschool boy. First his stepmother died mysteriously, and then others in his circle became ill — his father, his sister and a school friend. It was pretty obvious something extraordinary was happening and Young was accused of poisoning them with arsenic. He told the local toxicologist how incompetent he was. He was very opinionated."

"I can see one parallel already," Halliwell said.

"Yes, but he went on to say it was obvious he hadn't used arsenic because the symptoms were typical of another poison, antimony."

"Crazy."

"Arrogant, anyway. He boasted he'd used it on his stepmother. They decided the boy was criminally insane and locked him up in Broadmoor. He convinced the authorities there that he was interested in science and wished to spend time in the prison library studying chemistry and medicine. After nine years the Broadmoor psychiatrist decided this scholarly young man had made a full recovery and was fit for discharge. He was neat in appearance, knowledgeable and serious and there was no difficulty placing him in a job as assistant storeman in a photographic works in Hertfordshire."

"With access to chemicals. Here we go," Ingeborg said, seeing the point at once.

"Exactly. Christmas had come early for Graham Young that year. It wasn't long before the head warehouseman became ill with stomach pains and died in St. Albans hospital of what they decided was 'peripheral neuritis.' "

"A nerve thing?"

"It is, weakness, numbness and pain, often the legacy of a number of different illnesses. But the real cause was thallium poisoning. Young had moved on from antimony. His researches had told him this would do the job better. Thallium is a heavy metal, similar to lead and mercury, but colourless, tasteless and easily dissolved in water. As the newest recruit, he'd been made the tea-boy."

"Bad choice," Ingeborg said. "I suppose they got it in their cuppas."

"Twice a day sometimes. It's cumulative."

"Nasty," Halliwell said. "How did he get hold of thallium in the first place?"

"Good question. Although it's sometimes used in the manufacture of lenses, this company used a different method. There wasn't any in the store where he worked, so he ordered his own supply from a London pharmacist. He dosed his victims methodically, little by little, gradually increasing the amount and keeping a record in his diary."

"A diary? He wrote it down, like Pellegrini?"

"Like him, yes. That's good scientific practice, logging each stage in the process. He didn't stop at one victim. He poisoned the replacement storeman the same year."

"Killed him?"

468

"Yes."

"Same way?"

"He'd found a method that worked, hadn't he? After that, it was open season. Six more workmates developed symptoms of numbness, stomach cramps and hair loss. Some sort of bug was suspected, but one of the management feared some chemical used at the works might be responsible and a medical team was called in. They invited all the staff to a meeting and who do you think had most to say?"

"Showing off again?" Ingeborg said.

"And how! He demanded to know why they hadn't considered thallium poisoning."

Halliwell said, "That's dumb."

"It's attention-seeking," Ingeborg said. "He couldn't bear to have anyone else take the credit."

"Still dumb."

"It's the dilemma Pellegrini writes about in these notes," Diamond said. "He commits a perfect murder and wants the world to know how clever he is."

"Was that how he was caught?" Halliwell asked.

Diamond nodded. "The management checked him out. They didn't know he'd already done time for poisoning, but when they dug out his original job application it

469

stated that he'd studied chemistry and toxicology. After that they called in the police and his previous was revealed. They searched his home and found more than enough to convict him, quantities of thallium, antimony and aconitine and, most damning of all, the diary."

"Was it cryptic, like Pellegrini's?" Halliwell asked.

"More explicit, along the lines of, 'I have now administered a fatal dose. I gave him three doses altogether.' Such attention to detail didn't do much for his defence case. He claimed he was writing a crime novel. Oh, and there's another parallel: Young's first victims, his stepmother and the store-keeper, were both cremated, making it unlikely the murder would be discovered. However, the store-keeper's ashes were sent for analysis and, thanks to a new forensic technique called atomic absorption spectrometry, traces of thallium were found."

"So there was never any question of his guilt?"

"You're joking, I hope? After his conviction he announced that he could have killed many more if he'd wished. To quote him: 'But I allowed them to live.' "

"Generous."

Ingeborg smoothed back her hair with

both hands and gripped it. "You've told us this for a purpose. Graham Young managed to fool a lot of people, but gave himself away through boasting. Pellegrini is smarter."

"From all we know so far."

"But highly conceited, if this stuff is anything to go by."

"He won't crack easily," Halliwell said.

Diamond shrugged. "Can't tell until we interview him."

Ingeborg was nodding. "So we hit him with what we know."

Not the best choice of words for a recovering coma patient, but Diamond knew what she meant. "And the more we have up our sleeves, the better chance we have. We need to delve deeper, investigate his past and look at every death with a possible link to him."

There was a moment when nothing was said.

Ingeborg frowned. "When you say 'we,' are you talking about the three of us? That's a massive undertaking."

"I don't underrate it."

"Can't we turn this into a major inquiry now we've got the evidence of the journal?"

"Not yet," he said.

She frowned. "Why not?"

"As you said a moment ago, we're relying on illegally obtained evidence. He's got to be persuaded to make a confession statement."

Halliwell said, "The guv'nor's right. If Pellegrini denies everything and wants his day in court, we're mincemeat."

"Yes, but . . ." Running out of words, Ingeborg let go of the hair and let it slide over her shoulders.

Halliwell added, "And we really must discover the method he uses. Isn't there anything in these pages that gives it away?"

"No more than you've just read," Diamond told them. "If we can believe him, they don't know anything about it, which I take to mean they don't suffer — unlike Young's victims, who were put through serious pain."

"Confirms what we worked out for ourselves," Ingeborg said. "It's some sort of knockout drug. Has to be. They're found dead in bed without marks. What do those clinics in Switzerland use for assisted death?"

"Pentobarbital," Diamond said. "They administer an antiemetic first, and then about an hour later the lethal dose. The patient goes into a coma and dies."

"Peacefully?"

He nodded.

"How would Pellegrini get hold of the

472

stuff?" Halliwell asked.

"Get with it, Keith," Ingeborg said. "You can buy anything online: landmines, Kalashnikovs, a US army tank if you want."

"Can't we find out from his computer?"

She sighed. "Don't you think I spent enough hours on this already?"

Halliwell was in dog-with-bone mode. "Is there a second computer somewhere in the house? He must have a laptop or a tablet he uses for emails."

"Are you suggesting we break in again?" she asked.

"Please," Diamond said. "We didn't break in. I borrowed the key."

Ingeborg swung back to him. "That's the workshop key. You don't have the key to the house?"

"No."

"We could get inside with the help of that cleaning woman you met."

"Mrs. Halliday?"

"She must have her own key. She'd let herself in the day you called. It's worth a try, guv. Did she say where she lives?"

"Fairfield Park."

"Let's find her, then. We need to do it fast if he's coming out of the coma."

22

First he phoned the hospital and this time he didn't get the usual ward sister. No need to start with the bulletin about Hornby's well-being.

"Mr. Pellegrini's condition has improved in the past twenty-four hours," he was told, and it sounded as if the sister was reading from notes. "He is responding to auditory and visual stimuli and he's clearly trying to communicate. It's too early to say if he'll make a full recovery, but the signs are promising."

Ingeborg had been right. There was reason for urgency.

"I'll visit him later."

"You won't."

"I beg your pardon."

"All visiting is stopped for the rest of today."

"Why is that? I was allowed to see him yesterday."

"Patients emerging from comas can get agitated and confused. He may need to be sedated."

"I thought the whole idea was to wake them up. I can help with that."

"You'll allow us to decide what's medically appropriate, sir?"

"Well, yes," Diamond said. "But how soon can I expect to get some sense out of him?" Immediately he knew how callous he'd sounded and rephrased the remark. "That is to say, as he's trying to communicate, when can we look forward to hearing from him?"

"Impossible to say. Recovery rates vary enormously."

"Hours rather than days?"

"Don't push me, sir. I answered your question."

"Sorry, sister. But I need to see him again at the first opportunity. I'm the police officer dealing with the incident. Detective Superintendent Diamond. Would you make a note of my name? Anyone calling here needs to ask for me in person."

Before he put down the phone Georgina had glided wraithlike into his office and was pulling up a chair.

"Was that the hospital?"

"It was," he said, and added smoothly, "I

475

haven't forgotten you asked me to keep tabs on the man found at the scene of the collision. It's better news. He's definitely coming out of the coma."

"Thank God for that," she said. "I was fearing the worst. I must tell the IPCC team."

He'd almost forgotten Grabham and Squeeze. "Be sure to tell them visiting isn't allowed yet."

"I'm sure an exception will be made in their case."

"No chance. I can't even get in myself. He mustn't be distressed."

"I can understand that," she said with a smile. "You distress *me* on a regular basis. Do we know any more about this poor man?"

He had to rack his brain to remind himself how much she had been told. "Retired engineer, widower, lives alone in Henrietta Road."

"I know that much," she said. "What was he doing out on the road at such an early hour?"

He could safely tell her about the HOPS, and did so without once leading her on.

She listened and was satisfied. "That clears up the mystery, then."

"Er, yes." If Georgina believed there was

no more to uncover, who was he to disabuse her?

"You can get back to what you do best."

He waited for another sarcastic dig, but she spared him.

"Investigating crime," she said.

"Business as usual, ma'am."

Within the hour he was at Pellegrini's house with Ingeborg and Mrs. Halliday. The helpful help — as Diamond thought of her — had been collected in a patrol car from her flat in Fairfield Park.

"Believe me, we appreciate this," he told her.

"I'm pleased to do it," she said. "I enjoyed the ride. I usually cycle over. Anything I can do to help Ivor get his memory back has got to be good."

Ingeborg gave her boss a sharp look. She would never entirely fathom his deviousness.

Mrs. Halliday produced her house key and let them in. "I can't let you into his workshop. That's where he spends most of his time, but it's private, like."

"I remember. You called it his holy of holies."

"I've never so much as flicked a duster in there."

"We don't need to go in," he said in all honesty.

"Where shall we start, then? I showed you the library, didn't I?"

"With the rolling ladders. Yes. Where does he go when he isn't in there or the workshop?"

"His bedroom. He's got an enormous telly in there and a phone."

"We'll start there. We may find some object that will trigger his memory when I take it to the hospital."

She led them upstairs, talking as she went. "Even when Trixie was alive they had their own bedrooms. He suffers from insomnia, you see. He likes to get up in the night and turn on the TV."

"Does he have any favourite programmes?" Ingeborg asked.

"Anything to do with trains, I expect. Sometimes they show old films at night, don't they?"

"*Murder on the Orient Express?*"

"That would appeal to him, yes."

"*Brief Encounter?*" Diamond said. His preference was always for the older films.

"Beautiful," Mrs. Halliday said. "I weep buckets each time I watch it."

"*The Lady Vanishes?*"

"We shouldn't have started him on old

478

films," Ingeborg said. "He'll go on forever."

He didn't because they'd reached Pellegrini's room. "I gave it a good clean the other day," Mrs. Halliday said. "Not that he's untidy. He's one of the tidiest gentlemen I've worked for."

This was borne out by the absence of any clutter. It could have been a hotel room ready for a guest. Double bed, chest of drawers, built-in wardrobe, plasma TV, a poster of the Cornish Riviera Express.

"Not much here we can take to the hospital," Diamond said.

Ingeborg picked up a small framed photo from the bedside table. "This must be Trixie."

A slight woman in her sixties, with permed white hair and rimless glasses. She was in a twinset and tweed skirt. She looked as if she wouldn't know what to do with a Fortuny gown.

"Can't show him that," Diamond said. "It might distress him. Isn't there anything else?" He opened the wardrobe and spotted some neckties neatly arranged on a special hanger. "One of these might do." He picked off one that was light brown in colour with rows of small yellow circles with the letters *GWR* inscribed in grey. Not a thing of beauty.

"He ought to recognise that," Mrs. Halliday said.

"Good suggestion." Diamond folded the tie and put it in his pocket. "We can hang it on the railing above his bed." He looked at the old-fashioned rotary-dial phone on the bedside table. No stored numbers. "Did he use a mobile?"

"I never saw him with one. If he did, it would be in his little office in the spare room."

Another office.

Diamond's gaze flicked to Ingeborg.

"Where's that?"

Mrs. Halliday led them along the corridor and opened a door. The first thing Diamond noticed on the desk was precisely what they'd hoped to find: a laptop.

A disappointing day had suddenly redeemed itself. "This will do it," he said, flipping open the lid. "What's the screensaver? I wouldn't mind betting it's a bloody train," he muttered to himself.

How right he was: front view with a fine head of steam polluting the countryside.

"This is ideal."

"I can't allow you to take that away," Mrs. Halliday said. "It might have personal stuff on it."

"Don't you worry about that, my dear,"

he said, sounding awfully like a conman. "My colleague Ingeborg has a clever little gadget that will copy this and any other memorable images he's stored. She's a wiz at technical stuff."

Ingeborg may have cringed at such deceit, but she'd come prepared with the hard drive.

"Won't take more than a few minutes," Diamond went on. "I wonder if there's anything else here." He needed to find a distraction while Ingeborg transferred all the data.

"This." Mrs. Halliday reached up to a shelf above the desk and picked off a soft toy, a huge, hideous pink squirrel in a railway guard's uniform with cap and waistcoat and a plastic whistle sewn between the front paws. "I found him in a car boot sale and gave him to Ivor for his birthday. Isn't he the cuddliest little armful you ever saw?"

It was more armful than cuddly, and not little, about the size of a St. Bernard.

He managed to say, "Very fetching."

"I made the uniform myself," she said. "It's all authentic. The cap took me a long time. When I got him he had a large nut between his paws — a padded felt nut about the size of an orange — and I had the idea of giving him the whistle instead for reality's sake. Ivor was really taken with him. He calls him Nutty. He made the shelf specially. He says Nutty can sit up there where I can see him each time I clean the room."

"How thoughtful." Nutty had been thrust into Diamond's arms. He could understand Ivor's difficulty on being presented with this misguided labour of loyalty. And why it was kept above eye level on the shelf. He thought about replacing it there, but Mrs. Halliday had other ideas.

"Take him with you to the hospital and stand him near the bed where Ivor can see him."

"The nurses might trip over him."

"On the bed, then."

"I doubt if they allow things like that in intensive care," he said. "They have rules about hygiene. They won't even let you take flowers in."

"There's nothing unhygienic about Nutty. I spruced him up before I gave him to Ivor. He's been through one of those big commercial washing machines," she said. "He was too large to get into mine. He's germ-free. You can smell the detergent on him. Have a sniff."

Nutty's state of hygiene wasn't worth fighting over.

It was easier to give in. "I can only ask."

He held on to the thing.

"Not by his ears," Mrs. Halliday said. "Tuck him under your arm."

Ingeborg must have heard this going on, but she kept a straight face and concentrated on copying the entire contents of the laptop.

"Is he able to eat?" Mrs. Halliday asked — and for one surreal moment Diamond thought she was speaking about Nutty.

"The last I heard they were feeding him through a tube."

"As soon as he's on solids we can get Elspeth Blake to send in one of her quiche Lorraines. He'd enjoy that."

"I expect they regulate what patients eat." He turned to Ingeborg. "Have you finished?"

She nodded and disconnected the lead.

"What else can I show you?" Mrs. Halliday asked.

"We've got more than enough now."

"Is it safe to talk, do you think?" Diamond asked as Ingeborg powered her Ka southwards on Henrietta Road towards the city.

"Why, what's the problem?" she asked.

"Him in the back."

She laughed. Nutty had taken over most of the back seat. "He could be a whistleblower, couldn't he? He's got the whistle.

All he needs is some puff. What are you going to do with him?"

"I'm not taking him to the hospital." He paused for thought. "Actually he looks comfortable where he is."

She crashed the gears. "He's not staying in my car."

"We can't have him in CID," Diamond said. "Georgina will want to know where he comes from."

"We know where he comes from: a charity shop. They'll take him."

"Can't do that. He doesn't belong to us."

For harmony's sake he agreed to transfer Nutty to his own car when they reached the staff car park.

"How long will it take you to go through the disk?" he asked.

"Depends, doesn't it? Could be really quick, but if any of the files are encrypted we could be looking at a couple of days."

He hoped not. This was crunch time. If Pellegrini used the laptop for his emails and the Internet, his guilt would surely be exposed. Even a technophobe like Diamond knew modern computers list your search history. That's how paedophiles are caught. And if the Internet didn't nail him, his emails surely would. It was vital to know all the dirt before Pellegrini emerged fully from the coma.

Eager as Diamond was to find the smoking gun in this case, a part of him remained uneasy. The sense of touch has a remarkable ability to stimulate our emotions. That pressure of Pellegrini's fingers when Trixie's name was spoken had been profoundly moving at the time and wouldn't fade from his memory, however obvious it had become that the man was a killer several times over.

"Make a start straight away," he told Ingeborg, "and let me know the minute you find anything."

Attached to his own computer screen he found a Post-it note asking him to contact Richard Palmer, the chief inspector he'd consulted about the body in the Avon.

"Some juicy news about the drowned woman," Palmer said when Diamond looked into his office.

Diamond corrected him. "The woman in the river. We don't know for sure if she drowned."

"Okay, Peter, be like that. Call her the woman in the morgue if you like. Anyhow, she's not just 'the woman' any more. I know who she is."

"Really?"

"I told you I sent her DNA profile to

485

Interpol. They got back to me this morning, or rather the Bulgarian police did. They matched it to a missing woman from Sofia by the name of Maria Mikhaylova, who left in 2010 and hasn't been heard of since."

Diamond tried to appear unmoved. Inside, his nerves juddered like one of Pellegrini's express trains going over points.

"The physical details match pretty well," Palmer was saying. "Height, build, colour. The age is close enough, thirty-seven compared to our estimate of between thirty and forty. I emailed her mortuary photo by return and they say it's her."

Run up a drain, Diamond thought. This can't be right.

"They're going to get back to me when they've spoken to the family."

He took a long, deep breath to compose himself. "Bulgarian, you say? But we already have a match with the woman known as Jessie, who as far as I know is British."

"Some of them speak excellent English," Palmer said. "She could have been here five years."

Why listen to this garbage?

"I'm not convinced. How is she supposed to have got here?"

"Can't say for sure, but Bulgaria is high on the list for trafficking."

"You mean for sex?"

"Sex or forced labour. Slavery, either way. It's possible she escaped at some stage and decided to get a job and make her home here. She was getting on a bit to be a sex worker. They may even have let her go. She's not going to live here under her Bulgarian name, is she? She calls herself Jessie and finds work as a carer."

No doubt this bilge made sense to Palmer, but it was going over Diamond's head. "You've had time to take this in. I haven't."

"You didn't meet her yourself when she was alive?" Palmer asked.

"Well, no."

"You want to find someone who did. Ask if there was any trace of a foreign accent."

Not a bad suggestion. He thought of Hilary. She hadn't said anything about Jessie sounding like a foreigner. He'd ask Keith Halliwell if he'd heard any such suggestion when he was knocking on doors in Little Langford.

Palmer was adamant. "It can't be anyone else. DNA is a hundred percent accurate. There's no other person in the world with the same profile."

"An identical twin."

"You're splitting hairs now. If she has a twin, which is unlikely, the twin would also

487

be Bulgarian, so you're stuck with the same problem. Face it, Peter, your Jessie is Maria from Sofia. Try and look grateful."

In his days as a smoker he'd have lit up. He badly needed some kind of therapy. He went to the nearest coffee machine and pressed the buttons for the blackest caffeine brew it would give.

He clutched the paper cup so hard that some slopped over the rim and hurt his hand. He was muttering to himself. He knew he had to adjust. You make assumptions and they get challenged by the facts. No future in arguing with the science.

After several swigs of coffee he began to accept the inevitable and tell himself that Jessie's nationality wasn't such a big deal after all. There was no reason why she couldn't be Bulgarian. Nothing had been known about her life before she took her job as Cyril's housekeeper, not even her surname. The rest of what Richard Palmer had been saying about the trafficking and the sex trade was guesswork, the spin he'd put on the few reliable facts he'd got from the Bulgarian police: that she was a missing woman in her late thirties whose appearance was similar to Jessie's.

The one fact that mattered was that she was dead.

Dead and identified.

He binned the cup and went in search of Ingeborg.

She'd downloaded the data from Pellegrini's laptop and was clicking through files at mind-boggling speed.

"How's it coming?" he asked.

"These are his sent emails," she said. "He's methodical about accurate subject-lines and that helps. Loads of boring railway stuff. But I looked first at his document files and found he'd downloaded the Internet forum on murder methods — the material we know about because he printed it."

"So he used the laptop for that?"

"Yes. And saved it."

"Can you put a date on it?"

"Hang on a mo." She worked the keyboard, found the file and checked the account details. "Created thirteenth June 2014. Not long after Max's death."

"*After* Max went? Interesting. I was thinking he must have researched all this before he started his killing."

"It was before Cyril's death. And Jessie's. Maybe he was just brushing up on new ways of killing people."

"What was the date again?"

"Thirteenth of June."

"That was actually the day of the funeral.

Max's funeral. So Pellegrini was studying murder methods on the day he attended his friend's last rites."

Her eyes rolled upwards. "Some friend."

"Has he saved anything else of interest?"

"Any amount of train-related stuff."

"Of interest, I said. Nothing encrypted?"

"If there is, I haven't found it yet. I was hoping the emails might contain something helpful, but they haven't yet. He's probably wise to the risks. Email was never designed with security in mind. Every message you send passes through various servers before it gets to the recipient. Any of them could intercept your personal correspondence."

"To say nothing of hackers."

"Or government agencies."

"You're not expecting to find much? Well, there's new information today about one of the victims." He told her what he'd just learned from Palmer about Jessie's Bulgarian roots.

"Surprising," she said, and showed straight away that she'd got the point. "DNA doesn't lie. Does it make any difference to the case against Pellegrini if Jessie is from East Europe instead of somewhere in Britain? I don't believe it does."

"But we've learned that Jessie wasn't her real name."

"You're thinking she was here illegally?"

"Palmer does. He put together a back story that made her a working girl who was trafficked and escaped and created this new identity for herself."

"Does he have evidence for this?"

He shook his head. "Guesswork, but not all that far-fetched."

Ingeborg had tensed. "Horribly persuasive."

"And if there's any truth in it," he said, "we can't rule out the possibility that she was killed by her former gangmaster and not Pellegrini. After all, the MO is different. His other victims weren't chucked in the river. They were found dead in bed."

She was silent, thinking. "But we don't know she was in the sex trade. That's Chief Inspector Palmer's theory and I don't know if we should buy it. He's piling speculation on speculation."

"Yes, and let's not forget there was quite a debate in that forum about drowning and how difficult it is to prove at postmortem. Pellegrini was clued up on this."

"It's a departure from his usual MO."

"True. But Jessie — I'm going to carry on calling her that — was younger than his other victims and less likely to die in bed. He had the problem of where she was going to be found."

Ingeborg twisted a strand of hair around her forefinger. She wasn't convinced yet. "Realistically, he's elderly to lug a body about. It wouldn't be easy for him to tip her in the river. How would he have got her out to Swineford? He doesn't drive any more."

"He'd arrange to meet her on some pretext."

"Such as what?"

"I'm speculating myself now. He offers her a job, or money. Let's remember she's just lost her livelihood. He may have suggested she join him as his housekeeper. He invites her to meet for a drink at Swineford. He knows the place well because of the steam trains, the Avon Valley Railway. It's a good location for what he has in mind, secluded and beside the river. They meet at the Swan some quiet evening and talk it over and he offers to show her the little station, which means a stroll along the riverbank. By then he's added something to her drink. They don't get far before she feels unsteady. All he has to do is push her in. He's capable of that, especially if she's losing her balance already."

"Hmm."

She didn't sound impressed.

"One possible scenario," he said. "I'm not

saying it's foolproof."

"How does he get there in the first place?"

"Taxi. That's his mode of transport. And when he's ready to leave, he calls for another."

"And Jessie? How does she get there?"

"She drives. She has her own car. We know that because she used to drive Cyril to Bath."

"Yes, but where does she leave it? In the pub car park?"

She'd seen the flaw.

And so had he. "Her car is still going to be there. That is a problem. It would have been reported before now." He squeezed his eyes shut. "Well, there may be an answer. After pushing her in, he picks up her handbag and removes the key to her car and returns to the car park and drives away. We know he could drive at one time."

"No disrespect, guv," she said, "but on balance I'd rather keep an open mind about how Jessie got into the river."

"Are you thinking a gangmaster did it?"

"Or a client. Or she jumped. We don't know enough."

He let her get back to the computer.

This day kept throwing up new problems and time was racing by. He needed to get a grip on the fundamentals of the case before confronting Pellegrini. He was strongly tempted to treat Jessie as a side-issue, unconnected with Pellegrini, and concentrate on the deaths of Max and Cyril.

And yet Jessie had been a main player. She'd visited Max's house regularly with Cyril. She may well have known Cyril was stealing items of jewellery to fund his gambling debts. It wasn't impossible she had been aiding and abetting him in the thefts. While the two old men played Scrabble she had the opportunity to root around the house for things to steal.

And she'd met Pellegrini at Max's funeral. That meeting may have made her death inevitable. Pellegrini, too, had been stealing Max's property. The Fortuny gowns were evidence of that. Was the funeral reception the occasion when Pellegrini discovered he wasn't the only thief?

That afternoon in the house in Cavendish Crescent there had been some sort of incident involving Jessie. Diamond had heard about it from Mrs. Stratford, the actress who cleaned for the Filiputs — and from Jake, the gay railway enthusiast who lived in the signal box. In the unseemly scramble for railway souvenirs Pellegrini had upset coffee over Jessie's skirt and she'd left the room and changed into something else. She hadn't returned.

Why?

Surely because she was gifted with a last chance to roam the house looking for more things to steal while the party was in full swing downstairs.

What if she'd been caught red-handed by Pellegrini? He, too, must have realised this was his final visit to the house, an eleventh-hour opportunity of theft.

Or was it the reverse? Had Jessie discovered Pellegrini in the act of stealing?

Either outcome was fraught with danger. Exposure would be devastating for each of them. They had so much to lose if the police were called.

So there had been no hue and cry. It had been resolved another way.

Jessie couldn't have known she was dealing with a killer.

All of this had to be set against the practical difficulties Ingeborg had raised. The MO was different. The victim was female and younger than the others. Pellegrini, at seventy, was taking on someone who could match him physically.

But the idea of murder was rooted in Diamond's thinking. His way forward was clear. Get to the truth of Jessie's death.

He went back to Richard Palmer's office.

The chief inspector eyed him with amusement. "Found the identical twin yet?"

Diamond wasn't in a jesting mood. "I'd like to see the postmortem report."

"You still have doubts?"

Palmer accessed the report on screen and moved out to allow Diamond to use his chair.

His preferred reading didn't include material such as this, but he worked steadily through the forensic pathologist's findings. In effect, there were two reports: an interim one dictated at the time of the autopsy or shortly after, before the test results were obtained, and a second, with fuller information and a summing up, including discussion of the possible causes of death.

The description of the body was basically similar to the missing person appeal on the police website, but there were additional details. Some superficial injuries had been noted consistent with her having fallen into the river, travelled downstream and met obstructions. Nothing external or internal indicated she had been assaulted prior to entering the water, but the involvement of someone else couldn't be ruled out.

As to the cause of death, it was impossible to be certain. The pathologist had looked for the classic signs of drowning. There was water in the stomach and oesophagus, but you would expect some from passive percolation regardless of whether the person had been dead or alive. The water within the body didn't contain debris such as weeds and algae. No stones or weeds had been gripped in the hands, which would have indicated cadaveric spasm, and therefore drowning. The characteristic froth that forms in the air passages wasn't present, but still didn't make for a conclusive diagnosis.

The samples tested in the laboratory had yielded no findings of importance. A diatom test, for the microscopic algae present in water, had proved nothing either way. Nothing in the body fluids had suggested she was already dead prior to immersion.

"Drowning cannot be ruled out in this case," the pathologist summed up, "but neither can it be ruled in. The circumstances in which the body was found make it probable. However, there is insufficient evidence to be certain."

"You thought she'd got drunk and fallen in," Diamond said after rising from Palmer's chair. "There's nothing here about alcohol."

Palmer clung to his theory. "I told you before, it metabolizes quickly. We can't be sure how long she was in the water. Twenty-four hours would do it unless she drank the pub dry."

"Have you heard any more from Bulgaria?"

"About her past?" Now the chief inspector jutted his chin like a politician who is asked the question he was waiting for. "I was spot on."

"They got back to you?" Diamond said with a grunt of annoyance. "Why didn't you let me know straight away?"

"I was getting it on file while it was fresh in my head."

"She really was in the sex trade?"

Palmer stood with arms folded, the embodiment of smugness. "They confirmed it, the familiar story, depressing, but all too common. She came from an orphanage somewhere out in the sticks, got into petty crime as a juvenile and made her way to the capital, where she was soon taken over by traffickers, promised a better life and driven with other girls across the border into Turkey. Forced into prostitution, escaped and was taken over by some other minder who was worse than the first lot. He shipped her out of the country and she found herself in Milan and then Rome, still selling her body. There the trail goes cold."

"This was when?"

"About 2010, they reckon."

"You got all this from the Bulgarian police?"

"About an hour ago."

Diamond glared at his self-righteous colleague and felt too bruised to protest any more about poor communication. "The Bulgarians know all this and we know shit about her life in Britain?"

"It's not for want of trying."

"Oh, come on. She could have been on the game here as long as five years."

"It's not illegal, Peter."

"But pimping is. Someone was controlling her."

"You tell me."

"All right, I will. She ends up in Britain, probably after a nightmarish journey in a container and presumably without papers. And some gorilla puts her to work, right?"

"Something like that."

"But at some stage she gives up the sex trade and finds work as a housekeeper."

"Housekeeper so-called," Palmer said with a sneer.

Diamond wasn't having that. "She really was a carer by the end of her life. The old guy was ninety. It was a proper job with a regular wage paid for out of his late wife's estate." He dragged a hand over the dome of his head. "I need more about her time in Britain and how she got to be in the West Country. If she was here any time at all, she must have had some run-ins with the police."

"Probably under another name."

"There was a time when every force had its vice squad and you'd know who to ask. These days the only vice squad left in Britain is a punk band."

Palmer grinned.

"Avon and Somerset must have someone with responsibility for policing the sex industry in our manor."

"Here in Bath it's me," Palmer said.

"You? Why didn't you say so?"

"I don't crow about it."

"Who are the major pimps, then?"

Palmer blew a soft raspberry. "It all changed when Bob Sabin died."

"Everyone's heard of Sabin."

"He had an empire that stretched way beyond Bath, did Bob. After he died, the bulk of it was taken over by his sidekick, Eddie Woodburn."

"Woodburn. The name is familiar."

"You can forget it now. Eddie took a bullet to the head shortly after and there was mayhem. We thought we were in for a gang war, but it was settled. I won't say peacefully because I don't believe for a moment it was peaceful. Charles Gaskin divided the spoils with Gerry Onslow."

Diamond knew both names and thought of them as pond life, but hadn't needed to meet them. Organised crime was a constant menace dealt with on a regional basis by a unit known as Zephyr. Palmer would be reporting to them. "How long have Onslow and Gaskin been running the show?"

"Woodburn was shot at the end of last year, so it's three or four months. Not long."

"Long enough. Which of them should I speak to?"

"You're not serious, Peter?"

"Got to find out if they regarded Jessie as unfinished business and put out a contract on her. If they didn't, it's odds on that my man Pellegrini is her killer."

"Wouldn't it be simpler to ask him when he comes out of the coma? It would be safer, for sure."

"No. I need to know the score before I speak to him. Who shall I try, Onslow or Gaskin?"

"I don't know about Gaskin, but Onslow is local."

"That settles it, then. Where does Onslow hang out?"

23

Bath has many amusing ironies. The best is the fact that thousands of tourists arrive because of the Jane Austen connection while the author herself could hardly wait to quit the place with "happy feelings of escape." Another is that for three decades no one could bathe in Bath — because the spa water was deemed dangerous.

This was remedied in 2006 when the New Royal Bath opened. The massive glass cube a few steps across the street from the Pump Room has a clean bill of health, is stunningly modern and houses five floors of pools and treatment rooms using the warm spring water that fell as rain ten thousand years ago, is heated more than a mile below ground level, and is the source of the city's existence.

Mind, the project had a series of embarrassing false starts. Part-funded by a millennium grant, the building was envisaged as a spectacular way of marking the year 2000, and six years later it still wasn't open. Delays and spiralling costs made it into a battleground between the designers and the contractors while horrified ratepayers looked on. The farcical high point was the visit of the Three Tenors in 2003. Perfect timing, it was thought, for a grand opening. Pavarotti, Domingo and Carreras were duly filmed beside the rooftop pool (but not in it) holding glasses of the spa water, but the champagne had to be put on ice because the wrong paint had been used and a legal injunction meant new contractors had to be brought in to do the work. Fully three more years passed before the doors were opened to the public.

Gerry Onslow, the most feared man in the West Country, wasn't bothered about the forty-five million the building was said to have cost. He reckoned he was paying off the overspend himself. He had exclusive use of the place several evenings a week after the public had left and the doors were officially closed. How much this cost him was a secret known only to the management and Gerry, but it must have been substantial.

He always came with a team of heavies who made sure he was not interrupted. They guarded the main entrance, the changing rooms and the pool area. No one was so foolish as to enquire if they were armed.

This evening Gerry was in the Minerva pool on the lower ground floor. Although the visually exciting rooftop pool has the best views and the water temperature is the same as downstairs, the Minerva has more appeal on a chilly April evening. Another factor in Gerry's thinking was that any evil-minded person with a long-range rifle could take a shot from the roof of the Abbey tower.

He wasn't there to swim. This was all about easing away the stresses of a compli-cated week of trafficking, laundering money, making offers people couldn't refuse and watching his own back.

He floated.

In the buoyant water, he could have been lying in bed, he was so relaxed. He filled his lungs with the warm air and treated the water like a mattress. He wasn't built like an athlete, but fat is less dense than muscle and more helpful for floating. Gerry didn't think of himself as fat and didn't want anyone else to think it either, so let's say discreetly that here in the water the laws of physics were in his favour.

Out in the middle, he felt safe. The mas-sive trumpet-shaped white pillars rising from the turquoise pool and bearing the weight of the entire building gave a feeling of stability. He liked staring up at them and thinking about the business he supported.

So he was totally unaware of the manatee-like shape gliding underwater towards him. The first he knew of it was when something brushed against his foot.

Startled, he drew his legs up to his chest and tipped like a barrel, glimpsing the creature's shadow below him. But he couldn't stop himself from swallowing a pint of water before he got control of his body and managed to stand upright, with his feet on the bottom. The pool's depth was the same throughout, only four feet six.

A smooth, oval head broke the surface within touching distance and water cascaded from it.

The manatee spoke.

"Easy, Gerry."

"What the fuck . . . ?"

The creature was human, but not reassuringly human. To Gerry's eye it was uglier than any sea monster.

Yet there was just a chance this might be someone who had been allowed in by mistake.

"You shouldn't be here. The bath is closed."

"Not to me."

Spoken with menace. No mistake.

A manatee would be preferable to this.

Gerry looked round for his minders. Nowhere in sight. They'd cocked up, the toerags. They would be burnt toast in the morning.

Forced to humour the invader, he said, "Who the fuck are you?"

"Peter Diamond, Bath CID."

"Police?" Gerry shrilled. Panic set in. They must have found out about Charlie Gaskin, his so-called "oppo," who had taken a bullet to the head last month and was now part of the foundations of a new high-rise building in East Twerton.

Peter Diamond said, "I'd have brought my warrant if it was waterproof."

"Get outta here."

"No thanks. I went to some trouble to get in."

"How the hell . . . ?"

"Hiding in a towel room for over an hour. I need a quiet chat with you and this is the ideal situation."

"What d'you mean — 'ideal'?"

"I know you're clean, don't I?"

"Ha bloody ha."

"And if your minders take a pot-shot with their handguns, they're as likely to hit you as me, so they won't try."

"Who told you I was here?"

"Common knowledge. Take my advice, Gerry, and vary your routine. Shall we do this in the whirlpool?"

A feature of the Minerva was a bowl-shaped structure in the middle of the pool.

"Why should I fucking talk to you?" Gerry asked. His teeth were chattering, but not from cold.

"Because I know enough to put you away for a long time — but that isn't in the plan if you cooperate. I want answers to questions, off the record. I have no hidden tape recorders, no wires, see?"

The policeman spread his palms and it was true. All he was wearing was a pair of baggy blue swim shorts.

There was still no help in sight. Grudgingly, Gerry waded towards the dormant whirlpool and took a position inside, with Diamond in his wake.

"Don't panic if it starts up," Diamond said, when comfortable. "It's on a timer."

"I know," Gerry said. "I'm a regular."

"I heard. And you have it all to yourself, as befits a man of your status. You can afford luxuries now you're top of the heap."

Something close to panic crept up Gerry's spine.

"What heap?"

507

"Would you rather I said 'the firm'? Or 'the empire'? Bob Sabin called it his family, didn't he?"

Gerry felt like saying "no comment," but that would have confirmed he had a major crime to hide. Instead, he kept his mouth closed.

Diamond said, "Wasn't that his name for it — family? We know the only family he truly had was his widow, Dilly, and in the end she didn't get treated like family. I was told she got the Rottweilers and damn all else. I was talking to Larry Lincoln only the other day. Some people thought Larry was like a son to Bob, but he didn't get much, either — just a few names of people who were late payers. You and Charlie Gaskin were the main beneficiaries, but you had power bases of your own. You were the obvious heirs."

The mention of Gaskin — and in the past tense — was alarming. Gerry dug deep to deflect attention. "Dilly wouldn't have wanted to take over. I don't know how many wives Bob got through. She was the latest, the one who outlived him."

"What happened to her?"

"She took off with her nice clothes and the bling. I don't know where."

"Nothing untoward happened to her?"

Gerry shook his head. "She'll be all right. She didn't stand in anyone's way."

"I'll lay out my cards, then."

Christ, here it comes, Gerry thought.

"I'm interested in a certain Bulgarian woman."

"A woman?" This wasn't in the script.

". . . who contributed to your income by selling her assets, her natural assets. Are you reading me?"

"No." Huge relief. Unless he was boxing clever, the policeman hadn't come about the Gaskin killing. They didn't know yet.

"The name is Maria Mikhaylova."

Gerry's mind was still on the buried corpse in East Twerton. "Say that again."

"I'd rather not try. You heard it and if you say you don't remember, you're a liar. She was on your payroll some considerable time. She arrived here in 2010 or soon after, blonde, thirtyish, average height and build."

"I know a thousand women like that," Gerry said, growing in confidence. "You gotta do better than that."

"You ought to remember this one. She scarpered."

"When is this supposed to have happened?"

"Eighteen months to two years ago. She changed her name and got another job, but

509

you didn't know at the time."

"How would I remember, then?"

"You found out eventually when the payments stopped."

Gerry was willing to talk about Maria for the rest of the evening. "I'm a tycoon. I got more important stuff going on in my life than some girl going AWOL."

"The reason you remember Maria is you put out a contract on her only last month. You're a tycoon. You make the big decisions. She was found dead in the river a mile downstream from Swineford. Does that ring a bell?"

If it did, it was a warning bell. "Not really," Gerry said.

"Don't give me that. It's in all the papers — not her name — but the fact that her body was found in the Avon. Was she dead already or did she drown?"

This could be trickier than it first appeared. Gerry went silent again, deciding how to react.

Diamond had spread both arms along the rim of the whirlpool. "Off the record, Gerry. I'm not about to nick you for this one. I know it won't stick."

So had this been shadow-boxing? Was Gaskin's fate the charge that would stick?

Gerry felt shaky again. He didn't like this

situation. He was ready to talk about Maria. He wanted to talk about her. "What if it was an accident?"

"What indeed?"

"She was fully clothed."

"So you *do* know about her."

"Not the way you're telling it," Gerry said.

"Go on, then. I'm listening."

He started talking to save his own skin. "Maria from Bulgaria was known to me, yes. If she's the person you're on about, she was no trouble to anyone. She had a nice house south of the river in Oldfield Park. I happen to own some property out that way and she was one of my tenants. I'm not a hundred percent sure what line of work she was in —"

"Come off it, Gerry. We both know what she did and who was running her. She absconded and you couldn't allow that."

"Bollocks. She was living in the flat until the day she died."

Diamond blinked.

"That isn't possible," he said. "She decamped a couple of years back, like I told you. She called herself Jessie and took a job as housekeeper near Salisbury, in Little Langford. I have DNA evidence to prove it. We traced her back to Bulgaria and they checked their records. She was working in

Europe as a prostitute some years and then got over here as an illegal. All this is a matter of record."

"It's news to me," Gerry said. "I'm telling you Maria was living in the house I own at 22 Darwin Road and paying her rent."

"Until when?"

"Until she fell in the river."

"No, no, no, no." The policeman looked as if he was about to burst a blood vessel. "What are you suggesting here — she had a double life? She was based in Little Langford, housekeeping for an old man called Cyril Hardstaff, twenty-four-hour caring. I've spoken to people who knew her. I've seen the room she slept in."

"Have it your way," Gerry said, trying to humour him. "We can't be talking about the same bird."

For that he got a glare a judge might give the public gallery after an obscenity was uttered, followed by drop-jaw uncertainty, as if the gallery was empty. "You were collecting money from her all this time?"

"Regular as clockwork."

"This is the woman in Darwin Road?"

"Sofia Maria, I called her."

"Why was she killed, then?"

"Obvious, ain't it?" Gerry said. "She done it herself. Anyone else wanting to dispose of her wouldn't choose the river." Instantly, Gerry regretted what he'd just said. Talk of alternative disposal arrangements could easily turn to building sites.

But Diamond was off on another tack. "Have you heard of Cyril Hardstaff?"

"Not before you mentioned him."

"He was in hock to Bob Sabin. When Bob died, Eddie Woodburn was the main man, and Larry Lincoln took over as Cyril's debt holder."

"That scumbag," Gerry said. "Yeah, that figures. Lincoln was given some names to play with. Small potatoes, more trouble than they're worth."

"Cyril was stealing jewellery to raise the cash. Does the name Max Filiput mean anything to you?"

"No, mate."

"Ivor Pellegrini?"

Gerry just shrugged.

Diamond seemed to have exhausted all his options. He was like a suicide bomber who has got to paradise only to find they've run out of virgins. "I've got work to do. I don't have time to sit in a pool with you." He splashed out of the whirlpool and swam away.

Gerry took a few long breaths, looked upwards and crossed himself.

24

"Diamond in the thermal spa?" Ingeborg said with saucer eyes. "Who told you this?"

Keith Halliwell was certain of it. "Richard Palmer. He's an old mate of mine and I believe him."

"How does he know?"

"The boss talked to him late yesterday. Richard is the SIO on the dead woman found in the river. He's the one who contacted Interpol and found she was from Bulgaria."

"I know."

"Well, Richard had a theory that she was a sex worker."

"I heard about that from the boss. Load of rubbish, he reckons."

"But it turns out Richard is right."

"Get away. This is Jessie the housekeeper we're talking about."

Halliwell shrugged. "He asked the Bulgarian police to do some more checking and she was definitely on the game at one time."

"No kidding?"

"They're certain. Her picture is a perfect match."

"Poor soul."

"She'd been moved about Europe and was known to the police in Turkey and Italy. Then they lost track of her and it seems she was trafficked to England."

"Is that certain?"

"Well, we know she ended up in Little Langford, so it isn't rocket science."

"And the assumption is that she worked here as a prostitute before becoming Cyril's housekeeper? Wouldn't that have come to light before now?"

"She changed her name, didn't she?"

"Okay — I get that."

Halliwell nodded. "So the boss is digging like fury. And when he starts digging he can rip through concrete. He wanted to find out who could have been running her and Richard told him the main man, the biggest pimp locally, was Gerry Onslow — who is now Mr. Big after some carnage in the crime world."

"And they traced Onslow to the new baths?"

"Apparently he can be found there late most evenings when it's officially closed.

It's the one safe place to see him if you can get past his henchmen. That's what Richard told me, anyway, and that's what he told the boss — who went straight home to collect his swim shorts."

"Is he a swimmer?" Ingeborg's face creased at the image this conjured up. "God, I'd love to have been a fly on the wall. And did he get a result?"

"Don't know. He hasn't appeared yet."

Wedged into the last remaining slot in a long line of parked vehicles in Darwin Road, Oldfield Park, Diamond stared at the end-of-terrace house a little way up. How do you tell if the place is in use as a brothel? The closed blinds at all four windows might be a clue.

He swallowed an ibuprofen. He was not at his best this morning. He'd spent most of the night trying to get his head round the maddening conundrum of Jessie the housekeeper. The science had established that she and Maria the Bulgarian were the same woman. There's no arguing with DNA. Yet Gerry Onslow had insisted that right up to the time of her death Maria had been living as a prostitute at this address.

The obvious inference was that Onslow was lying, but why? By admitting he owned the flat and virtually confessing he'd been living off her earnings for some time, he'd put himself at risk of prosecution. His whole demeanour had suggested running a brothel was small fry to a man of his status. He was clearly more concerned at covering up more heinous crimes.

And if he'd killed her himself, or ordered her death, he would surely have been only too relieved to grab the alibi Diamond had offered — that she had been living in a small village in Wiltshire.

Nothing added up.

Better deal with the matter in hand.

By now, Maria was two weeks dead. It was likely some other sex worker had been installed in the house. There's no sentiment in the selling of flesh.

Diamond left his car, marched over and pressed the bell on the blue front door. Double chimes sounded inside, but that was all he heard.

He tried twice more.

A voice close by said, "You're too early in the day, my friend. She'll be sleeping off yesterday's business."

A bearded character in a flat cap and raincoat and holding a folded newspaper was speaking across the wall from next door.

"You're the neighbour?" Diamond said.

"For my sins, yes. Didn't know I was next door to a knocking-shop when I first moved in. I soon found out. But they don't bother me. Live and let live, I say. My advice to you is tie a knot in it, at least until after lunch."

"I'm not here for that," Diamond said. "I'm a police officer."

"Yeah, and I'm the Bishop of Bath and Wells," the man said with a chuckle. "You can be honest with me. Man of the world, I am."

"Do you ever speak to your neighbours?"

"I have done, yes. My cat Pussy went missing once. I had to go and ask. There was a slight misunderstanding over what I was calling about, but once we were over that, she was normal as you like. She'd been feeding the little varmint for weeks."

"Did you get her name?"

"She didn't give it. Wouldn't have meant much to me, I expect, being foreign."

"She's a foreigner?"

"Most of them are these days, aren't they? They come over the Channel and take our jobs. I blame the government."

Not a helpful route to go down. "How do you know she's foreign?"

"The way she talks, bleeding obvious."

From an inner pocket Diamond took out

the picture of Maria from the police website. "Is this her?"

The neighbour put on his glasses to scrutinise it. "This is the one who feeds my cat, no question. She's not there right now. I reckon they need holidays more than the rest of us, but Pussy is pissed off about it."

Diamond's headache had suddenly got a whole lot worse. He hadn't truly believed until this moment, and it made no sense.

"There's another one been there some time," the man went on. "Redhead with tattooed arms. I haven't spoken to her."

"This one" — Diamond jabbed the picture with his forefinger — "was definitely living here until recently, was she?"

"Two, maybe three weeks. I'm having to buy extra cat food."

"Does she own a car?"

"I never saw her in one."

"How long do you reckon she's been your neighbour?"

"She was installed before I moved in two years ago."

"And does she spend most of her time in the house?"

"She needs to. Blokes are calling all week long. I have to mark off my parking space with cones. It's not illegal, is it?"

"Reserving a parking space?"

"No. Paying for some how's-your-father."

"Depends," Diamond said. He pressed the bell again.

"She won't answer," the man said. "This time of day they're out to the world."

It dawned on Diamond that he no longer needed to speak to the other tenant. He'd learned enough from the neighbour. Just as Gerry Onslow had claimed, Maria the Bulgarian had been selling her services as a prostitute here in Oldfield Park all the time Jessie the housekeeper was supposed to be thirty miles away in Little Langford.

Crazy.

He pocketed the picture, nodded to the man and returned, muttering, to his car.

Back in Keynsham, he phoned the hospital to get the latest on Pellegrini's condition.

The sister who sounded like a station announcer came on the line. "Mr. Pellegrini had a very good night and is progressing well, so well that he is being moved from Critical Care to a general ward on the same floor. He started eating solids last night and had a good breakfast this morning. His brain function seems to be returning, although his short-term memory is uneven. He was seen by the doctor an hour ago and it was decided to allow visits from designated persons once he is installed in Brad-ford Ward."

"What does that mean — 'designated persons'?" Diamond asked her.

"Close family."

"He's got no family. His wife died some time ago."

"Particular friends. People he'll recognise. Visits from close family and friends are part of the healing process."

"I need to see him urgently. I'm Detective Superintendent Diamond."

"I know who you are, Mr. Diamond," she said as if it was distasteful.

"And . . . ?"

"I don't think it's appropriate. Does he know you?"

"We haven't spoken, if that's what you're asking, but I got closer to him than most people ever will. I gave him CPR at the scene of the accident and visited him several times when he was unconscious."

"I doubt if that qualifies. He's not ready to answer questions. I've already had to put some people off."

"Really? Who do you mean?"

"Trying to pull rank. It doesn't wash with me, saying they're a public body and calling themselves watchdogs."

Dragham and Stretch. They'd been quick

off the mark.

"Going over the accident that put him here would be far too distressing," the sister went on. "We'll see how he copes with the visitors he knows."

"Visitors he knows?" Diamond said in alarm. "Who are they? I told you, he's alone in the world."

"You're mistaken there. Two old friends from his railway society have asked to come and he's happy to see them. These are people he'll respond to."

She could only mean Jake and Simon Pool, the amiable gay couple who lived in the signal box. They were the only other members of his GWR society left alive. Decent of them to visit. But were they putting themselves in danger? It was hard to see how. Together, they ought to be safe from Pellegrini in his weakened state.

He thought about telling the sister her precious patient was a serial killer, but decided it wouldn't sway her. They can take high moral stands, these health professionals.

He told her he would phone later. "I'm not pestering you for no good reason, sister. There are matters crying out for attention."

"There will be no crying out in Bradford

Ward," she said. "Don't call before tomorrow."

Sod that, he thought. What time are you going off duty? But all he said was, "I'll bear that in mind."

Deep in his gut he knew more work needed to be done before he could charge Pellegrini.

"I finally finished checking the laptop and there was nothing more of importance," Ingeborg said. "If I never have to read another sentence about old trains, I won't feel deprived."

They were having a brainstorming session, as Diamond had put it, at Verona. He'd started on a late breakfast and the other two were watching him eat, Ingeborg over a skinny latte and Halliwell a cappuccino.

"His online diary is as good as a confession," Halliwell said. "Talk about a smoking gun."

"Tainted evidence, unfortunately," Ingeborg said. "We can't just let ourselves into people's houses and steal the data from their computers."

"No problem."

Diamond stopped his chewing to give a faint smile.

"What do you mean by that?" Ingeborg said.

Halliwell wasn't smiling. "We can use some guile here and go through the motions of arresting him and applying for a warrant to search his house and workshop."

"On what evidence?"

Halliwell carried on as if he hadn't heard. "Then we can take away his hard disk and get the diary decrypted all over again and in the eyes of the law we've got him bang to rights."

"You're talking as if search warrants are discount vouchers," Ingeborg said. "They don't hand them out in shopping malls. There's a small requirement known as reasonable grounds. All we can offer is strong suspicion."

"What's your suggestion, then?"

"Belt up and listen, both of you," Diamond said, putting down his knife and fork and wiping his lips with the paper tissue that came with the meal. "Something is seriously wrong with our thinking. We've been duped."

Some of what he revealed in the next few minutes was known to them already. His visit the night before to the new thermal bath to surprise Gerry Onslow had been relayed already by Richard Palmer. But they hadn't heard about Onslow's startling assertion that Maria had worked as a prostitute in Oldfield Park right up to the time of her death. And they didn't know about Diamond's early morning visit to Darwin Road to confirm the truth of the claim. He told them what he'd heard from the neighbour.

"Not possible," Ingeborg said. "We know she was living in Little Langford."

"Onslow is lying," Halliwell said.

The pair of them were united now.

"I thought the same. That's why I went to the house to check, and everything he told me is true," Diamond said. He stopped to let the waitress take his plate. "But there's more. Just as I was about to start the car I looked up at the window of number 22 and someone pushed it open and looked out. I left the car straight away and hurried over and got a torrent of abuse because she thought I was a would-be punter disturbing her sleep."

"This was the redhead?"

He nodded. "When I said I was police she thought better of it and came down and opened the door."

"Was she dressed?"

"I'm not going into that. I fussed her up a bit, got invited in, made her a coffee and I had no difficulty getting her version of what really happened to Maria. These two were both on the game and sharing the house, Maria upstairs, Tracy, the redhead, down. On the night Maria died, Tracy was between clients, in the kitchen having a smoke, when a young man came downstairs. He said he'd been with Maria and she'd suddenly had some sort of seizure and passed out. He'd tried to revive her, but he couldn't."

"A likely story," Ingeborg said in her all-men-are-rats tone.

"Tracy dashed upstairs to check and there was no question Maria was dead. They talked about calling a doctor, but it was obvious she was past help. Everything about the young guy's behaviour convinced Tracy he hadn't done anything to harm Maria."

"Sudden death syndrome?" Halliwell said.

"Beating up a whore syndrome, more likely," Ingeborg said.

"I don't think so," Diamond said. "These women are experienced. They know how to spot a violent punter. There were no marks. Tracy was in tears talking about it. Anyway, they both knew calling a doctor would lead to all kinds of complications for them both, so she suggested asking for help from someone she knew. She called Onslow and he came at once and took some swift decisions. He told the young guy to scarper and say nothing to anyone about what happened. The body was naked, of course, but with Tracy's help he got it into some day clothes, for decency's sake, as he put it. Meanwhile he'd called for reinforcements. Maria's body was carried downstairs and driven away in a van. The next morning a woman Tracy knew as Dilly collected all Maria's clothes and possessions and stuffed them into plastic bin bags and drove off with them."

"Dilly," Ingeborg said. "The widow of that old crime boss, Bob Sabin."

"I expect so."

"Did you tell Tracy the body was found in the river?"

"Yes, and she was visibly shocked. She'd got along well with Maria and knew she came originally from Sofia. Tracy herself is Romanian. They were both trafficked. She'd heard about Maria's experiences on the game in Turkey and Italy."

"Did you ask about Little Langford?"

"Of course. Tracy knows nothing about it. She said it was impossible Maria was leading a double life. She hardly ever left the house." A smile as broken as a snapped twig appeared on his lips. "The thing is, I believe her."

Frowns and silence.

Ingeborg was the first to find words. "What are you saying, guv — the forensics lab cocked up?"

"Or we did," Diamond said. "There were two different women and the hair sample I sent for analysis wasn't Jessie's after all. It was Maria's."

Halliwell folded his arms defiantly. "That's not possible. It was Jessie's hairbrush. You found it under her bed at Little Langford."

"This is going to be difficult for you to get your heads round, but I've had all night to think about it. The killer obtained a brush belonging to Maria and planted it under Jessie's bed in the expectation someone would find it and send it for DNA analysis and get a false result."

Ingeborg was shaking her head. "Pellegrini placed it there the evening he went to Little Langford? But Jessie was still alive then."

"She was out when he arrived," Halliwell said.

"Oh, come on. How on earth did he get hold of a prostitute's hairbrush?"

"He must have been one of her clients. They both lived in Bath."

She rolled her eyes. "Ridiculous. He's seventy years old."

"Doesn't mean he's given up sex. At that

age, he'd need to pay for it."

"I don't believe a word of this," she said. "Why would he do such a thing?"

"Because it was in the blueprint. You've read his diary. Everything he does is thought through like some engineering project. He set out to fool us, and that's what he achieved." Halliwell glanced Diamond's way. "But only up to now. Thanks to the guv'nor's good work, we aren't totally suckered."

Diamond had lit the touchpaper and stepped back in the hope of a flash of insight he hadn't envisaged. The short spat between his two colleagues hadn't sparked anything new. They'd repeated the line of reasoning he'd been through in his own mind.

"You're right to mention the diary," he said. "There was an entry about misdirection, remember?"

Ingeborg was on to it at once. "The conjuror's trick. 'I've baited the trap and we'll see if it works.' "

"Right. Doesn't this have the feel of a trap?"

"Just what I'm saying," Halliwell said. "He fooled us."

Ingeborg spoke the actual words of the diary entry. They'd all been over the text so many times that she knew them by heart.

" 'A situation has arisen giving me the chance to insure my secrets against discovery. It's the conjuror's trick of misdirection, simple but effective. The nice thing is that I am uniquely placed to pull this off.' He must have been in the habit of visiting Maria. He nicked that pink plastic brush with some of her hair attached."

"Now she believes me," Halliwell said to Diamond. "She just said Pellegrini paying for sex was ridiculous."

Ingeborg ignored him. "He took it to Little Langford when he visited Cyril and must have said he was going upstairs to visit the bathroom and instead went into Jessie's room and planted the brush under her bed. 'I've baited the trap and we'll see if it works. No worry if it doesn't.' "

"This was what he meant by misdirection," Halliwell said. "Making us believe Jessie was doubling up as a tom. 'Today I'm rather pleased with myself.' He would be, the tosser."

"The calculation behind it!" Ingeborg said. "Let's not forget Cyril and Jessie were both still alive when Pellegrini visited the house."

"Under sentence of death as far as he was concerned," Halliwell said.

"What I'm saying is that he did his bit of

misdirection with the hairbrush, sneaking it under Jessie's bed, the same evening he murdered Cyril. It's chilling. He was already planning to kill her as well."

"Except," Diamond said.

Nobody spoke for a moment.

"Except what?" Halliwell said.

"There's a flaw in all this. When is Pellegrini supposed to have nicked the brush from Maria?"

"On one of his visits for sex. It wouldn't be difficult, finding a brush she used."

"If that's true, how did he know in advance that she would die in someone else's arms and end up in the river?"

25

"Another problem," Diamond said. "If Jessie wasn't the woman in the river, what happened to her? We know she reported Cyril's death the morning after Pellegrini visited, but then she upped sticks and left. No one has seen her since."

"Dead," Halliwell said as if it was a well-known fact. "He went back and murdered her."

"At Little Langford?"

"Obviously."

"How exactly?"

Halliwell shrugged. "We never discovered his method, did we? We looked at all those suggestions on the printout in his workshop — the air bubble in the bloodstream and the sharpened icicle — and none of them fitted the facts."

"It's got to be simpler than any of those," Ingeborg said. "He says so in the journal. They don't see it coming and they don't know anything about it."

"What does he mean by that?"

"Painless, I should think."

"Like some powerful drug?"

"Look at the logistics for a moment," Ingeborg said. "You're saying he killed Jessie at Little Langford the day after Cyril was murdered, right?"

Halliwell nodded.

"First, he had to get there."

"Taxi, same as before," he said. "He went to the rank and took a taxi."

"What, and asked the driver to wait outside the cottage while he committed a murder? 'I won't be long, driver. Just got to total the housekeeper.' "

Her sarcasm went unchallenged.

She tightened the screw. "Well? He had to think about getting home afterwards, didn't he?"

A smile spread across Halliwell's face. He had the answer. "No, he didn't tell the driver to wait. He had alternative transport. Jessie had a car of her own. She used to drive Cyril around in it. It wasn't left at the cottage, so Pellegrini used it for his getaway. We know he could drive. It's probably still parked on some street in Bath."

"With her body inside?"

"Christ, I hadn't thought of that." He

scratched his head. "No, he wouldn't bring her back to his own territory. He's too smart to make that mistake. Far better to leave her at Little Langford."

"Where? You've been there. The boss has been there. Neither of you found another corpse."

"The garden is a wilderness. She could have been dumped in the bushes."

"Didn't you make a search?"

"We weren't looking for another body at the time."

Ingeborg switched to Diamond. "You started this, guv, asking what happened to Jessie. She hasn't been seen or heard of in more than six weeks. Do you think he killed her?"

"It looks that way," he said. "He went to some trouble to plant the hairbrush in her room so we'd get a false DNA result. Keith is right. It's worth going to Little Langford and making a search. Find Jessie's corpse, and we'll have all the proof we need."

Inside ten minutes all three were heading out of Bath in Ingeborg's tangerine-coloured Ka. Diamond, being the boss, not to say the largest, was in the front passenger seat. Halliwell, wedged in the back, was not alone.

"What the fuck is this?" he said when he found himself next to Nutty, the monstrous squirrel.

"It shouldn't be there," Ingeborg said. "Someone I won't name promised to transfer it to his car last night. Conveniently he forgot."

The unnamed someone stayed silent.

"Can you move it?" she said. "It's blocking my rear-view mirror."

"What do you want me to do — cuddle it?"

"Good idea. And take it with you when you get out."

Diamond was oblivious to all this. Mentally he was already at Pellegrini's bedside having the crucial face-to-face that would settle everything.

The crunch.

He fully intended it should happen before the day was out, whatever the nursing staff said. Another night would hand Pellegrini an advantage, a chance to prepare a defence. Much better to catch him off guard.

He took out his phone and called the hospital. The station-announcer must have gone off duty because the voice on the line was the other sister's, never a pushover, but approachable, given the right prompts.

"Yes," he was saying presently, "he's fine,

soon to be reunited with his owner, we hope. How's the recovery progressing?"

"Better than anyone expected. He was moved this morning to a private room in a general ward."

"That's Bradford Ward?"

"Yes, it's adjacent to this one, so I can slip in and see him. He can hold a conversation now, which is a huge step forward."

"Does he remember much?"

"A lot, but there are some blanks. That's to be expected. He can't at the moment recall anything about the accident that put him here. Par for the course in a case of severe concussion. And although he remembers his home and his friends and his late wife, he's at a loss when I talk to him about Hornby."

"You don't say."

"I'm sure he'll get that memory back. He looks more alert by the minute. Are you planning to visit him?"

"Later, I hope."

"We've lifted all restrictions. Well, I have, as soon as I came on duty and saw the improvement. Two of his railway-enthusiast buddies are with him as we speak and a lady friend is on her way. She asked if he's allowed chocolate sponge. We should all have friends like that. When do you hope to get here?"

"Later. I'm on a trip out Salisbury way right now."

"Shall I tell him to expect you?"

"Please don't," he said at once. "He won't know me from Adam."

"But you rescued Hornby. He ought to be told about that."

"If he doesn't remember who Hornby is, there's no point. I want my visit to be a surprise. You can keep a secret, sister, I know you can."

After he'd ended the call he was braced for the inevitable question.

Halliwell voiced it. "Who the hell is Hornby?"

"Did you ever see a film called *Harvey*?"

"Before my time."

"James Stewart."

"Black and white, I expect, if the boss rates it," Ingeborg said.

"It was about this guy who befriends a six-foot-three-inch invisible rabbit," Diamond said.

"Don't talk to me about rabbits," Halliwell said. "I'm sharing a seat with one."

Ingeborg said with scorn. "Squirrel."

"Squirrel, then."

"Are you sure?" Diamond said.

"Sure about what?"

"Sure who's sitting next to you?"

Ingeborg giggled as they overtook another car.

Halliwell said, "Give me a break."

Diamond said, "I only mentioned it because Hornby, like Harvey, is real to some people and not others."

They were zipping along in the small car, way too fast for Diamond's peace of mind, but he couldn't really object. Already they were through the Warminster bypass and heading up the Wylye valley.

His stress was partially about what lay ahead. He'd never met Jessie, of course, but having seen where she lived and thought a lot about her, he'd formed an impression of the woman. Maybe the Jessie in his thoughts was no more grounded in reality than Harvey or Hornby, yet he could picture her driving Cyril along this same road on the Scrabble afternoons, trying to persuade the old rogue to cut down on his gambling. Some hope! He could see her getting bored in the little cottage with only a ninety-year-old for company, glad of the chance of an evening off when Pellegrini arranged to visit. His Jessie was a believable personality. The possibility that he and his team would shortly find a body was upsetting.

Had she been a thief? he wondered, not for the first time. Had she actually helped Cyril repay some of his debts by stealing items from the Filiput house? With better opportunities than Cyril himself, she may well have done so.

That episode after the funeral — when coffee was spilt on her purple wool skirt and she left the room with Mrs. Stratford, the actor-cum-cleaner, to change — must have given another opportunity to roam the house, but it wasn't her doing. Pellegrini himself had caused the spillage. Jake and Simon had used the phrase "tipped coffee over her skirt" — as if he'd done it deliberately.

Deliberately?

Was that possible? What a mean trick if it was true. Presumably he wanted her out of the room so that he could get up to something. But what?

Diamond visualised the incident as it had been described, first by Mrs. Stratford and later by Jake. The lawyer, Miss Hill, had explained Max's last wishes about the railway memorabilia and invited the guests to help themselves to the old posters and photos. Mayhem had followed. Pellegrini had elbowed Jessie in his eagerness (it was said) to get to the precious items on offer.

Jessie had changed into overalls. She hadn't returned to the funeral reception. It was left to Mrs. Stratford to come in from the kitchen and collect Jessie's handbag.

And that, surely, was what it had all been about. By accident or design Pellegrini had made an opportunity to go through that bag.

The truth about the killings, the whole ugly truth, shot through Peter Diamond like a million volts.

26

"Turn it round."

Ingeborg, taken by surprise, said, "What?"

"The car. Do a U-turn. We're going back."

"We're almost there, guv."

"I know. There's nothing for us at this place. Do as I tell you."

Ingeborg allowed two motorbikes to hurtle past in the other direction and then did as instructed with a screech of tyres. "Where are we heading?"

"The RUH." He had his phone out again. "Put your foot down."

This had to be serious. Diamond urging any driver to put their foot down was as likely as him taking to the stage at Covent Garden in the *pas de deux* from *Le Corsaire*.

His direct line to the sister didn't work. She wasn't answering.

Called to some new emergency?

Please no.

Back to the main hospital number. "This

is the police. Can you put me through to the Critical Care unit? I can't get the sister in charge."

A wait while they tried.

"Try the ward adjacent to it . . . I'm trying to remember the name . . . It's where you're put when you're starting to recover . . . Bradford, that's it."

He kept the phone jammed to his ear and said to the others, "It's a general ward and he's in a private room." He was speaking into the phone again. "Who is this? The sister? . . . Who's in charge, then? Let me speak to the senior person, whoever that is."

His two colleagues waited to be enlightened. Clearly whatever was going on at the hospital had priority over everything. Ingeborg was forced to give her attention to the driving. Her car wasn't fitted with blues and twos, so other drivers weren't aware she'd be ignoring speed limits and rules of overtaking. The A36 through the Wylye valley isn't as twisting as the river it runs beside, but it comes a close second.

Diamond had got through to someone more senior on Bradford Ward. "You have a patient called Pellegrini, right? Until a couple of days ago he was in Critical Care. Can you see him from where you are? Is anyone with him? Okay, now listen to me.

This is the police. Close the ward and stop all visitors from entering. Yes, everyone. An extreme emergency. I'm sending officers to seal off the ward. It's mandatory that you take this action now."

He prodded the keys again and got Keynsham and made himself known. "I need to seal Bradford Ward at the RUH until I can get there. I'm currently on the A36, a good twenty minutes away. Treat this as a high emergency. Get some armed officers there as soon as possible . . . Yes, the hospital has been informed. Do it now."

"Can you do that?" Halliwell asked him after he'd taken the phone from his ear.

"Do what?"

"Close a hospital ward."

"I've just done it, haven't I?"

"But on what authority, guv? You know what hospitals are like. They have their own protocols."

"You heard my end of the call," Diamond said. "Didn't I make myself clear?"

"I wonder if they'll act on it."

"Of course they will. 'An extreme emergency' I said. The lives of the patients come above everything else."

"They'll want to confirm it with Keynsham. I doubt if they'll act on one call to a staff nurse — or whoever you spoke to."

There was sense in what Halliwell was saying.

Troubling sense.

"I couldn't get hold of the sister I know," Diamond said. "She'd take me seriously. I'll try her again." He keyed in the direct number.

Still no answer.

"What I'm getting at," Halliwell said, "is that if some hospital manager was to check with the station, nobody knows what the hell is going on. The ACC isn't in on this, is she?"

"Christ no. Georgina doesn't know."

"So it's not like an ongoing operation everyone is up to speed with."

He was right. Now it had been pointed out, Diamond could see his emergency unravelling as the hospital hierarchy tangled with the management tier in the police. "I'd better fess up with Georgina. God, where do I start?"

When he tried Georgina's direct number, she was engaged, very likely in conversation with the hospital.

A nightmare of failed calls.

"Where are we now?" he asked Ingeborg.

"Beckington, guv. We're closing in."

"Ten miles?"

"About that."

"When we get there, it's gate one, the main entrance. Pull up there and when we get inside, Critical Care is straight ahead, not far up the corridor, and Bradford Ward is next to it. I'm not sure what to expect. If they haven't sealed the ward it could be too late. The sister said he's expecting two lots of visitors, two railway buddies, who I took to be Jake and Simon, and a woman friend, who is almost certainly Jessie."

"Jessie is alive?" Ingeborg said.

"Alive and set on killing Pellegrini."

"Jessie?"

Ideally, he would not have sledgehammered them like this. Under the pressure of what awaited at the RUH there was no way of letting them in gradually. Only God knew the shock Diamond had felt when he'd finally grasped the truth, but at least he'd worked it out for himself. His two colleagues were forced to take it on trust.

He kept the facts terse and to the point. "She's our serial killer. She did for all the others, wrote the journal, planted the bogus DNA, and almost got away with it by leading us to think she was dead. She's been waiting to see if Pellegrini recovers because he knows far too much about her. She can't allow him to live and this is the first chance she's had to get to him since he came out of the coma." He took a breath. "Now do you see why I want to close the bloody ward?"

Neither spoke. There's a limit to how many revelations anyone — even a trained detective — can take in at a time.

"Take it from me, all this is true," Diamond went on. "Everything checks. There isn't time to take you through it, but I will. Right now, we must stop her from committing another murder, if we're not too late."

Profound shock takes people in different ways. In the back seat, Halliwell reacted like a troubled infant by chewing something soft and fleecy that turned out to be one of Nutty's ears. At the front, Ingeborg did well to avoid running into the back of a post office van.

They were making the ascent that is Claverton Down, swerving past slower vehicles at every opportunity. The innate terrors Diamond suffered from high speeds were as nothing to his concern for Pellegrini's survival. He tried using the phone again and was thwarted. He felt like tossing the wretched thing out of the window.

In silence, they careered down Bathwick Hill and the city opened up in front of them. They'd made brilliant time, but every minute that passed could be the minute murder was being done. Pity the hospital was located on the other side, out at Weston. At the bottom of Bathwick they passed St. Mary's church hall, where the railway society held its meetings and Captain Jarrow presided. The meeting with that old soldier seemed a lifetime ago to Diamond.

Ingeborg took her own route through the centre. There were a dozen ways she could have chosen and only volume of traffic made the difference at this stage. Her judgement worked for them: along a northern arc, using Weston Lane, avoiding the afternoon congestion on the Upper Bristol Road.

Sharp left at Combe Park and they'd made it to the hospital. Through gate one.

She halted at the drop-off point outside the main entrance. They all quit the car and sprinted past wide-eyed visitors and staff through the atrium, round the side of the café and up the corridor to Critical Care.

Bradford Ward was on the left.

No one was guarding the entrance. They got straight in.

Diamond grabbed a male nurse by the shoulder. The trolley he was pushing swung off course and almost hit a visitor on her way out.

"Patient Pellegrini. Which way?"

"Who?"

547

"Just admitted from Critical Care."

"Oh." The nurse pointed. "Second left. Who are you?"

He didn't get an answer. Diamond followed Ingeborg into the private room.

Unoccupied.

Or so it appeared. On the bedside cabinet two white mugs and an empty plate with a few crumbs suggested someone had been there.

Ingeborg grabbed the pillow and tossed it aside. Underneath was the deathly pale, slack-jawed face of an old man Diamond recognised as Ivor Pellegrini. He must have been smothered.

"Get help."

Halliwell dashed out while Diamond placed his index and middle fingers against the hollow between Pellegrini's windpipe and the main neck muscle.

With nothing to do but watch and hope for a faint beat of life, Ingeborg stood back. After the rush to the room, her own heart was pounding. So strong was her concentration on the figure in the bed that she barely noticed a slight sound behind her.

"Who's that?"

Diamond must have heard her, but he was too intent on what he was doing to look round.

She turned her head fully and glimpsed a female figure in dark clothes, with red hair, quitting the room.

In their beeline to the bed, they'd failed to notice someone else against the far wall. They must have interrupted the killer at work.

Ingeborg moved so fast in pursuit that Diamond didn't know she'd gone. He turned to say, "I can't find a pulse."

Instead of Ingeborg, Halliwell had returned with a nurse.

The medics took over.

Ingeborg retained a fleeting impression of the woman she was pursuing, above all the shoulder-length red hair. White-skinned, average in height, black suit, flat shoes — or so she thought. She hadn't seen anything of the face. Didn't match the description of Jessie, who had short, brown hair with blonde highlights. But this person had to be stopped. She had definitely been in that room with Pellegrini.

Why hadn't the ward been sealed, as Diamond had ordered? Could have saved the old man's life.

Concentrate, she told herself. Somewhere up ahead is that woman.

Anyone who had just smothered a man

wasn't going to hang about. Better look for a redhead in a hurry, striding out fast, if not actually running. Probably heading through the atrium to the main entrance.

Ingeborg ran, dodging people who hadn't seen her coming. She hoped she wouldn't collide with some luckless outpatient on crutches.

For a moment she saw the woman framed in the spring sunlight at the entrance, the red hair swinging as she turned left and out of sight. In that direction she'd be heading for one of the car parks. Made sense.

No more than fifty yards to make up. But the first car park wasn't far off.

Outside the building, a cluster of security people had surrounded the Ka, which was improperly parked, of course, the doors still hanging open. The explanation could wait. Ingeborg needed to use it. She felt in her pocket, brandished her ID and yelled.

"Police, stand back!"

Dodged past two uniforms, slammed one door shut, jerked another fully open, got in, started up and powered away.

She'd sacrificed some precious distance to the suspect, but she had a plan, outrageous, dangerous, and the best she could do in the situation. She would stop all movement of traffic.

A short distance along the narrow two-way road leading to the car parks, she glanced in her mirror, decided it had to be now, jerked the steering wheel right, slammed the brakes and swung the Ka across the centre of the road and squared up broadside on, blocking all progress either way.

Immediately, brakes screeched, horns were sounded, windows wound down and no doubt the air was blue with curses at the crazy woman who was in the act of abandoning her vehicle in the worst possible place. Ingeborg couldn't hear for the din of the horns.

She waved — a gesture that might mean anything — but seemed to be saying all was fine and dandy, whatever the inconvenience. Then she marched up the centre of the road along the line of cars backing up and stared into each vehicle, oblivious of what they were shouting at her.

She was fired up, concentrating on the task of finding the redheaded driver, who should by now have moved out of the car park and been caught in the tailback, unable to move.

Unfortunately, the trap was full of innocent victims: wide-eyed old ladies, bald-headed men, a couple of turbans, two eyes peering from a burka, a mother with three screaming kids in the back, middle-aged blondes, distracted brunettes, a nun, a doctor in an emergency car, a good cross-section of the population. Any minute someone was going to jump out and grab her.

She reached a point that she calculated was too far along the line. The redhead ought to be in the thick of the hold-up if she hadn't found some other way out, or was still in the car park, boxing clever.

Frustrated, Ingeborg turned and retraced her steps along the verge on the other side of the cars. She'd take a close look at everyone in the front passenger seats. She thought she'd checked them all.

Ten or twelve cars along the line, she got lucky. She happened to look down at an empty seat in a Fiat just as the driver's hand snaked across and snatched something away.

A flash of copper that shimmered with the movement.

A red wig.

Ingeborg reached for the door handle just as the driver exited on the other side and made her escape bid.

Definitely the woman in the black trouser suit and flat shoes, but now without glasses and with her own hair exposed as short and brown with blonde streaks. She was bolting across a patch of lawn towards the hospital building.

Ingeborg started after her and knew at once she had the speed to catch her.

Maybe thirty yards on, she launched herself into the tackle that ended the chase. The woman buckled at the waist. They both hit the grass and Ingeborg made sure she was on top, cushioned from the fall. She grabbed a wrist and secured an arm-lock.

"You're nicked, Jessie — or is it Elspeth Blake?"

In the private room in Bradford Ward, a team of doctors were trying to resuscitate Pellegrini using a defibrillator, watched by Peter Diamond and Keith Halliwell.

The only positive thing anyone could have said was that he was in the right place. The medics knew what to do, they had the record of his natural heart rhythm and they understood how fragile he was.

To Diamond's eye, this was a scene out of numberless TV hospital dramas. Any moment the senior doctor would remove the paddles, turn to his colleagues and shake his head.

It would be a terrible anti-climax, a cruel outcome for all the doctors and nurses who

553

had spent days helping their patient out of the coma.

But it wasn't played that way. Presently there was nodding between the team. They'd detected a response.

"Let's get out of their way," Diamond said to Halliwell. "They'll want to move him back into Critical Care."

27

Diamond had asked Ingeborg to join him in the interview room at Keynsham. She'd proved yet again what a vital member of the team she was. Making the arrest had been a challenge enough, aside from dealing with the angry drivers on the hospital road. She'd succeeded by force of character, making the arrest without handcuffs, hailing the security men and getting them to remove the Ka as well as Jessie's Fiat 500 and restore the flow of traffic.

As for the woman known to them as Jessie, she'd already made clear she knew her rights. She wanted legal representation — her own, and not one of the duty solicitors. Diamond had informed her — and she appeared to know already — that as an officer of superintendent rank he had the power under the Police and Criminal Evidence Act to question her for up to thirty-six hours about a serious arrestable offence.

The good thing was that she was vocal in asserting her rights. She hadn't yet retreated behind the dreaded "no comment."

So it began with her alone across the table, composed and still managing to look attractive, for all that had happened, her mouth playful, ready to take any shape she desired from disapproving to amused to amoral. At their only previous meeting, when she was posing as a do-gooder, her expression had promised rather more than he would have expected from a lady of the church.

After the formalities were gone through, Diamond asked the sort of question that would have made "no comment" ridiculous.

"Tea or coffee?"

"Coffee. Black, no sugar."

The officer by the door went out to fetch some.

"Were you bruised by the fall?"

A shake of the head.

"We met briefly at Mr. Pellegrini's house," he said. "You in your red wig as Elspeth Blake from the church. I was drooling over the homemade quiche, remember? Tell me I'm not mistaken and you baked it yourself."

"I'm a Cordon Bleu cook," she said.

Promising. He'd already decided to play to her ego. "Multi-talented, then. I haven't heard a single complaint about your house-keeping. Your talent for getting the confidence of lonely old men goes back a long way, doesn't it?"

Too obvious a question. She shrugged and said nothing.

"I'll cut to the chase," he said. "I've read your diary. I call it a diary, anyway. You call it notes. Classy, intelligent writing, I must say, even though you take some side swipes at the police. And you were right about us. We didn't have a clue for a long time. Pellegrini was on to you before I was. Clever old guy, he was your nemesis. I can understand why you did what you did today. Can't condone it, of course, but I see why it happened."

He paused as the tray of coffee was brought in. China mugs for Ingeborg and himself as well as the suspect.

And digestive biscuits. Maybe Keynsham wasn't a total write-off.

When he resumed, he said, "You probably want to know how we got hold of the diary. That was thanks mainly to Pellegrini, as you suspected, and it all goes back to the little incident at Cavendish Crescent after Max's funeral when he tipped coffee over your purple skirt. He'd make a good detective, would Pellegrini. You were in your Jessie

557

persona then and he had suspicions you were stealing choice items of jewellery from the house, pieces that had once belonged to Olga Filiput. Poor old Max had just about despaired of keeping track of them. Pellegrini's plan was to get hold of your handbag and see if you'd nicked another necklace. We both know you hadn't. You're too smart to take a risk like that. Instead there was something else in the bag."

She said in a resigned tone of voice, "The flash drive."

He nodded. "It was a Eureka moment when I worked out that this was what he must have found. Made sense for you, storing your wit and wisdom on a memory stick no bigger than a lipstick and keeping it with you at all times, encrypted as an extra precaution, even if no one else knew of its existence. Unfortunately for you, Pellegrini took his opportunity. He didn't know at the time that the little memory stick contained better evidence of your crimes than a sack full of stolen jewellery and he never did find out. He downloaded the contents to his laptop at home and hit an immediate problem. The bloody thing was gobbledegook, so he never got to read it."

She couldn't stop herself rolling her eyes and saying, "Tough."

"But you knew he wasn't the sort to give up. Left to himself, he'd decrypt it, so you needed to eliminate him. I don't know how many attempts you made. At least three to my knowledge."

"Prove it," she said. She was getting involved in the narrative, keen to discover how much she'd got away with.

"First, let's discuss your method. You talk about it in the diary being beautifully simple, but you don't describe the process in detail — I suppose because you were writing for yourself and you knew damn well how it was done. You make them drowsy first with some tranquilliser administered in food and then you smother them with a pillow. How am I doing?"

The hazel eyes slid upwards in reproach. "You really think I'm about to tell you?"

"No need. Our forensic people will analyse the cake crumbs on the plate beside his bed. I've got to admire those culinary skills. The date-and-walnut cake he had with him on his tricycle ride the evening of the collision must have been one of yours. I know it wasn't meant to cause a fatal accident, but it did. He was supposed to eat the cake at home and drift into a state where you could easily kill him when you called later. Silly man, he went out and took the cake with

him and stopped to eat it som
the route. He was riding unstea
the road when the police car hit
"You can't blame me for that,"
"I don't. I'm sure you went to t
the same night expecting to finish
and found he wasn't in."

He could tell from her look that he
it right.

"But it didn't stop you trying again.
didn't know he was in hospital the morn
you arrived with the quiche and ran in
me with Mrs. Halliday, the home help. You
made your retreat at the first opportunity,
taking the doctored quiche with you. I'm
glad now, but I would have cheerfully
shared a slice at the time. Date-and-walnut
cake, a quiche Lorraine and what was
today's offering?"

"Chocolate sponge."

"Of course. The hospital told me. You
don't give up easily."

"He could have died naturally, from the
accident," she said.

"Yes, and saved you a job. What a bum-
mer when he started coming out of the
coma. Still, you got here at the first opportunity ready to finish him off."

"Is he . . . ?"

"No." He paused, looking keenly for the

reaction. "They revived him. He'll live."

She closed her eyes, doing her best to ride the blow. One more death wouldn't have troubled her, but Pellegrini fit enough to make a statement would.

"A hospital isn't the ideal place to kill anyone," Diamond said. "They're rather good at reviving people."

Beside him, Ingeborg smiled.

The suspect didn't.

"Your method has much to commend it. No marks are ever found on the victim unless he puts up a fight — and of course your victims are far too relaxed to resist. Any pathologist will tell you the smothering of someone who doesn't fight back is just about impossible to diagnose after death. Pellegrini is a fortunate man, twice rescued from the brink."

"I wouldn't have picked him," she said.

A strange choice of words. He had to think what she meant.

Her meaning was clear when she added, "He became a threat."

"By getting suspicious of you?"

"I was forced to take risks."

"Softening him up by posing as the good Christian lady?"

"He wasn't in my plans. I knew the others better and had more control."

561

Diamond was pleased to have this on tape. She'd virtually admitted her guilt. He wanted more. "When you say 'the others,' how many were there?"

A slow smile played over her lips. "You tell me."

"From reading the journal, I'd say you've been doing this a long time. You don't get to be the wife of a crime baron without staking out a position of influence."

"How do you know that?" she said, the amusement gone in the blink of an eye.

"That you had another identity as Dilly Sabin? I worked it out."

Ingeborg almost spluttered over the coffee she was sipping. Diamond was way ahead of her.

He explained. "How else would you have got to know Cyril? He was up to his ears in debt to Bob Sabin, but he'd obviously found some source of money because he was making repayments. I may be wrong, but my reading of your relationship with Bob is that it was past its sell-by date. He made clear that you wouldn't inherit the proverbial brass farthing — and you didn't. When things go sour with a man as ruthless as that, something has to be done. Did you feed him cake or something more fitting for a crime baron? *Bombe surprise,* perhaps?

Toad-in-the-hole? Anyhow, Bob went peacefully, same as the others."

Beside him, Ingeborg took another sharp breath. She was learning so many things she hadn't grasped until now. If she'd ever needed reminding of the sharp brain of her sometimes infuriating boss she had a prime example here.

His eyes hadn't wavered from the suspect. "There was definitely some sympathy for you in the criminal world. To quote Larry Lincoln, you were given the double-shuffle."

Jessie, or Elspeth, or Dilly, gave a shrug.

"But you had your own plan as usual. After killing Bob, you'd clear off to the country as housekeeper to Cyril Hardstaff. He was quite a charmer anyway, easy to get on with, and your salary was guaranteed by his late wife's trust fund. More importantly, Cyril had an Aladdin's cave somewhere. Didn't take you long to track that to Cavendish Crescent and Max Filiput. You drove your new boss there for the Scrabble sessions and had a good look round while the two old gents were arguing over seven-letter words. It made a change from Little Langford, I imagine. Life must have been boring there."

"Deadly," she agreed.

"You made the best of it and then things

went belly-up again. Max wasn't as gaga as you'd first thought. He'd started to notice things were disappearing from the house. He got himself into quite a state about it."

She actually nodded at that.

Diamond added, "Do you know, for some time we thought Pellegrini was the thief? He had three valuable Fortuny gowns, worth a small fortune, hidden in his workshop. How wrong we were. It only dawned on me recently that Max must have asked Pellegrini to take care of them for him. He feared they, too, would be stolen."

"He needn't have bothered," she said.

"Why not?"

"Impossible to fence. No use to me."

"Max didn't know that. As I was saying, he was getting jumpy about the thefts. He suspected one of the railway club must be the thief and he confided his suspicions to Cyril, who was worried and told you. This was alarming. It was obvious the finger would soon be pointing at you and Cyril if something wasn't done to silence Max. Another murder became necessary."

She sniffed and looked away, as if the whole process was wearying her.

"The set-up made things easy for you," Diamond went on. "I'm tempted to say a piece of cake. You often made tea for the two old men during the Scrabble after-noons. Simple to see that Max got some tranquilliser. And even simpler to return later and finish him off. The key to the house was kept behind a drainpipe near the front door."

"You don't miss much, do you?" she said and it wasn't clear if it was meant as sarcasm or a compliment.

"So you let yourself in, go upstairs, do the business and leave. The cleaner, Mrs. Strat-ford, discovers the body next morning. From all appearances, it's a peaceful death, just like your other victims. Old man at home in his own bed with no sign of vio-lence. Dr. Mukherjee takes a look, certifies life is extinct and puts it down to heart failure and narrowing of the arteries. No need for an autopsy."

Jessie reached for another biscuit.

"Some days later, you drove Cyril to Bath for the funeral, which ought to have been just a formality, like everything else up to then. It wasn't. You didn't realise Ivor Pel-legrini would be playing detective. You'd never even met the guy. Your trips to the house had always been on different days from the railway people. Unknown to you, Max had treated Pellegrini as a confidant and even asked him to take care of those valuable gowns. The funeral reception was the last opportunity for any of you to be inside the house and clear out any remaining items of jewellery. Pellegrini was on the lookout for the thief. He may well have decided by then that the anoraks in the railway club were in the clear, which left you and Cyril as the prime suspects."

"We've been through this," she said. "He stained my skirt, I stupidly left the room without my bag and he found the flash drive."

"Which meant — from your point of view — he couldn't be allowed to live," Diamond said. "And if you needed any more convincing, he made the trip to Little Langford and got talking to Cyril. All your tidy arrangements were under threat. You were sent out for the evening while God knows what was discussed between the two of them. I don't believe you panicked, but you had to take emergency action. Cyril was killed the same night. His usefulness was over anyway. In the morning you were gone — but not before laying a trap for anyone who would come looking."

"The hairbrush," Ingeborg said.

"Near genius," Diamond said, but the face across the table was expressionless, no longer susceptible to flattery.

He pressed on. "There was sympathy in the underworld for the harsh way you'd been treated after Bob's death. You'd stayed in touch with some of them, like Larry Lincoln. Kept an ear to the ground. And when a working girl known as Maria from Sofia died literally on the job and ended up in the river, you offered your help removing all trace of her. You collected a sack full of her possessions, including the hairbrush with some of her hairs attached. This happened a few days before you murdered Cyril and you're far too smart to miss an opportunity of faking your own death. It worked, too, until we compared your recent history and Maria's. Even a woman as versatile as you are couldn't be on the game in Oldfield Park at the same time as caring for dear old Cyril in Little Langdon. We rumbled you in the end, but it took some doing."

"Is that it?" she asked as calmly as if enquiring whether dinner was ready. Her composure hadn't been shaken at any stage.

"Going by your diary I strongly suspect it isn't. We've still got hours of work to do, finding out when you started and who you killed in years past. You're not new to this, are you?"

She didn't need to say, "No comment." It was in her eyes.

"You're not going to tell us where it began and how many there are and how many false identities you've lived under, but you definitely knew what you were doing when you killed a man as powerful as Bob Sabin. I was about to add 'and got away with it,' but you didn't."

Her eyes gleamed a response.

Diamond smiled at her. "And it's over now. If neither of you ladies wants the last biscuit, I'll take it."

28

The woman known variously as Jessie, El-speth, Dilly and other identities yet to be revealed, was charged as Dilys Sabin and remanded in custody. The extent of her murderous career would remain unknown until at some future date her exceptional ego needed nourishing by the revelation that she was unequalled as a female serial killer. She was certain to spend the rest of her life in prison with the consolation that she was a celebrity of unending interest. Psychiatrists would study her, publish books and articles, and be anointed as professors for their insights into her disordered personality.

Peter Diamond had never had much time for that kind of analysis. He had some explaining of his own to do to another formidable woman, his boss Georgina, and it was more about his own motives than Dilys's.

"I can't understand why you kept all this to yourself," the ACC complained when she finally cornered him. "Don't you think I deserved to be taken into your confidence?"

"And placed in an impossible position, ma'am?" he told her. "Couldn't do that to you. There's such a thing as loyalty."

"Loyalty? The loyal thing to do would have been to tell me about your suspicions the minute you had any."

"You had your work cut out dealing with Flogham and Flay."

She made a sound like a deflating tyre. "Please. Mr. Dragham and Miss Stretch."

"If they'd got involved, we'd have had our hands tied, to put it mildly. Have they gone now?"

"For the time being. They had hopes of interviewing Mr. Pellegrini, but they'll need to come back at a later date if they do. It's abundantly clear anyway that our driver wasn't the main cause of the accident. With luck, we may not see them again."

"Do you have the latest on Pellegrini?" he asked.

"I phoned the hospital and spoke to the ward sister in Critical Care. He's recovering well, considering all he's been through." Georgina gave him a penetrating look. "Who exactly is Hornby?"

"The toy manufacturer?"

"I'm asking *you,* Peter."

"He died years ago, but his name lives on. Model trains. Most of these railway fanatics play with them. It's a symptom of the disease."

After the weekend, Pellegrini was well enough to receive visitors and Diamond was the first. He wouldn't be content until he'd had certain matters clarified.

The patient was seated in an armchair in the day room of Bradford Ward, leafing through a copy of *Heritage Railway* magazine. The pages shook a little and he was slumped, but he straightened on seeing he had a visitor and his eyes lit up. "I understand you saved my life," he said after Diamond introduced himself. "It's weird. I can't remember any of it, but I'm more grateful than I can say."

"No need," Diamond said. "We're drilled in first aid. I should be grateful to you for the chance to brush up on my technique. So is everything a blank?"

"Everything that put me in here. I'm told that's to be expected. I don't like it. I'm a stickler for detail, always have been."

"You wouldn't want to know about most of it," Diamond said, thinking of his unauthorised visits to the house. "How is your memory for events before the accident?"

"Pretty sound, I think."

"So what turned you into the best amateur detective since Lord Peter Wimsey?"

He raised a smile. "That was my old friend Max Filiput. He died, poor fellow. I went to the funeral. It seems a long time ago."

"You had your suspicions he was murdered?"

"No, I'm telling it wrong. When Max was still alive he had suspicions of his own that things were being stolen from the house. He'd inherited quite a collection of antiques and jewellery from his late wife, Olga, who came from a wealthy family. Max, being the sort of fellow he was, hung on to them out of a sense of loyalty to Olga, but he wasn't interested in them as possessions. He shut them away and didn't look at them again. Then for some reason he opened a drawer where he thought some item was and couldn't find it. He didn't trust his memory enough to go to the police, but he was worried. He asked me to take care of certain items of great sentimental value, antique gowns that he thought might be at risk. As far as I know the things he entrusted me with are still stowed away in my workshop. I must do something about them when I get home. They'll be part of his estate. He left everything to a very good cause."

"The National Railway Museum."

He smiled and nodded. "Typical of Max. An inspired idea."

"Who did you think was stealing from him?"

"He's dead himself now, so I suppose it won't hurt to say. A fellow called Cyril who used to visit Max to play some board game. I met him at the funeral. Personable character who actually delivered a remarkably fine eulogy, but I thought he was a shade too full of himself. He and his chauffeur lady may have been in league, taking opportunities to deprive poor old Max of his prized possessions. That was my reading of it, anyway. Wide of the mark, would you say?"

"Not at all," Diamond said. "That isn't all you suspected them of, is it?"

Pellegrini flushed and smoothed his pale hands along the chair arms. "Well, it was uncharitable of me, but I was suspicious about Max's death. He went quite suddenly, just at the time he convinced himself that pieces of jewellery were systematically disappearing. It crossed my mind how convenient it was for Cyril — if indeed he was the thief — to have Max out of the way.

Fanciful, no doubt, but once the idea was planted, I had to pursue it, even though my old friend had died peacefully in his own bed. I went about it in my usual way, doing some research, looking on the Internet for methods of murdering people. Clever methods, I mean, likely to escape detection by professionals such as yourself."

Exactly the confirmation Diamond had needed, and he'd got it without admitting he'd made a copy of Pellegrini's hard disk.

"Did you find anything?"

"There are forums where people discuss this sort of thing in a superficial fashion. It's not scientific by any stretch of the imagination, and I didn't learn anything of relevance, but I downloaded some of the material and read it again. My best hypothesis was that some sort of toxic drug was administered, something that metabolised rapidly and wouldn't be detectable at postmortem. I'm not a chemist and I wouldn't know what. Mind you, there was no post-mortem on Max. His doctor decided he'd died naturally. So you see, I was up against it, but when I get the bit between my teeth, so to speak, I don't give up."

"Did you take it further, then?"

"In a bull-in-a-china-shop fashion. At the funeral reception I got it into my head that

Cyril's chauffeur lady called Jessie may have taken one last opportunity to steal more of the jewellery."

"Ah, yes," Diamond said. "The coffee incident."

"I deliberately spilt some over her clothes at a moment when her handbag was on the floor. She went outside to change."

"Leaving the bag in the room? You picked it up, expecting to find a stolen necklace or something similar?"

"More fool me, there was nothing of interest inside except a USB, a computer flash drive."

"You took it?"

"The temptation was too much. I wasn't sure if there was anything on it, but just in case there was a clue to her identity, I kept it. No use to me at all, as it turned out when I slotted it into my laptop, because it was encrypted."

"But you didn't give up?"

"I don't — ever. A week or so later, I went to see Max's solicitor, a Miss Hill, who had arranged the funeral. Ostensibly I was there about Max's request for me to dispose of his ashes, but I mentioned his concerns about the possible thefts. She had an inventory of the jewellery collection at the time of Olga's death and it became clear that upwards of ten important pieces had gone missing by the time Max died."

"As many as that?"

"Miss Hill was looking for an innocent explanation, saying Max was getting confused in his last months and may have given them away or even sold them."

"Unlikely," Diamond said.

"I thought so. I suggested asking the police to investigate, but she was as tight-lipped as only a solicitor can be. I may be wrong, but I rather thought she didn't intend to take any action in the matter. And of course she was under no obligation to tell me anything."

"I've met Miss Hill," Diamond said. "I know what you mean."

"Well, eventually I visited Cyril Hardstaff at Little Langford to have it out with him."

" 'Eventually' is right. The funeral was in May last year. Why did you wait so long?"

He sighed heavily. "For the greater part of last year, I was preoccupied with troubles of my own. My poor wife Trixie was developing serious dementia. My life was on hold. She needed constant care. Everything had to wait, including Max's ashes, I must add. She died in November."

Diamond nodded and passed no comment. Trixie's death certificate had finally arrived with the morning mail. She had suffered a stroke and died in hospital.

"You were telling me about your visit to Little Langford."

Pellegrini nodded. "I only got round to it in February, when my life was returning to normal. I took a taxi and saw Cyril on his own. He admitted everything almost as soon as I brought up the subject of the missing jewellery. He'd got into trouble through gambling and was deep in debt to some very unpleasant people. He'd started stealing in desperation, an item at a time, knowing Max was hardly aware of what was there. He pleaded with me for a chance to put things right."

"Difficult."

"Yes. Put me on the spot. The main loser at this stage would be the legatee, the National Railway Museum. I said we'd both better sleep on it. The next morning Cyril was found dead."

"Discovered by his housekeeper."

"Yes, and she was impossible to contact. That was where my part in the matter ended. I still had Max's ashes to dispose of. I'd collected them from the funeral director months before, but I'd better not say where I planned to scatter them in case I get into trouble with you."

"That won't happen," Diamond said. "I'm nothing to do with National Rail. This was the night of the accident, which your brain has blanked out?"

"I'm afraid so."

"If it's any consolation, I can tell you the urn was empty when it was found, so I think you must have kept your promise to Max."

He beamed with pleasure. "That's a relief."

"You were prepared for a long night. You'd packed some food, including a banana and some cake. Do you remember where the cake came from?"

"That would have been the lady from the church."

He still had no inkling of the truth.

"Elspeth Blake."

"Is that her name? I didn't get the chance to thank her properly. She became friends with my domestic help, Mrs. Halliday, and started calling out of the goodness of her heart with things she'd cooked. Between you and me, I wasn't comfortable accepting charity. I'm not in need of it. And I don't normally buy cake for myself."

"Difficult to turn down a kindness?"

"Exactly. She seems to have kept an eye out for elderly men who live alone."

And how! Diamond thought. "Was it good cake?"

"Delicious. I should have thanked her personally, but I kept her at arm's length. Until I could think of some way of putting her off, I let Mrs. Halliday deal with her."

This answered a question Diamond would have needed to ask at some point. Pellegrini had never got close enough to think the lady looked in any way similar to Jessie the chauffeur. With a wig, glasses, contacts and different make-up and clothes, a woman can turn herself into someone else. The thing you can't disguise is the voice, but he'd scarcely spoken to the Elspeth Blake persona.

"Had she been visiting your house for some time?"

"A couple of weeks, I believe, no more."

"We think the cake contained a strong sedative."

"Really? Why was that? I have no trouble sleeping."

Such innocence.

The old man had suffered enough shocks already, so Diamond didn't enlighten him. "When you're feeling better we must get together again. I won't trouble you now with the nitty-gritty of what happened. It was as cunning a series of crimes as I've come across. Unless you have any other question, I'll leave you to get some rest." He got up and moved to the door.

"There is one thing I'd dearly like to know," Pellegrini said.

"What's that?"

"Who is Hornby?"